TRICKED

PRAISE FOR THE IRON

"This is the best urban/paranormal fantasy I have read in years. Fast paced, funny, clever, and suitably mythic, this is urban fantasy for those worn out by werewolves and vampires. Fans of Jim Butcher, Harry Connolly, Greg van Eekhout, Ben Aaronovitch, or Neil Gaiman's American Gods will take great pleasure in Kevin Hearne's Hounded. Highly recommended"
John Ottinger III, editor of *Grasping for the Wind*

"I love, love, love this series"
My Bookish Ways

"*Hounded* completely justified its hype and was a favourite of mine amongst this year's Urban Fantasy debuts. Not only did it liven up the subgenre's landscape, but it also announced Kevin Hearne as an author to watch . . . *Hexed* is an excellent sophomore effort by Kevin Hearne who is quickly becoming one of my favourite authors. I highly recommend picking up the Iron Druid Chronicles"
Fantasybookcritic

"This is one series no fantasy fan should miss. Mystery, suspense, magic, and mayhem . . . If you read one book this summer, read *Hounded*. Then, read *Hexed*, because you won't be able to help yourself"
SciFiChick

By Kevin Hearne

The Iron Druid Chronicles

Hounded
Hexed
Hammered
Tricked
Trapped
Shattered

TRICKED

**THE
IRON
DRUID
CHRONICLES**

KEVIN HEARNE

orbit

www.orbitbooks.net

ORBIT

First published in the United States in 2012 by Del Rey,
an imprint of The Random House Publishing Group
First published in Great Britain in 2012 by Orbit
Reprinted 2012, 2013, 2014

A CIP catalogue record for this book
is available from the British Library.

ISBN 978-0-356-50196-3

Printed and bound by CPI Group (UK) Ltd, Croydon, CR0 4YY

Papers used by Orbit are from well-managed forests
and other responsible sources.

MIX
Paper from
responsible sources
FSC® C104740

Orbit
An imprint of
Little, Brown Book Group
100 Victoria Embankment
London EC4Y 0DY

An Hachette UK Company
www.hachette.co.uk

www.orbitbooks.net

For Alan O'Bryan,
who bravely stands in front of my word vomit
and tells me to clean it up.
He is an outstanding alpha reader
and the finest of friends.
This is not a trick.

Pronunciation Guide

There's a reason the Navajo Code Talkers were so invaluable to the Marines in WWII. Their language, while beautiful, is really difficult to describe, filled with little glottal stops and special characters and mind-shredding verb constructions like the optative-semelfactive. They have no adjectives but rather use their verbs in an adjectival way. To illustrate how complicated it can get, there is no Navajo word for the verb *to give* but rather eleven different words that vary depending on the size and shape of what is being given. I don't use many words of their language in this book, but I've done my best to give you a clue about the few you'll see below. None of them are verbs. Also note that there are regional differences in pronunciation, just as there are different dialects in English, so some of these pronunciations may differ slightly depending on where you are in the Navajo Nation.

Navajo

Áłtsé Hashké = Aht SEH hash KEH (Translates to *First Angry,* or perhaps *First Mad* or *First Scolder.* It's the proper name of one of the First People, Coyote.)

Áńł'įįh = unn TEE (Means the *Witchery Way,* or *the Corpse-Poison Way.*)

Ch'įįdii = CHEE dee (A ghost, but specifically the part of

one's spirit that wasn't in harmony with the universe at the time of death.)

Diné = dih NEH (Means *the People*. It's what the Navajo call themselves; the term *Navajo* was slapped on them by the Spanish and it stuck. In this book, art will imitate life; the Diné will call themselves Diné, and everyone else—including Atticus—will call them Navajo.)

Diné Bahane' = dih NEH bah HAH neh (Means *Story of the People*. It is the Navajo creation story, parts of which are sung in various ceremonies.)

Hataałii = hah TAH hlee (This translates to *singer*, a person who sings at ceremonial occasions and creates sandpaintings, important in many rituals from blessing structures to restoring balance in those who have lost it; in crude terms, a medicine man.)

Hózhǫ = hoh ZHOH (This means *very good*, or *great energy*, everything spiffy and balanced in the world, which English sometimes translates to *blessing*. To be honest, it doesn't translate well into English; it's just one of those words that are too big for Anglo-Saxon noises.)

Hózhǫji = hoh ZHOH jee (This means *Blessing Way*.)

Níłch'i = NIL cheh (Literally, *air*, but in stories this is the name of the wind. And, yeah, that *l* with the cross through it doesn't really get pronounced like an English *l*, but it's more of a guttural noise behind your molars; using an *l* is just an expedient approximation.)

Stunning Sandstone Edifices

Tyende = tee YEH in DEH (This mesa is located about ten miles southwest of Kayenta. Incredibly beautiful sandstone—just don't be in a wash after a rain. Get to the high ground FAST, because they aren't kidding about flash floods.)

Wolverines of Especial Interest

Faolan = FWAY lawn (This isn't a Navajo name, by the way; we're back to the Irish here.)

Tuatha Dé Danann

Ogma = OG mah (Pronounced *og* as in *log*. It's not like the Ó in Aenghus Óg. That had a diacritical mark over it so you'd pronounce it as a long O. This one's short. Ogma is credited with teaching Druids Ogham script, among other things.)

Chapter 1

The best trick I ever pulled off was watching myself die. I did a respectable job of it too—the dying, I mean, not the watching.

The key to dying well is to make a final verbal ejaculation that is full of rage and pain but not tainted in the least by squeals of terror or pleas for mercy. This was my father's wisdom—about the only shred of it that has managed to lodge firmly in my mind all these years. He died while trying to steal somebody else's cows.

It would be an ignominious end today, but before the common era in Ireland, it was honorable and manly to die in a cattle raid, as such theft was called. Before he left to meet his doom, my father must have had some dark premonition about it, because he shared with me all his opinions about dying properly, and I will never forget his final words: "A man's supposed to shit himself *after* he dies, son, not before. Try to remember that, lad, so that when your time comes, you won't make a right girly mess of it. Now fuck off and go play in the bog."

Like many silly codes of bravery and manliness, the meat of my father's instruction on how to die well can be distilled to a simple slogan: Die angry at maximum volume. (Dying silently is out of the question; the world's last Druid should not go gentle into that good night.)

During infrequent spates of morbidity, I used to speculate on my eventual manner of death. I figured it would happen on a city street somewhere, cut off from the power of the earth, unable to summon a magical mulligan that would let me see the sunrise. But at the same time, I hoped it would be in a cool city with a bitchin' name, like Kathmandu or Bangkok or maybe Climax, Michigan. I never thought it would be in a dried-up place called Tuba City.

Situated in the southwestern portion of the Navajo Nation in Arizona, Tuba City rests on a red sandstone mesa with no visible means of economic support. The first question I asked when I saw it—besides "Where are all the tubas?"—was, "Why is anybody living here?" The red rocks may have a stark beauty to them, but beyond that Tuba City is nearly treeless, dusty, and notably lacking in modern amenities of dubious worth, like golf courses and cafeteria-style dining. It does have a reservoir and some pastures nestled into a canyon, but otherwise it's puzzling why nine thousand souls would adopt an address there.

On the north end of town, where the BIA Road intersects with Indian Route 6220, a large white water tower juts out of the desert. It overlooks a few dilapidated trailers on the very edge of the city, and then there is naught but a rocky mesa with scattered shrubs gamely trying to make a living in a few inches of sandy soil. I'd flown to the top of the tower as an owl, carrying a wee pair of binoculars in my talons, and now I was camouflaged in my human form, lying flat, and peering northeast into the barren waste where I was about to die.

The dying had to be done. The Morrigan had seen it in a lucid vision, and she doesn't get those unless it's really dire and inevitable, like James Earl Jones telling you in his Darth Vader voice, "It is your desss-tiny." And, frankly, I probably deserved it. I'd been very naughty recently and, in retrospect, epically stupid. Because I couldn't bear to break my word, I'd taken Leif Helgarson to Asgard to kill Thor and he managed to pull it off, but we killed a few extra Æsir in the process and turned Odin into a drooling vegetable. Now the remaining Æsir were slavering for me to shuffle off my mortal coil, as were several other thunder gods who took Thor's demise as a personal affront to all things thundery.

After building flaming funeral ships for their dead and resolving to avenge them—for some people approach vengeance like an all-you-can-eat buffet—the Æsir sent Týr and Vidar after the surviving members of our company. I had no idea where Perun or Zhang Guo Lao were hiding, and I hadn't an inkling of whether Hrym and the frost giants ever made it out of Asgard. Leif was safe, because they saw Thor smash his skull with Mjöllnir; thanks to the peculiar regeneration capabilities of vampires and the dutiful attentions of Dr. Snorri Jodursson, Leif hadn't quite died, but it would be some time before we knew if he'd make a full recovery.

I, on the other hand, wasn't safe at all, because I had people to look out for. Perun could spend the next century as an eagle and they'd never find him. Zhang Guo Lao, I'd heard, was capable of true invisibility when he stood still; since he could go full ninja, they'd never get him either. I could go to a nice plane somewhere and be safe—I could even take Oberon and Granuaile with me—but without true contact with the elementals of earth, Granuaile wouldn't be able to advance her training as a Druid, and the world desperately needs more Druids. So my choices were to stay on earth and die or leave earth and let the world slowly die of neglect—which wouldn't truly help, since all planes connected to earth would die at the same time.

I decided to stay and die. Loudly.

Týr and Vidar found me quickly enough once they

knew who to ask for. I'd blown my cover somewhat spectacularly some months earlier by killing Aenghus Óg, so by now almost anyone paranormal or supernatural could have pointed them to Arizona. They chased me up to Tuba City, towing along five thunder gods for backup: Ukko from Finland, Indra from India, Lei Gong from China, Raijin from Japan, and Shango from Nigeria. All of them are very powerful gods and quite beloved by their people, but few are the tales in which we hear of their wit or perception.

Indra was quite the character, for example, and undoubtedly the most powerful of the lot currently. He had a reputation for lovin' the ladies, a tendency I couldn't criticize myself, but he got himself into some awful trouble for it once. He chose to lay down with the wife of a magician, who of course found out immediately that Indra was "in da house" and assigned him a punishment worthy of Dante: Since the thunder god could think of nothing but vaginas, the cuckolded husband cursed Indra with a thousand vaginas all over his body. Indra had to walk around like that for a while, until Krishna took pity on him and commuted the sentence by turning all the vaginas into eyes. Still, think of the optometrist appointments.

The Morrigan observed, "They may be sharing the brain of a nuthatch between them." She was perched on the water tower beside me in the shape of a battle crow, making sure that I "died" precisely as her vision foretold. We'd both been worried initially about her vision of my death—she because it meant she'd break her oath to keep me alive, and I for obvious reasons—until I remembered the Plan. I'd conceived the Plan before the Morrigan shared her vision with me but realized only later that the Plan could fulfill her vision of my death without me actually having to die for it. Now we watched with faint amusement as someone who looked like me cursed the circling thunder gods and asserted that they all were spawned from the puffy red asses of baboons. The gods sent bolt after bolt of lightning at him with no apparent effect as he stood in a puddle of mud.

"Give them a little credit, Morrigan," I said. "They found me here, after all."

"Only after you allowed them to by parading around this foolish copy of yourself. It still took them a week, but, very well: They are sharing the brains of two nut-hatches."

The Atticus O'Sullivan they assaulted was a near-perfect replica. The tattoos on his right side were a precise copy of mine. The slightly curly mane of red hair would have shone luxuriantly in the sun had it not been pouring rain on him, and the goatee blazed with character on his chin. He was foulmouthed and had his Irish up, and he had my wallet and my cell phone in the pockets of his jeans. There was an iron amulet on a silver chain around his neck, with five square charms on either side of it and a fulgurite talisman in the back protecting him from the lightning. The fulgurite was real, but the amulet and charms were little more than costume jewelry. He did, however, carry Fragarach in his right hand—the real Fragarach, not a facsimile—for extra special verisimilitude.

Yet a clever enemy would not have been fooled. He didn't have Oberon or Granuaile by his side, for one thing, and he wasn't casting a single Druidic binding—not that this bunch would know it if he did. They were still trying to fry him electrically.

"What are they thinking?" the Morrigan asked. "If the first hundred lightning bolts don't work, the hundred-

and-first one will?"

"That strategy would require them to count," I said, "which is improbable if they're sharing two nuthatch brains."

"Good point," the Morrigan conceded.

Týr, the Norse god of single combat, waved off the thunder gods to approach my double with a shield and an axe. Vidar, Odin's son, armed with a long sword, followed close behind. The thunder gods floated down to the muddy earth behind the faux Atticus to cut off any escape.

Poor Týr clearly didn't know anything about Fragarach. The only people who saw me use it in Asgard died immediately afterward, and thus he'd never been told that my ancient Fae sword cut through shields and armor like a chainsaw through mozzarella. Týr crouched behind his shield as my double charged, thinking to take the blow and then strike back quickly with his axe. He took the blow all right. He took it right through the center of his body, as Fragarach sliced down through his shield, his forearm, and his torso. Everyone—including my double—was startled that Týr was now half off. Literally.

But Vidar, the god of vengeance, recovered first. Yelling, "For Odin!" he thrust his long sword into the unprotected left side of that handsome Irish lad's rib cage, definitely stabbing a lung and maybe the liver too. The man who was supposed to be me cried out his pain magnificently—"Garrl! Urk! Auggh!"—and tried to raise Fragarach for another blow, but the strength wasn't in his limbs anymore. Vidar yanked out his sword with a slurping noise, and the Druid poseur collapsed in the mud.

They apparently knew enough about Druids not to leave it there. They didn't want me healing from a wound that would be mortal to anyone else. So they all descended on the body and chopped it up into pieces with whatever gigantic, godlike phallus-weapon they had, far beyond my capacity to heal.

"Yeesh. What a mess," I said. "Cue the Chooser of the Slain."

"Yes, let's finish this," the Morrigan said, leaping off the tower and flapping through the rain as Vidar finally ceased his butchery and shook his fist at the sky.

"Vengeance is miiiine!" he roared.

I snorted quietly at him from my vantage point. "Dream on."

The Morrigan is a spooky creature by default, but she can turn up the spookiness to eleven whenever she wishes. Her eyes glow red and minor harmonics creep into her voice, vibrating on a frequency guaranteed to produce shuddering fits, liquid bowels, and tiny screams of fear. At least that's what her voice o' doom does to normal people. Gods are able to take it a little better. Still, they flinch. The Morrigan shifted to her human form about twenty yards away from the cluster of gods, a svelte seductress with milk-white skin and coal-black hair, and advanced toward them.

"I have come for the Druid," her voice boomed and scraped, and the gods jumped at the sound, crouching into defensive positions. They didn't relax either when they saw that the Morrigan was unarmed—she was naked, in fact—so maybe they each had a brain after all. She didn't need to be armed or clothed to do them serious harm. Indra's thousand eyes were busy, presumably searching her for weapons.

"Who are you?" Shango demanded. It was pretty easy to hear them, despite the distance and noise from the storm. They were all trying to intimidate one another, so they were using GodSurround Sound and scored a little reverb off the ceiling of clouds.

"I am the Morrigan, the Celtic Chooser of the Slain," she said, approaching them fearlessly. "The Druid's shade is mine to claim, as is his sword."

"His sword?" Vidar spluttered. "That is mine by right of conquest!" He was a little late to claim it. The Morrigan was already picking it up.

"It is the rightful property of the Tuatha Dé Danann. The Druid stole it from us." She left out the part where she helped me steal it, I noticed.

"And I won it of him. It belongs to me now," Vidar said.

"Be careful, little god," the Morrigan's voice grated, menace crackling in the charged air. "Do not mistake me for one of your Valkyries. You have slain the Druid and avenged your people, as was your right, but you may not tread on the rights of the Tuatha Dé Danann."

Vidar bristled. He didn't like being scolded by a naked woman in front of all the macho thunder gods. If he let it stand, he would lose major testosterone points. Was he smart enough to let it go? He clenched his jaw, held out his left hand, and beckoned. "Give me the sword, woman, or I will take it." Nope. Not smart at all.

The Morrigan's smile was wide and wicked as she settled into a defensive stance, Fragarach raised behind her head. "Come and take it, then."

Now he was neatly trapped in a prison of his own devising. Yet he still had the key; all he had to do was laugh at the Morrigan and say, "I was only joking. Begone with your faerie sword, I care not," and he'd get to return to Asgard a hero, maybe even take over the joint. He could walk into Gladsheim and tell the remaining Æsir, "I slew the dude who slew Freyr and Týr and crippled Odin," and then they'd fete him and praise him and he'd definitely get laid. The last thing he should do is listen to the voice of machismo and give battle to a goddess whose primary power is to *choose who dies in bat-*

tle. Did he think he was invincible somehow? Did he not understand that all the Norse prophecies were null, the Norns were dead and so were many of the gods who were supposed to fall in Ragnarok? He was no longer fated to kill Fenris in the final gore-spattered brouhaha. If my trip to Asgard and the butchered remains of Týr showed anything, it showed that the Æsir could now die at any time.

But no, the dumbass charged. "For Odin!" he cried, thinking perhaps it was a lucky thing to say since it had worked so well against the fallen Druid. But the Morrigan wasn't off balance and out of position like the faux Atticus had been, and she had all the power of the earth at her command in addition to the powers of a goddess. As Vidar swung at her, she darted quicker than the eye could track to her right, out of the path of Vidar's sword. She spun around in a blur, past his shield, and swung Fragarach from behind him with two hands, shearing his torso in twain and sending the top half sailing fifty feet as the bottom half staggered another step and collapsed. The Morrigan reset herself facing the thunder gods as Vidar's head and shoulders smacked wetly to the earth. Her posture dared them to attack, but they had no such intentions. They collectively said, "Ahhh," and gave her a round of golf claps for the spectacular slaughter.

"An excellent swing," Shango said.

"You warned him but did not toy with him. I approve," Lei Gong added.

"Flawless form, worthy of the finest samurai," Raijin said.

"Marvelush dexterity and wondrous strength," Indra opined before belching thunderously.

"That shit was *awesome*!" Ukko said, smiling through his beard, and I decided I liked him, even though he wanted me dead.

"No one else will object if I take Fragarach with me?" the Morrigan asked. The thunder gods all shook their heads and assured her that they thought it best she keep it.

"I mush be going," Indra said. "But before I do, can you assure us that thish man is, in fact, quite dead?" He gestured to the chunks of flesh on the ground that used to look like me. The motion caused him to sway unsteadily on his feet, and I realized that his slight speech impediment was due to inebriation. A few of his thousand eyes were already passed out or blinking rapidly in an effort to stay awake. So the legends were true; Indra liked to hit the *soma* hard. "He casht ashpersions on my—urp—parentage," he added, as if that explained why they'd practically diced the faux Atticus. Indra had pummeled bits of him to paste with the mighty club he carried.

"He is thoroughly dead," the Morrigan replied. "His shade has already left this plane."

"Then I am shatishfied that justish is done," Indra said. "It was a pleasure meeting you, Morrigan. Perhapsh in a happier time, you and I could—"

The Morrigan's eyes flashed red, daring him to finish. Indra's thousand eyes blinked.

"Never mind," Indra said. He took his leave and rose into the sky. The other thunder gods quickly followed suit, offering quick pleasantries before ascending to the thunderheads above, leaving the Morrigan alone with the carnage of a winter afternoon. She surveyed it, rain sluicing the blood off her body and Fragarach's blade, and laughed.

Chapter 2

Congratulations, the Morrigan's voice croaked in my head. That was new. Neither she nor any of the Tuatha Dé Danann had demonstrated the ability to communicate telepathically with humans before. What had changed? *You have survived your own death,* she continued. *Five thunder gods will spread news of your demise throughout the world's pantheons, and you will finally be free to live a boring life.*

Could she hear my thoughts in return? *Sold! I'll take it!* I said, in the same way I would have spoken to Oberon. *Boredom sounds great right now!*

Apparently, she could hear me just fine. The Morrigan waved the tip of Fragarach around at the chopped pieces of faux Atticus. *Are you sure this native god will rise again?*

Positive, I affirmed. *You can't kill Coyote. Well, you can, obviously. But he just keeps coming back.* That was the heart of the Plan I'd made with Coyote: He'd assume my shape, die in my place, and I'd do him a favor on the reservation. A pretty big favor.

This mangled flesh will re-form? the Morrigan asked.

Nope. Coyote's magic, like our shape-shifting, tends to ignore the Law of Conservation of Mass.

All the Old Ways do.

Yep. He'll re-spawn in a completely new body and

have a brand-new set of clothes to boot. I don't know how he does it. Maybe he has a warehouse full of spare brains and body parts down in First World and a wholesale deal with Levi's. There were many versions of Coyote running around North America, but this particular iteration of the Navajo tribe's was one of the oldest and most powerful.

Beware, Siodhachan, the Morrigan said, calling me by my Irish name as always, *trickster gods are not usually so helpful. There will be a price to pay for this service he's done you.*

Oh, I'm well aware. But Coyote and I arranged it all beforehand.

No. I mean there will be something else, she said.

I doubt it. I was very careful in our negotiation to specify the limitations of my service.

That may be so, Siodhachan. All I am saying is that tricksters have a way of working around deals. Be on your guard.

I will. Thank you for playing your part.

Through my binoculars, I saw the Morrigan give a half shrug in the rain. *It was amusing. More amusing still will be bringing the news to Brighid.*

She may be delighted to hear of my death, I pointed out. *She was less than pleased when I refused to become her consort.*

A rich, throaty laugh bubbled out of the Morrigan. *Yes. I remember.*

What will you do with Fragarach? I asked.

I will return it to Manannan Mac Lir. He will be surprised, I think, and then he will spend a year reminiscing about the elder days when we forged such things.

Any chance I could get it back after that?

None, the Morrigan said, her tone firm. *Even the tiny brains of the thunder gods would figure that one out.*

No, you must give it up to secure your safety. And you still have the other.

Yes, that's true, I said. Moralltach, the Great Fury, couldn't cut through armor and shields, but it killed with a single blow. I had watched it work its magic on Thor. Still, it wasn't as sweet as Fragarach. I would miss that sword, but the Morrigan was right. Giving it up was the only way to convince people I was truly gone.

Something in the Morrigan's posture changed, and I was suddenly grateful that I was still up on the water tower and she was far enough away that I needed binoculars to see her well.

Come here, Siodhachan. Her voice in my head changed its tenor, turning all husky and chocolate, like a late-night DJ's.

Um . . . why?

I have just killed a god. I want to celebrate with sex in the mud and the blood and the rain.

That's when it clicked in my head: What had changed was that when we had shagged a couple of months ago—at length, and at her insistence—she had performed some bindings in a proto-Celtic language that had healed my demon-chewed ear. She could have easily bound her mind to mine at the same time—and clearly, the evidence proved she had. I was less than anxious to give her another opportunity to perform such shenanigans. *Wow. That's tempting,* I said, *but I need to go meet Coyote when he re-spawns.*

Oh. So soon? Are you sure? Her left hand drifted over her body, drawing my attention to it. The Morrigan can beat a succubus when she wants to, in terms of stimulating desire in men. I knew this because my iron amulet protected me completely from succubi but only blunted whatever Horndog Lust Ray she was pointing at me now. Without the amulet, I'd already be her willing slave. As it was, I barely held on to my mental faculties;

physically I was extremely attracted, much to my embarrassment and discomfort. Some people might like them, but I, for one, am no fan of boners in the rain.

I am sorry, I lied, *but I am bound. You could always make a gift of yourself to one of the mortals here.*

They never last long, the Morrigan said morosely.

So have ten or more. Twenty if you want. You can suck 'em dry like those little juice pouches and toss 'em away, I said, then winced at the imagery. I felt a brief stab of guilt, but I rationalized it by reminding myself that I'd be the juice pouch if I didn't distract her.

Mmmm. Twenty men in the mud. Sounds delicious. Her lust stopped focusing on me and began to broadcast like the call of a siren. I sighed in relief.

You're welcome. See you later, I said, then muttered an inadequate apology to the men who'd be arriving shortly to please the Morrigan. They'd not walk away unscathed, and some of them would probably get drawn into the investigation of what happened out there to Atticus O'Sullivan. Since this was murder on federal land, the FBI would be getting involved. There would be lots of tracks and evidence to pursue in all that mud, especially after the Morrigan had her fun with all the men she lured into the rain, and it would look like the mob or a cult had decided to execute me. That thought was actually kind of fabulous.

Leaving the binoculars behind, I bound my shape to an owl and flew south to my hotel. It's not pleasant flying in rain like that, but I had to get out of there. Once safely in my room, I greeted my wolfhound, Oberon, who'd been watching *Mystery Science Theater 3000* on TV. Then I took a cold shower and tried to think about teddy bears and baseball and those little bouncy air castles you can rent for kids' birthdays—anything but the Morrigan.

Since it's always better to clog up someone else's drain

with dog hair, I thought it would be a good time to give Oberon a bath as well. He hadn't had one for a while, and I didn't know when we'd have an opportunity like this again.

"Hey, Oberon," I called, filling up the tub for him, "it's time for your bath!"

<It is?> He sounded doubtful. <Do you have a decent story?> Oberon wouldn't sit still for baths unless I told him a story—a real story about historical figures. He never settled for faerie tales.

"I'm going to tell you the true story of a man named Francis Bacon."

<BACON?> He came running so fast that he couldn't negotiate the sharp turn into the bathroom very well, and he slammed into the door awkwardly and then splashed into the tub, soaking me after I'd just finished drying off.

<Oh, this is going to be great! I can tell I'm going to like this man already. He had to have been a genius with a name like that. Was he a genius?>

"Yes, he was."

<I knew it! I have an instinct for that kind of thing. But I hope this story doesn't end with him chopped into bits and sprinkled on a salad. That would be tragic, and a story about bacon should be uplifting.>

"Well, Francis Bacon was quite inspirational to many people," I said, pouring water on Oberon's back. "He's the father of modern empiricism, or the scientific method. Before he came along, people conducted all their arguments through a series of logical fallacies or simply shouting louder than the other guy, or, if they did use facts, they only selected ones that reinforced their prejudices and advanced their agenda."

<Don't people still do that?>

"More than ever. But Bacon showed us a way to shed preconceived notions and conduct experiments in such a way that the results were verifiable and repeatable. It gave people a way to construct truths free of political and religious dogma."

\<Bacon is the Way and the Truth. Got it.>

As I shampooed Oberon's coat, I explained how to craft hypotheses and test them empirically using a control. And then I stressed safety while I rinsed him off.

"It's best not to experiment on yourself. Bacon practically froze himself to death in one of his experiments and died of pneumonia."

\<Right! Bacon must be heated. Knew that already, but thanks for the reminder.>

I love my hound.

Chapter 3

I have a thing for breakfast. *Thing* is a word I usually frown upon; I consider it a crutch for the chronically confused, a signal flag that says *I don't know what I'm talking about,* and, as such, I studiously avoid it, like cheerleaders avoid the chess team. But in this case I feel justified in using it, because there isn't a precise word in English to convey the character of my feelings. I suppose I could say that I regard breakfast with a certain asexual affection, a gustatory relish that's a bit beyond yearning yet well short of pining—or some other verbal brain-fondle that penny-a-page hacks like Charles Dickens used to take delight in crafting—but no one talks or thinks like that anymore. It's far faster and simpler to say I have a thing for breakfast (or eighties' arena rock, or classic cars, or whatever), and people know what I mean.

Oberon shares my thing for breakfast, because in his mind it equals hot, greasy meat of some kind. The culinary art of the omelet is lost on him—as is the sublime pleasure of parsley potatoes or a cup of fresh-squeezed orange juice. Regardless, when we wakey-wakey, we always make time for eggs and bakey.

<Oh, great big bears,> Oberon said, yawning and stretching out his back legs at the same time. <I'm going

to need half a yak and an industrial winch to keep my eyes open this morning.>

Where am I going to find half a yak?

<Duh. Attached to the other half. Hound 1, Druid 0.>

Oh, you want to keep score today? I'm going to win this time.

<Never let go of your dreams, Atticus.>

Tuba City—alas!—doesn't have a wide variety of places to eat. There are some chain restaurants peddling fast food, and then there's Kate's Café. The locals eat there, so that's where we went after we collected Granuaile from her hotel room, a few doors down from mine.

As you enter Kate's, there's a register and waiting area, and to the right of that is a long white counter with bar stools and a window to the kitchen behind it. The menu is displayed above the kitchen window on one of those old-fashioned marquees with red plastic letters spelling out items and prices. If you keep going past the counter, there's a rectangular space that serves as the main dining room, full of gunmetal-gray vinyl booths and tables. The walls are painted a sort of burnt orange, kind of like sandstone with lots of iron oxide in it. I camouflaged Oberon, and he squeezed himself underneath one side of a booth while Granuaile and I slid in on the other side.

<I wish you'd get me one of those seeing-eye-dog aprons so that I can walk around in plain sight and be comfortable,> Oberon said.

But then I'd have to pretend to be blind, and that would be inconvenient.

<Inconvenient is squeezing myself under this table. Why can't I be a tasting-tongue dog or a smelling-nose dog?>

I smiled. *Because a lack of taste or smell isn't considered a handicap to humans.*

<Don't I know it. Humans can smell hardly anything

at all. But, hey, I think they must have pretty good sausage here. I smell chicken-apple!>

Nah, I doubt it. I'm sure they have frozen links or patties, just like everyone else.

<It's here! You can't fake that smell!>

I don't see it on the menu.

<So it's off the menu! But I'm telling you they have chicken-apple sausage!>

A slow, drawling voice tinged with amusement interrupted. "You're both right. They don't have chicken-apple sausage, but it's here." A slim Navajo man in a black cowboy hat peered around the corner of the main dining area; a brown paper bag liberally stained with grease dangled in his hand.

<Saint Lassie smiles upon me! It's Coyote, with a bag of goodies!>

"Hey, Coyote," I chuckled, and he smiled back. "Come and join us." Like me, Coyote could hear Oberon's words, but his comment that we were "both right" had me wondering if he could hear my side of the conversation as well. It was uncomfortable to think that maybe he could read my mind, but perhaps I could chalk up the thought to my paranoia. He could have easily inferred what I was saying based on Oberon's side of the conversation.

"Don't mind if I do," he said, and then he turned on the charm to greet Granuaile. "Good morning, Miss Druid. Nice to finally meet ya." Coyote had seen Granuaile before, but at the time she'd been communing with the elemental Sonora, and she'd missed Coyote's brief visit entirely.

"Oh. Um, I'm not a Druid yet. Call me Caitlin." She looked a little starstruck, but that was understandable. Coyote was the first immortal she'd met.

"Caitlin?" Coyote squinted at me as he sat down gingerly so as not to disturb Oberon. "Thought you said her name was Granuaile."

"It is, but we're using different names now," I said. In the past I had taken the trouble to mimic his pattern of speech, drawling my words a bit and dropping g's off the ends, but I saw no need to do that now. Our deal had already been struck, and any advantage that would have given me was gone. "We're in hiding, see. It would kind of waste all your effort yesterday to make it seem like I died if you keep calling me Mr. Druid. You should call me Reilly." Granuaile and I were supposed to be known to the world now as Reilly and Caitlin Collins, brother and sister. We had driver's licenses and fake documents to prove it, courtesy of my lawyer down in Tempe.

"Aw, hell with that, Mr. Druid. I ain't gonna call you anything different."

<Preach it, Coyote! He's always Atticus to me. Say, what's in that bag you got there?>

"Think your hound might be hungry. Mind if I give him something to chew on?" he asked, pointing at the bag on the table.

"Sure, go ahead," I said. "I appreciate the thought, and I know he does too."

"Well, I told him I'd bring him some the next time I saw him."

<That's right, you did! Thanks, Coyote!>

Try to snarf quietly.

<No worries, Atticus. I will snarf surreptitiously. And I should get bacon, because my adverb was two syllables longer than yours, plus a bonus for alliteration.>

I grinned. *It's a deal. You're the best hound ever.*

<I rock on with my fur on. And it's Hound 3, Druid 0 now.>

What? Where'd you score two?

<I was right about the sausage, and Coyote won't call you Reilly either.>

Okay, but I was also right about the sausage, so it's 3–1.

Coyote opened the bag and withdrew the sausages, placing them on the seat next to him where Oberon could easily get to them. The waitress arrived at that point to take our orders, and the three of us tried to keep talking constantly to disguise the smacking, chop-licking noises that Oberon was making. She picked up on it anyway and regarded us uncertainly, trying to fig-ure out who was making the juicy sounds and whether or not she should be concerned or even offended.

Coyote ordered four sides each of bacon, sausage, and ham, plus coffee.

"Do you want any eggs or toast?" the waitress asked.

"Hell, no, keep that shit away from me," Coyote said, then remembered who he was talking to and added, "I mean, no, thank you. 'Scuse my language."

Granuaile asked for a gorgeous stack of pancakes, and I ordered a fluffy omelet with cheese, bell peppers, onions, and mushrooms, with skillet potatoes and dry wheat toast on the side. I also ordered three sides of bonus bacon for Oberon.

The waitress did her best to keep her expression neu-tral, but I could tell she thought we were the weirdest people she'd ever served—and perhaps perverted too, considering that one of us kept making licking noises. That discomfited me; I wanted to blend in and be forget-table, and we were doing a terrible job of it. What if, in the course of their investigation, the FBI came around here asking about unusual people? As far as I knew, the killing site hadn't been discovered yet, but it couldn't be much longer before it was. What if they published some picture of me in the local paper and the waitress recog-nized it? I voiced these doubts to Coyote after the wait-ress left, and he scoffed.

"Ain't nobody 'round here ever gonna talk to the

feds," Coyote said. "The way it works is, if the feds want something, we don't wanna give it to 'em, unless they want directions off the rez. We give those out nice and easy."

"All right, if you say so. I imagine you'd know better than anyone."

"Yep." Coyote grabbed a couple of napkins and courteously wiped down the seat, now that Oberon was finished with his chicken-apple sausages.

"So you held up your part of the trade very well yesterday," I said. "The deal was, I'm supposed to move some earth for you in return, so long as it doesn't hurt anybody physically, emotionally, or economically."

"That's right, Mr. Druid. You ready to hear the details?"

"Shoot."

"All right, then. Look at this town—or, hell, anywhere on the rez—and what do you see?"

"Lots of red rock and shepherds. You see groups of houses here and there, but you can't figure out what everybody's doing for a living."

"That's right. There aren't any jobs here. We can open casinos or we can open up mines. That's where the jobs are. But, you know, those mines are all big companies beholden to shareholders. They don't care about our tribe. They don't care about anything but their bottom line. And once they've stripped our land clean, they'll move on and strip somebody else. There's no vision for a sustainable future. So I came up with one."

The waitress came back with Coyote's coffee and he thanked her and took a sip before continuing. "The American Southwest could be the Saudi Arabia of renewable energy, you know that? We have enough solar and wind potential on the rez alone to power most of the state, if not all of it. Problem is, nobody's going hard after it. Everybody's makin' too much money off oil and coal and buyin' congressmen with it to make sure it stays that way. Besides, you need a ton of capital to start a new energy industry. So that's going to be your job, Mr. Druid. You get us the capital to get going, providing a few mining jobs in the short term, and then we're going to invest all that money into renewable energy and infrastructure, creating plenty of jobs in the long term. And it'll all be owned and operated by *my* people, the Diné," he said, using the term that the Navajo called themselves.

"I see. And how am I going to provide capital, exactly?"

"Gold. You know the price o' gold has tripled since 2000 or so?"

"You want me to create a gold vein on the rez so you can mine it?"

"That's right."

I didn't have to pretend to look distressed. "You know I can't really do that, right? I'll have to ask an elemental to do it, and it might not agree." I could move small amounts of earth myself through some basic binding, just shifting topsoil around, but I wasn't particularly fast at it. Finding large amounts of gold, concentrating it, and moving it long distances through the earth was far beyond my compass.

"I don't need to hear your problems, Mr. Druid. All I need to hear is that you'll get it done, because that's the trade we agreed to."

"I'll do my best, of course. But if the elemental says no—"

"Then you'll convince it to change its mind. There ain't no room here for negotiation. A deal's a deal."

"All right," I said, holding up my hands in surrender. I hoped the elemental in this part of the state would be amenable to a scheme like this. It wasn't Sonora, with whom I'd worked for years, but rather Colorado, and

I'd had very little contact with it, or her . . . whatever. Granuaile had me questioning all my pronouns.

Mollified, Coyote changed the subject. "You still friends with that vampire down in Tempe?"

I narrowed my eyes. He was referring to Leif Helgarson. "Yes," I replied. "Why do you ask?"

Coyote shrugged. "How's he doin' these days?"

"He's recovering from a strenuous journey. Jet lag, I guess." Which was true, if jet lag equaled getting his head smashed to pulp by Thor.

Coyote smirked. "Right, Mr. Druid. Let's call it jet lag."

"What about it?"

"Well, I've noticed he ain't protectin' his territory like he used to. We got us vampires all over the place now."

"All over the place? Which place? Can you be more specific?"

"Well, we got us two right here in Tuba City, which is two more than anybody needs. There's one in Kayenta and a couple more over in Window Rock. I bet there's three or more in Flagstaff, and that's only northern Arizona. That's seven or eight more vampires than there used to be for sure, and your friend ain't doin' a damn thing about it. Who knows how many you got crawlin' 'round Phoenix and Tucson? Probably a whole lot more."

"Are they killing people here?" Granuaile asked.

"Not yet," Coyote replied, shaking his head. "They're just takin' little sips and scaring people."

"I'll ask about him next time I talk to my lawyers," I said. Hal Hauk, my attorney, was now alpha of the Tempe Pack and could get an update from Dr. Jodursson posthaste. "Maybe he's getting better."

"Maybe he ain't, and that's why we have all these new ones lookin' to take over."

"Anything's possible," I agreed.

A trio of servers arrived with our food and looked curiously at Coyote, the guy who'd ordered twelve sides of meat. The tabletop quickly filled up with plates, and Coyote ogled them greedily.

"Can I get you anything else?" the waitress asked, a curious half smile on her face.

"Yeah, wow, this sausage is really good," Coyote said. He was already chewing on an entire patty he'd folded into his mouth. "Four more orders o' that, if ya don't mind. I'll be ready when it gets here, I promise."

<Atta dog, Coyote!> Oberon said. <Did she bring the bonus bacon, Atticus?>

Yes, she did. Hold on, it's coming.

The waitress returned to the kitchen, shaking her head, and I passed my bacon over to Coyote so he could put it on the seat for Oberon.

My omelet looked scrumptious, and I promptly showered it with Tabasco to perfect it. Granuaile slathered her pancakes in butter and maple syrup and sighed appreciatively. For a while we did nothing but celebrate gluttony. After we'd tucked in long enough to take the edge off, I broached a subject that had been pestering me.

"What I don't understand," I told Coyote, "is how you came up with this idea in the first place. This long-range planning, this sudden altruism—well, it doesn't sound like your sort of enterprise, if you don't mind me saying."

"Umf," Coyote grunted around a mouthful of ham. He held up a finger, telling me to wait, there was more to come after he'd swallowed. After he gulped down the ham and chased it with a swig of coffee, he said, "Know what you mean, Mr. Druid. It's a fair question. An' it came about because I asked myself a differ'nt question, like why I'd never bothered to do somethin' good for my people."

"Hold up," I said. "What made you ask yourself that question? I mean, you've been around a long time, Coyote, and you could have asked yourself that centuries ago if it was in your nature. What changed your outlook?"

"Oh. That." He looked shamefaced and mumbled something about oompa loompas.

"Pardon me?" I asked.

"I said *Oprah Winfrey,*" Coyote growled, his irritation clear. Granuaile's jaw dropped, and Coyote pointed a finger at her. "Not a word outta you, Miss Druid." She wisely took a large bite of her pancakes and chewed as if he'd been discussing nothing more than the nice weather outside.

<It's okay, Coyote, I secretly find her inspirational as well,> Oberon chimed in. <It's a shame she's no longer on the air. I had a dream once where I was in a studio audience full of famous dogs—I was sitting right next to Rin Tin Tin—and she gave all of us our very own cow. "You get a cow, and you get a cow, everyone gets a cow!" And then, to make it sweeter, she gave everybody their own Iron Chef to cook it up. I scored Bobby Flay, and Rin Tin Tin got Cat Cora. The Tramp got Morimoto but he was pissed because he wanted Mario Batali, and I was like, "Tramp, you got a *free cow,* dawg, you have absolutely nothing to bitch about here," and he was all, "Look, Oberon, I've moved up in the world. I've sold a shitload of DVDs and I've single-handedly made mutts adorable, so I'm not going to settle for a guy who specializes in fish. I want an Italian who knows his way around a rack of ribs." Can you believe that guy? Total diva.>

Coyote and I chuckled over this, and Granuaile knew Oberon had said something amusing, but she refrained from asking what it was. She was still trying to keep her amusement over the Oprah revelation from showing on her face.

Sensing this, perhaps seeing the flicker of a smile at the corners of Granuaile's mouth, Coyote chose to move on. "Look, Mr. Druid. A long time ago, I fucked things up for people. Brought death to the world, you know, made it permanent. It's tough to live that down. I've always done things to satisfy my own hungers; seems like I'm always hungry," he said, gesturing to the stack of empty plates in front of him. He paused as the waitress arrived with his four additional orders of sausage and cleared away his dishes. Then he continued, "But I see now there are other hungers than mine to feed. An' I want to do somethin' about it. I want to do somethin' that is one-hunnert percent good. People will look an' say, where's the downside? What trick is Coyote playin' now? But there won't be any. An' that'll be my finest trick of all."

Coyote ate his sausage even faster than before, then got up to go to the bathroom and didn't come back. That meant I got stuck with the bill; I should have seen that one coming. The trickster was waiting for us out in the parking lot with a grin on his face.

"Took you long enough," he said. "You ready to go?"

"Yeah, let's do this."

Coyote called shotgun and was visibly surprised when I moved to the rear door. "She's driving?"

"Yeah. It's my car," Granuaile said, then arched an eyebrow. "Is there a problem?"

"Hell, no."

"Good." She beamed at him briefly, then ducked into the driver's seat.

<You almost died again, Coyote. Close call,> Oberon said.

At Coyote's direction, we drove on 160 northeast

toward Kayenta, but before we got there we turned off
on a dirt road just on the far side of a massive sandstone
wonder called Tyende Mesa. It was rough, dry country,
covered in red rocks and infrequent attempts by plant
life to make a go of it. The trees were scrub cedars and
junipers; there wasn't the cactus you'd find to the south
in the Sonoran Desert. People tend to picture the state of
Arizona as all saguaros and rattlesnakes because that's
the sort of postcards they keep seeing, but saguaros
don't grow on the Colorado Plateau. Parts of the plateau are pretty lush with pine, like the southern tip of it
known as the Mogollon Rim, but on the reservation the
topsoil is shallow and sandy and mostly unable to support large trees, except in the bottoms of old washes.

The road was extremely rough in places. Discarded
tires bore mute testimony to the fact that the thin layer
of sand covered sharp rocks. We crossed a one-lane
metal bridge that spanned a narrow defile—a flash-flood
canyon that eroded anew every time it rained and the
water trailed off the bare rock of the mesa—and, shortly
after that, Coyote directed us to pull over onto a cleared
patch on the left side of the road. There, the mesa rose
up steeply in a sort of terraced fashion until it flattened
out again, then two magnificent buttes jutted up almost
like the dorsal fins of some massive, mad creature, an
avatar of erosion swimming in sand. The flash-flood
wash we had crossed no doubt began between those
buttes. In the other direction, the plateau was flat and
covered with various bunch grasses and a few stunted
trees, all the way to Kayenta and beyond. We took some
canteens with us and began hiking up the mesa toward
the buttes.

"First thing I need you to do," Coyote said halfway
up, "is make a nice smooth graded ramp here to speed
up the construction of a road. Down there where the
car's parked," he pointed to the flat, arid plateau, "we're

going to build the work camp that will eventually become a town. And once we build the factories for our solar and wind companies, it'll be a proper city. A carbon-neutral one too." He put a hand next to his mouth and whispered as if he were sharing a secret, "I learned that carbon-neutral shit from a hippie in Canyon de Chelly."

We continued to hike until we crested the first terrace. The next layer, sort of like a wedding cake, loomed on either side. We walked west down a valley dotted with scrub cedar for about a quarter mile, until Coyote stopped and spread his arms wide to indicate the northern butte face. "Here is where you make my people rich," he said. "Move the gold underneath this mesa. We'll put the entrance to the mine in that little cave right there." He pointed to a small depression at the base of the butte that qualified more as a niche than a cave.

I shook my head. "You know, Coyote, this makes no sense geologically. You can't put gold underneath this kind of rock. Geologists will scoop out their eyes with a melon baller and ruin their shorts when you start hauling precious metals out of here, because it will put the lie to everything they know. Then you'll have prospectors searching for gold underneath every chunk of sandstone around the world and getting pissed when they don't find any."

"I don't care, Mr. Druid. This is the place."

"It has to be here? We can't pick a spot elsewhere on this huge reservation that makes more sense in the natural world?"

"It has to be here. I've gotten permission to build here from the Kayenta chapter, I've gotten you permission to live here while we do it, and my workforce and business connections are all in Kayenta. This here is where we change the world, Mr. Druid."

<But no pressure or anything, Atticus.>

Chapter 4

As we were hiking back down the hill, three white work trucks rolled up behind the car. They were full of people in jeans and orange T-shirts, some wearing cowboy hats and others wearing hard hats. One man in a hard hat started giving directions, and the workers moved to get stakes and sledges out of the truck beds along with surveying equipment and one of those portable toilets. A woman and an older man stood next to the man in the hard hat. They weren't wearing orange shirts, and thus I concluded they weren't technically part of the work crew.

All three of them were very happy to see Coyote. They shook hands and traded smiles full of affection for one another. Their faces turned expressionless, however, when Coyote began to introduce the white people. He remembered our fake names, thankfully.

"Reilly and Caitlin Collins," he said, "this here is my construction foreman, Darren Yazzie." The man with the hard hat nodded at us and mumbled a "Pleased to meet you." He was a well-muscled fellow in his mid-twenties, his eyes mere slits in a sort of perpetual squint from working outside all the time. He wore his hair long and braided in the back in a single thick queue.

Coyote pointed next at the woman, who appeared to be in her late twenties or early thirties. She wore a thin black Windbreaker over a yellow polo shirt. Her hair was pulled back and tied in a simple ponytail, and she had a pair of eyeglasses with thick black rims resting on her nose. A hundred subtle cues of body language told me that there was a keen intelligence behind those eyes; I knew she was important to this project before Coyote said a word. "This," he said, "is Sophie Betsuie, the head engineer."

"Hello," she said, shaking our hands firmly. "Nice to meet you."

The elderly gentleman had character carved into his face, arroyos and washes of years trailing above and below his mouth, around his eyes, and down his neck. His black cowboy hat sported a silver band set with turquoise in the front, and he had a buttoned-up broadcloth shirt tucked into his jeans. He had a giant chunk of turquoise floating at the base of his throat, because he'd apparently missed the memo that said bolo ties were out of style and quite likely had never been in style at all. His belt buckle was an enormous silver job worked in fine detail, though I couldn't say what the design was, since I didn't take time to examine it carefully. I was too distracted by his aura, which had the telltale white light of a magic user in it.

"That's Frank Chischilly," Coyote said. "He's a *hataałii.*"

<Did he say hot tamale?> Oberon asked as I shook hands with Frank.

No, he said hataałii. *In the Navajo language, it kinda sorta means a medicine man.*

<Who needs medicine?>

Excellent question.

"I'm honored to meet you, sir," I said.

"Likewise," he replied. To Granuaile, he didn't offer his hand but rather tipped his hat and said, "Miss." His voice was scratchy and warm, like a wool blanket.

"What brings you out here, Mr. Chischilly?" Granuaile asked before I could.

"Well, he has to be here," Coyote explained.

"Oh," Granuaile said, nodding, then added, "Sorry, but why does he have to be here? I'm not too clear on what that thing was you called him. Are you a tribal official, Mr. Chischilly?"

"Nope," he said, a faint trace of a smile on his chapped lips. "I'm here to do the Blessing Way ceremony, once we get a hogan built up there."

"Cool!" Granuaile said, a huge grin lighting her face, and then it disappeared, replaced by uncertainty as Frank's vague amusement vanished. "Oh. I mean . . . I didn't mean to assume. I would love to watch, but I'm not sure if that's allowed. I actually don't know what the Blessing Way ceremony is, so forgive me if I just sort of stepped on your toes there, I feel really stupid if that makes you feel any better, and—"

Chischilly raised a hand to stop her stream of apologies and gave a shrug. "Hey, it's okay with me if it's okay with Mr. Benally."

Before I could ask who Mr. Benally was, Coyote said, "It's okay with me."

Interesting. Granuaile and I pivoted on our heels to face Coyote with our eyebrows raised, and Oberon said, <Hey, if everyone around here is going to use a fake name, then I should have one too!>

"Thank you, *Mr. Benally,*" I said, emphasizing the name.

<I want to be introduced to these people as Snugglepumpkin. You have to say it seriously too, Atticus; you can't laugh.>

Sophie Betsuie chose that moment to ask, "Is this your dog? What's his name?"

"Snugglepumpkin," I said.

Sophie snorted in disbelief but recovered rapidly, wiping a nascent grin off her face. "Oh. That's really his name?"

<Tell her yes! Play it straight.>

But why?

<Just do it!>

I nodded somberly. "That's his name."

"Oh. Well, that's . . . simply . . . *adorable*." Sophie put her hands flat on her thighs and bent her knees a bit as she looked at Oberon. Her voice took on that saccharine-sweet tone people use when they talk to something they think is cute. "Yes, you're adorable, aren't you? Are you a good boy, Snugglepumpkin?"

Oberon wagged his tail and came over within petting distance.

"Oh, yes, you *are* a good boy, yes, you *are*." She stopped making sense and instead made high-pitched squeals of delight as she scratched Oberon's giant head; the rest of us stood and watched as a woman with an advanced degree completely lost her mind.

Okay, explain to me what you're doing, I said.

<I'm testing a hypothesis, and so far it's working. It states that any human female who can be classified as a "dog person," when confronted with a friendly-looking dog of any breed bearing a ridiculously cute name, will begin to make sounds at least two octaves above her normal register within thirty seconds of meeting said dog. She went there in less than ten seconds.> He sounded particularly smug about that last part.

Oberon, you shouldn't have done this.

<I am Snugglepumpkin. Hear me roar.>

When she snaps out of it she's going to be embarrassed, and we just met her.

<Bacon is the Way and the Truth! But I'm beginning to have my doubts. These noises she's making are kind of annoying.>

Bark once and she'll stop out of surprise.

Oberon barked.

"Oh! You're getting excited, aren't you, Snugglepumpkin? I'd better stop, then."

<Hey, good call, Atticus.>

"So how long you think it's gonna take you to get that road graded for us up to the top of the mesa?" Coyote said, redirecting us back to business. "I wanna start buildin' that hogan as soon as possible."

"Should be good to go by tomorrow morning," I replied.

Sophie frowned. "I beg your pardon? You're going to have a functional road built to the top of that mesa by tomorrow morning?"

This was also news to Darren Yazzie, whose workers would presumably be accomplishing all this. "Wait, how are we gonna do that? We don't have the right equipment out here."

Whoops. Coyote had already clued me in that these people weren't aware of his true nature—or mine—but I'd answered him without adjusting for "normal" ears. I covered brilliantly: "Uh—"

"I think we're talkin' 'bout two differ'nt things," Coyote interrupted, a sly smile on his face and a glint in his eye that told me he was enjoying my mistake. "Don't mind Mr. Collins here. He's just a geologist. Completely worthless when it comes to buildin' shit. He can 'splain the fuck outuva rock though, heh heh."

I shot Coyote a glare while Granuaile coughed to hide a laugh. Darren and Sophie confined themselves to smiles, but Frank Chischilly chuckled hoarsely.

<I think he got your goat, Atticus! And I've been meaning to ask you about that expression. When people get your goat, what do they do with it? Do they eat it or hold it for ransom or what?>

See, this is why I enjoy Oberon's constant commentary. Much of the time it's a bit distracting and funny enough that I might laugh inappropriately in the face of people who can't hear what he says. But in this case, it saved me. If he hadn't been around to point out that I looked irritated, I might have said something stupid and escalated things with Coyote. Instead, I excused myself by saying, "It was nice to meet you all, and I hope to speak with you later. I have some work to do right now though." I turned and strode up the incline to the base of the mesa, Oberon and Granuaile following in my wake.

Typically you never get your goat back, I explained to Oberon. *So you're left with two choices. Either you let it go and get another metaphorical goat, or you try to get their goat in a sort of eye-for-an-eye revenge thing. Most people get another goat.*

<Wow. Sounds like a sweet deal for the metaphorical goatherders! Those guys must be livin' large.>

"That was an interesting encounter," Granuaile observed, once we were safely out of earshot. I grunted sourly, and my apprentice laughed. "You're going to build that road tonight out of spite, aren't you?"

I grinned, amused that she could read me so easily. "If I can get the elemental to cooperate, I will. Then I want to see our so-called Mr. Benally explain it to Sophie and Darren, because I'm supposed to be a geologist who can't build shit."

"I think it's funny how he messes with you," Granuaile said.

"You do, eh? Well, we'll see how you like it once he starts playing his tricks on you. They're not always harmless tricks, you know. There's a dark side to all tricksters. Coyote laughs at other people's misfortune more than anything else, and this little name and occupation game of his could be the setup for something bigger down the road."

Granuaile's amusement faded. "We're protected against him, though, aren't we?"

"Protected how? You mean magically?" I snorted. "Coyote doesn't need magic to trick us. The only thing we can do is try to stay ahead of him. Gotta be smarter than the anthropomorphic canine."

<Whoa, did you just talk smack about canines?>

No, I said that Coyote's a dog in the shape of a man.

<Oh, yeah, well, I feel sorry for him when he's like that. He probably can smell hardly at all! This is why we need smelling-nose dogs, Atticus. They'd serve the burgeoning arthro . . . uh, powerstick canine market.>

Anthropomorphic.

<Right. That's totally what I said. You don't get a point for that.>

"Crap," Granuaile said. "Now I'm going to be paranoid about him pulling something on me."

"Ehhhxcellent!" I said, steepling my fingers together like Mr. Burns on *The Simpsons* who's always talking to Smithers. Then I switched genres. My voice took on the high nasal tones that comic-book villains tend to have when adapted for the Saturday-morning cartoons. "You should cultivate paranoia, because they really *are* out to get you!" I dropped my hands and resumed walking and talking normally. "He'll notice that, by the way. He'll smell your anxiety and fear, so you need to relax without appearing to be consciously relaxing."

"Right, sure. Now that we're talking about it I won't be able to."

"Insidious, isn't it? But you can do it. It's a Druid thing."

"Whatever, sensei."

"I'm being semi-serious. Once you're bound to the earth and you can see in the magical spectrum, you'll be dealing with two different sets of stimuli. I showed you what it was like before, remember? Right before those

German witches tried to kill us, I bound your sight to mine."

"I remember."

"Now remember how disoriented you were. That's major-league cognitive dissonance, and you'll need to embrace it and master it if you want to accomplish anything. You'll also want to project complete calm to enemies when you're planning to stab 'em in the pancreas. And if you ever want to shift planes with anyone, you'll have to hold their totality in your mind along with your own. The essence of Druidry is training the mind to both handle contradictory input and construct contradictory output."

<That would make her a politician, not a Druid.>

What? Oh. Well—

<Hound 4, Druid 1.>

I continued to lecture a bit more, to disguise the fact that I was getting my ass handed to me by my dog. "One of the reasons I require you to learn so many languages is that you can use each of them as a different headspace; they're going to provide you with a framework in which to multitask, and they'll also help you avoid mistakes. You'll want to use Old Irish for your magic and English for everyday use, so that you're firmly separating your bindings from your regular speech. Then you're going to want to pick a language to use for elementals that's different from either."

"But I've already started using English when talking to them," she replied, sounding a bit worried. Two elementals had given her a small piece of themselves so that she could speak with them before she got bound to the earth.

"That was only with Sonora and Ferris," I pointed out. "There are plenty of other elementals out there, and if you continue to use English with them once you're connected to the earth, you'll wind up calling them accidentally and broadcasting your emotions when you don't want to."

"Why does the language matter at all? Speaking to them is all emotions and images anyway."

"Again, each language is a different headspace; it patterns your thinking and gives it a unique signature. So once you make contact with an elemental in a certain headspace, that's what they become attuned to. For Sonora and Ferris, you'll always need to think in English. But if you stick with English as you meet new elementals, you'll unconsciously start to call them when you'd rather not—they'll pick up on your thoughts when you're angry or overly excited and wonder if you're talking to them. And it won't be long before you'll start to annoy them."

"Oh. What language do you use when you speak to elementals?"

"I use Latin. Since it's a dead language, the pattern of my thoughts doesn't change with the popular culture. But you can use Greek or Russian or whatever you'd like."

"Latin sounds good," she said, and I gave her a nod of approval. She was progressing well with her Latin. And in . . . zeal, I guess. I don't know how else to put it. She was different somehow since my return from Asgard, but I couldn't pin the tail on the donkey named Why. We had found very little time to talk about anything except what might have happened to Mrs. MacDonagh and how we would survive the vengeance of the Norse. I had probably spent more time than I should have brooding in silence over both problems. Circumstances had hardly allowed me to conduct Granuaile's training peacefully or, indeed, in any way conducive to shaping a mind for Druidry.

An unwashed, bearded phantom of my memory rose to scold me, a loaf of bread in one hand and a yew staff in the other, his wee, beady eyes glaring at me from under grizzled brows. It was my archdruid, who I'd assumed was dead these many centuries past but still lived on in one sense as a rather loud voice in my head. His staff blurred, and I could almost feel the pain of one of his sharp raps to the skull: "Pay attention, Siodhachan!" he said. "You're cocking it up again!"

He was right. But Granuaile's training would have to stay on my back burner until I could finish cooking what Coyote had ordered. We stopped at the base of the mesa and sat down, yoga style. Oberon stretched out and panted, his tongue lolling to one side.

"I'll have to spend a bit of time working at this," I explained.

Granuaile squinted up at the sky to check the sun—a routine precaution for the fair-skinned living in Arizona, who must live in fear of crispy skin—and saw that a thin layer of stretched cotton clouds diffused the January sun's weak rays. She gave a short nod.

"All right. I have plenty more Latin to learn," she said. "I'll go get my laptop out of the car. But before I do, I need to ask: How much can you tell me about the Blessing Way ceremony?"

It was a difficult question, and I frowned before offering up a disclaimer. "I'm not an expert on this. More like a vaguely informed outsider."

"Good enough. I'm clueless."

"Well, first you have to understand that the training period for a *hataałii* is even longer than that for a Druid. We're talking twenty years or more. There's lots of memorization, lots of practice, lots of collecting the proper materials for the rituals. So what does that tell you about Frank?"

"He's probably smarter than me and ten times more patient."

"Heh! I think he might be wiser; let's say that. And I

bet he knows more about the medicinal properties of native plants than I do. But you probably nailed the patience thing. Some of that comes with age." I took a breath to order my thoughts before I continued. "Okay. There are many different kinds of these ceremonies. The Blessing Way is an entire branch of ritual practice. The Navajo word for it is *hózhóji*. You can perform the Blessing Way on a mother and her newborn, for example, or on a soldier going to war, or you can bless a building and make it holy, like Frank is going to do. There's also the Enemy Way, which is used to get rid of evil influence—or on people who have been away from the tribe a long time and need to reconnect to their roots. But what all the ceremonies have in common are songs and prayers, which call to the Holy People, remind people of their origins, and bring them into harmony with the universe. Often there's a sandpainting of the Holy People to help things along—it's the only time they're allowed to depict the Holy People visually, so all those sandpaintings the tourists buy are just art for art's sake; they're not anything of religious significance. They have a word in their language, *hózhó*, which encompasses everything good, and we simply translate to 'blessing.' But it's beauty, peace, harmony, order, good health, happiness, and more. I should probably add that there is also another branch of practice, called the Witchery Way, that turns everything on its head—let's hope we don't run into anyone practicing that. So Frank is going to lead the Blessing Way, but you'll see it's not a tremendously formal occasion where people are bowing their heads and kneeling as some old crone leans down on a pipe organ to fill the air with a sense of piety. People will be talking or eating while he's singing. They'll be socializing and filling the place with love. That's all part of it. And we can do that too—we'll just stay out of Frank's way as he does his thing." I intended to watch him carefully. The magic in his aura indicated that he wasn't an average *hataałii*—but, then, I shouldn't have expected anyone average to be in the company of Coyote.

"Sounds good. Thanks, sensei. I'll let you do your thing now." Her footsteps crunched away behind me and Oberon sighed.

What's the matter, buddy?

<I'm bored. There's nothing to smell out here but you guys. It's all rock and bunch grass and there are hardly any animals to hunt. Plus they don't have cable.>

You poor, poor doggie. So take a nap.

<I'm not tired.>

Why don't you conduct another experiment?

<I haven't finished the one I've already started. Sophie is hardly a sufficient sample size, Atticus. You should know that.>

Perhaps you should explain what you're trying to accomplish. I don't understand how you're contributing to human knowledge.

<I'm trying to demonstrate the importance of names on human psychology and behavior. If you had introduced me as Oberon, or Spinecracker, or Hearteater, she would have kept her voice low.>

Well, that's quite a leap—

<I know, it's just my hypothesis. So I need you to introduce me to large numbers of strange women. But you're not allowed to flirt with them! You might skew my results. Are there large numbers of strange women nearby? I'm still bored.>

I sighed. *You can go harass the construction workers if you want. I even give you permission to sniff their asses.*

Oberon stopped panting and pricked up his ears at me. <Seriously?>

Sure, why not? They're construction workers. They'll

tease one another about it, especially if you sneeze afterward. But if you startle them, they might knock you upside the head, so watch out.

Oberon levered himself off the ground, his tail wagging. <Okay, this sounds like fun. Thanks, Atticus.>

No problem. He trotted away, leaving me alone to establish contact with the local elemental. We were on the Colorado Plateau, a large region stretching across four states, so I had already assigned it the name of Colorado in my mind. I took a deep breath, put myself in that Latin headspace, and sent a message through the tattoos that bound me to the earth: //Druid greets Colorado / Wishes health / Harmony//

There was a long pause before I got an answer. I was getting ready to repeat my greeting when it came. //Colorado greets Druid / Welcome//

I frowned at the short rejoinder. Elementals aren't talkative as a rule—they don't talk at all, really, I simply do my best to render their images into words—but Colorado sounded reticent, perhaps even a bit surly. Usually elementals are overjoyed to hear from me. They tell me to relax, ask me to hunt, wish me harmony, and so on.

//Query: Health? / Harmony?//

//None// came the reply.

Well, shit. I tried to remember the last time I'd spoken to this elemental and came up blank. I knew I'd traveled through here with Coronado and Don García López de Cárdenas in the sixteenth century, but after that . . . This might be my first visit since. I wondered if elementals felt jealousy. Might Colorado be feeling petulant because I'd spent so much of the past decade talking to Sonora, Kaibab, and the other elementals of Arizona, but not to him?

//Query: Source of discord?//

Deafening silence. Yep. Colorado was having an elemental hissy fit. Emergency flattery needed.

//Druid happy here / Will stay for long visit / Find harmony//

That got a response. //Query: Druid will stay?//

//Yes / Druid visits for long time//

//Query: How long?//

Damn it. Promising a lengthy stay would get me quickly into his good graces, but I didn't know what I could promise anymore. Still, provided that the Norse and the rest of the world believed me dead, the reservation would be a good place to stay and complete Granuaile's training. I chose a happy turn of phrase. //Druid wants to stay forty seasons / Perhaps more//

Wanting wasn't the same as promising.

//Joy / Contentment / Harmony// Colorado said.

//Harmony// I agreed. Ice broken. Granuaile returned and sat down beside me as Colorado took great delight in showering me with a list of complaints. He'd had less than average rainfall the past few years, his water tables were getting dangerously low, and to make matters supremely irritating there was the matter of the coal mines, which not only opened wounds on his surface but exacerbated the water problem.

And since he'd last seen me, he'd suffered fifteen extinctions. Not nearly so many as other elementals, not by a long shot, but he mourned them no less. I commiserated with him throughout the afternoon and into the evening before asking him to do anything. The sun had headed off to bed early, the workers had all headed back to Kayenta, and Oberon was napping next to Coyote by the time I wondered if he'd help me build a road from the plateau floor to the top of the monocline.

A graded slope for his long-lost Druid buddy? Hey, no problem! Colorado couldn't wait to show off, and he knocked it out in about a minute, amid a great clash of rocks and dirt that woke Oberon and Coyote and roused Granuaile from the campfire she'd built some distance away. Coyote was now in his animal form, and he began to yip in amusement at how quickly the road took shape.

"It's too bad I can't build shit," I told him. "Because now you'll have to explain how this got here without me."

Coyote fell over laughing and howled, and Oberon regarded him with bemusement.

<What's so funny about moving rocks around?> he asked. <Is there some kind of joke to it that you never explained to me?>

No, Coyote just appreciates a good trick. He put me on the spot earlier and now I've turned it against him. How did the ass-sniffing go?

<Oh, it was great fun! Lots of laughs. I scored a peanut-butter sandwich too. But nobody had milk; how do you like that?>

I thanked Colorado for his wonderful work and told him we would speak again in the morning. I'd be hanging around and training an apprentice, and I was counting on him to help me teach her about the earth's needs. He was nearly overwhelmed with gratitude and pride at this news and said it was the best day he'd had in centuries.

While I'd been in a trancelike state all afternoon, paying full attention to Colorado, Granuaile had slipped away to town and come back with a few groceries. She had a basic grill propped over the fire, thanks to a couple of rocks, and she was making hamburgers sprinkled with garlic powder. In a cast-iron skillet resting on one half of the grill, she sautéed mushrooms and onions in olive oil.

<Will you tell her I like my cow plain?> Oberon said. <No need to ruin it with fried fungus, and those onions will give me Heinz body anemia.>

I think she knows that already, but I will tell her. I was used to watching Oberon's diet and unbinding the caffeine in his tea, but he was conscientious about keeping track of his allergies in case I missed something.

Coyote shifted to his human form and chuckled. "That was pretty good, Mr. Druid. But why'd it take ya so long? Woulda been better to do it when ever'one was still here."

"You got a completely solid road made to the top of that mesa in less than a day and you're complaining about how long it took?"

"Ain't complainin'," Coyote said. "Just sayin' your timing coulda been better."

"I'll remember for next time, Mr. Benally."

Coyote told us stories after we ate—some of them old, like his encounter with Horned Toad and with Bluebird, and some of them new, like teaming up with Rattlesnake to scare a traveler who'd stopped on the roadside to relieve himself.

After I told a story about my involvement at the Battle of Kalka River, and Oberon shared how he'd landed on that rescue ranch in Massachusetts where I'd found him, we were ready to hit the sack. Said sacks were in Granuaile's car; she'd stowed sleeping bags in there in preparation for this road trip, because we knew at some point we'd be staying outdoors. Granuaile hauled them out, I used a wee bit of power to smooth out the ground, and we stretched out for the night. Coyote took his canine form and curled up with Oberon near the fire, and Oberon was so pleased by this that he completely forgot that he was ahead in our little game and neglected to declare victory. That meant I might be able to catch up tomorrow. I couldn't wait to see how Coyote explained the road in the morning.

He disappointed me. To my chagrin, he brazenly, baldly lied about it. "It's always been there," he said, when Darren Yazzie asked how in the world we'd built a road overnight. Sophie Betsuie chimed in and said, no, it wasn't there yesterday, she remembered talking about it. And then Coyote turned everything into a dominance game.

"You callin' me a liar?" he said, a threatening growl in his voice. And that's all it took, because he was the boss.

Sophie wanted to call him a liar, bless her heart, but she couldn't. But she wouldn't cave and say he wasn't a liar either. She just turned around and walked away, making her position clear without saying anything.

Coyote shot a smirk at me. He hadn't been made the least bit uncomfortable by the situation. We were allies, sure, but he was also intent on getting the better of me whenever he could.

Now that the road was there, work trucks brought up lumber to build a large hogan. They were building it semi-traditionally, with a hard-packed dirt floor, but in terms of construction, they were going a decidedly modern route by bringing up a small crane to get the logs placed quickly—they'd already been cut and sized, kit style.

Frank Chischilly began singing some of the traditional songs; as the posts were placed in clockwise, beginning at the east, he sang to them. He had unrolled his *jish* for the Blessing Way, a buckskin medicine bundle containing everything he would need for the ceremony. Much of it he left untouched for now, but there were rattles and feathers, some stones, and tiny pouches that contained herbs and pollens, colored clays, and sand for sandpaintings.

I watched him do his routine at the southern post in the magical spectrum. Nothing unusual happened until he finished, and then a brief flash of white light appeared along the ground between the eastern post and the southern post. It faded quickly, and I had no idea what it signified other than some magical energy had been expended there. I didn't think that was normal for *hataałiis;* Frank was something extra.

I placed myself at Darren Yazzie's disposal and helped out, and we got everything framed up with a couple of hours of sunlight left. We still needed to insulate it and put something on the roof besides plastic sheeting, but the structure was up and looking good. Granuaile was excited, because Frank would continue the Blessing Way that night and she'd be able to observe more closely. She'd spent most of the day on her Latin and trying to keep Oberon entertained.

As Darren's crew was moving all the big equipment into a hastily fenced area for the evening, the *hataałii* was standing at the top of the road, about thirty yards away from the hogan site, nursing a bottle of water and looking down at the floor of the plateau. He called to us hoarsely, his eyes fixed on something to the north. Granuaile, Coyote, and I jogged over to him, but Oberon got there first. His hackles rose and he began to growl at whatever he saw.

<Atticus, we should run.>

Why? Who's there? Moralltach was stored in Granuaile's car below. I wasn't ready for a fight. But as I drew even with Oberon and put a calming hand on the back of his neck, the blood drained from my face when I saw a lone figure limping toward us across the dry red rock. It looked like a little old lady, and she could not have been more out of place; it was like watching Elmo ride in to the Sturgis biker rally in South Dakota.

Granuaile joined us a moment later and gasped. "How did she find us?"

"You know her?" Frank asked. "Coming from the north like that, it's a bad omen. An' I can tell from here she's got an awful bad vibe." I took note of that; if he was speaking literally, then he must possess some sort of rudimentary magical sight.

<I'll say. She could be a Sith Lord with a vibe like that. Or a Wall Street executive.>

Coyote squinted at her and agreed. "That ain't a little old lady."

"I used to know her," I admitted. "She's supposed to be dead."

Frank spat on the ground. "You sayin' she's a zombie or some crazy shit like that?"

"Not a zombie, but some crazy shit? Yeah, I think she qualifies."

"You ain't really a geologist, are ya, Mr. Collins?" Frank asked in a wry tone. He had a sideways grin on his face, one of those looks that said he expected me to lie and that he wasn't going to be fooled—or offended—if I did. If he could see something magical about the widow, then he could certainly see that I wasn't an average Joe. So I didn't try to pretend. It was all Coyote's story anyway.

"No more than Mr. Benally here is a benevolent entrepreneur," I said.

Frank chuckled as Coyote told me under his breath to shut up. That meant Frank must not know Coyote's true nature—but he probably knew Coyote wasn't normal either. "So what the hell is that out there?" the *hataałii* asked, pointing with a brief jut of his chin instead of his hand.

"I don't know what it is. But it's time I found out."

The figure approaching on foot from the north looked like the widow MacDonagh, but I knew it wasn't really her. I sprinted downhill to get my sword.

Chapter 5

After my return from Asgard, Oberon told me that the widow had died. Poor Mrs. MacDonagh had been fighting a long list of ailments before I left, and she succumbed to them during my absence, passing on in her sleep. But then Oberon told me that she rose from the dead, behaved strangely, never spoke and never ate. And she never had a single sip of whiskey. I knew at that instant she'd been possessed—though by whom or what, I wasn't exactly sure. All I knew was that whoever had taken possession was waiting for me to come back and get my dog. It could have been the Hindu witch, Laksha Kulasekaran; she had the ability to do something like that. But I doubted Laksha would break her word to me so offensively and invite my displeasure, and the timing suggested to me that it was someone (or something) else more dangerous. And, on top of that, Jesus had told me during our conversation in Rúla Búla that my activities in Asgard would attract unwanted attention.

I retrieved Moralltach from Granuaile's car, unsheathed it, and strode forward to meet the erstwhile Mrs. MacDonagh. Oberon, Granuaile, Coyote, and Frank Chischilly followed at what I hoped was a safe distance. Turning on my faerie specs, I saw that the widow no longer carried a human aura about her. There was a fairly humanoid shape to what I saw, but it bloated and pulsed and changed constantly, like one of those fractal screen savers, and it was rife with the white noise of magical power. Whatever possessed her was powerful; I strongly suspected it was a god.

What was left of the widow looked much the worse for wear. Her floral cotton dress was stained and unraveling at the hem. The light in her eyes was gone, and her face hung slack until I stopped ten yards away and lifted my sword.

"Who are you?" I demanded.

The stricken face stretched itself in a grisly imitation of a smile. The lips didn't precisely fit properly around the skull anymore, and I saw more tissue than I should have. It didn't reply in English; instead it spoke in Old Norse, and my worst fears were realized.

"I do not speak that tongue," it said. The voice was not the kind lilt of Katie MacDonagh but rather a wheezing rasp of malevolence, as if someone had taken a fistful of sandpaper to her vocal cords. "If you are the hound's owner, then I'm sure you understand me. Do you speak Old Norse?"

I nodded and replied in that language, which meant everyone else was out of the conversation. "Who are you?" I asked again. It couldn't be an omniscient sort, or it wouldn't have had to track me here using Oberon. That ruled out Odin, but it left almost everyone else as a possibility.

The creature in the widow's body chuckled, or rather made a sound like ice cracking in the spring, while the body shook with merriment.

"Come, now. I rule the old and infirm, the diseased and palsied, all the slain unchosen by the Valkyries, all whom Freyja abandons outside her hall at Fólkvangr. This form I take is no disguise. Surely you can guess."

With no little effort, I stifled a shudder. "Hel," I

breathed. The daughter of Loki, ruler of the dead in Niflheim.

The horrible smile yawned again. "Yessss."

"Why are you in Midgard?"

"I am here because of you . . . What shall I call you?"

"You can call me . . . Roy."

"That is not your true name."

"Let it suffice for now. What happened to the widow?"

"The woman who wore this skin? She passed on to the Christian lands as she wished. Her soul was not mine to take, only the body."

"The body isn't yours to take either. It's offensive that you should wear it. Release it and then we will talk."

"Nonsense," Hel replied. "I cannot walk around in my true form. People never wish to talk to me that way. They scream or gibber or vomit but never talk. However offensive you find me in this old woman's skin, we can at least converse without you losing your sanity."

I didn't insist she drop the widow's body now, because she might not be exaggerating. But neither did I like to think she would hold on to it. The widow's family deserved some closure.

"We will talk, then. But you will return this body to the place you found it out of respect for the dead."

The ice-crackle laugh returned. "What use could the dead possibly have for your respect? Perhaps I will grant you the favor, though. I suppose I could do it by way of thanking you for this sojourn through Midgard."

"I had nothing to do with it."

"Are you not he who slew the Norns and crippled Odin?"

"Yes."

"It was they who kept me trapped in Niflheim. Now I may visit any plane connected to the World Tree, and I have you to thank for it."

I lowered Moralltach slowly. She didn't seem intent on

attacking me quite yet. "You've come all this way just to thank me?"

"No. I've come because I'm curious. You wiped out the Norns and many of the Æsir, but I don't know why. Did you hate them?"

"No. I was led into Asgard through a chain of obligations, and once it became a kill-or-be-killed situation, I survived. That is all."

"That is all?" Hel looked bemused. "No vendettas? No quest for power or riches?"

"Not for me, no." The vendetta had been Leif's. And Gunnar Magnusson's, but he'd paid for it with his life. As for riches, we couldn't have cared less. We left Thor's hammer and belt behind—they were Leif's to claim, if anyone's. No telling who had them now. I had taken Odin's spear, Gungnir, by right of conquest, but it wasn't as if I was going to sell it on eBay.

"You seek no seat in Asgard, no reward from Niflheim?"

"No. As I said, I was drawn into the conflict but did not seek it out."

"Yet you have made it easier for me to achieve my goal," Hel said.

"What would that be?"

"Ragnarok, of course! Now that the Norns are dead, along with Thor and Heimdall and others, true victory is possible for the sons and daughters of Loki. I can start my preparations in earnest. Who is left to oppose us? Midgard and the other planes will be remade as my father sees fit. I tend to think he will burn it all and start over. It is time to marshal my forces, and so I wonder: Would you like to join us? Do you want to be there, at that new beginning?"

I took a step backward as if she'd pushed me, because the question was that repulsive to me. I struggled to keep my face bland and seem thoughtful when I wanted to grimace in disgust, because offending a goddess of the dead is neither wise nor polite. Best to let her down easy. I cleared my throat. "A new beginning," I said, nodding a bit as if the idea had appeal. "I've thought of it sometimes. I've wondered what it would be like if the people who abused the earth for personal gain were gone." That was as far as I could go, and I waved such thoughts away. "But these are idle speculations, the basest form of wishful thinking. I cannot judge who deserves death. And there can be no new beginning without destroying much that is beautiful and innocent and worthy of praise. I cannot be a part of such destruction."

The poor widow's face fell slack, and Hel's next words were frosty. "You will oppose us, then?"

"If you give me cause."

Hel brought her hand—or, rather, the widow's hand—up to the left side of her rib cage. It sank a bit into the fabric of her dress and clutched at something there, and then she gracefully drew out a large knife etched with runes. There was no scabbard that I could see; she had pulled it straight from her substance somehow. I raised Moralltach to guard myself and heard a collective intake of breath from the spectators behind me.

Hel laughed at our reaction. "Your Fae sword has a name, doesn't it?"

"Yes. Moralltach."

"This is Famine," Hel said, pointing it at me. "Perhaps no match for a sword. You are the better warrior, I am sure, in any case. I'm not famous for my dueling skills. But this knife will be the death of you, regardless." It began to twitch in her hand. "You see? It is drinking in your scent. The next creature it wounds will hunger for your flesh, and no other food will satisfy it."

Perhaps she expected me to quail in fear or beg her for mercy at this point. She seemed to anticipate some sort of reaction, so I remained still and alert for any attack, saying nothing. The daughter of Loki tilted her head quizzically.

"Do you doubt that I know of a creature to whom your sword means nothing?"

I shrugged.

Hel hissed in frustration. "So be it. Roy." The knife stopped twitching and she sank the "happy dagger" into its sheath—namely, her abdomen. Showing no ill effects from this, she turned and loped away to the north, in an extremely awkward and unsightly gait but at a surprisingly fast clip the widow never could have managed.

<Ah. Good job, Atticus, you scared her off!>

Not really. I'm in trouble.

<But she's running *away*, Atticus.>

Right. She's running to find someone to kill me.

<Oh. Shouldn't you stop her, then?>

I suppose I should.

"Sensei? What happened?" Granuaile asked. I didn't have time to explain if I wanted to catch Hel. Gods Below, listen to me—why would I want to catch Hel?

I gave chase anyway, eliciting cries of dismay from those behind me, who had no idea what was going on. I heard them pursue me, even as I pursued a wee Irish widow across the Colorado Plateau. I steeled myself to remember that the sweet little old lady was a malevolent goddess who didn't belong on this plane of existence. And no matter how I wished it were otherwise, that goddess was skittering around here because of me.

I'd been warned that my actions in Asgard would have dire consequences. The Morrigan told me they would, and so did Jesus—but he'd also said that only I could prevent the worst cataclysms from happening. Those cataclysms, I saw now, had to be the coming of Ragnarok; my actions had made the Norse apocalypse *more* likely rather than less. The forces that were supposed to stymie the onset of Ragnarok were either dead or crippled, thanks to me—and now there was no one around to deal with Hel on earth save myself.

On top of that, there was that prophecy of the sirens of Odysseus: If I was interpreting events correctly, they had foretold that the world would burn thirteen years from now. Perhaps their prophecy coincided with the advent of Ragnarok? The sons of Muspellheim were supposed to set the world on fire, according to the old tales. Would Hel have her forces marshaled by then? Would it even take her that long? Regardless, I felt I had to stop Hel, if for no other reason than that she'd personally threatened me. I needed that knife—and I wanted the widow's body back. It hurt to see her used as an avatar of death.

Drawing some power from the earth, I increased my speed and began to gain on her quickly. Hel heard me drawing closer and cast a glance over her shoulder. Seeing me there, she abruptly stopped, and the little-old-lady façade sloughed away like a summer dress around her ankles. I slammed on my brakes hard as a twelve-foot-tall horror erupted from the top of the widow's head and roared at me. It could be nothing but Hel's true form, and she was half hot, half rot. Her right side was lithe and supple and built to cause major traffic accidents on the Pacific Coast Highway, with a full half head of lustrous hair, an attractive eye, and other goodies. If I were a giant and looking to date half a woman, I'd ask her out. But her left side—split right down the middle, mind—was like a particularly purulent zombie corpse, with bones and muscle fibers showing and some writhing-maggot action. She was the embodiment of the old saw that beauty is only skin deep. I spied the scabbard for Famine lodged between her lowest ribs, the handle sticking out into the air. If the hot side smelled like coffee and cinnamon rolls, it didn't get through the stench of putrefying flesh the rot side was throwing down. I took a breath to exclaim something profound like "Whoa, shit!" but the smell triggered my gag reflex and I staggered away from her, retching. Behind me, I heard similar startled cries choked off by heaves and juicy splashes of vomit spilling on the ground. Hel lurched a couple of steps my way and made as if to pull Famine out of its sheath, but when I raised Moralltach defensively, demonstrating that her smell hadn't completely overwhelmed me, she thought better of it. She blasted me again with an unholy Balrog belch, then she shrank back into the widow's skin, which resealed itself at the top of the head, and resumed her macabre flight north.

I was tempted to let her go, but then I reminded myself of the stakes.

In order to save the world, I would simply hold my breath next time I got close.

Hel lengthened her stride until she seemed to be executing a never-ending triple jump instead of running. I began to close the distance, with Colorado's energy providing the assist. When Hel spied me behind her for the second time, she didn't erupt again from the widow's head in an attempt to intimidate me. Instead, she stopped, turned, lifted her dead left hand toward me, and said with an unfocused gaze, *"Draugar."*

That word brought me up short. It was the plural form of *draugr,* and those weren't the sort of creatures you wanted two or more of. Even the singular would ruin most anyone's day. I waited a moment for something heinous to appear. Nothing did. The unholy grin split the widow's face one last time, and as Hel cackled at me I heard an alarmed squeal from the rear. It was Granuaile.

<Atticus! Help!>

I stole a glance back and saw three corpses with dark

blue skin between me and my friends, advancing toward them with a fair bit of menace—the corpses'outstretched arms weren't pleading for hugs. Apparently Hel could summon *draugar* at will. Already large and overmuscled for corpses, they were growing, their arms swelling like Peeps in the microwave. I didn't want to turn my back on Hel, but I didn't see what choice I had. My dog and my apprentice—not to mention Frank and maybe Coyote—were in danger.

But Hel didn't want to jump on my back. She just wanted me off hers. She turned and ran again to the north, leaving me to fend off three insanely strong zombies—not the George Romero kind that hungered for braaaains, but juiced-up Norse ones capable of magic in some tales. Oberon was barking, his hackles raised as the *draugar* approached them.

Don't bother barking. They can't feel fear. Harry them from behind or the flanks. See if you can knock them down, but don't let them grab you, I told Oberon as I sprinted to help.

<Gotcha,> he said, and then he scrambled around to the side of the nearest one—which completely ignored him and focused instead on Granuaile—and took a couple of quick strides to gather speed before launching himself at the *draugr*'s torso.

Why don't high school math teachers ever come up with cool problems like this? If a 150-pound Irish wolfhound launches himself at seventeen miles per hour at a 250-pound *draugr*, will that dead motherfucker go down? The answer is Hel yes. Oberon actually scored a twofer, because the *draugr* he rode down to the ground clipped the knee of a second blue boogeyman. My hound nimbly leapt away from the clumsy attempt to grab him and circled back around to place himself between the *draugar* and Granuaile.

"Run!" I shouted at her, now that I was in range.

"Just go!" Without any weapons or training, Granuaile wouldn't stand a chance against these lads, and thankfully she obeyed. The advice should have held true for Frank Chischilly. He wasn't a young man, and he was breathing hard already from trying to keep up with us this far. Coyote was urging him to bail. But he had pulled out a wee *jish* from his back pocket, and he was untying the rawhide knots as he backpedaled away from the third *draugr*. Coyote looked like he was trying to convince Frank to stop, but I couldn't tell what was being said, because they spoke in Navajo. The last thing I saw was that Frank had worked the knots loose and dumped the contents of the *jish* on his head. Said contents appeared to be nothing more than various colors of herbs and pollen and sand.

Then I had to concentrate my attention on the first two *draugar* that Oberon had knocked down. After a few moments of disorientation, they did not lumber to their feet so much as dissolve into mist and re-form again—except that when they re-formed, they were standing up instead of lying prone. I was still behind them and gaining fast.

<That's how they showed up,> Oberon explained. <They kind of rose up out of the rock, like steam, and then, *blam*, they're blueberry death on the march.>

Let's see if they can go all misty on a sword blade, I said. Iron hurt them but wasn't always fatal, from what I'd heard. This was the first time I'd ever run into *draugar*. Though I'm sure Hel had other forces at her command, *draugar* would be the bulk of her army. They wore heavy helmets with chain ventails to protect their necks; it was low-cost stuff but enough to prevent easy decapitation. Otherwise they wore nothing but the ragged remnants of tunics and breeches that they had died in long ago. White bone shone through here and there where the blue necrotized flesh had torn or rotted away.

I came in from behind and hacked at the arm of the *draugr* on the right, expecting the blade to shear through fairly easily, but it sank into flesh and bone and got stuck as if it was lodged in soft wood. Caught by surprise, the *draugr* jerked away, and suddenly I was disarmed, Moralltach dangling impotently from the arm of this corpse. The Fae magic began to work, the blue flesh turning black, but it only made the creature shudder. Its flesh was already necrotic, the creature already dead, so the enchantment was unable to kill it again.

"I miss Fragarach," I said, as both *draugar* turned to face me. Empty eye sockets and gaping skeletal smiles grimaced at me as they lurched forward. The one I'd hacked at made no effort to wrench the sword out of its arm. The arm was swelling, sealing the blade in if anything.

Can you knock down the blue one and buy me some time? I asked Oberon. *I need to take care of this black one first.*

<Easy,> Oberon said. He was behind them now. Juicing up my speed and strength, I charged the blackened *draugr,* who opened his arms wide to welcome me. Oberon charged the blue guy, and as he leapt up onto his opponent's back, I dove down and to my right, wincing as the rock tore at my skin. My dive put me next to the *draugr's* legs and, bracing myself with my hands and forearms, I spun around to kick the back of its knees; it crashed down heavily onto its back, right next to me. Its left elbow rammed into my back ribs and drove all the breath out of my lungs, but I was thrilled to see the hilt of Moralltach hit the ground first on its other side: That impact forced the sword to pop out of the thing's arm and fall backward. Before the creature could decide to turn into mist, I snaked my left arm across its throat and

then pulled with all of my might as I tried to fill my lungs again. It flailed at me, putting that left elbow to good use, but I wasn't letting go. A couple of cracking vertebrae, a sudden lack of tension, and I had torn its head from the body. I rose with it, gasping, and located the blue *draugr* not five yards away, newly re-formed out of mist after Oberon had knocked him down. I threw the head of his buddy at him and it caught him in the face; he staggered backward a couple of paces. That allowed me time to locate Moralltach and retrieve it. As I set myself to meet the *draugr,* I heard a massive bellow to my right. I risked a quick glance toward the sound and saw the most incredible possession I've ever seen.

Frank Chischilly was suddenly unbelievably strong, because he held what must have been a two-ton boulder above his head with one hand. As I watched, he jumped high into the air with it, one of those super anime leaps that are wholly unnecessary but completely awesome, and then came down with that boulder in his hand like he was dunking a basketball—a two-ton sandstone basketball that he slammed onto the head of the third *draugr.* The creature just disappeared under that rock, and Frank crouched down to land on top. If he'd been in the movies, he would have stayed there and risen slowly, heroically, as the dust cleared, but he leapt right down off that boulder and charged the last *draugr,* who was coming for me. Frank's shirt strained at the buttons as muscles he didn't have before threatened to burst out. His eyes were completely white and glowed a bit. I switched my vision to the magical spectrum, and Frank didn't have that cute little white line in his aura anymore; he was almost entirely made of white magic now, at godlike levels. He whipped around his right arm in a backhand swing at the *draugr*'s head, and when his fist connected, it was like he had teed off on the fourth hole. The head sailed away into the north sky, in the direction that Hel had run, and the dead blue corpse sank to the ground. Frank roared at it, and the veins on his trunk-size neck stood out; the turquoise stone of his bolo tie snapped off the cord and went zinging away, and his massive quivering pecs reminded me of Lou Ferrigno's. His opinion of the *draugr* established, he turned in a circle, searching for more foes. He looked faintly disappointed not to find any more—Hel was gone—and those glowing eyes examined us again for an uncomfortable few seconds, to make sure we weren't legal targets. And then he began to deflate, the light winked out of his eyes, and he coughed once, violently, before slumping into a faint. Coyote darted in quickly to catch him; he was a frail old man again.

Chapter 6

"Okay, Coy—Mr. Benally, I mean—what the fuck just happened?"

"I should ask you the same thing, Mr. Collins!" Coyote snarled. "Who was that lady and what were those things?"

"Tell me about Frank first. Is he going to be okay?"

"Yeah, he'll be all right," Coyote said, the anger in his voice modulating to regret. Frank's chest was still moving up and down. "Wished he hadn't of done that, though. He ain't gonna get another shot, and I was kinda countin' on him to use it on somethin' else."

"What'd he do?"

"He called Changing Woman and told her we had monsters here. Let himself be a vessel, see? So she sent her son, Monster Slayer, to help us out, a onetime limited engagement." So that *had* been a god inside him. An aptly named one.

Granuaile's footsteps approached from the south. "I'm assuming it's safe now? Ugh," she said, looking at the headless corpses. "What are those things?"

"They're sort of like zombies on Red Bull with a little bit of ghost mixed in," I said.

Frank moaned and his eyes snapped open. Then he closed them again and raised a hand to his head, saying something in Navajo that made Coyote laugh. He must have a killer headache. Coyote helped him up to a sitting position and patted him companionably on the back.

"All right, Mr. Collins," Coyote said. "It's your turn. Who was that lady?"

"Yeah," Frank said. "I nearly crapped my pants."

"That was Hel," I said, "the Norse goddess of death."

Frank turned to Coyote to see if he was buying it. "He's not bullshitting?"

"Naw, this guy don't usually tell stretchers about gods," he answered. Then he asked me, "What did she want with you?"

"She, um, wanted my help, I guess."

"Help with what?" Granuaile said, her lip curled. "Personal hygiene?"

"Um . . . destroying the world." I tossed Moralltach aside and sat down heavily in the red dust next to Frank, executing a double face-palm. Saying that out loud took quite a bit out of me. What had I done when figures like Hel approached me as a potential ally? My primary reason for going through with the Asgard trip had been to preserve my honor by keeping my word. But I saw no honor in an unstained name now. If Ragnarok began because of me, no one would remember or care that I followed through on my promises. There would be no kind historians to write apologetics for me.

Usually I try to suppress any emotions that savor of regret, because they are invariably aperitifs to a main course of depression, and for the long-lived, that's a recipe for suicide. But that doesn't mean they can't sneak up on me sometimes.

And, like, gang-tackle me.

I felt a slight spell of vertigo as the enormity of what I'd done hit me. I wept silently behind my hands for Mrs. MacDonagh, for Leif, for Gunnar, for Väinämöinen, for the Norse, and for the untold suffering to come because of my bad decisions. Druids were supposed to be forces of preservation, not destruction, and I could not dance around the fact that my stupid pride had turned me into a misbegotten cockwaffle.

Granuaile squatted down next to me and put a gentle hand on my shoulder. "Well, clearly she didn't like what you had to say about that," she said.

"Just checkin' here," Frank said, his voice thick. "Geologists don't normally get invited to help destroy the world, do they?"

Behind my hands, I shook my head. "No," I said. "No, they don't." I pressed my tears away with my palms and then dropped them to my lap. "But don't ask me who or what I really am right now. I'm supposed to be dead."

"Well, it seems to be a day for dead people to be walkin' around," Frank said. "And disintegratin'." He pointed over to the *draugr* bodies, which were turning into ash and mixing with the dust of the plateau.

"What was the deal with that freaky knife she had?" Coyote wondered aloud.

"It's called Famine. She said the next thing she cut with it wouldn't rest until it had eaten me."

"Ew," Granuaile said.

Oberon tried to cheer me up. <I'm going to give her a point for originality. "Druid: It's what's for dinner!" But then I'm going to take away three million points for how she smelled.>

Frank Chischilly narrowed his eyes. "Did she say if it works on only one thing or on as many things as she cuts with it?"

"That's a pretty specific question. Why do you ask?"

"Because there's a couple of skinwalkers livin' north of here. She's headed right for 'em."

<What's a skinwalker?> Oberon asked.

Granuaile scrunched up her face. "Aren't they shape-shifters of some kind? They use an animal skin?"

Chischilly nodded. "They have to use a different skin for each shape. They keep to themselves mostly, unless you invade their territory."

"You say there's two nearby?" I asked.

"Up past the ranches a few miles thataway." He pointed in the direction Hel had gone.

I shifted my gaze and glared at Coyote. "So I guess I know why you're so anxious to have the mine here," I said. "Its primary qualification isn't the proximity to Kayenta's workforce; it's the proximity to the skinwalkers. You figured I'd take care of them for you once they show up to defend their territory."

Coyote shrugged, not bothering to deny it. "I can't go after 'em myself. If they killed me, then they'd just be that much more powerful."

Frank Chischilly frowned, clearly not understanding how killing a man could make the skinwalkers more powerful. But I understood. Skinwalkers can't use a man's skin—they already have their own. Coyote wasn't a man, though, and that's what Frank hadn't quite figured out yet: Coyote was one of the First People, and whenever he died he always left his remnants behind. If the skinwalkers got hold of a Coyote skin, as opposed to a regular coyote skin, there was no telling what kind of shredding they could do with his power. And the Morrigan, I noted, had been right about thrice-cursed trickster gods. They were torrential fucksluices spraying their happy juices on the innocent and the damned alike.

To distract the *hataałii* from asking an uncomfortable question of Coyote, I asked him one instead: "How would you handle a skinwalker, Frank?"

He was so surprised by the question that he started to chuckle, and that morphed into a hacking cough. When the fit passed, he said, "You can't handle 'em. Just protect against 'em and wait for dawn."

That made them sound like vampires. "They can't be killed?"

Frank hawked up something green and spat on the ground. "Maybe they can, but I never heard of anyone pulling it off. Least not by any normal way you'd kill a man. They're wicked fast."

Granuaile asked, "They only come out at night?"

"Usually. Sunlight won't kill 'em, but they sure don't like it much."

"So you've run into them before. You have personal experience."

Frank nodded. "Long time ago."

"How'd you deal with that one?"

"We reversed a curse on it. We never woulda stood a chance otherwise. But it shot a bone bead into someone and then came back to make sure it was working the next night. We got it then, when it was standing still."

I squinted at him. "Got it how?"

"Shot it with the same bead. The bead was cursed. They're basically witches, and if you know how they worked a spell on someone, you can probably turn it back against them. These two ain't like the ones I've seen in the past, though. They don't use ceremonial magic. They just physically punish people. Can't fight back against 'em that way."

"Well, if they tend to come out at night, we'd better get inside before sundown."

"Yep," the *hataałii* agreed, and then he patted his chest as Coyote helped him stand. "Damn. Where'd my bolo tie go?" he said.

"It kind of popped off and sailed away over there," Coyote said, pointing.

As everyone looked around uncertainly, I shot a quick thought to my hound.

Oberon, think you can find it and bring it to me?

<Sure thing! Blue rock. I can do blue.> He trotted off in the direction of the turquoise's last known trajectory.

I rose from the ground and retrieved Moralltach, but Frank stopped me before I could take a step back toward the hogan site. "Whatever you are, Mr. Collins—if that's your name—I get the feeling that you were brought here as Plan B." His eyes shifted to indicate Coyote. "Except now you're Plan A."

I favored Coyote with another glare. "Yeah, the plan is sort of revealing itself to me as we go," I said. "How many of the others are in on this plan, Frank?"

"Oh, you mean Darren and Sophie and everybody? They all know about the skinwalkers."

"Damn it, Frank," Coyote grated softly.

"What? He wasn't supposed to know? Then why's he here?"

"Too late now. Tell me everything," I said.

"Well, Mr. Benally says we're buildin' a mine and stuff, but we're also baiting the skinwalkers with where we're buildin' it. Not everyone believes in them, you know. Lot o' people think they're just myths—I mean a lot o' the Diné who buy into the idea that there ain't nothin' in the world but science. And they also think I'm crazy and oughtta be locked up for sayin' they're real. But Mr. Benally believes me, and so does Sophie and the rest of this crew. What about you, Mr. Collins? Would you be willing to believe in skinwalkers?"

"Yeah, I'd be willing to believe most any monster is real—or was real at some point."

"Yeah, I figured," Frank said. "Guy who talks to Norse goddesses oughtta believe in a monster or two."

"I'm going to stop at the car for a minute. Meet you up at the site," I told Frank. He waved and started up to the mesa, but I held Coyote behind with my eyes.

"You, sir," I said, "have all the dignity of a badger

with the clap. Shark shit has more fiber than you. I'm going to tie you nuts-first to a monkey's cage and make a mix tape of the resulting noise. Then I'm going to take a bag of marshmallows and a pair of granny panties and—"

Coyote held up his hands in surrender and spoke in low tones to prevent the departing Frank from over-hearing. "I hear ya, Mr. Druid, but, look, it really don't make any differ'nce. You wanted to make a trade and you agreed to the terms."

"I didn't agree to kill any skinwalkers for you."

"And Frank didn't agree to kill those blue-skinned zombie things."

"No, but I didn't lead Frank here to confront them either. Don't expect me to give you any bonus services. The skinwalkers are your problem."

Coyote chuckled. "Well, they might be your problem now too, if that goddess o' death takes her knife to 'em. Can't blame me for that, Mr. Druid. She didn't show up here at my invitation with her hungry silverware."

Oberon returned with Frank's turquoise in his mouth. <One slobbery stone,> he said. <Will you be paying Treat on Delivery today?>

"Thanks, Oberon," I said, wiping the turquoise off on my jeans. "Let's go see if we can find you one in the car." I turned my back on Coyote without saying another word. He didn't want to know what I was going to do with those granny panties.

Surprisingly, Granuaile did. "Sensei, what were you going to do with those marshmallows and panties?" she whispered as we walked together. "I mean, I'm sure it had to be dire, but it just didn't sound as threatening as the potential havoc a monkey could wreak on his sack."

"There was more to that recipe," I admitted. "He cut me off before I could get to the Icy Hot and the gopher snake."

"Ew. What would you do with that?"

"I will leave it to you as an exercise."

I decided it would be best to keep Moralltach on me from now on. It wouldn't be conducive to maintaining the fiction that I was nothing but a geologist, but that wasn't much of a priority now, if it ever was. Frank and the rest of them could think whatever they liked about me; they'd never guess the truth.

Of more concern to me was who Hel might talk to now that she'd discovered the slayer of the Norns in Arizona a couple of days after said slayer was supposed to have died. My elaborate attempt to disappear through faking my death would all come to naught if Hel spread it around that I was still walking the earth. She needed to be faked out as well—or eliminated. But trying to invade Niflheim to take on Hel in her home territory didn't sound like a win to me. She'd have a nearly infinite supply of *draugar* at her command, a moon-devouring wolf hiding in her basement and itching for action, and the original Helhound, Garm, would probably consider me to be a light snack.

Retrieving the scabbard from Granuaile's trunk, I sheathed Moralltach and slung it over my back, fastening the leather strap across my chest. I fished out a treat for Oberon before I closed the trunk and tossed it into his mouth.

<Hey, Atticus. Do you automatically feel more like a badass with a sword strapped across your back?> Oberon asked. Using the new road, the three of us began to walk up to the proposed mine site.

I paused to think about it. *Well, I suppose I do,* I replied.

<A sword wouldn't do me much good,> Oberon reflected sadly. <But if I had one of those shoulder-mounted rocket launchers that Predators have, I'd feel much better. Can you get me one of those?>

Your shoulders aren't wide enough, I explained.

<Mount it on my back. When I want to fire, I'll lower my head.>

Hmm. That sounds plausible. It would require a rather elaborate harness, though. Would the discomfort be worth it?

<Of course it would! There is always a price to pay for badassery. Neo was a badass in *The Matrix* and *The Matrix Reloaded,* but the price he had to pay was *The Matrix Revolutions.* Still, the benefits outweighed the drawbacks, and I hypothesize that would also be the case here. Think of what I could do to those insufferable cats that prowl on top of fences and taunt dogs world-wide! For the price of some discomfort and chafing, I'd be a legendary canine hero!>

Yes, Oberon, I imagine you would, but, unfortunately, those rocket launchers exist only as props and CGI.

<Aww. You could have said so at first. I was getting my hopes up and then you ruthlessly smooshed them.>

Hound 4, Druid 2, I said, glad to finally score a solid point.

<Hey, wait! I won yesterday!>

You didn't call it, so the game continues.

<Fine. I'm calling it tonight and you're going to owe me a porterhouse.>

The workers on the mesa noticed the sword, and so did Darren and Sophie, but no one said anything about it; they were too polite.

Asking Oberon to stand sentinel outside, I entered the hogan with Granuaile to survey the interior. Hogans are not particularly large buildings, only about 250 square feet inside, but they're important to ceremonial life and thus crucial to the beginnings of large enterprises like this one. This hogan was one of the more modern plans, built in an octagonal shape; the walls were fairly free of gaps, since they were constructed with precut logs, and the roof was a latticework of beams covered over with black plastic sheeting at this point, a four-plane design. Tomorrow the roof would be finished and covered with mud, insulating it well, and the exterior walls would be covered too. I thought it interesting that this particular hogan included no windows; circulation came solely from the door and the round chimney built at the meeting of the various beams. In the center of the floor was a fire pit, and Frank Chischilly was hunched down over it, tending a small fire. Lava rocks were arranged closely around it, and Frank had sprinkled some herbs on them. The burning herbs sent fingers of fragrant white smoke up through the chimney.

He shot a glance up at me and then spoke to Granuaile. "We're going to stay in here tonight," he said. "Safer that way."

Granuaile noted the profound lack of facilities. "Guess I'd better visit the privy before sundown, then."

"Yep. We'll be startin' the sing as soon as everyone's ready."

"Anything I can do to help?" she asked.

Frank's eyes flicked over to me. "Well, if you happen to know any way to keep out or repel evil spirits," he said, perfectly serious, "that would be helpful."

That was an interesting challenge. "What kind of evil?" I asked, not knowing precisely what to ward against.

Frank stared at me in disbelief and then spat into the pit before asking, "Ain't there only one kind?"

"No, there's all kinds of evil, just like there's all kinds of good. What I need to know is where the source is. We're not dealing with the Christian hell here or *rakshasas* from the Vedic planes. Where is the evil coming from? This plane or somewhere else?"

"Oh, I see what you mean now. The spirits come from First World."

"That's Black World, right?" I asked. I knew some of the basics of the Navajo faith, but I was by no means an expert. Their creation story follows the Emergence pattern, where people emerge into this world after climbing through several subterranean levels, evolving as they go. According to what little I knew, our plane is Fourth World, which is sometimes called Glittering World or White World. Granuaile appeared lost but didn't interrupt to ask.

"Yep, that's Black World," Frank said.

"How'd they get all the way up here?" I wondered.

"Answer to that depends on who you ask. You want my guess?"

"Absolutely."

"I think they been here all along, since the world was first bein' made. We know that monsters an' spirits from the lower worlds came here to Fourth World in the beginning. But Changing Woman sent her sons, Monster Slayer and Child-Born-of-Water, to kill 'em all. I think they got most of the monsters—they left old age, hunger, cold, and poverty behind on purpose."

"Ah, but they didn't take care of all the spirits, right?"

"Right. Those spirits from First World, they were spirits of the air, but mostly ornery insects—angry beetles, ants, locusts, dragonflies, and the like. They got kicked out of all the other worlds for fightin' all the time, always wantin' to dominate someone else. Most of 'em got turned into real bugs, but some didn't and remained spirits. And the way I figure it is, when a soul turns as black as Black World, these old spirits find them a comfortin' touch of home, and if they're called to move in, they will. That's what a skinwalker is: a mean asshole with a meaner spirit squatting inside."

<I've run into some of those at the dog park,> Oberon said. <They're usually attached to Chihuahuas.>

"Hmm. All right, I've never dealt with anything like this before, but I'll see what I can do."

The *hataałii* didn't say anything, merely nodded and turned his attention back to the fire. Granuaile and I exited and rejoined Oberon outside. We walked off a short distance and spoke in low tones so that no one could hear, save perhaps Oberon.

"You have a way of warding against skinwalkers, sensei?" Granuaile asked.

I shook my head. "Not specifically. I've never been down to First World or run into a skinwalker before. It's been centuries since I've had to deal with any sort of Native American magic. I've been hiding in cities to stay away from the Fae, and all the shamans or holy men are hiding out on the reservations."

"When was the last time you dealt with any?"

"Well, there was this rain god of the Maya who gave me a bit of trouble."

"The Maya! Do you know what happened to them?"

"Not for certain, but they might have left this plane. They had a priest who could do it. But this is a completely different belief system," I said, waving back at the hogan, "and so the rules of the magic are different as well. If I wanted to work up something to ward specifically against a skinwalker, I'd have to confront it first and see the pattern of it in the magical spectrum. General wards against magic from another plane may or may not work. And that's the problem with wards, Granuaile." I figured I might as well embrace the teachable moment. "You can't ward against everything, and sometimes the bad guys will win through or around it despite your best efforts. So you know what happens in that case?"

"The bad guys win?"

"What, automatically? Getting past your wards means you're instant toast?"

"Well, no, I'd fight first."

"Exactly. You fight. The problem is you don't know how."

Granuaile huffed, her pride wounded. "I've taken some kickboxing lessons."

I grinned at her. "Ah, you have? Bring it." I set myself in a defensive stance.

My apprentice scowled at the idea. "You'll use magic."

"I promise I won't. Not even a little—"

She didn't lack for initiative. She pivoted and shot a kick at my gut before I finished the sentence. I pivoted as well and her toes grazed my belly, no more. I knew she was the athletic sort, but I hadn't seen her exert herself until now. She was fast. Lunging in, I socked her in the stomach before she could recover and she staggered back, wheezing. I didn't press my advantage, and she didn't seem eager to continue.

"You know a bit more than kickboxing, don't you?" she said.

I nodded. "Considerably more. We could do the whole Pai Mei thing if you want, but I'd rather not hurt you and I don't have the flowing white beard to pull it off respectably."

<If I grow out the hair underneath my chin until I look like Pai Mei, will you brush it to keep it silky yet intimidating?>

It will drag on the ground and get dirty every time you go to smell something or eat. It will be a mess.

<Oh. Good point.>

Thank you. Hound 4, Druid 3.

<Awww!>

"That's all right, sensei, I'll take your word for it," Granuaile said, clutching her stomach. "Do I have to carry water up the mesa or something? Wax my car? Paint the rocks?"

"No," I said, smiling at the movie tropes. "I don't

think I need to break your will. But we do need to train your muscles and get you accustomed to fighting with weapons."

"I'm going to need a sword, then?"

"We will train with swords, yes, but I don't think that will be your best weapon. Your size and reach will put you at a constant disadvantage in a sword fight. I think a staff would be better for you, and we will see what you can do with a throwing knife."

"How will a staff and some throwing knives help against some brute who bull-rushes me with his shield up? Or a smart guy with a gun?"

"An excellent question. Every weapon has its drawbacks. We'll prepare you for all kinds of antagonists."

"What about automatic weapons? Can you pull a Neo and dodge bullets?"

<Told you Neo was a badass.>

"Nope. I cheat if I have the time. I dissolve the firing mechanism with a spell of unbinding."

"And what if you don't have the time?" That was an even better question—a dawning ray of paranoia that should be encouraged. "What about snipers?" she added, and I almost burst with pride. I settled for clenching my fist and drawing it down close to my body.

"Yesss! I ask myself that question every day and everywhere I go. Well done. And the answer is, you look around." I pointed up at the buttes above us to the north and south. "I can't stand where they're placing this hogan, because we're in the ideal spot to get picked off. You have to see the snipers before they see you, take cover, and then unbind their toys into hunks of useless metal."

"But if you don't see them in time, or if they have one of those fancy plastic guns, you can't do anything."

"Right. Except duck. Druids aren't invincible, or else there would be more of us around."

Granuaile turned to consider the hogan, which was lined in the red glow of the setting sun.

"So how do you create a ward, anyway?"

"You can think of it like a Boolean search on the Internet. You begin by defining your boundary—'all life is okay in here'—and then you layer on the exclusions. 'And not frakkin' Cylons and not douche bags and not Imperial Stormtroopers.'"

"That's it?"

"That's what a ward is. The tricky part is defining your terms. How does the ward know the difference between a douche bag and a boy from Scottsdale?"

"Oh, I see." Granuaile nodded. "They're practically synonymous."

"Right. Much of the time spent constructing wards is devoted to defining your terms magically. And you can't define the magical signature of something until you've run across it once and laid your eyes on it in the magical spectrum. So I have no ward against skinwalkers. Trying to construct one now would be the equivalent of a null program."

"But you do have a ward against douche bags?"

"Alas! Turns out they're not malignant magical creatures at all, just naturally occurring phenomena, an evolutionary mutation of modern society."

Granuaile cocked an eyebrow at me. "Evolutionary? You're suggesting that douche bags are naturally selected?"

"Sure. Vestigial remnants of hunter behavior manifests itself as douchebaggery in males when confronted with the emasculating role of modern man, where they are no longer expected to provide food, shelter, or even spiritual guidance for their families but rather stay out of the way until it's time to perform in the bedroom."

"Really?" Granuaile cocked a single eyebrow at me, her voice drenched in wry skepticism.

"Maybe. I just made that up." I turned to Oberon. "I should get a point for that."

<No, Granuaile's not playing! You can't do that!>

"I don't think so, sensei. Sounded pretty pointless to me."

<Whoa, maybe she *is* playing. Hound 4, Druid 3, Clever Girl 1.>

Once the equipment was stowed, Darren Yazzie's whole six-man crew—each of whom I assume was handpicked by Coyote—was going to spend the night on site as part of Chischilly's Blessing Way ceremony. They unloaded a couple of coolers from their trucks and moved them inside, lit up a few kerosene lanterns for ambient light, and popped open some sodas. They had bedrolls and joked with one another about who was going to snore the loudest. Darren announced he was going to make a quick run into town to grab a couple of party trays full of veggies and some more ice, which was acknowledged only by Sophie; she smiled fondly at him, and I got the sense that he was doing her a favor. Frank didn't hear him at all, absorbed as he was with arranging his *jish* for the ceremony.

"Why do they need to stay?" Granuaile asked. "I mean, I get that it's a necessary part of the ritual, but why?"

I shrugged. "My guess is that they lend their strength and energy to the protections. The more people present, the stronger the blessing. Or the binding. I'll be watching as it progresses."

Frank started singing as soon as he was ready, while there was still a touch of dark rich blue in the western sky. As I'd thought, this didn't produce immediate silence among the crew. They may have quieted down a bit, and a couple of them were paying attention, but it was casual interest. The ceremony was conducted in

Navajo—a language I do not speak aside from a few stray words—but Frank was singing and working on a sandpainting on top of a sacred buckskin. It would be one of the Holy People, though I wasn't sure which one yet.

I turned on my faerie specs to see what magical energies, if any, were being employed, and discovered that Frank was doing something much more complicated than I expected.

To a Druid's eyes, all magic, regardless of origin, is an exercise in binding and unbinding. Other systems differ from Druidry in what they're able to bind and how, and usually they call on different energies from Gaia's, but all those circles and pentagrams and sacrifices accomplish a binding of some sort. Customarily there is a religion involved and a generous helping of faith. Shamanistic systems, like those of many Native American faiths, often seek to bind people more closely to the spirit world for healing and protection or else unbind them from the influence of a malign spirit. I find them all fascinating and a little bit scary, because, except for my own shape-shifting—which involves my own spirit—I have no influence on the spirit world. A Druid's bindings are physical. But what Frank was doing was occurring almost entirely on the spiritual level.

My suspicion that everyone would play a part in the ritual was confirmed; whether they knew it or not, whether they were actively participating or not, some portion of their energy, their spirit, was contributing to the protection of the hogan. It took no effort on their behalf; Frank was gathering it, channeling it, and redirecting it, and he was doing this through his singing and his sandpainting. Since I had never seen this ceremony performed by any other *hataałii,* I didn't know if it was normal—but I suspected Frank might be in a league of his own. In my sight, the energy flowed from the others in multicolored undisciplined globs toward Frank's sandpainting, and then it flowed outward from there as fine white rays of light. These rays shot toward the base of the walls. The ceremony wouldn't be complete until the fourth day, according to Frank, but his preliminary songs during construction and his current singing was already energizing a rudimentary protection along the base—and a good thing too. Oberon, who was inside with us, barely had time to warn me before the attack began. I was about to pop open a can of liquid sugar when his ears pricked up and he growled.

<Hey, Atticus, something's coming—>

A bestial feline scream rent the night and a crunching impact shuddered the north wall of logs, rattling the roof and eliciting more than a few curses of surprise. It was quickly followed by another impact directly behind where I was standing, which enveloped me in a cloud of sawdust and shot splinters into my back.

Chapter 7

As any war veteran will tell you, there is a vast difference between preparing for battle and actually facing battle for the first time. You can be told that reading Victor Hugo will sap your will to live, but you can't understand what that means until you've read a few chapters and your eyes have glazed over and someone has to revive you with a defibrillator. Sophie and the six crewmen might have understood intellectually that skinwalkers possessed superhuman strength and speed, but to see it in action freaked them out a little bit. The creatures had nearly punched through the walls on their first try.

Frank Chischilly cast a pleading eye over at Sophie and kept singing. He couldn't stop what he was doing without stopping the flow of magic; he had to keep singing, had to keep sandpainting.

"Keep on with the ceremony!" she bellowed. "Join in, help Frank where you can. It is our best defense." They nodded, and some of them offered up their voices along with Frank when they knew the words; the choruses were repetitive.

Any idea what's outside? I asked Oberon.

<Smells like some kind of cat. But they smell wrong somehow.>

I turned around, thinking I would ask Coyote, only to

discover that he wasn't in the hogan at all. Come to think of it, the last time I remembered seeing him was right after I told him off.

"Where's Mr. Benally?" I asked one of the workers.

He shrugged. "He left a while back."

"Gods-damned sheep-loving tricksters," I muttered. Always figuring out ways to get other people to fight for them. But then I got a chill. What Coyote feared wasn't death but what the skinwalkers would be able to do if they acquired his skin. His absence indicated he thought there was a very good chance for the skinwalkers to get hold of it tonight—which meant we were all in movie trailer territory, where that guy with the low, twelve-pack-a-day voice informs you that you're "in a world . . . of terrible danger."

I was on the east wall near the door, opposite Frank. I moved around to the north side of the hogan as the attacks resumed on the logs there. They were absurdly percussive; the sound reminded me of small battering rams. I could hear wood cracking, splintering, chunks of it flying away outside, and saw the trauma reflected inside. If they were doing this with nothing but flesh and bone, then they were operating on the strength level of vampires, and the walls wouldn't last very long. I activated two charms on my necklace, squatting down and peering through a gap that had developed between the logs. The first charm was night vision, so that I could see what was out there. The second was faerie specs, because this was my first chance to get a handle on how the skinwalkers' magic worked.

It took me a while to find them; they were moving so fast that they blurred in my vision. Once I did spot them, I wasn't sure what I was looking at; each was a gruesome mash-up of three different creatures, and if Frank hadn't told me about the old spirits from First World, I wouldn't have been able to interpret what I saw. The physical form causing all the damage was a bobcat, warped and mutated into ferocity beyond its natural bent—so that was the skin they were currently wearing. But underneath that skin, I saw something dark and scabrous, a mottled horror of crouching, insectile menace with orange eyes; underneath that, crippled almost beyond recognition, subsumed to the other two and its nobler nature quashed beneath a blanket of bile and aggression, was a human.

The demon-eyed thing was the glue binding the other two; it's what allowed the human to shape-shift using an animal skin. I wondered how it would appear in Frank's magical sight. Something snicked into place in my head—perhaps it was the way the dark tendrils of the insect thing had wrapped itself around both the bobcat and the human—and I realized that this was a magical symbiosis. Alone in the Fourth World, that dark spirit of the air could exert its will about as well as a substitute teacher on a room full of jaded seniors. But with the willing cooperation of a corrupted human, it could overpower most anything. My strategy, magically, should be to figure out a way to sever the spirit from either the human or the bobcat. It was unlikely that any one of them could harm us acting singly; bound together, however, the skinwalkers were practically juggernauts until sunrise.

Frank's magic wasn't severing anything, however; his Blessing Way was laying down a ward around the hogan.

I dropped to all fours to see precisely what those threads of light were doing once they slipped under the lowest log. I had to unbind the cellulose in front of my eyes to give myself a peephole of sorts, but once I did and put my eye to it, I could see Frank's work clearly on the ground outside. His ward was building from the ground up; already there was no way the skinwalkers could get in by digging underneath the hogan. But the protection hadn't found its way above ground level yet. Crisscrossed on the earth, I saw a webwork of glittering threads, obscenely bright in the darkness, like someone had taken those glow sticks kids use at raves and fueled them with plutonium. I tried to filter the light out to see what was at the core of it, but there didn't seem to be anything else. One of the skinwalkers slammed into the logs directly opposite me, and I admit I jumped, but then it yowled as it touched the ward on the ground and skittered away.

The light, I realized, might be all there was to it. In First World, or Black World, light was in short supply— anathema, in fact, to all the dark spirits of air that lived there. Make some light in the magical spectrum, and the mojo of First World was neutralized. It sounded simple, but it wasn't. I don't do shiny mage balls or handheld fire globes or soft, friendly light whispers in any spectrum. Those aren't in a Druid's bag of tricks. Clearly, though, some kind of effective light was being produced by Frank Chischilly and the others participating in the Blessing Way. I couldn't duplicate it, nor could I think of any other way to ward against the skinwalkers in the short time we had before they burst through—I gave it less than five minutes, at the rate they were tearing through the logs. I wouldn't be able to come up with a magical bullet to sunder the humans from their First World symbionts either, in so short a time. What I could do, though, was bind the logs back together and perhaps make them tougher to shred in the first place. It would be a time-consuming and draining effort, but all I had to do was keep it up all night.

"Ha-ha, that's easy!"

<What's easy?>

I said that out loud?

<Yes.>

Never mind. It was merely positive thinking.

I'm not sure if there's any onomatopoeia that properly describes the sound of an unholy bobcat punching its paw through a log. *Punt-thrack-rawr?* But that sound exploded near my head, and I got a few wood chips in the face by way of punctuation. The next one or two hits would clear a hole, and then all they needed was to widen it enough to get through. No time to waste; Granuaile and Oberon said something to me, but I had to shut them out and give my undivided attention to keeping the skinwalkers outdoors.

I focused on the log, down to the level of its substance that I normally dismiss as visual noise. There I began to bind it back together, like to like, the simplest binding there is, and though the next impact actually got most of the paw through the wood, I was able to fill it in after that faster than they could punch through it. Once the skinwalkers realized what was happening, their pissy kitty howls went up an octave and switched to the key of apeshit. They backed off for a time, considering, and then I lost track of them. The next impacts came on two completely different walls. The ones after that were in yet another location. They were betting I couldn't divide my attention and strengthen two or more spots at once. But I noticed a pattern to their attacks that I hadn't seen before: They were always hitting the same log in terms of vertical distance from the ground. It was the fifth one, every time. It made sense when I thought about it: They had to hit the log hard, leaping off the ground outside the influence of the Blessing Way ward, and then leap back or ricochet out past the ward each time. If they went too low, they wouldn't have the arc to miss it safely on the rebound. If they went too high, they'd have no problem falling safely, but the force of their hits would be greatly reduced due to simple physics. So if I could strengthen that fifth log on every wall, they'd be at a supreme disadvantage.

Their strategy of trying to weaken multiple points actually worked to my advantage now. I could let them chip away while I tried something different. Keeping my Old Irish headspace going for binding purposes, I carved off a piece of my attention so that I could communicate in English and still keep track of things in the magical spectrum.

"Granuaile, grab that shovel over there"—I pointed to one leaning against the door—"and scoop me out one of those lava rocks from the fire pit. Bring it over here, quick."

She moved and didn't question, knowing that I must have a reason for the request and she'd find out what it was soon enough. Best apprentice ever. Oberon didn't say anything; he knew the businesslike tone, and he knew the faraway look in my eyes that said I didn't really see him right now. Some of the Navajos followed Granuaile with their eyes and flicked querying glances my way, wondering what the hell we were up to, but they were not about to interrupt the Blessing Way ceremony at this point to ask her. They let Granuaile take a rock from the pit and haul it over to where I was standing.

"Great. Now lift it up to this log here and wedge the shovel blade against it so the rock leans against the log."

Granuaile looked at the smoking hot rock and then at the dry wood and couldn't get around her doubts. "Won't that set it on fire?"

"Nope. Trust me. Don't move the shovel away until I say it's okay."

"All right, sensei." She did as instructed and then I quit dividing my attention, turning back fully to the magical spectrum. As the skinwalkers attacked various points on all the walls, I began to unbind the rock into its component silica and carbonate parts. As it dissolved into dust and the stored heat vented upward like a furnace blast, I channeled the material into the outer walls of cellulose in the log, essentially petrifying it and upping its strength considerably. There wasn't nearly enough silica in the rock to petrify the whole log, so I concentrated it in a two-foot area and made it about four inches deep. The skinwalkers would have a much tougher time punching through that, even with their unnaturally strong muscles and bones—and if they did manage it, they would probably injure themselves in the process. Once I'd used all the silica, I divided my focus and let Granuaile know she could lower the shovel.

I didn't know how much of that the Navajos caught, but I figured I wouldn't have to worry about explaining the effectiveness of magic to this particular group. They might wonder what I'd done and how, but they'd never doubt the possibility of it. Their faith, after all, combined with Frank's singing and sandpainting, was constructing a far more effective ward against the skinwalkers than anything I could come up with.

"Need another rock?" Granuaile asked.

"No, let's wait and see if this works first." I placed myself directly behind the petrified portion of the log and raised my voice to taunt the skinwalkers. "Here, kitty, kitty!" I made kissy noises. "Come and get me over here!"

One of them obliged. One second I saw nothing but darkness to the north, and then in the next fraction of a second there was a sickening *thud,* of a distinctly duller and lower tenor than from previous impacts, and then a skinwalker fell gracelessly to the ground—directly on top of the ward surrounding the building. The bobcat screamed and scrambled away from it, but it was literally burned by the contact. It held still for a moment to assess the damage, and that allowed me to check it out as well. There were white lines seared across its fur now, in the weblike pattern I'd seen before in the ward. It was only a narrow strip, as if he'd been thrown on the grill for a few seconds, but his awkward, slower movements proved he had been crippled by it—by that, or by crashing headlong into petrified wood. He wouldn't be jumping at the hogan with nearly the strength or ferocity he'd had up to that point, if at all. Allowing myself a tiny smile, I checked the log; it was fine.

"Yeah, get me another rock," I said. "That worked out well."

Granuaile moved to comply, but Frank shook his head urgently and Sophie spoke for him. "No more rocks," she said. "We need what's left for the ceremony." They were still burning herbs on top of the rocks, and apparently they were more important to the process than I thought.

My apprentice looked at me helplessly. "It's okay," I said. "I'll make do. The odds have evened out a bit in any case." With only one skinwalker attacking the hogan, I could keep up with the damage being dealt to the structure. It would be a long night of work, but it was manageable. I sighed with relief; we would get through this.

I sighed too soon.

The crunch of gravel under tires and the rumble of a V8 reminded us that Darren Yazzie had gone to Kayenta for a few goodies, and now he was returning at a spectacularly unfortunate time.

Eyes widened around the hogan and voices faltered, but Frank Chischilly sang on. Failing to complete the ceremony properly might offend the Holy People—and that would rather defeat the purpose of having a ceremony in the first place.

"It's Darren!" Sophie said, putting a hand up to her mouth in worry. "I asked him to go to town for me— I didn't think we'd be dealing with them so soon!" She

moved toward the door, and one of the crew members—
I'd never been introduced—slid over to intercept her.

"Ain't nothin' we can do for Darren except hope he
figures it out and turns around," he said. "Anyone who
goes out that door will die. Ain't nothin' faster than a
skinwalker."

He was right. Those things were faster than Leif and
therefore faster than anything I could manage with the
aid of magic. Moralltach or no, I couldn't keep them
from taking me down. They were so alien to the magic I
was familiar with that I wondered if even the Tuatha Dé
Danann could handle them.

<Stay, boy,> Oberon commanded.

Don't worry, I'm not going anywhere.

Granuaile fished her cell phone out of her jeans and
hope bloomed on her face. "There's actually a signal
here!" she said. "We can call him."

It was far too late for that, signal or no. The hammer-
ing on the hogan ceased, and we heard a thunderous
impact against metal and shattering glass. I rushed to
the east wall, where the door faced the road, and peered
through a gap in the door's hinges. Frank kept chanting
over Darren's startled cries. Through the wee gap, I
couldn't see much except for his truck's headlights
cresting the lip of the mesa. The lights shuddered violently as the skinwalkers rocked the vehicle. A yell,
two gunshots—he must have had a pistol in his glove
compartment—more broken glass, a bobcat scream,
then a human one, and then the headlights reeled crazily
and disappeared. A rolling, crashing noise followed, as
Darren's truck tumbled off the graded road and down a
half mile of rocky hillside. I doubt he survived it; my
only hope was that one or both of the skinwalkers had
taken the plunge with him.

Frank kept singing, but everyone else had fallen silent.
Sophie was doing her best to be stoic about it, but I saw

tears on her cheeks and she'd probably be plagued by guilt for years if she didn't get help.

I patched up all the logs with bindings while we waited to hear something that would tell us the fate of the skin-walkers. There were no more bobcat growls or attacks on the hogan. A tense half hour passed with no sounds from outside, all of us wishing the silence would last another minute and yet feeling that it couldn't possibly last any longer. What broke the silence, finally, wasn't a bobcat. It was a human voice—or, rather, two of them, on the outer edge of what could be called human. The voices were hoarse and throbbing with menace, and they spoke in Navajo on the north side of the hogan.

Peering through the cracks, I saw the skinwalkers in their human form. Though they kept moving from place to place in a blur, they would stop briefly here and there, as if they were following some unseen connect-the-dots pattern on the mesa. In their brief flashes of stillness, they were lean, of stunted stature, and unclothed. That didn't mean they were underwhelming; their menace was simply concentrated, like frozen orange juice forti-fied with Vitamin Evil, and their eyes kind of reflected that, a liquid fire glowing out of their sockets with no pupils. The bobcat skin was gone, so now it was just them with that spirit wrapped all around and through them; their human auras were tainted with black ichor. I was curious to see where Hel must have cut them, but neither of them looked wounded. Whatever it was they were saying, they kept repeating it, and lots of eyes shifted briefly in my direction before looking away, pre-tending that I wasn't there. Frank winced the first time he heard it but then grimly continued to work on his sandpainting and lead the singing.

I flipped my faerie specs off. "What are they saying, Sophie?" She pretended not to hear and, in so doing, set an example for the others. No one would meet my eyes.

They began chanting in time with Frank—he'd apparently reached a sort of call-and-answer section in his "sing." And I think it would have been a casual passage under normal circumstances, but in this case they were belting it out and supporting from the diaphragm, an unconscious agreement that they should drown out the skinwalkers with their raised voices. Somehow, the skinwalkers' voices cut through it without increasing their volume.

<What's going on, Atticus?> Oberon asked.

I don't know, buddy. I don't speak their language.

<Those things out there don't smell like cats anymore. They're human but tainted with something else. Kind of like burnt rubber.>

"Sophie. I need to know what they're saying." I got no reply. "Come on, somebody help me out here. I can handle it."

The man who'd prevented Sophie from going out to save Darren—and getting herself killed in the process—finally took a step toward me and offered his hand. I shook it and nodded once to him gratefully.

"Ben Keonie," he said.

"Um . . . Reilly," I said.

"I think Sophie wants to finish the sing," he explained, as she and the rest of the crew continued to chime in at the appropriate places. "But I can tell you what those things out there are saying if you like."

"Yes, I'd appreciate that."

"They're saying, 'Feed us the white man.' "

Chapter 8

Fucking Hel.

Oberon leapt in front of me and began to growl at Ben, teeth bared and hackles raised. <If anyone tries to feed you to the skinwalkers, they're going to get fed to the wolfhound.>

Whoa, calm down, Oberon. Stop growling. You can see he's not even considering it.

<That's because he's considering my teeth.>

Okay, I'm sure he gets the idea. "Stop growling," I said aloud. Oberon quieted and wagged his tail contentedly, looking up at me.

<What's the meat I get for impressive displays of loyalty? Is it lamb? Because I think I earned a rack or at least a leg right there, drizzled with an ancho-chile sauce and a dollop of mint jelly.>

That's it. I'm using parental controls and blocking the Food Network.

"Sorry about that," I said to Ben. He shook his head and gave a tight little smile. It was no big deal.

"Who are you, man? How do those skinwalkers even know you're here?"

"Well, that's . . . um . . ." I didn't want to explain to him that I was on several gods' Most Hated list and that one of them had recently turned me into a bobcat Fancy Feast. Because then I'd join Sophie in shouldering blame for Darren's death, plus I'd feel guilty about endangering the lives of everyone there, even though they had intended to lure the skinwalkers out in the first place. "We should probably wait and talk to Frank about that. He knows why, and he can explain it best, I think."

"At—I mean, Reilly?" Granuaile said. "If they're in human form now, what's stopping them from opening the door?"

That was an *excellent* question. Aside from the hinges, plenty of wire bound it shut, but I thought they would have at least tried it by now.

"I don't know," I murmured. "Let's go see." I flipped my faerie specs back on, so as I got closer I could see the door silhouetted by the white glow of magic. The glow wasn't at the very top, but it was on either side and definitely at the bottom. "It's the ward laid down by the Blessing Way," I marveled. "It starts at ground level and then moves up, starting with the door. Hogan doors always face east, so it would be simple to structure the spell that way. Clever. If they reach for the door now, they'll be burned."

Granuaile nodded but had no further questions. I switched back to normal vision and waited for the song to end, as the skinwalkers continued their creepy loop of demanding extra-rare Druid.

I tried to squat out of the way on the north side. It kept the skinwalkers lurking over there, since Hel's damned knife had somehow turned me into ambulatory ambrosia. Oberon and Granuaile came over to squat beside me.

"Now what, sensei?" Granuaile asked, sotto voce.

"Now we have a long, sleepless night ahead of us. And if they start thrashing the hogan again, I repair it. Just keep it up until sunrise, when we hope they'll go away."

"What if they don't?"

"Then I try to figure out a way to mess with them magically without doing any direct harm. But I think they'll go. The thing that makes their eyes glow doesn't like light."

With a flourish of Frank's hand and a final shout in unison, the first song ended. Frank sank down, exhausted. Before he could say anything, the skinwalkers' litany changed, and this started a series of murmurs among the Navajos.

Frank shook his head though as they came to the end and began to loop once more. "That's all bullshit," he said, his voice rasping a bit more than it had before. He looked around at Ben, Sophie, and the others. "Even if we could be sure they're not lying, which we can't, they'd never be honest with the deal."

<What deal?> Oberon asked. <If they're making a deal with your life, I'm going to have something to say about it.>

Let's wait and see.

Sophie said, "But what if he's alive, Frank? If there's a chance we could save him, shouldn't we at least try to figure something out?"

Frank's voice was full of sympathy. "He's not alive, Sophie."

"But how do you *know*?" she said, her tone desperate.

"I'll tell them to prove he's alive right now. You'll see." Frank set aside his sand for the moment and carefully rose to his feet, coming over to stand next to Granuaile on the north wall. He faced the wall and shouted something in Navajo.

I get it now. The skinwalkers want to trade Darren for me. Frank thinks they're bluffing and Darren is already dead. He's asking them to prove Darren is still alive.

<And if he is?>

We'll have to do more than sit here and wait for dawn. We'll have to try to save him.

<But not if it means giving you up, right?> When I didn't answer, Oberon pressed for an answer. <Right, Atticus?>

The skinwalkers hissed, apparently upset that Frank wasn't interested unless Darren was breathing. They spat out something else, and, whatever it was, it set Sophie to crying anew. Frank shot her a look that said, "I told you so," but then the lines on his face rearranged themselves into the topography of regret. He gingerly knelt down next to his *jish* and announced he would begin to sing again.

Darren's dead, I told Oberon. *You don't need to worry about me.*

<Oh. Well, I'm sorry to hear about Darren. He smelled like a very nice guy.>

I was sorry too. But I wasn't going to be allowed to mourn him now, nor was Frank going to get started on that new song.

A sound like steel tearing erupted from the throats of the skinwalkers and they attacked the wall again, this time with spirit-juiced human fists. They weren't as effective as the bobcat forms, and I had no difficulty rebinding any damage they did.

The futility of it sank in after a few minutes and they subsided, but while everyone else was comforted by this, it worried me. I've met more than my fair share of demons and monsters, and usually they're so full of juvenile rage that they're incapable of dialing down the aggression until they've killed something. You can't ever talk your way out of a fight with creatures like that, but you can predict their behavior reliably and use it against them. Up to now they'd attacked us using the "Hulk smash!" school of martial arts. Silence and peace just meant they were going to try something else. But what? The ground was covered. The door was safe. The walls were getting there. That left . . . the roof.

The roof wasn't finished by a long shot. That plastic sheeting wouldn't slow them down much, and those lads were so slim they could drop down through the trusses and beams without any trouble. But they'd have to stand still for a moment to tear a hole through the plastic, and during that time they'd be vulnerable. I rose from my crouch and addressed the room.

"Does anyone have a gun?" The looks I got in response suggested that I'd asked about something profoundly distasteful, like trickle-down economics or the poetry of William Blake. "Okay, how about a knife?"

Ben had a decent knife clipped to his belt. He nodded at me and handed it over, hilt first.

"Thanks," I said. I grabbed the shovel Granuaile had used and unscrewed the wooden handle from the blade. I used the knife to whittle the end of the handle down to a sharpened point, unbinding the cellulose a bit to make the work go easier. I had a makeshift javelin in less than thirty seconds. Switching the javelin and knife between my two hands, I held the tip of the javelin over the fire to heat it up a bit and kept an eye on the ceiling.

Granuaile and Oberon figured it out by watching me.

"Oh, no, the roof . . ." she breathed.

"That's right," I said. "That's their best shot." I gently tossed the knife at her feet. "If they get through, they're coming after me because of the compulsion Hel put on them. And once they do that, stab 'em in the back and duck."

"Will that kill them?"

"Probably not. But it will distract them, maybe give me a chance to draw my sword or save my life—you know, that kind of thing." I flashed a quick grin at her to try to lighten up the message. It didn't seem to relax her very much. The tip of the javelin was beginning to smoke and glow orange: good. I moved back to the north wall to encourage the skinwalkers to attack on that side, if they were coming at all. I boosted my reflexes and strength with temporary bindings, hoping they would be enough to let me get a decent shot. I'd get only one.

<How are they going to get up there?> Oberon asked.

My guess is an alley-oop. One of them will toss the other up. They're strong enough to manage it. They proved it a few seconds later.

Take two Fords from the 1940s and scrape them against each other at an excruciating three miles per hour, then feed that sound through the amps at a Motörhead concert: That's what the skinwalker sounded like when he landed on the roof directly above me and tried to paralyze us all with fear as he tore at the plastic sheeting. Most everyone flinched, startled by the noise and the direction it came from. I didn't hesitate once I saw the skinwalker silhouetted against the dark cobalt of the starlit sky; I threw the javelin straight up, hoping it would connect, then reached back to draw Moralltach from its sheath.

The javelin flew true, but the skinwalker was so fast that it was able to jerk back and take it in the shoulder joint instead of the middle of the chest. My boosted strength served me well; the javelin plowed straight through to the other side, no doubt ruining the skinwalker's shoulder, and the impact bowled him backward off the roof. He shrieked as he fell. He missed the ward of the Blessing Way, unfortunately, but I figured neither of them would view attacking the roof as a good idea anymore.

<Heh. I think you made your point, Atticus.>

Gods Below, Oberon, that was horrendous! You just violated the Schwarzenegger Pun Reduction Treaty of 2010.

<What? No, that didn't qualify!>

Yes, it did. Any pun relating to a weapon's destructive

capabilities or final disposition of a victim's body is a Schwarzenegger pun, by definition. That's negative twenty sausages according to the sanctions outlined in Section Four, Paragraph Two.

My hound whined. <No! Not twenty sausages! Twenty succulent sausages I'll never snarf? You can't do that—it's cruelty to animals!>

You can't argue with this. Your pawprint is on the treaty, and you agreed that Schwarzenegger puns are heinous abominations of language that deserve food-related punishments for purposes of correction and deterrence.

<Auggh! I still say it's your fault for renting *Commando* in the first place! You started it!>

Who started it is immaterial. You violated the treaty by continuing it.

<This is terrible. Terrible! But, wait, it's the end of the day and I'm still up, 4–3! That means I earned back ten penalty sausages!>

That is a ridiculous figure, Oberon. One.

<Eight.>

Three.

<Five!>

Fine. You may discount five penalty sausages by virtue of your minor victory.

Oberon lay down and put his paws over his eyes. <Oh, great big bears, negative fifteen sausages! It's a nightmare, that's what it is.>

His words were more true than he realized, but for far weightier reasons than the loss of meat products. If I was reading things right, skinwalkers were the worst nightmares of the Navajo world, all their other monsters having been dispatched long ago by Monster Slayer, and I am sure there was nothing more horrifying in their minds than being taken by one. It was a nightmare for me too, because there wasn't anything I could do magically to defeat these guys, and physically they were far faster and maybe stronger than me. I was unprepared, like a bad Boy Scout. Their magic was as old as mine, if not older, crafted independently and far removed from the European traditions with which I was familiar.

I remembered a bizarre day of my education, when the archdruid taught me how to unbind vampires, beguile dragons, and tame manticores. "You'll probably never need to use this," he said, "but if you ever run into one of the beasties, you'll be glad I took the trouble. Now, *stop* looking at that girl over there and pay attention, gods blast you!"

I had been an unruly and easily distracted apprentice at times. But I was fairly certain there was nothing in Druid lore that would help me deal with this. It would take days or weeks of experimentation to come up with something new and effective, but I didn't have that luxury. Nor did I have anything to chuck skyward should they try the roof again; I was fresh out of shovels or anything else that could be converted to a projectile weapon. Well, maybe I could fling the discarded shovel blade like a square Frisbee.

Thankfully, the skinwalkers had no intention of attacking again. They had plenty of wounds to lick, not to mention a sharpened stick to yank out of a torso, and they weren't (yet) hungry enough for my flesh to continue their assault in such a state. They made plenty of spitting and cursing noises as they staggered away, and mildly hopeful expressions bloomed on the faces of the Navajos.

Frank let that feeling settle in and get comfortable before he said anything. "They'll be back. If not tonight, then tomorrow." That caused some restless shifting of feet. "An' if you're thinkin' you might call in sick tomorrow, think about it again. This project here can't fail. It ain't just your job at stake, it's everyone's. Besides, that man out there woulda wanted us to finish. An' you know we can finish it right." The workers all nodded solemnly, Sophie choked back a sob, and Frank led them in a new song.

Granuaile shot a querying glance in my direction. *"That man?"* she whispered.

I replied in the same low tones. "He's talking about the construction foreman. The one the skinwalkers killed."

"You mean Dar—"

"Shh!" I held up a hand to stop her. "Some cultures, including Navajos, don't speak the names of the dead."

Granuaile checked to see if our murmured conversation was being overheard. "Why not?"

"The reason varies from culture to culture. But with the Navajos, they don't want to attract the ghost of the man by calling his name. They call the ghosts *ch'įįdii*, and they're not benevolent. You take all the bile and discord and unrest a person has inside of them, every evil thought and all the impulses they repress during their life, and that's what escapes upon death to become a *ch'įįdii*."

"Ew. Those things are just floating around?"

"Well, they disperse if nothing keeps them here. But they have to be in the open to do that. When someone dies inside a hogan, no one will live there anymore, unless it gets blessed and renewed."

"Oh, because it's haunted? Things that go bump in the night? Like poltergeists and such?"

"No, nothing like that. *Ch'įįdii* can make you sick with their malevolence. They call it ghost sickness or corpse sickness. Skinwalkers use it, actually, to kill people."

"How do they do that?"

"You heard Frank tell me he reversed a curse on a skinwalker long ago by shooting a bone bead into it?"

"Yes."

"Well, what they're really doing by shooting pieces of bone into you is inviting a *ch'iidii* into your body. *Ch'iidii* linger around the bodies, see; they're anchored to them until they have a chance to disperse. So if you're shot with a piece of a corpse, you'll get corpse sickness and die. And there are stories about witches sneaking up to hogans and dumping corpse powder down chimneys—that's ground-up bones mixed with ash. Everyone inside breathes it in, and the family is wiped out. That's all part of the Witchery Way."

"That is some seriously evil shit," Granuaile said. "Are these witches like you're used to in Europe?"

"No, the Navajo witches are mostly men. And what they're doing is inverting the wholesome rituals of the Blessing Way—they'll make their paintings using ash instead of sand, for example. It's similar to conducting the Black Mass."

Granuaile frowned. "I'm starting to see why you don't like witches."

"Yeah. I keep hearing that there are good ones out there, but I haven't met any, with the possible exception of Malina's coven."

"Have you ever seen a *ch'iidii*? I mean in the magical spectrum?"

"No, I've never had occasion to."

She looked down at the ground and said quietly, "Guess you'll have a chance in the morning."

Chapter 9

Most of us managed to get three or four hours' sleep once the skinwalkers were gone. Frank called a temporary halt to the ceremony and told us to get some rest. My sleep was plagued by troubling dreams of shapeless, smoky demons that never felt the bite of my sword but whose claws and teeth found ample purchase on my skin. They were like congealed darkness, and I could neither bind them in place nor unbind their substance—for how does one control an absence of light?

Once dawn arrived, the Navajos greeted the sun—a tradition that stems from their belief that the gods rise with the sun, and the reason that hogan doors always face east—and we went to see what happened to Darren.

We found him lying on the road, torn from his truck and his body savaged by the skinwalkers. His blood had sunk into the earth, red dust made doubly red. Down the hill, north of the road, Darren's truck was a mess of crumpled metal and shattered glass.

Sophie Betsuie lost her composure and returned to the hogan, crying. She was beating herself up with a club made out of the words *if only,* and I knew what it felt like. If only I hadn't done this. If only someone else hadn't done that. I hoped she would learn sooner, rather than later, that you can't unchoose anyone's choices, least of all your own. All you can do with your past is try to grow out of it.

Darren's crew gave the body a wide berth as they walked down to their trucks, some of them already talking on cell phones, calling the police and perhaps family members.

"Can you see it?" Granuaile asked, one hand absently petting Oberon. "The *ch'iidii*?"

"Let me check." I flipped on my faerie specs and looked at the space above Darren's body. What I saw made me shudder. It reminded me uncomfortably of my dreams.

"Atticus, what is it? Can you see it?"

"Yeah. Sit down, I'll bind your sight to mine."

She sat cross-legged on the ground next to Oberon, and I concentrated on her aura until I could isolate the threads of her consciousness. Choosing the ones that represented her sight, I bound them to mine, and she breathed in sharply as her vision was wrenched from her perspective to mine. Then she scrambled backward, crablike, once she saw the *ch'iidii*.

"Gah! That thing—it looks evil!" she cried.

"I know," I said. An inky cloud—funnel-shaped and with a pair of pale, blank eyes that faced us consistently—swirled counterclockwise over Darren's body. It was unnerving to see such steady regard in the midst of that restless motion.

"But he seemed like such a nice guy," Granuaile said. "How could that have been inside him?"

"We all have our dark sides."

"You mean I have something like that inside me? That will float above my body when I die?"

"Not unless you believe it will. That which is immortal in us all must express itself somehow when we die. He believed in *ch'iidii*, and thus you see it here."

"That is so fucked up."

"Eh, let's not be so quick to judge. It's not that bad. The way he saw it—the way the Navajos see it—the good parts of him were already in harmony with the universe, see? Much of their spiritual lives are spent trying to achieve that which is *hózhǫ́*, or spiritually balanced and beautiful—and isn't that what we all want, regardless of what we call it? This remnant is nothing but the shadow of his baser nature. Contrast that with some people who send their entire souls to a plane where they are tortured and burned for eternity. You could judge that if you wanted, but it would be nothing compared to how they judged themselves."

Granuaile sat in silence for a while, digesting this. She'd never confronted anything so concrete in her philosophy classes. Frank Chischilly came over and stood next to her but didn't say anything. He could see we were studying Darren's body. When next she spoke, Granuaile's voice was sad and subdued. "What are we going to do about him?"

"You're going to sit there," I replied. "I am going to see if I can help this *ch'įįdii* disperse a bit quicker, send him on to his peace. We cannot wait for it to disperse on its own—I don't know the half-life of things like this, anyway."

"What? Hey," Frank protested, spurred to speech by my intrusion on his territory. "You can see the *ch'įįdii*?"

Granuaile spoke over him. "You're going to unbind it somehow?"

"Not with any spell. I'm merely going to give it a taste of cold iron." I took a few steps forward and the *ch'įįdii* shifted, eyeing my approach.

"Hey, Mr. Collins, you'd better not get too close. Don't touch him," Frank warned. "If you do, the *ch'įįdii* might take it as an invitation to enter your body."

"I won't," I assured him. Careful not to touch Darren's body at all, I extended my fist directly toward the

ch'iidii. The blank white eyes locked on my arm. Wispy
tendrils of soot reached out, wrapping themselves sinu-
ously about my hand and forearm. I felt them; they were
damp and freezing and suffused with pollution. I could
well believe that something like this, once inside a person, could cause an incurable disease. But those tendrils
lost their solidity in the next second, vaporizing as the
cold iron in my aura sundered the magic holding it together. It attacked me more fiercely, realizing that I was
harming it somehow, but it was silent and spooky and
cold. In less than a minute, all that was left of Darren
Yazzie's dark side dispersed into the morning sun.

"That was good," Granuaile declared. "Without that
hanging over him, he seems more at peace now."

"He is," I said. "Frank, his *ch'iidii* is gone. We can
move him safely."

"I can see it's gone," he said. "Though I'm not sure
how you saw it or how you did that."

I sighed, frustrated with myself. "I should have bound
your sight to mine so you could see it. Didn't think of it
at the time, but let's fix that now. Nobody's watching,
and I think I can trust you to keep your mouth shut, so
I'm going to give you a glimpse of what you were up to
last night."

Frank frowned at me. "What the hell are you talkin'
about?"

"Brace yourself and don't freak out. I know you have
some kind of magical sight, but I'm willing to bet mine's
a bit different. Here, give me your arm so you don't fall.
Granuaile, will you get his other side? I'm going to return you back to normal and do Frank."

"Got it, sensei." I unbound her sight, and she smiled
at Frank as she rose from the ground and looped her
arm through his. It's tough to get too surly when Granuaile smiles at you, but he still scowled at her, and a quer-
ulous note leapt into his voice.

"Now, hold on here, nobody's *doin'* me, that's for damn sure—"

"Relax, Frank, you're about to see the wonder of your medicine for the first time. You'll be the first *hataałii* to ever see evidence of the Blessing Way like this. I'll explain as we go. Ready?"

"No, I'm not ready, because you're not making sense, you crazy bastard—whoa!" He lurched forward and would have fallen had we not supported him. "What happened? What's wrong with my eyes?"

"Nothing's wrong with them. You're just seeing through my eyes right now, and at the moment I'm looking at the world in the magical spectrum. I've filtered out most of the noise, so it shouldn't be too overwhelming. But let's turn around here and go back to the hogan so you can see how the Blessing Way protected us last night."

We led Frank over to the door, and I focused in on the ward around the door first. "See all that white webwork? That's your doing. We learned last night that it's an extremely effective ward against spirits from the First World. It burns them."

"It does?" Frank said in a tiny voice.

"Yep. Saw it firsthand when one of the bobcats fell on the ground here." I pointed at the ground near the first log and focused on the webwork there. "You say it takes four days to complete the ceremony?"

"Yes, four days for public buildings."

"Well, then, I'd assume that by the end of four days this ward will completely envelop the hogan, roof and all. You won't need me around then."

"What are you, Mr. Collins? For real."

Sophie was still in the hogan and might hear us, so I dissolved the binding and returned his own sight to him, then beckoned him to follow me some distance away.

Once we were safely out of earshot, I told him, "I'm a Druid."

I waited for the customary dismissal, but instead there was an awkward pause. "I don't know what that is," Frank admitted.

I laughed. "That's all right. I guess you could say my job is to protect the earth from assholes."

"Oh, I see." Frank paused, then said, "Kinda seems like the assholes are winning, don't it?"

"That's because I'm vastly outnumbered."

"Ha. Know what you mean."

"Can I ask you something, Frank?"

"Sure, go ahead."

"What you were doing last night—that ward you were laying down—is that normal for a *hataałii*?"

"Well, not exactly. I'm singing the songs and doing everything a normal *hataałii* does, but I'm kinda like that chef on TV who's always throwing garlic in the recipe and shouting, 'BAM!'"

Granuaile smiled at him. "So you just kick it up a notch?"

"That's right. Normal plus hot sauce. That's me."

"Where'd you get that hot sauce, if you don't mind me asking?" I said.

The shadow of a wince passed across Frank's face. "You'd think I was crazy if I told you."

"Frank, I'll believe darn near anything. You saw a Norse goddess of death yesterday. That wasn't the first deity I've run into—just the ugliest and the smelliest. If I can wrap my head around that, I can probably handle your secret."

Frank turned his head and spat contemplatively. "All right. I was down in Canyon de Chelly a couple years back and I got ambushed by a buncha hippies."

"Real hippies?"

"Naw, I mean those New Age turds who wanna hijack native religions for their own use 'cause nothing in the great white world speaks to them. They flock around at the solstices and try to find someone to teach them healin' ceremonies, askin' people for illegal shit like eagle feathers 'cause they got it into their heads that there's some huge black market in feathers on the reservation. Six of 'em found me in the canyon, and whoever told 'em to find me there deserves a swift kick in the cooter. I was sittin' down, see, doin' a sing, a little private prayer, and you know how it is—once you start you ain't supposed to stop, 'cause it's an insult to the Holy People. Well, those hippies found me and didn't wanna wait for me to finish. They started sayin', excuse me, sir, yo, dude, hey, old man, can we talk for a second, and of course I ignored them and kept singin'. If I gotta make a choice between bein' rude to the Holy People and bein' rude to six white people, I'm gonna be rude to the white people every time."

"Right," I said, nodding in agreement. I wouldn't interrupt one of my ceremonies either.

"Well, they didn't wanna take the hint. They got more insistent, shouting at me. Tapping me on the shoulder. Then one of them chucked me hard on the side of the arm, here"—he pointed to his right upper arm—"and it knocked me over sideways, startling me and stopping my sing."

"That's terrible!" Granuaile said. "Roundhouse kicks for everybody!"

Frank grinned at her. "That's more or less what happened, heh! Before I could sit up again, I felt this wind—my hat blew away—and I heard a noise, kinda like a door shutting on a storm outside. Then all their feet left the ground and they were blown back, flat on their asses, and they didn't move."

"Oh! Were they dead?" Granuaile asked.

"Naw. Just unconscious. I sat up and faced the east,

and there she was. It was Changing Woman, and I knew this without her saying anything. I apologized for stopping my song and she forgave me, said she understood. She'd come to give me some gifts. She knelt down in front of me, and she touched my eyes here at the corners," he said, putting his fingers at the outside edge of his eyes, "and said I would be able to see things I'd never seen before. I started cryin', because, you know, *damn,* it was Changing Woman. She touched my throat and said the Holy People would hear my songs better from then on. She touched my right hand and said my sandpaintings would always be perfect. And then she gave me a special *jish.* Said that when I spoke the words and used it, one of her children, Monster Slayer, would come to Fourth World again, once and once only. Said I would know when it was time.

"When I saw that giant thing climb out o' the top of that little ol' lady's head yesterday, I thought it was time. That was somethin' that didn't belong in this world."

"You're right about that," I said.

"Yeah. But now I don't know if I did the right thing. Mr. Benally knew about it—he's one o' the few people who believed me—and he was tryin' to tell me, no, don't waste it now, save it for the skinwalkers, but I didn't listen." He hooked a thumb in the direction of Darren's body. "Now I'm thinkin' maybe I shoulda waited, you know?"

If only.

"Even if you still had the *jish,* Frank," I pointed out, "you couldn't have saved him last night without interrupting your sing."

"True," he said. "But that don't make me regret what happened any less."

There was nothing I could say about his regret, except to perhaps offer the advice to suppress it savagely. It keeps you functioning.

"What happened to the hippies?" I asked, to distract both of us from our regrets.

"Oh. Well, Changing Woman told me they'd wake up eventually, but she didn't say when. It was summertime and hotter than a branding iron down there, and part o' me thought it'd serve them right to get sunburned, since they wanted to be red men so badly. But then I thought they might get seriously burned, and I didn't want to be responsible for that. So I did my best to drag them into the shade. One of them was too damn huge and I couldn't move him, so I put my hat over his face and hoped he'd be all right."

"That was kind of you," Granuaile said, smiling at him. "I know from experience that a bad sunburn can make you terribly sick, so that was a good precaution."

"What could you see after Changing Woman touched your eyes?" I asked.

"Most things were the same. But some things weren't. I saw some colors around my *jish* that weren't there before. I could see which homes had been blessed well and which ones hadn't. And whenever I did ceremonies after that, I could kinda see what I was doing, see everyone's spirit and how the songs and the sandpaintings could change them, bring them into harmony with the Holy People, and unite the spirit world with the physical. And sometimes I'd run into people who had colors around them too. People like you. People like that lady with the death goddess inside."

"How about Mr. Benally?" Granuaile said.

Frank squinted at her. "Well . . . yeah. Him too." He looked at me. "You know who he really is, don't you?"

"I think so," I said. "He—"

"Wait," Frank said, holding up a hand. "Don't say any names. That's important."

I didn't understand, but I wasn't going to argue with

him. If he thought it was important, far be it for me to gainsay him.

"I think he's one of the First People," I said, hoping that wasn't stepping over any lines.

"Yep. I think so too. Problem is figuring out which one. They're capable of trickin' a fella pretty good. Let's say no more about it."

I shrugged. He seemed to have a pretty good idea it was Coyote, so I wasn't going to force the issue.

"You'll be all right for a while?" I asked.

"Aw, sure. Where you goin'?"

"Gotta walk the dog." Oberon's tail swished energetically through the air at this announcement. "Might head north."

Frank looked at me sharply. "You be careful."

I nodded acknowledgment at him and called Oberon, who'd been quietly watching all this time. "Ready to do a little bit of hunting, buddy?"

<Sure! Hunting for what?>

I switched to mental communication. *Skinwalkers. Let's see where they went. If they're hiding in a cave, maybe I can get Colorado to collapse the entrance and solve our problem for us.*

<Okay, but I need a drink first.>

"All right, let's go," I said. Granuaile joined us as we walked down to the car. We stepped softly around Darren's body. Oberon whined once, then put his nose down to the ground.

<They came this way. They used the road. That burnt-rubber scent is easy to follow.> We paused at Granuaile's car and poured some bottled water into one of those collapsible dog bowls. We also took the opportunity to fill our tanks with some beef jerky and crackers. Then we took an extra couple of water bottles each for the trip ahead.

<Ready,> Oberon announced. He trotted back to the

base of the hill, snuffled around a little bit, then turned north. <Footprints here, strong smell, occasional blood drops too from that one you speared. This is going to be simple.>

I expect it will get harder soon.

"What's the plan if we find them, sensei?" Granuaile asked. We broke into an easy jog to keep up with Oberon.

"Depends on the situation," I replied. "I'd prefer to call in an air strike, but unfortunately that's not a viable option. Don't worry, I'm not planning on poking them awake and suggesting a duel. Whatever we do, it will be from a safe distance and completely cold-blooded."

The trail ended on a small knoll three miles away. My improvised javelin was there, stained with blood, and there were plenty of tracks and smells for us to decipher. I wouldn't be able to smell any of it while in human form.

"Fair warning: I'm getting naked," I said to Granuaile as I unslung Moralltach and stripped off my shirt. "I need to shift and find out what Oberon's smelling."

Granuaile made no reply, but she let out a wolf whistle when I shucked off my jeans. I shifted quickly to my hound form so she wouldn't see me blush.

I sneezed immediately, as I often did when I changed to a hound. The potent sense of smell that comes with the form is far more jarring than suddenly walking on all fours. What hit me first was the burnt-rubber scent Oberon had described, except there was something fouler mixed in. It was like placing your face next to the exhaust port of a city bus just when it accelerates from a stop; it was asphalt and rubber and oil and everything black and smelly in a single, lung-destroying cloud. But underneath this were other scents: the blood and sweat, fear and anger of two humans, two bobcats . . . and something else.

\<Atticus, you smell that?\> Oberon asked.

\<You mean the thing that kind of smells like chicken but not really?\>

\<Yeah. It's a big bird, whatever it is. But it doesn't smell like a hawk or a raven. Not a crow either.\>

\<Hmm. I see the bobcat prints here, the human prints too. . . .\> These were mostly smudges and scuffs in the sandy dirt; there was nothing like a perfect print in the mud waiting for us there. \<Look for bird tracks. Careful where you step.\>

\<Well, I think I found some. These aren't bobcat claws.\>

\<Let me see.\> I padded over to where Oberon had his nose to the ground and considered the outlines of two large talon marks. It was an incomplete print—impossible to tell the species without a clearer picture, but it was definitely a larger bird.

\<You think they flew out of here?\> Oberon asked.

\<Yep. They used this little knoll as their staging area. Fly in here with bobcat skins in their talons and land. Shift out of bird skins and leave them here. Shift into bobcats and attack us. After they killed Darren, they probably came back here and shifted out of their bobcat skins too, because they had to talk. So I stuck one, and that's when they returned and shifted into birds again. Perfect way to prevent anyone tracking them home. But one was injured right at the shoulder, so his buddy probably had to carry him. I doubt he'd be able to fly in his condition.\>

\<Is that physically possible, for a bird to carry another one?\>

\<Sure, some of the bigger birds can carry their own weight or more. I can carry twice my weight when I'm in owl form.\>

\<Ah, but a five-ounce bird cannot carry a one-pound coconut. Got it.\>

<Probably had to make two trips. He would have had to come back and get the bobcat skins too.>

I looked up and around. There were any number of places to the north and west where the skinwalkers could be hiding, all kinds of little holes up in the mesa, lots of water-carved caves and the like. If Frank Chischilly had known precisely where they were, I'm sure he would have told me. Hell, if Coyote had known where they were, he wouldn't have had to resort to tricking me like he did. So now we had two choices: We could spend all day searching for them, with the distinct possibility of finding nothing, or we could go back to the hogan and approach the problem from a different direction.

<Damn. They're craftier than I thought, Oberon. I prefer my mortal enemies to be stupid.>

<Are we through here? Can I mark up the place?>

<Sure. In fact, I think I'll join you for the fun of it. Feels like it's been ages since I allowed myself to be immature.> Oberon and I went around lifting our legs on scrub cedar, boulders, and the javelin.

Granuaile wrinkled her nose at us. "That's really classy, sensei."

Oberon and I chuffed at her.

Chapter 10

Plan B was to get the gold moved under the mountain and then get out of there so that the skinwalkers would pursue me—the cure for Famine's curse—and leave the Navajos alone. The problem was, once I returned to the proposed site and broached the subject, Colorado didn't feel like cooperating.

//Reluctance / Discord / Hate mines// he told me. Well, fair enough. But I had to get him to agree, not only to fulfill my obligation to Coyote but to give myself a free hand to deal with the skinwalkers.

//Necessity / Urgency// I replied.

//Query: What necessity?//

It took some time to explain why Coyote's plan for solar and wind power was far superior to the current coal mining operation going on. To Colorado, a mine was nothing more than a giant hole with unconscionable water usage and a surefire way to destroy the habitat of anything living nearby. But he conceded that generating power from clean energy was better than generating it from coal—even if the government wanted to call it "clean coal," an Orwellian oxymoron if ever there was one. Still, he flatly refused to provide material for a precious metals mine while the coal mine continued to operate.

//Query: Coal mine ends, gold mine begins?// I asked.

//Yes / Coal mine must remain closed//

//Agreed / Harmony// I said.

//Harmony// Colorado gave the equivalent of a mental nod.

When I came out of it, the workers were breaking for lunch. They'd been working on the roof with a sense of purpose since Darren's body had been taken away, and Sophie Betsuie had stayed down in the flat with the surveying crew, laying out whatever plans Coyote had cooked up. Coyote himself had yet to make an appearance. Granuaile was working on her Latin, and Oberon had found someone game enough to play tug-of-war with him on a piece of rope. It was Ben Keonie, and he was now the foreman for the crew.

<Hey, Atticus, you watching this?> he asked.

Yes. You'd better let him win, Oberon. If you pull him down, he'll lose face with his crew.

<Oh. Good thing you said something, because I was about to yank him off his feet and then hump his leg, proclaiming him to be my bitch.>

Play nice with him and you'll earn back a sausage. Negative fourteen.

<Okay! This is fun anyway. He's making growly noises at me. He'd probably make a good dog.>

I called Granuaile over for a confab and explained that I'd need a ride down to Black Mesa. "Colorado's forcing me to pull a Monkey Wrench Gang before he'll agree to move gold here."

"What's a Monkey Wrench Gang?"

"You've never read Edward Abbey?"

Granuaile shrugged. "Nope."

"Well, they call it ecoterrorism now, and I would agree that if you blow stuff up you're being terrifying. But I'm not going to do that. I'm going to sabotage their machinery in a completely safe manner. It will effectively shut down their operation and they'll have to replace everything before they start again."

"You can do that?"

"Sure. They can't stop me. All I have to do is sneak in there and unbind the steel in the engines. Or bind the pistons to the cylinder walls. Turns 'em into big hunks of scrap metal, no way to repair it."

"Well, why don't you do that more often? Wouldn't that protect the earth?"

"I could spend my entire life doing it, shifting from place to place, and I still wouldn't stop them. I can do one big mine, maybe two, a day. So that's 730 mines a year if I don't take a day off and never spend two nights in the same place. Do you know how many mines there are in this country alone? Tens of thousands. And for every mine I shut down, another one will start somewhere else. Even the ones I shut down will reopen after a while. And that's doing nothing about developing and dams and overfishing and oil spills and clear-cutting virgin rain forest for cow pasture so some fat man in Rio can have a steak. There's no way I can keep up."

Granuaile tucked a wisp of hair behind her ear and sighed. "Kind of depressing when you put it like that."

"On the bright side, what Coyote's proposing to do here is a step in the right direction. He's right, you need a lot of capital to create a new energy infrastructure. The problem with generating so much electricity in a concentrated area is that there's no efficient way to transfer it to the rest of the country, and the government's not going to step up and do the right thing anytime soon."

"Been meaning to ask you about that, sensei."

"Ask what?"

"How do we know Coyote's going to use the gold the way he says he is? What if this is just a scheme to get rich and make a fool of you, and all that talk in Tuba

City was one big con job? He knows what you are and what buttons to push. Why are you buying his story at face value?"

I pointed down the hill. "They're certainly investing in something down there."

"Yeah, but it could be a casino for all you know. Or Coyote's paying them to put down stakes in an impressive pattern for our benefit."

"All right," I conceded, "it bears investigation. Coyote certainly deserves the skepticism. I'll have Oberon spy on them, because people say all kinds of crazy stuff to dogs." I switched mental gears to talk to my hound, who was still playing with Ben Keonie. *Hey, Snugglepumpkin!*

<Very funny, Atticus.>

Heh! Granuaile and I are going off site for a while. I want you to stick next to Sophie Betsuie this afternoon and report later on everything she talks about. Listen especially for anything regarding the project she's working on. I want to know what they're building.

<Don't we know that already? I thought it was going to be buildings they would use to build other stuff. Solar-power stuff.>

We're treating this like nuclear-arms reduction. Trust, but verify.

<I don't know, Atticus. She's going to pet me a lot and tell me I'm precious. Sounds like rough duty for a hound of my delicate constitution.>

Whatever, you big baby. Negative thirteen sausages.

<Twelve!>

Thirteen, with a possible bonus if your report is satisfactory.

<Deal! I'm on it!>

Oberon dropped the rope suddenly and Ben Keonie staggered backward a bit with the sudden release of tension. "Whoa!" he said, as he watched Oberon bound away down the hill.

"Come on," I told Granuaile. "Let's go." I filled her in on the plan, such as it was, on the way down to the Black Mesa mine. It was located about twenty miles south of Kayenta. She'd drop me off at a gas station located on the highway; I'd camouflage myself and run in the rest of the way to the mine property. She'd come back to pick me up at five. If I wasn't there by five-thirty, she was to get a room in Kayenta and I'd catch up with her at the hogan the next morning.

I left Moralltach in her car, because deadly Fae swords aren't very useful in disabling heavy machinery. Jogging in along the access road, I got passed by a couple of trucks but nothing else. It was the middle of a shift; they worked it round-the-clock six days a week, shipping the coal to a power plant in Page and producing a good chunk of the state's electricity. Since it was Saturday, I'd be hitting it right before they had a day off.

It was more of a sprawling complex than I'd anticipated. First up was a gated area full of hauling trucks and yellow machines of various stripes. The gate was open, and I slipped through unnoticed to pay special attention to every vehicle in the lot. I needed line-of-sight to complete the unbinding, and it wasn't a simple process like triggering one of my charms either. It took two minutes with the hoods or engine covers open to make it happen.

I had to get clever once I got around the running machines. I started banging on the engine covers loudly with a crowbar I'd found, and panicked operators would turn off their earth-shredding behemoths or conveyor belts to investigate the noise before it got any worse. They'd obligingly come down, open the engine compartment for me, and I'd unbind and then rebind the pistons, fusing them to the engine block while they stared uncomprehendingly at it. Once they were satisfied and returned to their station or cockpit to turn it back on, all they got were little red lights telling them of an engine failure. More investigation would ensue, and I'd move on to the next target.

Before I got to the end, they had shut down all the machines to preempt whatever mysterious mechanical failure was afflicting all the engines. Foremen were losing their minds because they were thinking about all the lost revenue for every minute those machines weren't stripping coal out of the earth. It would take them a while to figure out precisely what the problem was; they'd have to bust open the engine casings to discover that their pistons and cylinders were permanently wedded.

They had a coal-washing facility too, and I sabotaged that for good measure, even though it wasn't strictly necessary; without a steady supply of new coal coming in, it would run out of work in a day or so.

I allowed myself a satisfied grin. Public Relations men could sugarcoat it all they wanted, but strip mining was foul, and monkey-wrenching it felt good. Nobody had been injured, much less killed, yet I'd shut down the entire operation. Unfortunately, I'd also lost track of time. The sun was sinking below the horizon when I finished, which meant I'd already missed my rendezvous with Granuaile. I'd have to make my way back to Kayenta on foot. I could fly there as an owl, but then I'd have to steal a new set of clothes before I could show myself in public, and that sort of thing always made me feel cheap and sketchy. (Costing a corporate mining operation millions in lost revenue and equipment replacement made me feel great, by comparison.) Colorado would provide me with the energy for the run, but it would still be a good couple of hours on the road.

While going cross-country afforded a straighter path

back to Kayenta, I risked facing obstacles that I couldn't pass without shape-shifting, and I didn't know the lay of the land. I chose to stick to the roads instead. Once safely back to the highway and off the coal mine property, I considered dissolving my camouflage, because it was, frankly, an unnecessary drain on the earth. It was nighttime, I had no reflective clothing on, and no one would notice or care about a lone white man jogging well off the shoulder of the road. But paranoia made me keep it on. There were two skinwalkers out there with Famine's curse on them, and their tummies wouldn't stop rumbling until they tore into me.

While one of the skinwalkers might have been laid up and in no shape to hunt for edible Druids, the other one, I discovered, was quite able to stalk me, camouflage be damned. The speed and surprise of its attack overwhelmed me. I saw a flash of movement underneath a stretch of barbed-wire fence ahead of me, but before I could identify it as a kangaroo rat or a roadrunner or anything else, the bobcat it turned out to be drove me to the ground, its teeth at my throat. Before I could shout a completely pointless demand to get off, he'd already ripped out my windpipe and one side of my neck, my life's breath and blood spilling into the cold air. I weakly brought a hand up to prevent further attack, but he was greedily gulping down the mouthful of flesh he already had. I dissolved my camouflage, since it was clearly useless, and triggered my healing charm, focusing my efforts on rebuilding my trachea, but I doubted it would make a difference. The skinwalker would snuff me long before I'd be in any shape to put up any sort of spirited defense. I wished I hadn't left Moralltach in the trunk of Granuaile's car.

As I finished that thought and the bobcat finished swallowing my poor neck, its fur looked like it was bubbling, rippling as if it had those scarab beetles from *The*

Mummy running around underneath its skin. Its dead eyes—curiously, not orange the way they had been in human form—were focused on me, considering where it might take its next mouthful, when something slapped forcefully into its flesh, sending it tumbling and howling over my head. Belatedly I heard the crack of a firearm. It howled anew in response to a second shot, and the skinwalker fled, which was just fine with me. He might have ended my long life with one more bite. He might have already ended it with one.

I was drawing on the earth, feverishly trying to re-build my windpipe and stop the bleeding, all the while wondering why the Morrigan hadn't warned me of this. It occurred to me that this encounter, with what was outwardly an animal, probably didn't count as a battle to her, and thus it was out of her sphere of influence. I was on my own—with the possible exception of who-ever was out there with a sniper rifle. That person, how-ever, was a good distance away, judging by the delay in hearing the shots. To be in a position to take that shot, though, they had to be stalking me. Who was it?

Tired. So tired . . . My thoughts went fuzzy as my brain struggled with lack of blood and oxygen. But the rebuilding continued on autopilot now that my healing charm was activated, the bindings executed in hierarchi-cal order, healing circulatory and respiratory systems first, nervous systems next, and so on. Rebuilding mus-cle tissue was always last, and always the most time-consuming. I gasped in a giant, burning lungful of air when my trachea mended, staving off a blackout for a few more seconds. The walls were thin and fragile but enough to keep me breathing as I tried to splice together my torn carotid and jugular. That was more dire, and all my power went into restoring that circulation so I could think clearly and quickly again. I know I lost conscious-ness for anywhere from a few seconds to a few minutes, because there were no boots in my vision one second and then they were there the next, with no warning of approach from my ears. A dry voice tinged with contempt addressed me from above, and a flashlight shone into my eyes.

"Skinwalkers wanna make a Manwich outta you and you prance around in the dark all by yourself, no ninja stars or nothin'? You've gotta be the dumbest white man I ever met, and I've met more'n' my fair share." Coyote paused to spit juicily on the shoulder of the road, his boots shifting like sandpaper in the gravel. "Still, I ain't never been able to make a skinwalker hold still long enough to get shot afore this, so I s'pose I should congratulate ya for smellin' so damn tasty, heh heh."

Any witty retort I might have made was rendered impossible by my complete lack of vocal cords. I couldn't even look up and stick out my tongue at him, because my neck wouldn't move. Coyote knew this and rubbed it in.

"Man, he didn't put no ketchup on ya or nothin', just ate ya raw and sweaty, no fries with that or a slice o' pie afterward."

Coyote's boots shifted again, pointing northeast up the highway. "Hey, Mr. Druid, I know your dog is pretty big, but there's a truck-size hound with red eyes coming at us. He's six feet tall at the shoulder or I'm a horny toad. Ain't no skinwalker can get itself a dog skin like that. You got any ideas? Friend or foe?"

I couldn't see what he was talking about, of course. But if it wasn't a skinwalker, it had to be something sent by Hel, and the only hound Hel knew was . . . Gods Below! I scrawled two words hastily in the dirt by Coyote's boots. *GARM. RUN!*

"Run? Can't I just shoot 'im?"

I kept circling the word *RUN* with my finger until he got the message. I heard the rifle and flashlight clatter to the ground behind me, and Coyote grunted as he picked me up off the ground and slung me over his shoulder in a fireman's carry.

"You're turnin' out to be a giant pain in my ass, Mr. Druid." A strained wheeze puffed out of me as the whiplash from flopping against his back reopened my delicate windpipe and sent searing needles of torture along the short highway from my throat to my brain. Coyote laughed about it. "Guess I'm a giant pain in your neck, huh?"

Chapter 11

Coyote took four steps before he shifted us somewhere significantly different. Not only did we shift from an arid plateau in winter to a lush riverbank in spring, we arrived in the daytime. Fat bumblebees lazily pollinated the flowering bushes as the river sang its song over partially submerged rocks. Birds serenaded us and the wind sighed gently of serenity and fulsomeness. Coyote answered the question I wanted to ask.

"We are in Third World, or Yellow World, on the banks of the Great Male River, near the dwellin' place of White Shell Girl." He set me down on the smooth, sandy bank much more gently than he had picked me up. "Oughtta be a good place for you to hide up and heal for a while."

I wanted to shake my head, but of course I couldn't. I couldn't hold it up. But the power running through here was strong; this plane was bound tightly to the earth, and, had we the time, I could have enjoyed recuperating here. But it wasn't a safe place. Nowhere was safe from Garm. Unlike Hel, he wasn't bound to the nine realms of the World Tree. Supporting myself with one arm locked at the elbow, I scrawled another message in the sand of the riverbank.

Garm shifts planes.

Coyote read this and shrugged. "So what if he can? He don't know where we are."

I scowled and wrote furiously. *He TRACKS!*

"Aw, bull—" Coyote's dismissal got cut off by the sound of an epic belly flop combined with a surprised howl. Water *fooshed* into the sky as something elephantine displaced much of the river's flow.

"Son of a fucking bitch, Mr. Druid!"

Propped up as I was, I got my first look at the monstrosity pursuing us. It was Garm, Hel's personal widdle doggie: black fur over a thickly muscled, stocky frame and a muzzle curled at the lips to show slavering teeth with disturbingly red gums. His eyes were glowing egg yolks, burning Scut Farkus eyes to make your kidneys cringe. He rose from the riverbed, which was only three feet deep, and shook himself, showering either bank and making his fur stand out in spiky clumps. Coyote was hoisting me back over his shoulder, and I thought briefly about trying to run on my own while holding my head up with my hands, but I was too weak from blood loss to make a go of it. Garm spotted us and rolled out such a deep, vibrating bark that I thought it might be the etymological origin of the term *subwoofer*. He launched himself toward us, the water hampering his movements, and Coyote was able to take four steps and shift us away before Garm could close the distance.

We arrived someplace where the ground was as blue as the sky. Startled by our sudden appearance, blue pheasants erupted out of the blue grass and shat blue shit.

"This is Blue World," Coyote explained helpfully, but this time he continued to run away from the place where we'd shifted, and I had to concentrate on keeping my head attached and my fluids inside as I flopped over his back. "He'll be along soon, so we gotta figure somethin' out fast. Tap once for no, twice for yes, okay?"

I tapped his ass twice.

"Do you know how to kill it?" No. "Is this because o' that Famine thing that giant spooky bitch pulled? He'll keep comin' until he eats you?" Yes. "She said it was scent-based, right?" Yes. "Do you smell the same when you shift to an animal form?" No. I thought he was going to suggest I shift to an animal and stay that way, which might have been effective in the short term, but that was only half his plan. "So how about I copy your form again, all the way down to your scent, you shift to an animal, and then I run back up to White World and let him think I'm you?"

That was brilliant and . . . brave. Unexpected. It deserved a compliment, but I had to content myself with a couple of taps for yes.

"Can you shift, all torn up like that?"

I could, but it risked tearing my tender tissues again. I'd lost a lot of blood and didn't think I could afford to lose much more. I needed time I didn't have. If I didn't try it, though, there was no hope of shaking off Garm. I signaled yes, and as I did so, Hel's wet and extremely hungry hound popped into view behind us, about fifty yards away. He barked at us triumphantly, the sound vibrating our bones. I figured we had about three seconds.

"All right, then," Coyote said, "let's do it afore I think about it too much." He shifted us back up to Yellow World, and we were a little ways upriver from where we'd first arrived and fled. Coyote set me down near the bank and latched on to my arm.

"You hide out near here and I'll be back tomorrow," he said as he copied me. We had done the same thing earlier in the week to fool the thunder gods and the Norse; it worked despite my cold-iron aura, probably because he was targeting himself and he was beginning with skin-to-skin contact. Starting at his hand and rippling up from there, his rich brown skin turned pale and his clothes shifted to match mine. His neck sagged limply to the side, the same wound appearing, and it was disconcerting to see myself in such bad shape. On the plus side, Coyote couldn't talk anymore. When the copy was complete, he let go of my arm and gave me a thumbs-up, then twirled his finger around to indicate I should get on with it. I triggered the charm on my necklace that bound my spirit to the shape of an otter, hoping that shrinking my size would keep my mended vessels and trachea in one piece. It worked, but I felt like the victim of a first-year acupuncture student, needles of pain shooting through my entire right side. Trapped in my shirt, I squeezed through the head hole and began to crawl weakly toward the river, as Coyote staggered to his feet and then actually stomped, barefoot, away from the riverbank. He was trying to blaze the clearest trail possible, leaving my scent behind to lead Garm away from the river when he made his inevitable appearance.

The waters of the Great Male River were somewhat swift and I figured the current would carry me a good distance downstream when I attempted to cross it, but that was not necessarily a bad thing, considering that Garm would shortly arrive behind me. Of greater concern was surviving the crossing. My neck wound was still open, though it was now otter-size, and submerging it in water as I tried to swim with a weakened system wasn't the best idea I'd ever heard. If I passed out, I'd drown. If I didn't try, Garm might gulp me down like a fun-size candy bar when he showed up.

I waded into the cold water and discovered that I'd have to turn over on my back, because I couldn't hold my head up out of the water otherwise. I wasn't a quarter of the way across when I saw Garm splash into the shallows, where I'd been just moments before. He whipped his head around and those yellow eyes passed right over me, since he was obsessed with searching for a particular human at the moment. Seeing none, he put his nose down to the shore and searched for my scent. He paid attention to my clothes first, but then he spent some time at the water's edge, which puzzled me since I'd only come there as an otter. Then it struck me that my necklace was drenched in my scent, and I still had it on. Garm's head came up and looked across the water again. This time he saw me, and he growled, chops rippling over teeth the size of my hands. I kept swimming, moving my tail back and forth and putting distance between us, but I didn't think for one second that I could outpace him if he decided to splash into the river after me. I held what little breath I had and eyed him fearfully. Had I not screwed up fate, this was the dog who was supposed to fight Týr at Ragnarok. Now that Týr was dead, cut down by Coyote, who would stop him? Not a wounded otter in the Great Male River.

He put his nose down to the bank again as I neared the north side. He might be hungry for my scent, but he was after more than a snack; I didn't match the size or shape of his target. I wondered how good Coyote really was at copying; matching a scent is a tricky chemical business, and his assertion that he could do it did not make it so. Garm swerved away from the bank, following my otter trail back, *woof*ed when he caught a stronger whiff near where Coyote had stood, then bounded off in the direction Coyote had taken. He vanished from sight and I heard one more bark, then nothing above the chuckle of the river, plenty of birdsong, and the susurrus of the leaves in a soft wind.

Relief washed over me like the waters of the river. I was alone in Yellow World.

Unlike Blue World, it wasn't monochromatic. The environment was reminiscent of southwestern Colorado or the more verdant areas of northern New Mexico—

except for the birds. Here they were unusually active. Jays and woodpeckers and hummingbirds flitted about, chirped in challenge and triumph, defended their territory, and stole wee little bugs from one another. Their activity was such that I began to wonder if it might augur something in the original sense of the word. It didn't take me long to discern a pattern; though I'm not a fan of augury as a method of divination, it occasionally takes on the qualities of a baseball bat coming at your face—that is, you ignore it at your peril. Perhaps it was my vulnerable state that made me tune in; perhaps it was because this message was practically shouting at me.

The message I saw was betrayal. Betrayal was in my future, and fairly soon, if the birds were to be believed—and I wasn't in the habit of believing the dizzy little bastards, especially ones inhabiting a plane patronized by a trickster god.

Still, the augury made me uncomfortable. Who could betray me here, except Coyote? It didn't make sense; if he had wished to betray me, all he had to do was let the skinwalker eat me. Or run away and let Garm gulp me down. But maybe now, with Garm breathing down his neck, he was having second thoughts . . . ? If he led Garm back here, I would have to shift to an owl and try to fly; there would be no way to escape him in any other form.

Who else? Perhaps the Morrigan, who'd been notably present earlier but was notably absent now that I'd come closer to death than at almost any other time I could remember? It wouldn't take much to finish me off at this point.

Granuaile and Oberon were out of the question; their loyalty was ironclad. Perhaps the Sisters of the Three Auroras would break the nonaggression treaty somehow? That didn't make sense either, if they were busy relocating to Poland.

Speculating, I concluded, would be fruitless now. My priority had to be healing, nothing more. I shimmied underneath a blackberry bush and curled up as only otters can. I sighed once and let myself drift off to unconsciousness, allowing my system to repair itself.

Chapter 12

I woke in the night with a scabbed expanse of skin on my neck and the beginnings of muscle regeneration going on underneath. My breathing and circulation were fully restored. Vocal cords, I decided, should be the next priority. No muscle in my neck would save my life at this point, but a cry for help might come in handy. I listened to the dark for a while, checking for danger and perceiving none. I toyed with the idea of changing back to human form but abandoned it because I couldn't be sure yet that Garm—and, by extension, Hel—was satisfied that I was dead. If I turned back to my human form and Famine's spell wasn't broken, Garm might cross the planes to come after me again.

Moving slowly and as noiselessly as possible, I crept down to the river's edge to slake my thirst. I was hungry too, but I didn't want to tear anything open in the stress of a hunt—nor did I wish to announce my presence here any more than absolutely necessary. Having nothing else to do, I returned to the concealment of the blackberry bush and sighed into another recuperative sleep.

Coyote woke me in the morning, calling from across the river.

"Hey, Mr. Druid! Where are ya? Mr. Druid!" I poked my otter head out from under the blackberry bush to locate him visually. The voice of paranoia in my head—

and the memory of yesterday's augury—said he might not be alone.

Coyote was standing on the bank where he'd last seen me. He looked like himself again, blue jeans and boots and a sleeveless white undershirt, big silver belt buckle, and shining black hair falling from underneath a black cowboy hat. I watched him and the brush nearby to see if there was any movement. He kept calling, and his voice sharpened with an edge of irritation when I didn't reply.

"Don't make me hunt for ya! I ain't in the mood!" he yelled. Deciding it was worth the risk to show myself, I tested out my vocal cords and let out a high-pitched otter call. It sounded a bit rough but the volume was there. Coyote swiveled his head toward the sound and spotted me walking down to the bank. "Oh, there you are. Took ya long enough."

Pausing at the riverbank, I chittered at him again. Now that I was in the open, he could point me out to any unfriendly creatures he might have hiding nearby, if that was his plan. Instead, he just stood there, hands on his hips, bemused at my behavior.

"I don't speak Otter, ya dumbass. What are ya waitin' for? Get over here so we can get back to the rez. Unless I'm talkin' to a real otter, in which case I'm the dumbass and you can just stay over there."

I cheerfully suggested that he juggle hedgehogs, since he couldn't understand anything I said, and slipped into the river. Keeping my head above water was manageable this time, though it hurt like one of Torquemada's special tortures.

When I emerged, dripping, Coyote squatted down and spoke with more venom than I'd ever heard from him before. "Guess how much I like being eaten by a huge fuckin' dog, Mr. Druid," he said. "Chewed up an' swallowed, an' I didn't die until I hit the acid in his stomach 'cause he gulped my head down whole. I remember every horrible second of it. An' afore that I got turned into mincemeat by a buncha thunder gods. I've died twice now for you, an' both times were some o' the worst ways I could possibly go. You better be worth it."

Making otter noises would be insufficient reply, so I bound myself back to my human form and gasped at the pain as a few of the muscles tore again in the shift. My vocal cords held it together, but just barely.

"Thank you," I rasped as I lay on the riverbank, cold and naked. "Sorry about the trouble."

"Aw, don't thank me yet," Coyote said, a wry smirk on his face. "I'm takin' ya right back to them skinwalkers. They're prob'ly still hungry for Druid. An' if they ain't, they're still pissed about us bein' in their territory. They gotta be dealt with one way or another." He paused, thinking of something else, and gave two short barks of laughter before adding, "Plus your hound and your girl are going to kill ya for makin' 'em worry."

"She's not my girl," I said, which was probably not the smartest reply I could have made.

Coyote snorted derisively. "Yeah, whatever."

"She's my apprentice," I reminded him. For some reason this conjured a vision of Leif in my head, anxious to start a Shakespearean quote duel, and I could hear him say, "The Druid doth protest too much, methinks."

Coyote shook his head. "I don't care, Mr. Druid. Can you walk now?"

Experimentally, I pushed against the ground with both hands and discovered that I couldn't keep my head up or endure the excruciating pain the movement caused. Bunching the muscles in my shoulders and back affects the neck—check. I could cut off the pain, but it was there for a reason. I tried to lever myself up using only my left arm, on the theory that it was the side opposite the wound, but that was a no-go too. Bunching up the shoulders in any way made those torn muscles scream.

"Wait. Let's try something else." I rolled over gingerly onto my back and then held up my left hand. "Help me up. Just pull gently."

Coyote locked his hand in mine and pulled. The pain this time was more of a wail than a scream. I tried to keep my shoulders as relaxed as possible, and once I got my feet under me it wasn't so bad. What I needed was a brace.

"All right?" Coyote asked.

"Yeah. I'll have to move slowly, but I can walk with my head tilted like a zombie."

"Good. I got a truck parked and waiting in Fourth World."

"Any clothes in it?"

"Nope. You got clothes right there." Coyote pointed to my jeans and shirt on the riverbank, which had been thoroughly nosed and stomped on by Garm.

"Wet and muddy ones."

"So walk back naked, Mr. Druid, it ain't no matter to me."

Getting into my jeans was an exercise in patience for both of us. Cold and wet jeans are no fun to put on in any circumstance, but especially not when you have to keep your head as still as possible. I didn't bother with the shirt.

When I signaled to Coyote that I was ready to go, he said, "Okay, just put your hand on my shoulder and follow." I did so. We took four steps and were back on the side of the road a short distance from where the skinwalker had torn out my throat. A blue Ford half ton was waiting there, no doubt stolen. Coyote wanted to get in and drive back to the camp right away, but I insisted on messing up the earth where my blood was collected and dried. I used a little bit of power to churn the earth there and bury it completely, mixing it into the dirt while I was at it to prevent it from being used against me later.

"You think that skinwalker could have come back here and gotten to this blood while we were away?" I asked.

"Naw," Coyote said. "I got him pretty good. They're both laid up healin' somewhere. Prob'ly won't hear from either one of 'em for a couple days. But they'll be back soon enough. Maybe you'll be in decent shape yourself by then."

Maybe. Getting into the truck while keeping my head as still as possible was awkward, but I managed it with only a couple of spikes of sharp pain.

Coyote drove with the window down and leaned his head out a bit into the wind. "So, when will the gold be there, Mr. Druid?"

"Sometime after the coal mines shut down," I rasped. "The elemental wants them out of commission permanently. You'll have a big labor pool to draw from."

"An' if the coal starts up again, the gold shuts down, is that it?"

"Right," I said. Monosyllables, I decided, were good. Especially since I couldn't nod.

"That means you're goin' to have to stay here longer'n you thought."

"Yep."

Coyote grunted but said no more until we drove up to camp. Granuaile and Oberon came running toward the truck.

Before we opened the doors, Coyote turned off the engine and said, "By the way, Mr. Druid, you lost a day. It's Monday morning."

I'd been missing for two nights? They were going to kill me.

<Atticus! Where have you been?>

Oberon approached at a dangerous speed as I stepped

gingerly from the cab of the truck. *Slow down, don't jump on me, okay? I'm injured.*

<Where?>

Neck. Under the skin; you won't see it. I'll explain to Granuaile and you'll hear it all.

As she hurried to catch up, Granuaile's face was cycling through expressions of relief and worry and determination to make me pay. I held up my hands in case she wanted to throw her arms around my neck and hug me—or in case she wanted to grasp my neck in her hands and choke me.

"Where have you been?" she demanded, stopping several paces away and folding her arms in front of her.

"Sorry to make you worry," I grated, "but I'll be okay soon enough."

Her eyes flicked down to my wet, muddy jeans and noted my profound lack of shirt.

"What happened to you?"

"Someone took advantage of me."

Granuaile shot an uncertain glance at Coyote.

"Hey, don't look at me like that," Coyote said. "Far as I know he's still cherry."

I jumped in with a fuller explanation before Granuaile could react or Oberon could question that particular colloquialism. "On the way back from the mine, I got attacked by a skinwalker and then we got chased by Hel's hound, Garm."

Granuaile's jaw dropped. "How did you escape?"

"I didn't, really. Coyote saved me."

"Uh, what was that, Mr. Druid?" Coyote asked, cupping a hand behind his ear. "Didn't quite hear that."

"Yes, you did." I didn't feel like rehashing my brush with death while Coyote loitered nearby, so I gestured to Granuaile's car. "Let's go to town," I told her. "We have business to attend to and clothes to buy. I'll tell you everything."

"Hey, when are ya gonna be back?" Coyote asked.

"Before dark, don't worry," I said.

On the way in to town, I informed Granuaile and Oberon that I quite nearly died and that only Coyote's intervention had prevented me from being completely eaten by the skinwalker and Garm. He'd saved me twice and died for me twice.

"I owe him big now," I said. "Damn it."

"Well, that explains why it was quiet in the hogan last night," Granuaile said. "One skinwalker stabbed through the shoulder and another one shot twice. They'll be laid up for a while."

I gently begged to differ. "Not much longer, I expect. They'll have accelerated healing as well, and if they still have the Famine spell laid on them, they'll be desperate to reach me. I'm hoping that's not the case, though. How goes the Blessing Way?"

"It's almost finished. The hogan will be completely safe after tonight."

We reached the outskirts of Kayenta and Oberon wagged his tail, seeing the buildings. <Do they have a decent butcher in this town?>

"I imagine someone's working at it," I said. Granuaile darted her eyes quickly at me but then realized I must be talking to Oberon. She was getting used to my occasional non sequiturs.

"Where to, sensei?" she said.

"Head for the big box store. I can pick up some clothes and a neck brace there. Or, rather, you can. Don't think they'll let me in looking like this. It'd be nice to have a pair of sandals too."

"Got it." I gave her my sizes and she left Oberon and me sitting in the parking lot.

<Where are we going next?> Oberon asked.

Breakfast. There's a place on the highway called the Blue Coffee Pot.

<Will I get to come in?> Oberon asked. His tail wagged in excitement, thumping against the backseat.

I hope so. We'll get you camouflaged and you can squeeze in somewhere.

<Awesome! I can almost smell it already. The air will be thick with coffee and butter and sausage. Just what I need after three days of dirt and beef jerky.>

You could use a bath, I told him.

<I actually wouldn't mind one for once, even though we had one just a few days ago. Do you have a good story ready?>

I can probably think of something, I replied. *What sort of story are you in the mood for?*

<Something with ninjas in it!>

That's no fun. The ninjas are almost always invisible, and if they're not then they're wearing black pajamas and they don't want to talk about anything. How about a story with samurai instead? I can tell you about one of them.

<You knew a real samurai?>

Yep. I spent a couple years in feudal Japan until Aenghus Óg chased me out of there.

<Did the samurai you knew suffer terribly over minor points of honor and struggle to keep his face expressionless as his world came crashing down?>

Most definitely.

<All right, that sounds cool! I can't wait! Well, no, I take that back. I can wait until after breakfast. Priorities, you know. But, hey, before I forget, I need to report.>

You do? Report what?

<You asked me to hang out around Sophie in the clever disguise of Snugglepumpkin and find out what she knows. It was a mission and I chose to accept it.>

Ah, yes. Report, Snugglepumpkin.

<It's not a very good secret-agent name, is it? Oh,

well. What I found out is that she is secretly obsessed with lasers and wants to equip everything she owns with them. When nobody else was around, she would talk to me about her plans to mount giant frickin' lasers on top of her truck, her roof, and above her front door, to disintegrate missionaries and stray cats that come to take a dump in her front yard. She is a completely awesome lady. She even shared with me that she prefers T-bones to New York strips, and that means she is one of the finest human beings on the planet.>

Oberon. What did you find out about the building site?

<I was coming to that! Okay, they are laying out a massive compound, and I am not sure I understand it all. In one place they are building a factory for solar components; there's another for wind, and in another they are planning a rail depot—does that make sense?>

Yes, they need to ship out their products somehow.

<Okay, and then she also pointed one time to this space across from where the rail depot would be and said the storage facilities would be there, and behind that would be the transformers. Does that mean Optimus Prime has decided to help the Navajos achieve energy independence?>

No, the kind of transformers she's talking about transmit electricity. They are, sadly, inanimate structures.

<Oh. I thought that was too cool to be true. But, anyway, how did I do? Did I earn two sausages back?>

Yes, you did very well. You're at negative twelve now.
<Gravy!>

Gravy, indeed. It was comforting to know that Coyote planned to follow through on his plan—or at least he was thorough enough in his trickery to make sure that Sophie and her crew believed they were going to build all that.

Granuaile returned with a bag full of clothes and a

neck brace for me. I put the latter on first, and it eased some of the strain immediately. That would allow the muscle to grow back a bit faster.

"I didn't know what kind of shirt would be best, but I figured we shouldn't do anything like a regular T-shirt, which you'd have to squeeze over your head and put pressure on your neck. So I got this button-up one," she said, holding up a chocolate-brown shirt with a light tan vertical pinstripe design, "and then I also got these tank tops, because I figured those would be easy to pull on." She held a package of mixed black and gray undershirts. I considered both and then chose the undershirts, thinking the collar on the button-up would look a bit unwieldy and hang uncomfortably around the brace. I could stand to be cold for a while.

"Thanks," I said, taking the package and the rest of the clothes from her. "Turn around and stand guard, will you?"

"You're going to change right here in the parking lot?"

I cast camouflage on myself. "Sure. Scandal-free public nudity."

"Damn." She shook her head as I melted from view. "I can't wait until I can do that too."

"Only eleven years and nine months to go," I teased her as she turned around. I gladly shucked off my wet, muddy jeans and put on the new pair. I noticed she hadn't bought me any underwear; Granuaile either didn't think of it or she *did* think of it and decided that I should go commando.

I tore open the package of undershirts and gingerly pulled a black one over my head before tucking it into my jeans. Though I was now dressed in a similar fashion to Coyote, I figured he could keep the cowboy hat and I'd rock the tattoos. Usually I don't wear shirts that show them off, because they tend to draw attention and sometimes questions. "Where'd you get those done?" was an awkward one, because the truthful answer was, in Ireland around 50 B.C.E.

I slipped my feet into the sandals, then turned in a slow circle to check my surroundings, since my neck was now immobilized. No one was looking, so I dispelled the camouflage and pronounced myself ready to go.

Granuaile gave me a good once-over and her gaze felt less than innocent, but all she said was, "Much better," before walking around to the driver's side.

The Blue Coffee Pot was bustling for a Monday morning; we had to wait for a table. I asked the hostess if it was always like this, and she shook her head. "Coal mine's closed, so a lot of the workers are enjoying a day off."

"The mine's closed?" I said, letting a bit of incredulity flavor my tone. "Why?"

"It's in the paper," she said, nodding her head over to a rack filled with the *Arizona Daily Sun,* Flagstaff's newspaper. I bought one and grinned over the headline. BLACK MESA COAL MINE SABOTAGED, it read. The article claimed the shutdown was only temporary, until new equipment could be brought in, a few days at the earliest and two weeks at the latest, and there would be a raft of new security measures put in place to prevent something like this from happening again. The security measures wouldn't bother me; I'd simply have to make sure I went during full daylight and allowed myself plenty of time to get back out. And maybe I'd take my sword, just in case.

It was interesting, I thought, that it had taken a couple of days to make it into the paper. That bespoke some serious suppression on their end at first, but now they were looking for someone to blame.

On page seven there was an extended article about my mysterious death in Tuba City. That headline read: BI-

ZARRE TUBA CITY MURDER BAFFLES POLICE. Before I could get too far into the article, a table opened up and we were ushered over to a small two-top by the window. Once I saw where it was, I said, "Be right there, I forgot something in the car," then I went to get Oberon. I camouflaged him and explained that the space was going to be pretty tight.

<It always is. Sometimes I wish I weren't so freakishly huge. Do you ever wish you had a tiny dog?>

Nah. People find small dogs approachable, and I don't necessarily want to be approached. When they see you coming, they're more likely to cross the street. It's like I have Sasquatch on a leash.

<Sasquatch on a leash! I like that.>

You're welcome. That would be a great band name, actually.

<Or it could be a line of men's beauty products, like those musky soaps and colognes and stuff. *Sasquatch on a Leash: Control your Smelly Beast.*>

I opened the door for Oberon and let him walk in. *Watch out for people. Table's to the right, next to the window.*

<No problem.>

Granuaile startled a bit when she felt Oberon brushing past her legs to wrap himself around the center of the table but otherwise gave no sign that she had a huge Irish wolfhound lying on her toes. I carefully sat down, tucked my legs underneath the chair, and then scooched forward.

We ordered coffee, eggs, and a whole lot of meat sides. While we waited for our food, I returned to the paper and read aloud the article about my death.

TUBA CITY—Authorities are flummoxed by a strange murder scene in a small patch of desert in Tuba City, where the remnants of a man were found on Thursday.

The body of Atticus O'Sullivan, age 31—

"Thirty-one?" Granuaile interrupted.

"Well, that has to be based on the driver's license they found. I was twenty-one, according to the license, when it was feloniously issued to me."

"Ah, okay," Granuaile said, nodding in understanding. "Continue."

The body of Atticus O'Sullivan, age 31, was found mutilated and dismembered near a water tower. Examination of the area suggests that eight to ten different people were at the scene and possibly involved in the killing—one of them barefoot.

Friends identified the body based on hair and tattoos.

"Huh." I paused and looked up from the paper. "I wonder who identified me."

"It doesn't say?"

"No. It goes on, though. Check this out."

The FBI has jurisdiction over murders committed on reservation land. Though agents could not be reached for comment, authorities in Tempe noted O'Sullivan's recent troubles with the law.

Detective Kyle Geffert of the Tempe Police Department said, "Mr. O'Sullivan was shot by Tempe police a couple of months ago and was on the scene at the Satyrn Massacre in Scottsdale. Also, one of his employees died rather suddenly last November."

"Gods Below, can you believe that guy? He makes it sound like I killed Perry and deserved to be shot."

"Well, you didn't exactly endear yourself to him during that investigation," Granuaile pointed out.

"I know, but there's no call to go around smearing me now that I'm dead," I said.

"You might want to keep your voice down," Granuaile said in low tones, her eyes darting significantly to the tables nearby.

"Good point." Seeking validation for my own point that Geffert was out of line, I said in a hushed whisper, "Oberon, don't you have anything to add?"

<I'd like to add a few orders of bacon to the bill.>

"We haven't even gotten the first orders yet."

<Hey, you asked.> No validation for me, then.

"What else does it say?" Granuaile said over the rim of her coffee mug. The sun streaming through the window left golden highlights in her red hair and lit up her green eyes. The light dusting of freckles high on her cheeks was unspeakably charming and . . .

"Atticus?"

"Hmm?"

"The article."

"Oh, yes." I raised the paper to hide my embarrassment.

<Ha! She caught you staring again, didn't she?>

Shh. I have to read this.

O'Sullivan was the owner of Third Eye Books and Herbs in Tempe. The current manager, Rebecca Dane, was shocked to hear that her employer had passed.

"The last time I saw him, he said he was going on vacation to the Antipodes," she said. "I have no idea why he'd be in Tuba City."

Regular customer Joshua Goldfried noticed a change in Mr. O'Sullivan's behavior in the past few months. "Ever since the middle of October, it always seemed he was nervous about one thing or another.

He was always so good about being here, but he started to disappear for days at a time."

Mr. O'Sullivan was shot by a Tempe police detective in late October in his store and subsequently sued the city for $5 million. Hal Hauk, attorney for Mr. O'Sullivan, confirmed that the City of Tempe had just agreed to settle Mr. O'Sullivan's lawsuit against them for a seven-figure sum.

"Whoa. Does that mean you're rich?"

"I'm already rich. But, regardless, I instructed Hal to give my share of the settlement to the family of Detective Fagles. Wait, it gets good here."

Mr. O'Sullivan's murder was among the bloodiest and most brutal of any in Arizona history. While the murder itself may have been committed by a single person, the dismemberment and mutilation of his body afterward was undoubtedly performed by a group of people wielding different bladed and blunt weapons.

Mr. O'Sullivan was seen wearing a sword in Tempe by multiple witnesses before his death. Authorities from Tempe and Tuba City refused to speculate on a motive for the killing and denied that there was anything like a sword-based *Fight Club* organization.

Granuaile laughed at that.

<Well, of *course* they denied it,> Oberon said. <The first rule of Sword Fight Club is don't talk about Sword Fight Club.>

Our food arrived as we shared a chuckle over the article. As plate after plate was set down, I kept scanning the newspaper.

"Anything else?"

"Nah, it just continues to imply that I must have done

something naughty to deserve this. What's really interesting is that it doesn't mention the bodies of Týr or Vidar. Or any evidence of the Morrigan's orgy."

"I beg your pardon?" Granuaile's fork froze halfway to her mouth, and those green eyes, though still lit by the sun, carried a cool steel warning in them. I took heed.

"As I was leaving," I explained, "the Morrigan mentioned her desire for an orgy in the mud. I don't know if she actually had one or not, but she certainly seemed intent on it."

"An orgy with *whom*?"

"She was hoping to attract the locals," I said, leaving out the part where she originally hoped to attract me. "But now I'm wondering if she went through with it. She probably ate Týr and Vidar instead. She does that, you know, when she's in crow form. She eats dead bodies."

Granuaile blanched. "Ew. Gross." She looked down at all the sausage and bacon sides waiting on the table. "Kind of puts me off my appetite a bit."

<My appetite is like Sasquatch on a leash, and he's ready to break loose! Feed me, Seymour!>

Ah, right you are. Sorry, Oberon.

I camouflaged a plate of meat and then pretended I was picking something up off the floor when I was really putting something down for Oberon. He'd find it by smell, no problem.

"How could she put away two fully grown men, though?" Granuaile asked, in spite of herself.

I shrugged. "I never stick around to watch, and I never asked. It's a mystery."

After breakfast, it was errand time. We each rented a post-office box and then spent a tedious hour setting up bank accounts under our new identities, using what remaining cash we had. Armed with addresses and bank accounts, we each got new cell phones. Then I put in a call to the offices of Magnusson and Hauk, my attorneys. To get past the receptionist and actually talk to Hal, I had to identify myself as a "close friend of Atticus O'Sullivan" and stress that I was a new client who wished to put Mr. Hauk on retainer.

"This is Hal Hauk," he said, his voice distant and bored.

"Mr. Hauk. My name is Reilly Collins." Hal knew very well who I was. He was the one who'd given me my new driver's license, birth certificate, and Social Security number. He knew I'd be calling at some point to set up a "new" relationship once I got settled. This entire charade was for the benefit of anyone who might be listening in. "I'd like to put you on retainer and meet with you for a consultation, if that's possible."

"Where are you, Mr. Collins?"

"Kayenta. I'd like to see you today."

"Impossible for me, unfortunately. However, I can send an associate to see you this afternoon with all the necessary paperwork to get started."

"Can we see this associate here well before sundown?"

"Hmm. It's something of a drive, so we could probably make mid-afternoon if we hurry."

"Please hurry, then, Mr. Hauk. I have an important engagement at sundown."

"All right. I'll send Greta." Greta was a member of Hal's pack who seemed to get stuck with all of Hal's odd jobs. She wasn't a lawyer, but she was utterly trustworthy and utterly unimpressed with me. "Where shall she meet you?"

"The sub place on the main highway. We'll buy her a sandwich with extra meat and everything."

"That's extremely kind of you," Hal said drily. "She will be thrilled."

We made good-bye noises, I gave him my new number to pass on to Greta, and I snapped the phone closed with satisfaction. "That's good. Once we give him power of attorney, he can start moving funds from my other accounts."

"How many accounts do you have?"

"Hundreds, scattered around the world under various names. I got into the practice thanks to Aenghus Óg. The constant need to flee meant that I needed safe places to run, which often meant cities, and surviving there meant I needed funds. Hal knows about twenty of them."

"Do you really need so many now that Aenghus Óg is dead?"

"Eh. They're not doing me any harm. They're just sitting there earning interest. Might need them down the road."

Granuaile conceded the wisdom of this. "What are we doing next, sensei?"

"We have most of the day to wait until Greta can get here. Let's do some training for you and some play for Oberon."

We drove to a small undeveloped area in the township boundaries that supported a few rabbits and some extremely skittish ground squirrels. Oberon had a blast terrorizing them while I walked Granuaile through some martial arts forms that required a straight back and neck.

Kayenta was a dry place and a simple one. Austere, even. But I could see myself being happy there, if only the world would let me.

Chapter 13

There was a span of years in the 1980s during which I marveled at the almost supernatural powers of Steve Perry. While he sang for Journey, he made people believe in themselves, weep over long distance relationships, and inquire at transit stations about midnight trains. Together with his bandmates, he fully explored the hidden depths and nuances of the word *whoa*—teasing out shades of meaning and connotations that I would have been hard pressed to discover, even with two thousand years of attention to the problem—and I'm willing to bet that the pathos with which he imbued the syllable *na* shall never be equalled in the history of the human race.

He was a god of rock. He nearly solved all the world's problems with nothing but power chords and anguished cries into a microphone.

But his power to uplift the spirit did have a limit—a limit shared, I might add, by every other band—and that was the inability to ameliorate the soul-destroying visual discord of corporate fast-food franchises. Some acquaintance or another would periodically drag me into one of the horrors, and, under the malign influence of a décor scheme that assaulted my retinas with primary colors, Steve would be singing "woe" instead of "whoa" on my Walkman. His sound could not tame the visual fury of paper-wrapped cheeseburgers dressed in angry red ketchup and a lonesome pickle chip.

I should have remembered that before I suggested the sub joint on the highway as a good place for Greta to meet us. It was decorated in lurid yellow and a shade of green that I felt was unnecessarily belligerent.

"Ugh. This place hurts my eyes," Granuaile said. "It's offensive."

A camouflaged Oberon chimed in. <She's right. I can smell the vegetables in here and they almost drown out the scent of ham. That's offensive.>

What'll you have?

<Can I have the entire bin full of roast beast?>

Nope, sorry. Sandwich with double meat.

<Roast beast, then, with no frills.>

We had no sooner sat down with our sandwiches in a screaming-yellow booth than Greta entered and squinted at the glare.

"Damn," she said, pausing at the door and wincing. "It's ugly in here." She was dressed professionally and carried a brown leather courier bag slung over her left shoulder. Her hair had grown long since I'd last seen her, and she had it plaited into a thick braid. Seeing us, she lifted her chin in a terse greeting and came over to our booth, slipping the bag off her shoulder and into the seat we'd left her. She promptly put out her hand, palm up. "Boss said my early dinner's on you."

Granuaile's mouth gaped, but I'd half-expected this sort of behavior. Greta had never particularly liked me, and I expected she liked me even less since I'd taken a trip with her alpha, Gunnar Magnusson, and come back with his crushed body. I nodded and put a couple of twenties in her hand.

"So generous," she sneered, and went to stand in line without thanking me.

Granuaile bent close and whispered urgently, "Atticus, what the hell—"

"Patience," I said, interrupting her. "You do know that wolves have fantastic hearing, don't you?"

"Oh," she said in a tiny voice. "I'll just eat my sandwich." I smiled at her in thanks.

<Sure wish *I* had a sandwich to eat,> Oberon hinted from under the table.

Sorry, buddy, I said, properly chastised. *I got a bit distracted.* I unwrapped his sandwich for him and set it down on the floor on top of the paper. There was no one else in the shop to see me do this, besides Greta.

<I know. You do that a lot. You keep letting little things like the world around you distract you from the important things. Like filling the yawning abyss of my belleh.>

Greta returned with two double-meat foot-longs and a drink. One of them was a double roast beast, and she pointedly unwrapped it and put it on the floor for Oberon. It was a snide way to let me know she knew he was there, despite the camouflage. No doubt she'd smelled what he was having and ordered another. Our booth was out of sight of the employees, so she didn't have to hide what she was doing.

<Whoa! Another sandwich? Awesome! Tell her thanks! This is weird, though. Werewolves aren't usually this nice.>

"My hound thanks you," I said. "As do I."

"He is very welcome," Greta said. "I am sure he's quite hungry, after all," she added, a faint accusation in her tone. Granuaile narrowed her eyes at Greta but said nothing. I carefully kept my expression neutral.

<Ah, there's the werewolf attitude I know so well. Situation normal.>

Greta quickly, efficiently demolished her turkey sub, glaring at us all the while with unconcealed hostility. She

was here on the orders of her new alpha, and she would
do whatever he asked of her, but he hadn't asked her to
be pleasant, so she wouldn't be. Since I was outside the
Tempe Pack, she could throw all the challenging stares
she wanted at us. I could practically feel Granuaile
seething next to me, and I hoped she wouldn't rise to the
bait Greta was dangling. I shot her a quelling look,
pressed my hand down in the air to suggest she keep a
lid on it, and she nodded, message received. I'd have to
coach her later on how to handle werewolves.

Finished sinking our subs, we crumpled the paper
wrappings noisily and threw them away. Greta opened
up her courier bag and began pulling out documents
along with a pen. No friendly chitchat, just business.

"Fill these out with your banking information and so
on. Sign at the bottom," she said.

Seeing that she would volunteer nothing, I began to
ask her questions as I filled in blanks. "How is Rebecca
Dane doing with the bookstore?" I said. I'd given Hal
instructions to sell it to her for the random sum of a
buck seventy-two.

"Perfectly well. The same regulars visit the store as
before."

"How is Leif?"

"He's back."

I looked up from the documents I was signing. "No
kidding? He looks the same?"

"I wouldn't say that. But he smells the same. Dead."

Something in her tone didn't sound right. "What's the
matter with him?"

Greta shrugged. "Can't say. He's not a happy vampire. Probably because he has a lot more company these
days. He's not the only vampire in town anymore."

"I've heard something along those lines. Why doesn't
he take them out like he did before?"

"Says he can't do that this time. The politics have changed."

"Vampire politics?"

"He would hardly care about human politics, so yes. He wants to see you, but of course we didn't know where you were until you called this morning. Shall we tell him where you are when he wakes up tonight?"

"Um, no," I said. If the vampire politics had changed, in practical terms that meant Leif was no longer in charge. If he wasn't in charge, then Leif might have to share anything he knew with whoever was. "Definitely do not tell him where I am. Don't even tell him my new name."

Greta looked surprised. "You don't want to see him?"

"I didn't say that. I'd simply like to meet on neutral ground. Tell him to meet me at Granny's Closet tomorrow night, around eight-thirtyish. That's in Flagstaff."

"Sure, I know Granny's Closet," Greta said. "Great wings there. Cold beer."

"Indeed. What can you tell me about how my death is being handled?"

"By whom?"

"I want everything you know."

She rolled her eyes and sighed. We carefully did not take offense. "Hal has been busy dealing with the FBI. They've taken quite an interest in you now that you're dead. They're especially keen to know about your life before you showed up in Arizona as Atticus O'Sullivan, since you don't have a credit history or any other records before that time."

"Oh, if only they knew the size of that particular iceberg."

This earned me a brief flicker of a smirk. "Naturally, Hal knows nothing about your life before you became a client of the firm and wouldn't share it if he did. Detective Geffert, however, has been eager to share everything he possibly can."

"What a helpful lad he is."

"Yes. The theory he's pawning to anyone who will listen is that you were responsible for the Satyrn Massacre and this business in Tuba City was a revenge killing, and the reason you have no early records is that you're a sleeper agent from somewhere."

I shed my American accent and spoke like a lad from Tipperary. "A sleeper agent from Ireland? Hurting America by slaughtering affluent twentysomethings? For what purpose?"

"Yeah, he's a bit fuzzy there."

"That's the biggest load of bollocks I've ever heard." I resumed my standard American English accent. "What evidence is he offering?"

"He regrets that you died before he could build a decent case and arrest you properly."

"Ha! Excellent! What else?"

"I have something for you." Greta pulled out of her bag a lavender envelope with a wax seal and my name scrawled beautifully on the front in dark purple ink. I hadn't seen calligraphy of this sort since the nineteenth century. "It's from Malina Sokolowski."

"Ah. And where is she these days?" I examined the envelope in the magical spectrum, because—you know. Witches. As I suspected, there was a magical seal on it as well as the mundane wax one. Malina would know when the seal was broken.

"Don't know, except that she and her coven are out of town. I expect that might tell you something," she said, nodding at the envelope. "They kind of have the same arrangement with the firm that you have. They'll let us know when they settle down somewhere, but we can't tell you anything about it when they do. Hal wanted me to thank you for sending their business to the firm."

"He's very welcome. May I ask a question regarding the Pack?"

Greta's jaw tightened, but she said, "Ask."

"Have you ever run afoul of skinwalkers?"

She hadn't expected the question. She looked bemused and shook her head.

"Ah, well, kind of a long shot anyway."

Greta didn't pursue the matter with a polite inquiry. She looked down at the paperwork in a clear signal that we should hurry up and finish. It was a good idea, since we had to make it back to the hogan before sundown.

"I'll need Hal to transfer about forty thousand to each of our accounts," I said, finishing the documents and handing the stack over to Granuaile to sign. "He'll need to draw smaller sums from multiple accounts to avoid attracting the attention of the IRS. And I need it there tomorrow."

"Done."

"Please give my regards to Hal, Snorri, and the rest of the Pack."

"I will."

She said nothing more as she placed the paperwork back in her bag. With a curt nod to us that was supposed to serve as a farewell, she slid out of the booth and stalked out to the parking lot. I put my finger to my lips to tell Granuaile it wasn't safe to talk yet. While we waited for Greta to drive away, I opened the letter from Malina. There was a single sheet inside, written in the same impeccable hand as the address on the envelope.

Dear Mr. O'Sullivan,

We have taken your advice and have decided to move the coven elsewhere. If you ever need to contact us in the future, please do so through Mr. Hauk.

During our last divination ritual, we learned that the vampire situation will become extremely fluid and dangerous in the near future. There were hints that someone powerful—perhaps you—might be drawn into it somehow, and we urge you to avoid this, if at all possible, for your own safety.

> *Kind regards,*
> *Malina Sokolowski*

I showed the letter to Granuaile. "You know what this means?"

She scanned it quickly. "It means you shouldn't meet Leif tomorrow."

"That's right. But I owe him the courtesy of a meeting after all we've been through. And I'm curious to see what sort of shape he's in. You should have seen him. You know that comedian, Gallagher, who smashes watermelons with a sledgehammer? Leif's head was the watermelon."

Granuaile frowned. "I don't know that comedian, sorry."

<Poor Atticus. Another fruitless analogy.>

Augh! Oberon, that was dreadful!

<But not a Schwarzenegger pun! Fruit was never part of the treaty, so neener neener!>

"Why not just ask Hal to send you a picture from his camera phone or something?" Granuaile said. "You don't need to risk it. Wait until things stabilize."

"Well, you're coming to Flagstaff with me tomorrow anyway."

"I am?"

"Yep. It's time for you to die."

Chapter 14

Granuaile's face deflated. "I think my mother's going to be upset about that. Dad might shed a tear too. My stepdad will laugh, unless my mother's watching."

I reminded her that it didn't have to be that way. She could always go back to being a barmaid with a philosophy degree and hang around with normal people.

"No, that's not an option. The fact that I'm expressing my dismay over a necessary course of action doesn't mean I'm not willing to go through with it. But let's not talk about that right now; let's talk instead, if we're finally allowed, about what just happened. That woman was astoundingly rude to us. To you."

"Yes, she was." We exited the sub shop as an act of mercy on our optic nerves. As we drove back to the hogan, I explained to Granuaile the finer points of dealing with werewolves when one is a shape-shifter but still not part of the pack. Challenge with the voice, not the eyes, and you can get away with quite a bit.

<I still say everyone would get along better if werewolves would just accept snacks gracefully,> Oberon insisted.

To the werewolf, snacks are something to be taken, not given, I reminded him.

The hogan, once we reached it, was in considerably better shape. The walls and the roof had been coated with a thick layer of insulating mud, and in the magical spectrum the walls were covered completely by the ward of the Blessing Way. The only way the skinwalkers could hope to break through tonight without burning themselves was through the roof. They knew it, and they knew we knew it and would be waiting for them to try it. And, in all likelihood, they were still in no shape to try such shenanigans.

The ceremony was in progress when we entered. Frank Chischilly looked tired but determined. Ben Keonie and his crew were in there, and so was Sophie Betsuie. Surprisingly, Coyote was present in his role as Mr. Benally and lending his own mojo to the final night of the ceremony. He was wearing a gray hoodie sweatshirt but still had on his black cowboy hat. He smirked when he saw my neck brace and black undershirt. We received tight nods as greetings, and we gave them tiny smiles in return and tried to keep out of everyone's way.

The skinwalkers came but did not attack the hogan. They were still nursing injuries, as I suspected. We heard them out there in the night, both of them. They circled the hogan for about a half hour, snarling and hissing and issuing threats, and then the noises stopped. No one believed they had truly gone; they were simply waiting to see if anyone was stupid enough to go outside and check. No one was.

I wondered if their appearance meant that the Famine curse was still in effect despite Garm's meal or if they were here purely for revenge and to protect their territory. They did not renew their demands to feast on my flesh, so that was a hopeful sign.

The downside to being so well protected was that I couldn't see the skinwalkers anymore unless I used magic to create my own wee peephole. I would have liked to see if they were just as fast as before or if they had slowed a bit due to their injuries. The fact that they were out there at all was testament to healing powers that rivaled my own, but how bad off were they?

There was very little for us to do, yet we couldn't go to sleep with all the chanting, singing, and praying going on. I wouldn't want to take a nap around Coyote anyway—the only way to sleep comfortably near him is to make sure he's sleeping too. To pass the time, Granuaile asked me to talk about when I first came to North America.

<Yeah, I've never heard you talk about that!> Oberon said. <Too bad we don't have any popcorn.>

"All right," I said, speaking in hushed tones. "We might as well."

Long, long ago, when every collection of humanity smelled of shit and there was simply no helping it, I longed for a new, fragrant land. My longing was based on more practical matters than simply my sense of smell: My tattoos made me a target wherever I went in Europe, and I was running out of places to hide. The Romans had wiped out the Druids on the continent and burned all the groves that allowed us to shift planes, and on the islands, missionaries like Saint Patrick destroyed us through proselytizing and patience. I spent years traveling constantly, living off the land or eking out a meal from this farm or that, and slowly adjusting to the new reality: Druids were no longer the powers they once had been, and if I wanted to survive in the villages, I would need to pretend to be illiterate, know nothing of herbalism, and laugh at everyone's lame jokes.

I needed those villages; I decided that they were the lesser of many other evils. If I spent my time in nature, Aenghus Óg's blasted spawn would find me. After Rome fell and Europe began its long night in the Dark Ages, I wondered aloud in the Morrigan's presence if there might not be a nicer place to live for a while—somewhere I wouldn't have to dodge both Aenghus Óg and mobs of people looking for someone to burn at the stake. She said she would think about it, and the next time I saw her, she took me to meet the Old Man of the Sea, Manannan Mac Lir.

I was terribly nervous. Fragarach was his sword, you know, and he had much more right to feel affronted that I had stolen it than Aenghus Óg ever did. It turned out I didn't need to be afraid at all.

When the Morrigan introduced us, Manannan pointed at the hilt peeking over my shoulder and said in a slow, sonorous voice, "Heard you're keeping that away from Aenghus Óg. Good on you, lad."

"You're not angry?"

"Angry? Wave and tide, me boy, why would I be angry? Aenghus is a whiny tit, and everybody with a lick of sense in their head knows it. Ye have me blessing and then some." And then he grinned at me. He was taller than me, blue-eyed, with black hair and a full beard and a kind face suggested by laugh lines around his eyes. He wore a watery blue cloak swirled with patterns of lighter blue, fastened at his right shoulder with a silver brooch. "Come on, then, let's have some ale."

He led us to a poor stone hut on the edge of a cliff overlooking the Irish Sea. It didn't look like the dwelling place of a god. The doorway, however, shimmered at his command to form a portal to his home in Tír na nÓg, which was much larger than the interior of the hut and far richer than anything I had ever seen to that point. Lush woven rugs on wooden floors, exquisitely carved furniture, statues in bronze and glass and polished hardwoods displayed in niches and on shelves. We were served by faeries, for at that time I did not have my amulet and my reputation as the Iron Druid was still centuries in the future. Faeries actually liked me back then—at least, those who weren't descendants of Aenghus Óg did. These faeries owed their allegiance to Fand, Manannan's wife, who is often referred to as Queen of the Faeries. Manannan tended to prefer selkies and kelpies—go figure—but Fand loved them all.

We sat at a broad oaken table with ale and bread in front of us. "The Morrigan tells me you'd like to leave the neighborhood for a good while," Manannan said to me.

"Yes, that would be nice. Preferably out of a certain love god's sphere of influence."

Manannan's eyes glinted with amusement. "Yes, I understand. I have a proposition for you. I will take ye out of Aenghus Óg's easy reach if ye do something for me. Should keep ye busy for a couple of centuries, anyway."

"I am ready to hear it," I said.

Manannan took a contemplative sip of his ale, gathering his thoughts, then began. "Those sacred groves the Romans burned down—that was a lot of our work destroyed. Those bindings were crafted by the Tuatha Dé Danann long ago. Ogma did most of them on the continent, I believe the Morrigan did a few as well"—he paused while she nodded confirmation—"and I took care of Eire and England. There are still plenty of other ways to get to Tír na nÓg, doorways through caves and paths through forest thickets, but they are mostly for the use of the Fae and we have never taught them to Druids before; some of them cannot be walked by Druids at all. But we have become very worried that the Druids are dying out, and it's become clear that winning the battle against Christianity is hopeless. You are among the last, Siodhachan. And if you and the others are going to have a chance at surviving, you need a reliable way to escape when the Christians come for you. It's occurred to the Morrigan that the best way to make sure this happens is to teach you how to make your own paths to Tír na nÓg. I have agreed to do this. But I want you to make these paths in the New World."

"I beg your pardon?" I said. "Where is that?"

"Far across this ocean there is another continent, vast and unspoiled and green, where the elementals are strong, the people sense their connection to the land, and not a single Christian walks upon it. They do not know it exists. We have discovered it ourselves only recently. I will take you there and leave you, and you will explore it, binding it to Tír na nÓg as you go. Thus you will allow the Fae to cross the oceans and provide yourself and other Druids a powerful refuge. You can find apprentices there, no doubt, and train them without interference. Meanwhile, the Tuatha Dé Danann will undertake a similar binding project here, so that when you do return to Europe someday, you will have options available to you that currently do not exist."

"The New World sounds fascinating," I allowed, "but I have some questions."

"Speak."

"If I make these bindings to Tír na nÓg, won't Aenghus Óg's spawn be able to follow me there?"

"Yes, there is no way around the necessity; we want the Fae to be able to travel there. But you can make different bindings and restrict that travel to your advantage," Manannan explained. "Just as Druids can currently only use sacred groves to enter Tír na nÓg, you can limit Fae entry to the New World to certain areas. Then you can create many more bindings that only Druids may use."

"How many of these bindings would you want?"

"For the Fae? Say, only one every hundred miles. For Druids, make as many as you wish."

It sounded like a splendid opportunity to me, so I agreed. We decided together that the Fae could travel only in places with oak, ash, and thorn; where these places did not exist, it would be my task to introduce the proper trees, if the climate allowed. Where it did not, then the Fae had no business roaming there.

The Morrigan took her leave and I prepared a few things for the journey—mostly binding Fragarach into a waterproof package and doing the same for a knife, a set of clothes, and plenty of acorns, ash, and thorn seed pods.

When ready, we stepped back through Manannan's door-cum-portal to the stone hut overlooking the sea. We shifted to our bird forms—an owl for me and a great shearwater for Manannan—and then the god of the sea dove off the cliff. He plunged beneath the waves and shifted to his massive water form, the killer whale. Once he surfaced, I glided down, carrying my waterproof bag in my talons. I dropped it over his dorsal fin, and then I shifted to my otter form. I rode on Manannan's back all the way to the New World.

Manannan is unique among Druids and the Tuatha Dé Danann for being able to draw power from water as well as from earth. It was a gift given to him alone by Gaia, and his tattoos reflect this. He can swim without tiring. We took the shorter distance, heading north up to Iceland, where we spent a few days experimenting with bindings. Iceland was unbound at the time and the various elementals were small, so it was an ideal place for me to learn. Once I got the hang of it and we had shifted planes successfully from Iceland to Tír na nÓg and back, we continued our journey.

We landed in Newfoundland and made the first binding to Tír na nÓg in the New World there. Once that was completed, Manannan Mac Lir bid me farewell and shifted back to Tír na nÓg. Before he left, he suggested I do all the coasts first and tackle the interior later. So that is what I did; I kept the Atlantic Ocean to my left and headed south, linking the east coast with Tír na nÓg. I met many fine tribes and got to know some magnificent elementals. Gaia's bounty was made manifest to me all over again; it was like F. Scott Fitzgerald said, a "fresh, green breast of the new world."

It was not a week, however, before I grew lonely. I met an animal that was new to me, and only much later did people come to call them wolverines. But I bound my consciousness to his—like I have bound myself to Oberon—and called him Faolan, after the most loyal of the Fianna. It was an optimistic naming, for the wolverine Faolan was not naturally disposed to loyalty, but he was outstanding at warning me about the approach of marauding faeries and unafraid of taking them on by himself. It was also during this time that I began my long relationship with the iron elemental Ferris, who follows me around North and Central America whenever I'm on the continent. But one of the most interesting adventures I had on that initial trip of exploration happened years later in the modern-day state of Florida.

At that time, everything south of Lake Okeechobee was a swamp, a really lush one we now call the Everglades. The life there made the elemental quite powerful, and once I arrived, it warned me about the dangers you'd expect—gators and poisonous snakes—but then it also mentioned a wild sort of biped living there, albeit in very small numbers. When I ran into a native tribe and stayed with them, trying to learn a few words and communicate with them, they told stories of giant hairy men as well. The giants had been terrorizing them on and off for a year, always attacking at night, usually taking some of their food, and in one case kidnapping one of their women. The woman was never seen again.

Three nights after they told me this story, I was wakened by screams. I had to speak the binding for night vision—I had no charm for it yet—and then I followed the noise with my eyes to see two enormous figures carrying native women slung over their shoulders. The men were anxious to help, but they couldn't see well and they didn't want to hurl spears blindly toward the screams. I was the only one who could do anything. I took Fragarach and gave chase, Faolan keeping pace beside me.

These giants clearly had fairly decent night vision, but it was not quite as good as my magically aided sight; one of them stumbled on a fallen branch he should have seen and bore his captive roughly to the ground. Her screaming cut off abruptly as the breath got knocked out of her. His companion didn't spare a backward glance; he kept going with the other woman draped over his shoulder.

As the fallen giant was clambering to all fours and reaching anew for his stolen goods, I caught up and delivered some frontier justice: I swung Fragarach through his neck, and his head plopped wetly onto the native woman's chest as his body collapsed. I kept running, because if I stopped to check on her I'd lose the other one.

Faolan, will you lead her back to camp if you can? I asked.

<How am I supposed to do that?> he replied.

Make endearing noises at her.

<Like the ones she's making?>

No, that's screaming.

<She's very loud,> Faolan said. <She won't be able to hear me.>

Figure something out; just don't let her get lost or eaten by anything.

<She's not my cub.>

Pretend for me, please. I'll be back as soon as I can.

<All right, but I want a moose for this.>

There are no moose in this part of the world.

<I know. That was a hint. I want to go back to the snow. The bugs down here are as big as hares.>

The other giant had a good stride and some impressive endurance. Try as I might, I couldn't close the distance between us. But I wasn't going to tire anytime soon.

After a good mile or so, he turned around to check his six. He saw me behind him—one puny man—and not his erstwhile friend. He stopped and tossed his screaming captive to the ground. She scrambled away, but he didn't care. He roared at me and set his feet. He wanted me to bring it, and I was faintly disappointed; I wanted him to lead me to wherever he lived.

I stopped about twenty yards away and checked him out. I'd never seen anything like him, unless it was one of the Fir Bolgs back in Ireland. I think the Fir Bolgs might be slightly taller, but this guy would beat them in an ugly contest. He had a broad, sloping forehead, a wide mouth, and a coat of coarse dark hair all over his body, save for the palms of his hands. His lean, muscled limbs were proportioned like a human's, and so was his reproductive tackle.

Beyond survival, my first instinct was to find a way to talk to this guy. He was a giant vat of testosterone, so weird, and now that the natives were out of immediate danger, I wanted to learn more about him. He didn't have similar sentiments, unfortunately. He charged me, naked, armed with nothing but his ferocity and his actual arms, and completely ignorant of what the shiny thing in my right hand could do to him.

I treated him in much the same way Luke Skywalker handled the Wampa on Hoth: I took off his right arm at the shoulder and then got out of the way. Unfortunately, Fragarach doesn't cauterize as it cuts, and the wretch pumped out its lifeblood in a matter of moments.

My examination of the body confirmed that it wasn't a large, hairy human but rather a different creature. I hadn't been to Africa or the tropics at that point, so I couldn't even make a comparison in my mind to the various simian species. He wasn't precisely like them, in any case; he was fully bipedal and never used his knuckles for support.

I never did find out where they lived. I suspect, since the elemental told me he didn't know of any more, that I might have inadvertently killed the last two in existence—both males—and they were trying desperately to find a way to reproduce. Despite my intentions and the inevitability of their doom, it still depresses me to this day that I might be directly responsible for the extinction of a species.

The two native women got back to their tribe safely and they held a feast in my honor, but here is what I think really happened that night: I killed Bigfoot.

"No way!" Granuaile said.

"It's true. The modern fascination with Bigfoot, I think, all comes from that night centuries ago."

"Well, no, that can't be right," Granuaile said, shaking her head. "All those Bigfoot and Sasquatch stories come from the Pacific Northwest. There's nothing about the Florida Everglades in the literature."

"In the *literature*? You are claiming there is such a thing as Bigfoot Literature?"

"Fine. In the extant documentation, such as it is. None of the sightings occurred in the Everglades."

"All right, I will grant you that. Now, who do you suppose started all that stuff about Bigfoot and Sasquatch in the first place, hmm?"

<Oh, no. You can't be serious.>

Granuaile's expression indicated that she was less than credulous. "Atticus. The Patterson film is widely regarded as making Bigfoot famous. But it's also widely regarded as a hoax."

"And it was. It was me in an ape suit. I did a custom

job, put some fake hairy breasts on there, and once they lost me, I shifted away and laughed my ass off."

Granuaile's face remained stony. "No, I'm sorry, I'm not buying it."

"Who else can walk around in a suit like that and then disappear without a trace?"

"That's easy," Granuaile replied. "Keyser Söze." She blew on the tips of her fingers. "*Poof.* He's gone."

<If Sasquatch is really Keyser Söze, it's no wonder they never caught him!>

"No," I said, thumping my chest, "I did it. It was me."

"Whatever, Atticus. Why would you do something like that?"

"Because I get bored sometimes. I want to see how gullible people are. Come on, a giant apelike creature in the Pacific Northwest, when all the apes in the world live in tropical zones? Who would believe something like that?"

"A significant percentage of Americans."

"Clearly. But the truth is that there were two such creatures, both males, centuries ago just south of Lake Okeechobee. A subtropical zone."

Granuaile snorted derisively. "You expect me to believe that after you just told me you made up the whole thing about Bigfoot?"

<The greatest trick that Sasquatch ever pulled was convincing the world he didn't exist.>

"Fine. Sit there in your fortress of disbelief. Discovering a true Sasquatch was a tangent to the main story anyway: I bound the New World to Tír na nÓg almost entirely by myself, though it took me many years. Many mind-numbing, lonely years, Faolan's surly companionship notwithstanding. But there was another benefit to that mission I shouldn't neglect to mention. There were times when I was blown away by the virgin beauty of the land—kind of like that guy who lost his shit on the Internet at the full double rainbow across the sky. Remember that guy? He kept asking what it meant. And it is not so difficult a question to answer. It means that we are loved, like all living things that Gaia sustains. There is a poetry in the canopies of forests and in the gentle roll of hills, a song in the wind and a benediction in the kiss of the sun. There are stories in the chuckle of waters in creeks, and epics told in the tides of oceans. There are trees, Granuaile, that seem sometimes like they have grown all their lives just to feel the touch of my hand upon their trunks, they are so welcoming to me. You will feel that welcome in your hands someday. You'll feel it in your toes as you walk upon the earth. I cannot wait to see that love bloom in your eyes."

"It's there already, sensei. Sonora showed me. While you were gone to Asgard."

Tears glistened at the edges of her eyes, all mockery of my Sasquatch story forgotten. She knew precisely what I meant—she *had* changed; she understood. And she became almost unbearably beautiful to me in that moment.

"So it is," I said. I sighed and tried to get the train of my thoughts back onto its original track. "After I completed binding the western hemisphere to Tír na nÓg— a process of centuries—I always kept a lookout for additional places to bind to the Irish planes. Lots of those bindings have been ruined by development, but plenty are still around."

"Are there any near here?"

"There are some near Flagstaff. Or we could head west to the Kaibab Plateau. Not much else in the way of forests near here." She accepted this without comment, and Oberon jumped in with his own question.

<Atticus? What happened to your wolverine friend?>

That is another story, Oberon, and it's not a very

happy one. He was with me for nearly a hundred years, though. I do miss him, like I miss everyone.

<How many years have we been together? It must be forty-seven or something like that.>

I petted him and kissed the top of his head. *No, we have only been friends for twelve years.*

<That's all? I'm kind of jealous of him now. What does moose taste like?>

Kind of like caribou.

<Oh, I see! Um. What does caribou taste like?>

Like elk or deer, just slightly different.

<Can we go hunt moose or caribou when this is over?>

I don't see why not. It'll be cold though. They live far to the north.

<Bring it!>

The fact that the skinwalkers never approached the hogan and asked for a supper of Druid tartare convinced me that Famine's spell had been successfully broken; Hel now thought I was dead. According to what Frank had shared about them earlier, the skinwalkers were more concerned with defending their territory than with anything else. I knew they would have to be dealt with eventually, but when I thought of how I might be able to match their speed, my lower left eyelid began to twitch. That problem could wait a night or so and stew in my subconscious while I conducted some business in Flagstaff.

When it was time to greet the sun and the skinwalkers had slunk away to their evil lair—which I imagined was full of bones and skins—I pulled Coyote aside from the others.

"Need to go to Flagstaff today to take care of a bunch of errands. You'll be all right, won't you?"

Coyote scanned me up and down, searching, perhaps, for signs that I was going to abandon the project. "Well, yeah, but I thought you ran your errands yesterday in Kayenta."

"I have a few more to run. Should be back tomorrow."

Coyote pursed his lips. "Maybe I should help you run them."

"You're welcome to come along if you want. But I think you're more needed here."

"What is it you need to do, if you don't mind me askin'?"

"We gotta make my apprentice disappear. And maybe we can do something about that vampire problem."

Chapter 15

The key to faking deaths is a fine appreciation of arterial spray patterns. One might be tempted to simply smear a bit of blood here and there, but forensics fellows these days are a bit more sophisticated than they used to be. If they figure the scene is a fake, they'll tell the family and then said family will never hold that all-important funeral for closure. Without a body, the coroner would never issue a death certificate, but the police would at least designate it a cold case if you could convince them there was a high probability of death.

I have found that blood bags work very well at simulating spray with a strategically poked hole; apply pressure to the bottom of the bag, practice a bit, and before long you will be able to write stories of carnage and odes to gore.

A small fan brush—the sort that one dude used to paint happy little trees—can paint a picture of blunt-force spatters if you flick the surface properly. Don't use a toothbrush; those patterns are recognizable. You could even talk to yourself, as that painter did, while you flick blood around: "And maybe over here we have a nice stab wound. And, I don't know, maybe there's a few more back over here. Multiple stab wounds. It doesn't matter, whatever you feel like."

When it comes to the actual blood, my former policy

was that it was best to use somebody else's. You could even leave someone else's hair, as long as it was plausibly the same color, and that was the best practice because magic users would have no way to track you down. Can't do that anymore, however. Police routinely send all blood and other biological samples to labs for DNA matching, because some of those goodies might belong to the suspect. It's tougher to fool the coppers these days, but I enjoy the challenge.

Granuaile wasn't worried about constructing the crime scene, however. She steered me away from that topic.

"What I want to know is how you get around the documentation issues," she said. She was driving us down to Flagstaff as Oberon napped in the backseat.

"Documentation of what?"

"Of your life before you take on a new identity. I mean, you can't just show up. You need all this stuff. A credit history. How do you do it?"

"The lawyers do it for me these days. Werewolves in general have the inside line on identity changes. Since they have to uproot their entire packs occasionally and move to another territory, they all figure out some efficient way of getting the job done wherever they are. Hal's operation is among the best, but you can approach almost any werewolf anywhere and get help with IDs if you need to."

"All right, that's good to know, but how do they do it?"

"Well, let's make a list. You need a birth certificate, to begin with. Then some school records and immunizations. A driver's license. A passport, a visa, and a green card."

"What? A green card? Why do I need that?"

"Because no matter what names we use, we are always and forever from Panama."

"We are? Why?"

"Because that's where the corrupt officials are. At least the ones that Hal's pack uses. So you and I—Reilly and Caitlin Collins—were born in Panama to Irish expatriates who died tragically when we were young. We were raised as orphans. We have birth certificates and transcripts and everything. I got better grades than you in school, by the way."

She ignored this gibe and asked, "Did you do this when you started out as Atticus too?"

"Yep. Mostly all you need is the driver's license, a Social Security number, and a bank account. Throw cash at a bank and they don't really give a damn where you come from."

"How do you get the Social Security number?"

"Same thing. Corrupt officials. Kind of determined ones, though. It's tough to get around the internal security of the feds, but you can do it if you have the money to spend."

"But will these IDs stand up under scrutiny? I bet your background as Atticus O'Sullivan is getting searched right now."

I shrug. "It doesn't need to stand up. The moment it comes under serious scrutiny, you move on. It only needs to be good enough to fool people at first glance. If it looks authentic, you don't get the full background check."

"Who were you before you were Atticus?"

"Still me. Just a different name."

"Should I call you something else, like your original name?"

"No, Atticus will do. I like that one."

"Good, I do too. What's the worst name you've ever had?"

"Nigel. It was extremely uncomfortable. Never got used to it."

Granuaile laughed. "Nigel? When was that?"

"It was only three months in Toronto in 1953, but every day was a new adventure in embarrassment. You never want to be Nigel in Toronto."

When we got to Flagstaff, we drove to a medical supply store and Granuaile paid cash for some syringes, blood bags, surgical gloves, and other things we would never use. Padding the receipt would throw off the coppers if they ever got this far. I went in first, camouflaged, to make sure that there was no security camera to record the transaction. There was, of course, so I relaxed the silica bindings in the glass lens a wee bit and then allowed them to rebind once more in a different configuration. Light no longer passed through the lens in a sensible fashion, so it recorded nothing but visual noise from the moment Granuaile walked into the store. We ditched most of the purchases in an anonymous trash bin in a residential alley, keeping only what we'd need for the scene.

From there we drove to Shultz Pass Road on the north side of town and pulled over once we saw Shultz Tank below us to the right: a retention area full of stagnant water. There's nothing in the way of homes or businesses there; it's ponderosa pine on either side of the road, and the only traffic one can reasonably expect is mountain bikers and hikers heading to a trailhead somewhere—but even they were unlikely to show up on a weekday. Oberon trotted down the road a short distance to warn us of approaching traffic, commenting as he did that this area would be a great place for the death scene of a few squirrels. He kept to the shoulder, where a carpet of pine needles would conceal his tracks so I wouldn't have to erase them later. He knew where to meet us when we were finished.

I drew blood from Granuaile—not a full pint, but the better part of one.

"Aren't they going to find traces of you in here?" she asked, indicating the interior of the car.

"Yeah, but that's okay. I'm already dead, so I couldn't be the one who killed you. They'll be assumed to be old traces. But I bet this is going to get Detective Geffert all excited when he hears about it. Your death will just emphasize for him that I must have been up to something awful. But the loose end here is really going to be Oberon. They'll find traces of him in here too and wonder where he went, since he obviously hasn't been found abandoned or stray anywhere. Not much I can do about that."

Once Granuaile's blood was drawn and a bit of adhesive placed in the crook of her elbow, we packed everything we would take into a backpack and reviewed the plan as I drew on a pair of surgical gloves and carefully held a stitching needle between my lips. Performance theater. Granuaile left her handbag with her "old" ID and everything on the passenger seat. I searched for a suitable fallen bough among the ponderosas and found one, then meticulously covered my tracks on the passenger side of the car. I made no effort to cover the dim tracks coming out of the forest, even though they would be nothing more than faint impressions in the carpet of pine needles and bunch grasses.

Oberon, how we doing? Anybody coming?

<All clear, Atticus.>

Okay, we're about to start.

<Gotcha.>

Granuaile had to be inside the car for this or the glass wouldn't fall around her body properly. She'd get a few scratches, but that was okay. She did hold the backpack up between the window and her face, though; neither of us wanted that to get cut. She locked the door using her key fob, activating the car alarm, and then left the keys in the ignition. Let them puzzle out why she was parked here in a locked car. I didn't care.

Standing outside the car, bough held like a bat, I began to count down. Granuaile picked up her old cell phone and dialed 911. And I started beating the hell out of her window, which was a bit more awkward with a neck brace on than I'd expected. She screamed at the dispatcher that she was being attacked, Shultz Pass Road, oh my God, no, etc. And she didn't have to fake being terrified about glass exploding next to her head. While she yelled into the phone, I reached over the broken glass, careful not to cut myself, and unlocked the door manually before pulling it open. That caused the alarm to go off; it was Oberon's signal to leave his post and meet us at the rendezvous point and would also provide us some cover noise for the remainder of the call.

"Shut up!" I growled, trying to sound like some road-rage goon, then I swung the bough to *thunk* noisily into her steering wheel. Granuaile gave a startled yelp and dropped the phone, connection still live. She wordlessly handed me the backpack and I shrugged it on one strap at a time, switching the bough between hands as I did so. Granuaile had a few cuts on the legs of her jeans but otherwise looked to be in pretty good shape. I retrieved the blood bag from the top of the trunk and poked a hole in it with the needle I'd been holding between my lips. I sprayed some blood on one side of the bough and Granuaile helpfully stuck a couple of her hairs onto it. I dipped my gloved fingers into the blood, leaned into the cab, and carefully flicked a few drops around on either side of her head, pointing my fingers in the direction she was facing—because a blunt force blow to the face would hardly splatter drops behind her head. Satisfied, I dropped the bough into the dirt near the rear tire and then handed the blood bag to Granuaile, hole at the top so it wouldn't leak. Now came the tricky part. I had to drag her out of the car, presumably unconscious or even dead, and she'd get raked across some of the broken glass as she left the vehicle. She couldn't cry out if she got cut, because the phone call was still live, the 911 operator distantly calling out for her to respond.

She held the blood bag up near her right cheek, sort of like a squishy red shot put. I grabbed her left arm with mine and pulled. Then, as she went horizontal, I supported her rib cage with my right. Granuaile let the hole in the blood bag point down and she squeezed gently to create a trail out of the car. She kept her legs limp and did get lacerated through the denim on her left calf as she got dragged out, but that would just add verisimilitude at this point. With Granuaile now on her back in the dirt outside the car, I began to drag her by her left arm along the ground. She moved the blood bag just over her right shoulder and continued to let it flow out slowly. If she was being dragged, unconscious, by the left arm and had suffered a hit to the face, her head would loll to the right and bleed on that side. Once around the rear of the car, I pulled her downhill toward Shultz Tank. It was extremely uncomfortable for her, but the best way to accurately simulate dragging a body on the ground is to actually drag a body on the ground. Besides, we wanted stray threads and hairs and other trace evidence to be left behind in the path she was making through the pine needles.

Speaking of needles, I had to ditch the one I'd been carrying between my lips. Halfway down the hill and well outside the range of her cell phone's microphone, I took it out of my mouth and said quietly, "You're doing great. How you holding up?"

"Promise me I'll get to do this to you someday?" she asked, her voice all sweet and sugary.

"Sure, except maybe what's coming up next. I think that's really going to suck. The water looks foul."

"Great. Well, can you at least heal up my cuts before I go in? No telling what kind of bacteria are growing in there."

"Yeah, I can close up the skin, no problem. We'll get you on antibiotics as a precaution anyway. Hold on a sec." I knelt quickly and asked the earth to hold on to this needle for me. It accepted it, closed back up, and now the police would never find it—and even if they did, it was unlikely they'd connect it to the assault on the road when there was a giant bloody bough sitting next to the car.

<Hey, Atticus, I think I hear sirens on their way,> Oberon said. <You should hear them when your human ears get around to it.>

Okay, thanks for the heads-up, I told him, continuing to drag Granuaile downhill. "Oberon says the police are coming. We need to hurry."

A few yards from the waterline of Shultz Tank, I stopped and let Granuaile's arm go. She allowed it to flop down in the dirt. I walked around to her legs and looked for the cuts. The tiny punctures on her thighs were not much to worry about; the piece of glass that had dragged down her calf and shredded the denim had left a much more significant wound. Removing my gloves, I stuffed them in the pocket of my jeans and put a gentle hand on her leg. I usually don't like to do direct healing on other people, because the risk of screwing something up is too high, but convincing the skin to grow back quickly is harmless.

"Go ahead and continue to squeeze some blood out here to reflect a pause," I said, "and then empty the rest out when you're facedown and then in the water."

"Okay," she replied.

"All right, done here. You're closed up." I stood, gathered her feet in my hands, and pivoted her around so that she was lying parallel to the waterline. "Ready?"

"Let's get it over with," she said.

"Remember not to drop your feet once you're in. Dead people don't stand up in the shallows."

"I'll remember. Just get me out fast." We could both hear the sirens now. We needed to get out of sight before the police spotted us.

"All right. Here we go." I knelt down next to her torso and began to roll her down into the tank. Every time she was facedown, she squeezed out more blood into the earth. And then she took a breath as I rolled her into the scummy, stagnant water. I kept pushing her out so she'd be able to float freely, and I waded in up to my hips, careful not to soak the backpack.

I tapped her on the shoulder and shouted, "You can do a shallow tread," so she'd be able to hear through any water in her ears. Her head came up and she gasped, delivering her assessment of the water's freshness as soon as she could.

"It's fucking nasty!" she said.

"Sorry," I said. She really did look miserable, with fungi scum and who knew what else in her hair. I turned around and shrugged off the backpack, holding it in front of me. Granuaile threw her arms around my neck and pulled herself up, piggyback, the now-empty blood bag clutched in her right hand, and I waded out of there, making a glorious set of muddy footprints for the police to follow. They'd assume Granuaile's body was in the tank at first and figure out only a couple of days later that I must have carried her out with me. I jogged around the edge of the tank to the far side and then began climbing up, where Oberon waited for us in the shadow of the pines. Once on the relatively track-free surface of the pine needles, I dropped the backpack and asked Oberon to carry it for us between his jaws. That allowed me to hook my arm under Granuaile's legs and make really good time running. We heard the police pulling up to

Granuaile's car after we were only a hundred yards or so into the woods. We'd cut it pretty close.

We ran east through the forest for about three miles until we found a nice outcropping of boulders. "This will do nicely," I said. Once on top of the rocks, I let Granuaile down and asked Oberon to bring me the backpack. There was a change of clothes inside for both of us, as well as our assumed IDs and other assorted goodies like sunglasses and baseball caps. We retreated to either side of the outcropping to change and then stuffed the wet clothes into the backpack.

"We have to do something about my hair," Granuaile said. It still had funky alien chunks of something in it, pine needles, and a film of green algae on top. The rest of her looked great in a fresh shirt and jeans with brand-new sneakers. "It's utterly gross and I can't be seen in public like this."

She was right, but I thought it best not to agree too enthusiastically. "Okay, we'll get a hotel room so you can clean up before we go to the dealership. Sorry again."

From here on out she would run with me and I'd feed her energy so that she didn't get tired. We were going to head south and drop back into town on the east side of Flagstaff, where the auto dealerships were. Colorado graciously agreed to cover what tracks we made for a mile past the boulders; it didn't matter to me if my single set of prints was traced up to them.

After a half hour's stop in a cheap hotel room so that Granuaile could wash her hair and dry it, we walked onto the lot of a car dealership and told the salesman we'd pay cash for a hybrid SUV as long as he could guarantee delivery in a couple of hours. We used my neck brace as an excuse for why we needed a new vehicle and didn't have one to trade in.

"He totaled my old one in an accident," she explained,

and the salesman pretended to be sorry about that. She told him explicitly that he was not to run a credit check, because she didn't want to take the hit on her credit score. We'd pay cash via wire. We gave him Granuaile's account number at the bank, he made a call, and then he moved as quickly as he could to please Ms. Caitlin Collins. He even offered a few free hot dogs to Oberon, who was waiting patiently outside.

<Mmm, tubes of Grade C meat!> Oberon said. To keep him entertained, I drew a sign that said, *My name is Snugglepumpkin. I am friendly!* and propped it up next to him so that he could collect data as people walked by.

The salesman waved fondly at us as we drove off the lot a couple of hours later, no doubt thinking we were the biggest pair of suckers to ever walk into the dealership. We hadn't even tried to negotiate.

The sun said farewell with patches of pink and purple clouds. I felt fully healed now, so I took off the neck brace and chucked it into the backseat, where Oberon regarded it uncertainly.

<Is this a new chew toy?>

If you like, but there are plastic bits and I doubt those will be very yummy.

It was dinnertime, but we had a couple of hours before we had to meet Leif at Granny's Closet. I asked Granuaile if she was up for a gustatory challenge.

She eyed me suspiciously. "What do you mean? Chug a jar of habañero salsa or something like that? Because I'd rather save time and set my ass on fire with a match."

"No, much more interesting than that, not so painful. Do you like to try unusual foods? Stuff that you've never eaten before and probably never will again?"

"Ah, stuff you eat just so you can say later, 'I ate that once'?"

"Precisely. There's a place in town with a very unusual

menu. We can try that and then head to Granny's to chase it with some beers."

"Okay." Granuaile shrugged. "I'm game. Sounds fun."

<Hold on. Are you taking her to that one place that serves bizarre meats and cheeses made from mammals that aren't cows?>

Heh! Yes, I am. Remember the Nicaraguan chupacabra cheese?

<Okay, I'm betting five sausages that Granuaile can't make it to the fifth course.>

You're on. Say good-bye to those five sausages. I know she'll make it. She has a proud streak.

Chapter 16

The place in question was called the Double Dog Dare Gourmet Café. It's the only place I've ever found that provides patrons with a barf bag—and it's not because the food is ill prepared. To the contrary, it's exquisite. They just serve items that most Americans cannot fathom putting down their throats, and the reactions, when they happen, are all psychologically based. That being the case, they have a rather unique ordering system and service style.

Everyone gets a different menu from which to order, and you don't order for yourself—you order for your dinner partner. You pick five items from the menu by silently checking off a list and handing it to the waiter. All five of them are put on a single plate in very small portions, and then you get the plate put in front of you that your partner has dared you to eat—and vice versa. You don't get told what each item is until *after* you eat it. Hence the barf bags. It's all part of the charm.

The waiters are very careful to inquire about food allergies beforehand, and in some cases you have to sign a waiver before you get served.

When the ordering system was explained to Granuaile, she smiled and then she perused her menu with relish, determined to put me off my dinner. My smile mirrored hers; ordering was one of the best parts of the process. I toyed with the idea of having mercy on her, but I knew she wasn't going to have any on me, and, besides, I wanted to give Oberon a decent shot at winning his five sausages. Remembering that Granuaile was a bit sensitive to smells, I ordered the most pungent items I could think of, except for one fried item.

It was probably a bit unfair. I've been around and tried some unholy culinary atrocities in my time, so I knew I'd be able to hold down everything. She might surprise me with something, but nothing was going to make me ralph at the thought of it.

We took it easy on the drinks, ordering iced tea. Oberon was outside, camouflaged, sitting down out of the way of the door. I ordered him a full order of yak liver to go and let him know.

<Sounds good,> he said. <Hey, Atticus, not to alarm you or anything, but I think this woman about to walk into the restaurant is a vampire. She smells dead.>

I was sitting facing the door—an old paranoid habit—so I flicked my eyes over there casually as a sharp-featured brunette came in, accompanied by a doughy college kid. Checking her out in the magical spectrum, I saw that she was indeed a vampire; she had the dead gray aura with the two burning embers of vampirism about her heart and head. The college kid was just a clueless sort whose aura suggested that he was horny and hoping to get lucky later on. He'd get something, all right, but it wasn't lucky.

She wasn't all gothed out, the way people these days are trained to expect from vampires in fiction. She was wearing a pair of jeans with holes in the knees and a very tight American Eagle T-shirt underneath a thin white coat that was more for fashion than warmth. She was wearing Vans, for crying out loud. She was trying very hard to blend in and seem human.

I couldn't point her out to Granuaile or even say,

"Psst! Bloodsucker!" because the vampire would over-
hear. I had my own blending in to do.

Well spotted, Oberon. Negative eleven sausages now.

"Atticus?" Granuaile frowned. "What's wrong?"

I smiled at her. "Just remembered something," I said.
"I don't suppose you have a pen or anything like that in
your purse? I need to write it down before I forget."
This was a transparent excuse for anyone who knew
anything about Druids, because we don't forget. But I
was counting on the vampire not knowing what I was.

"Oh," Granuaile said. "Sure." She rooted around in
her bag and found a receipt that I could use for paper. I
flipped it over and wrote on the back: *Don't say anything about this out loud. She will hear. There is a vampire here. Don't worry; just thinking through the
implications. Will talk about it when we leave.*

"Thanks," I said, pushing the note to her. She read it,
nodded, and tucked it into her purse.

The vampire and her date/snack were seated two tables away to our left. She shouldn't be here, according to
Leif's behavior in the past; he exterminated all other
vampires in his territory as a matter of course. Was she
someone allied with Leif in the new vampire politics, or
was she an enemy? I could unbind her right now and the
college boy would have to watch his date melt in front
of him, but I thought perhaps I should wait, especially if
she turned out to be someone on Leif's side. I rather
doubted, however, that Leif was operating with anyone.
It was far more likely that she was one of many trying to
take Leif's territory for her own. And I suspected she
wasn't here by accident.

Our food arrived, and I grinned mischievously at
Granuaile as her plate was settled reverently before her.
She gave it right back as mine appeared before me.

"Okay, one thing at a time, right?" she said.

"Right."

"Age before beauty. Start with that stir-fry thing right there." She pointed to some suspicious cauliflower-looking bits mixed in with vegetables and fried brown rice.

"All right," I said, taking a generous forkful. Granuaile watched me put it in my mouth and chew, horrified fascination writ large upon her face.

The cauliflower bits weren't cauliflower. They were mushy, a bit gelatinous. But they had a nice, spicy flavor, if a bit pedestrian. Taste-wise it wasn't terribly unique, just an unusual texture.

Granuaile waited until I'd swallowed and then she said, "Congratulations. That was a bheja fry—goat brains."

"Brains? You made me eat brains like a zombie? Ugh!"

"Braaaaaaains," she moaned, eyes rolling up in her head.

"I bet you zombies would like them even more with these spices. All right, take that fried thing there, dip it in the cocktail sauce, and chow down."

Granuaile eyed it cautiously, as if it might suddenly decide to move. It looked like a large chicken nugget, but it wasn't. "What's under all the batter?" she asked.

"You find out after you eat it. Those are the rules."

She did as instructed, taking a tiny bite at first and quirking an eyebrow at me by way of inquiry.

"Eat the whole thing," I said.

She sighed and chomped down the rest of it. "That wasn't so bad," she said, dabbing at her mouth with a napkin. "What was it?"

"That was a Rocky Mountain oyster, also known as a Montana tendergroin."

"No. I just ate a bull's balls?"

"Only one, but yes, you just tore up a tasty testicle. Congratulations!"

Disgust suffused her expression for a moment, but it was quickly replaced by narrowed eyes and a cold promise of grief. She gripped the tablecloth and squeezed it, pretending, perhaps, it was my newly healed neck. "You will never tell anyone about this."

"No," I said. I fully intended to write it down, however. To keep her from extracting a promise not to record this in any way, I waved at my plate and said, "What shall I try next?" We worked our way through the culinary dares, and I kept half an ear open for what was going on at the vampire's table. The brunette didn't order anything, just ice water with lemon, and that sat on her table and sweated.

At one point, she turned her head and gave me a good stare. Leif had always told me my blood tasted different from that of modern men. I'm sure it smelled different too. The vampire didn't know what I was, precisely, but she knew my blood was as exotic to her as sloth steak was to me. Chances were she'd be stalking me after she disposed of her college boy—if she hadn't stalked me in here to begin with.

I paid for dinner, got Oberon's yak liver to go, and said, "Let's talk about that other thing when we get to Granny's." Granuaile nodded her understanding. We collected Oberon outside and I kept his camouflage on.

I'll need you to stay hidden while we're at Granny's Closet too. Keep your nose open for any more vampires and let me know.

<Okay. Do they have regular food in there? Yak is great, but it's kind of rich.>

Yeah, I'll get you a steak and bring it out, I said as we got in the car.

<Sweet. Did I win the bet?>

I answered him out loud to see what reaction it got. "She made it through all five courses, buddy. Sorry. You're back up to negative sixteen sausages."

<Dang it! I should have bet you some vegetables instead, then it wouldn't sting so bad. Though it wouldn't have been very cool to win vegetables either. Probably need to rethink this whole gambling thing.>

"Wait," Granuaile said. "Oberon bet against me? Thanks a lot, Oberon."

<Tell her she can take comfort in my suffering.>

We pulled into the parking lot of Granny's Closet and searched for a suitable place for Oberon to hang out. The lot stretched to the north of the restaurant, and we left Oberon on the north side. The entrance faced the west.

Once you stepped through the door, the dining area was to your left and the bar to your right, with the kitchen sandwiched in between. We ducked to the right and entered a room of dark wood and red filtered light. The bar was on the west wall, and half booths lined the remaining three—the kind where the seats on the walls are padded and two chairs rest on the other side of the table. The center of the floor was dotted with wee tables big enough to put down your drink and maybe a plate of wings, no more.

We took a table on the east wall and sat facing the room. A primped and pushed-up waitress took our orders over to the bar, where a rakishly handsome lad was mixing drinks. Granuaile eyed him with professional interest. And perhaps . . . something more. Her eyes flicked toward me and she caught me looking at her—she was extremely good at that—and then she looked down, a flush of embarrassment blooming up her neck.

I understood that this time she felt that she was the one who'd been caught. I joined her with a sympathy blush. Not so long ago, Granuaile and I had casually flirted with each other—well, I confess that perhaps it was not so casual on my part. When she was just a bartender and I was just a customer, both of us were fair game to be pursued. Now our relationship had shifted, necessarily, and I, for one, was having a bit of trouble with it.

The trouble was, I couldn't stop staring at her. Granuaile wasn't one of those exotic siren types of redheads, like a Jessica Rabbit or something; she was naturally beautiful, often wearing nothing but some mascara around her eyes and the gloss on her lips. I noticed how the soft glow of red lights shimmered on them; they were the sort of lips you couldn't *not* think about kissing. But now that she was my apprentice, every such thought caused a guilty twitch in my neck, as if someone had dropped a sleek, stinky ferret there. Guilt ferrets are bastards.

I didn't know if Granuaile was having the same kind of trouble I was. Still, I knew enough to recognize the tension between us, and it would be unwise to let it continue. Problem was, I didn't know how to address it gracefully. I was fairly certain it couldn't be done.

"Um, look, Granuaile . . ." I faltered, unsure of how to continue.

"Look at what?"

"Not that kind of look. Bollocks. Well, forgive me for saying something epically awkward, but I think it needs to be said. I don't want you to think that becoming a Druid involves a vow of celibacy or anything. Celibacy is a terrible idea, adhered to by people who hate themselves and want everyone else to do the same. You should do what you want to do, you know."

"I beg your pardon?" Her tone was light but her expression carried a warning. I ignored it.

"Don't play dumb. You know what I mean. And who I mean." I nodded my head toward the handsome bartender she'd been checking out.

Granuaile kept her eyes on me and they narrowed dangerously. "Are you giving me permission to have sex?" Her voice had a definite edge to it now. Rather sharp, actually: the kind of edge that saws effortlessly through aluminum cans, with a cheesy announcer saying, "*Now* how much would you pay for a knife like that?"

"No, I'm telling you that you don't need my permission."

"I should hope not!"

"Good, we're agreed." I hoped that would convince her to drop it, but no such luck. Her eyes flared at me.

"What? No, I don't think so. What brought this on? Do you think I'm some sort of sex-starved loser?"

"Well, you *are* American."

"What!"

Great festering tapir tits, that was a stupid thing to say. This was not going well, but there was nothing to do now but plunge deeper and hope I'd be able to swim out again. "I mean you have all these modern American hang-ups about the subject. You're getting all defensive about something that should be perfectly natural and relaxing."

"That is a cheap rhetorical device. By accusing me of being defensive, I cannot respond without proving your point, however unrelated it might be to the original topic. And the original topic under discussion here is your presumption that you have anything to say at all about my sex life."

"See, I told you this would be epically awkward. I was simply trying to explain that I'm not the sin police, and if you want to make a move on Mr. Drinky McDrinkypants over there, you can go right ahead."

Granuaile's lips drew into a tight, furious line. "If you were anyone else, I would slap you so hard you'd have two cheeks on one side of your face."

"Well, then, I sincerely apologize and commend your restraint. But you'll need to explain what I'm doing wrong here. I'm honestly not trying to insult you. I've never been in a relationship like this before, and I don't know how to handle it."

"What kind of relationship do you think we have?"

"*This* kind. Don't tell me you haven't felt the weirdness here. We used to flirt, Granuaile, and now we can't, because you're my apprentice."

"You just got done telling me you're not the sin police and celibacy is for people who hate themselves, and now you're saying we can't flirt?"

"That's correct."

"And you don't see a contradiction there?"

I shook my head. "Not at all. The student-teacher relationship is sacred. This is true across cultures and throughout history."

Granuaile scoffed. "You can't be serious. People have messed around with their teachers forever, and vice versa."

"Yes, but at the sacrifice of the relationship. Teaching and learning cannot continue once you cross that line. I would feel pressured to go easy on you to save your feelings. Or I'd lower my standards to ensure your success. You'd wind up being a much less powerful Druid, and I don't think either of us is the type to settle for mediocrity. So we cannot even get close to that line."

She looked away and down at her drink, carefully mastering her expression to be noncommittal. Perhaps she gave the barest nod of agreement. Whether she did or not, she wasn't happy. That meant we were in trouble; she was having the same difficulty I was, but until then I hadn't seen much sign of it from her. My neck twitched, and Granuaile's might have as well. Guilt ferrets are bastards.

<Atticus, something dead your way comes.>

Is it Leif?

<I don't know. Can't see him, but I caught a whiff of

dead. Comes and goes. There it is again. Must be coming from the other side of the building.>

I lifted my eyes to the bar's entrance and saw Leif walk
through, his hands thrust in his pockets as he casually
scanned the seats for us. I held up a hand to attract his
attention. He spotted me and tilted his chin upward to
indicate he'd seen us. He didn't move in our direction,
though. Instead, he carefully scanned the rest of the
room, seeking out traps or escape routes or perhaps
other people. It awakened my own paranoia, and I
began to look around as well.

Oberon, do you still smell dead people?

<No, it's gone now.>

According to what I saw in the magical spectrum, everyone in the bar was human except for Leif. Once we
were both satisfied, he approached us.

Granuaile had never met Leif—he was nocturnal,
after all, and she tended to stay in her condo at night—so
she had no way of knowing if he looked the same or not.
But as he grew closer, I had to school my features not to
reveal any of the horror I felt. Leif hadn't recovered fully
after all.

Chapter 17

I could still recognize him easily—even from a distance in dim light—but up close his complexion had the consistency of a Play-Doh sculpture, lumpy and clumsily shaped with chubby fingers. His hair, once full and shining with undead lustre, lay lank and greasy against his head. Patches were missing; I'd salvaged only a few hairs in Asgard, so it was remarkable that it had even grown back in this much, but the effect was to make him look diseased.

"I know I have looked better, Atticus," he said, extending his hand to shake, "but I have also looked much worse. And I am still healing, thanks to you." I wasn't sure he should be thanking me. Though I'd done my best to bind his head back together after Thor pulverized it into chunks of bone and brain, one could not look at him now without feeling seriously disturbed. The symmetry was gone. The shadows were wrong. One eye sat higher than the other—though it was a miracle he had eyes at all.

Taking his hand, I could not help but notice that his skin there was tight and smooth, in sharp contrast to his face.

"Leif, this is my apprentice, Granuaile."

He turned his unsettling gaze to her and nodded once. "It is my pleasure."

Granuaile bobbed her head in return, lips tightly pressed together. Perhaps she did not trust herself not to vomit; Leif's head was more disturbing than anything we'd eaten at the Double Dog Dare Café.

"Please, sit," I said. He took a seat opposite me, and the waitress appeared to drop off our drinks and take his order. She flinched when she saw his face, glanced guiltily down at her order pad, and flinched again when he ordered only water.

"So you will continue to improve?" I asked.

"Yes. The hair is coming in. The bones are still shifting around a bit."

"How's your memory?"

"There are gaps," he admitted. "Hal told me we were successful but that Gunnar did not make it."

My jaw dropped. "You don't remember killing Thor?"

He shook his head sadly. "I wish I did. But it gives me great pleasure to know that he is dead and that I was the instrument of his doom."

"What's the last thing you recall?"

"The frost giants stomping on Heimdall. Did they make it out?"

I shrugged. "They might have. Last I saw, they were chasing Freyja. So you're missing most of the battle."

"Yes. Can you fill me in?"

"Certainly." I spent some time rehashing our trip to Asgard—who died, who survived, and what happened afterward. Leif smiled when I recounted his face-off with Thor. His teeth weren't straight.

"So what now, Atticus?"

"What do you mean, what now? We move on. That's what I'm doing."

"It is not that easy. My situation is a bit dangerous."

"You mean the other vampires? I'm sure you'll take care of it soon enough. Give yourself a bit of time. You're not a hundred percent yet."

Leif sighed, intensely dissatisfied—whatever he wanted me to understand, I wasn't getting it. He cocked his head suddenly to the right, as if startled by a thought. "Did I tell you once that I was the shit? Or am I imagining that?"

"You said that once, yes," I said, smiling.

"Well, I am no longer the shit, Atticus." He twirled a finger at his face to emphasize the point. "I am excessively weakened, and I do not know when or even if I will regain my former strength."

"So these other vampires are out to destroy you?"

"Some are. Others are working for Zdenik."

"Zdenik? Your creator?"

Leif nodded.

I picked up my pint for a contemplative sip. "He's in Prague, right?"

"No. He's in Phoenix."

That almost caused me to inhale some Smithwick's into my lungs. I coughed a bit and put down the pint. "Um . . . why?"

"On our journey to Asgard, you'll recall, I went to visit him in Prague while you and Gunnar remained in the forest near Osinalice?"

"Yes. You said you were paying your respects."

"I also arranged for him to take over my territory in the event of my death or severe injury."

"Leif, that sounds like an extraordinarily bad idea."

"It seemed like a good one at the time. But now he's bought Copenhaver Castle on Camelback Mountain. You know it?"

"Hard to live in the valley without hearing about it. I heard it has a hot tub with room for twenty people. Bow chicka big orgy, eh?"

"Yes, but it also has a dungeon, which I believe was more attractive to him. He is renovating and fortifying the place. It is not the behavior of a vampire who is planning to return to his territory."

He said this in a way that implied I should be concerned. I was anxious to demonstrate that I wasn't, so I shrugged. "Well, you have only yourself to blame. You arranged for the takeover."

"The terms of the arrangement stated that he would return to Prague once I was fully recovered. Right now he is making the very credible claim that I am not and it would be irresponsible for him to abandon this territory to an all-out war. He argues that he and his lieutenants are doing me a favor by defending the territory from would-be usurpers. Yet he is bringing in more lieutenants than he truly requires. He has four of them now spread out through the state, and I am nominally in charge of the east valley while he takes care of the west."

"Are they older and stronger than you?"

"Not older," he scoffed. "They are all less than a half century old. I am not sure whether I can match them in strength or not, considering my condition. But they are all spending large sums of money on permanent residences. I fear that when I am fully recovered, I will face a flat-out refusal to leave."

"Fine, Leif. That's when you throw down and kick his ass."

He regarded me silently and drummed his fingers a few times on the table before saying, "You are being obtuse. I cannot kill my creator."

Granuaile frowned and broke in. "Pardon me for asking, but why not?"

Leif shifted his uneven eyes to study her. "It is a form of control vampires never relinquish over those to whom they grant undeath. He can command me to do most anything, and I must obey. It is similar to when I charm a human."

"Wow," I said. "I honestly didn't know that, Leif.

Never cared much about the social lives of vampires. The situation is regrettable, but I guess you need to find a new territory. Good luck with that."

Leif's eyes returned to me. "I was rather hoping for more than your good wishes, Atticus."

"What more do you want?" I smirked at him and gestured at the untouched glass the waitress had dropped off in the midst of our conversation. "Tell you what, I'll buy you that glass of water."

Leif did not appreciate my teasing. He said in a stone-cold voice, "I want your help in removing Zdenik from my territory."

My easy grin disappeared. "No way. That's not rational, Leif. There's nothing in it for me, and as far as I can see, there's nothing in it for you either. Don't you remember that talk we had in Siberia? You told me you came to Arizona to wait for me, all so that you could befriend me and secure my aid in your vendetta against Thor. Well, you've done that now: You've befriended me, Thor is dead, you've got your revenge, and there's no need to stay here anymore. You're still a badass, or you will be again very soon. You can take over any other territory in the states you wish, no sweat, and let Zdenik have this place. Hell, I bet you can take over a small country. Costa Rica is beautiful, why don't you go there?"

"You don't understand."

"And I'm fine with that, Leif! Perhaps you don't understand that I don't owe you anything. If anything, you owe me. Not only did I discharge my debt to you, I put your head back together and hauled you out of Asgard. You wouldn't be here talking to me now if I hadn't done that."

"I am both aware and grateful. Please allow me to explain."

"It would save time if I just told you 'no' now and took the explanation for granted."

Leif leaned forward and jabbed a finger at me, his lip curling in a Billy Idol snarl. "This state can support sixty-five vampires, under the Accords of Rome." Ah, what a delicious slip he made right there. This is the benefit of getting people annoyed with you: They say things they wouldn't normally say. I'd never been able to get Leif to admit before that vampires controlled their population, but now he'd gone and done it—and the ratio, based on that number in relation to Arizona's population, was one vampire per one hundred thousand people. It also told me Rome was the capital of the vampire world, as I always suspected.

Leif continued, "But I have been the only vampire here for centuries. This is practically virgin hunting ground. There are flavors and nuances of blood here that no one has sampled save me. These people . . . they taste of the sun. That makes the territory incredibly valuable on its own, Atticus. But add to that the prestige of taking it from *me,* and it is even better. Plus that group of Kabbalists called the Hammers of God have managed to stake a few of us, so that increases the challenge, and when you add in the news that the world's last Druid was rumored to live here, this territory is currently the most valuable on the planet. The Old World vampires are taking notice."

"I don't care."

"You should. Whoever winds up controlling Arizona will have plenty of cachet, but in these circumstances you are almost guaranteed to get the most ruthless, evil sort of vampire in charge—unless you help me."

"No, Leif."

He turned up his intensity. "Zdenik enslaves people and makes new vampires who commit every possible atrocity in his name. I neither enslave nor create new vampires. There is a definite difference between having me or someone like Zdenik in charge. And Zdenik is not the worst of them."

"Look, as far as I'm concerned, there isn't a vampire in the world who's worse than an oil executive, and I don't go around assassinating them either." Peripherally, I noticed that this earned me a sharp glance from Granuaile. "I'm through, Leif. I can't stick my neck out again. I just went to a lot of trouble to disappear, and my advice is that you should do the same."

So intent were we on our conversation that we did not pay attention to our surroundings as we should have. That allowed the vampire I'd spotted earlier in the Double Dog Dare Café to walk up behind Leif without being noticed until she spoke. She wasn't wearing the courtesy fashion coat anymore, but she still had on the American Eagle T-shirt. Her college-boy snack was absent. Her voice was thick and liquid with a Bohemian accent.

"This man can assassinate vampires, Leif? No wonder his blood smells unusual. Who is he?"

I would let Leif worry about her. I was worried about Oberon. Why hadn't he warned me that she had entered the restaurant?

Oberon? I got no answer. *Oberon?*

Chapter 18

"Ah." Leif looked embarrassed. "Natalia, this is, ah, a friend of mine."

"I assumed as much. Who is he?"

Leif was uncertain how to introduce me. He knew he couldn't use Atticus, but Hal hadn't told him our new identities. I didn't want this vampire to know them either, so I provided a name off the top of my head, gambling that this foreign vampire would be unfamiliar with heavy-metal drummers. "Lars Ulrich," I said, nodding at her. "Nice to meet you, Natalia."

"Do not speak unless you are spoken to," she snapped, her eyes boring into mine. She was trying to charm me, but that wasn't going to work.

"Awful bossy, aren't you?" I said, a small smile on my face. She blanched. "More than a little rude, in fact. Still, it's no reason for me to forget my manners. Would you like to join us?" I gestured to a small empty space next to Leif.

She eyed me suspiciously. "I prefer standing." Leaning toward Leif, she asked him, "Who is this Lars Ulrich who can resist my charms?"

My mind raced through possible scenarios. There was no way that we could talk our way out of this. Now that she'd identified me as someone who could kill vampires, my entire future was jeopardized. She would investigate, eventually discover the truth, and all my efforts to fake my death would be for naught. I had to assume, based on Leif's statements, her accent, and her behavior, that she was one of Zdenik's lieutenants. She couldn't leave alive. Or undead. Whatever. Once she was out of my sight, all it would take was one phone call, and I couldn't guarantee that I'd catch up to her before she could make it.

"That's just as well," I said, scooching over a bit so that I could stand. "I feel like getting some air anyway. Kinda stuffy in here. Shall we talk outside?"

"Here is fine," she said, shifting her position so that the seated Leif was between us, "or it would be if Mr. Helgarson would answer my questions."

Leif's earlier assertion that these lieutenants of Zdenik's were all younger than he was gave me an idea—she wouldn't be able to speak Old Norse. I had to hope that Leif hadn't lost the ability to speak it himself. Before he could stumble through some kind of answer, I spoke quickly to him in the language of his birth.

"I will bind her limbs and lips together," I said. "Stand up and make sure she doesn't fall." Thankfully, he remembered the language. Leif stood and Natalia took a step back as I switched to Old Irish and began binding the skin of her lips together.

As far as the earth is concerned, vampires are fair game. They're nothing but perambulating sacks of carbon and trace minerals that prey on living people, and, as such, I can do whatever I want to them and Gaia is completely chill with it. I didn't want to unbind Natalia here, because it would be excessively messy, cause panic, and draw unwanted attention to me. It would be better to remove her from the premises and make sure no other vampires were around. I also wanted to check on Oberon.

"Enough playing. Tell me who this man is or I will tell Zdenik," she said to Leif. And those were her last words. I completed my binding, and she discovered that it was simply impossible to open her mouth. Eyes widening in shock, she conveniently lifted her hands to her mouth for me, and I was able to execute a shorter, "repeat" binding, with just a small adjustment of the target: Now her hands were also bound to her mouth, and panicked noises were trying to bubble out.

"Grab her around the shoulders like you're buddies, but don't let her go," I said to Leif in Old Norse. As he moved to obey—she struggled a bit before he could secure his arm around her—I began one last binding on her jeans: I bound the inseams together so that she wouldn't be able to run. In this way, she was immobilized inside of fifteen seconds without a single punch thrown or a scream to summon would-be heroes.

Her desperate noises were attracting attention, however, some scowling faces wondering why that woman was so upset and whether the men had anything to do with it.

"It's her food allergy," I said in English, a bit louder than I needed to. "We'd better get her to the doctor. Come on." Some of the nearby patrons' expressions changed to pity for the poor lady with an allergy.

Now that he was clued in to the ruse, Leif played along. "Let's get you outside," he said consolingly, also speaking a little bit louder than necessary, to reassure anyone listening in. Using only his left arm to squish her side next to his, he basically carried her out of the restaurant, lifting her up a bit so her feet wouldn't drag on the floor. With her hands pressed to her mouth, Natalia plausibly looked and sounded like she was having trouble with something she'd eaten.

"Stay here," I told Granuaile before following Leif. "We'll be back as soon as possible."

"I'm coming," she said, moving to stand.

"No," I said firmly. "I really need you to remain here." If there were other vampires outside, I didn't want Granuaile to become an easy target. "Seriously."

She studied my face to see if there was any give in my expression and found none. She slumped back, clearly displeased but not about to fight me on the subject.

"Thank you," I said, then hurried to catch up with Leif.

Oberon! I called, mentally shouting as I darted past tables to the front door.

<Huh? What?>

Oh. You're okay?

<Yeah, I'm fine. Are we going now?>

I breathed a sigh of relief as I reached the exit. *Thank the gods of twenty pantheons. Why didn't you answer earlier?*

<I didn't hear anything.>

I called you twice, I said as I looked around for Leif. He was to my left, still carrying Natalia, heading next door toward a convenience store with a few gas pumps in the front; we'd left Oberon in the parking lot, to my right.

<Oh. Um.> His tone became apologetic. <I may have taken a short nap, Atticus. I'm sure it was very short though. Next time, remember to ask for the non-drowsy yak liver.>

Walk to the sidewalk and turn left, I told him. *You'll see me there. Follow behind and watch for vampires, please. Maximum paranoia. Don't forget the roofs.*

<Okay. I see you now. Only vampires I can sense are the ones in front of you. Leif and that one from earlier.>

All right. Keep me informed of any developments.

Leif paused at the end of the building and swung around to check on what I wanted to do. I jogged to catch up and pointed to the sliver of space between Granny's Closet and the convenience store.

"Dumpsters should be back there," I said in Old Norse. No use getting Natalia even more riled up. Yet.

As casually as we could, and with Leif still pretending that the arm around Natalia was protective, we walked the thirty yards or so to the back of the building and slipped out of sight of all the traffic on South Milton Road. We found the big industrial trash bins and I threw open the lid, startling a few hardy flies that were battling the chilly temperatures.

I'm dissolving your camouflage, Oberon. Please make sure no one follows us back here.

<Got it.>

"Toss her in," I said to Leif, purposely using English. Natalia heard that, made a supreme effort, and managed to separate her legs, tearing her jeans right down the inseam. I'd been expecting that, but Leif hadn't. He started cursing as she kicked at him, and I calmly bound her legs together again—now using her exposed skin. She wouldn't be tearing through that.

"What are you doing?" Leif said.

"I just wanted a quiet place to talk without someone interrupting with escape attempts. So. You have one of Zdenik's lieutenants helpless. What are you going to do?"

Leif looked wounded. "Me? Aren't you going to unbind her?"

"No. She's your enemy in your territory. You wanted help and I'm giving it because I can't let her tell anyone I'm alive. But I'm not your assassin. Do your own dirty work."

Leif shrugged and pushed her over so that she fell facedown onto the asphalt. He planted a foot between her shoulder blades, gripped her head on either side with his hands, and with a soft grunt pulled it off with a snap of bone and a wet, slurping sound. I'd bound the skin of her fingers so tightly to her face that some of them tore free of her hands and dangled from her lips, and in other cases the skin of her face tore loose and remained bound to her fingers. It was a quick, brutal, and messy extermination, as I suspected it would be. Leif tossed the bloody head into the trash and I began to unbind it, partly to get rid of the evidence and partly to make sure that this vampire would never respawn.

"Thank you, Atticus," he said, hefting the body and doing his best to keep blood off his clothes.

I finished the unbinding and watched in the magical spectrum until the red light of vampirism winked out in the skull as it dissolved among the food scraps and paper bags and plastic packaging.

"I don't really want to be thanked, Leif," I said. "I want to be left alone."

"I understand," he said, heaving the body into the bin. He kept talking as I spoke the words to unbind the body; if I didn't take care of the light in her chest, she'd come back in worse shape than Leif had, but she'd come back nevertheless.

"But you have to admit this was a simple exercise for us. Working together, we could clean up the state in a few days. Please, Atticus."

Natalia, who'd probably enjoyed thirty years of life and three hundred years or more of bonus existence sucking the blood out of the living, melted inside her T-shirt and torn jeans. I nodded once in the direction of her remains and said, "Sorry, but that's all the cleaning I'm going to do, Leif. That's one rival eliminated. Orchestrate the rest yourself. Though I still say you should simply leave. May harmony find you."

He didn't miss the note of finality in my voice as I

turned toward the gap between the buildings. "Where are you going?" he asked.

"I'm simply leaving," I replied, walking back to collect Oberon and Granuaile. "See how easy it is?"

I left him standing there and fully expected never to see him again.

Chapter 19

One of the nice things about waking up is the inherent serenity that comes with knowing you'll probably live until breakfast. It's true that sometimes you can wake up with a Brobdingnagian hangover and hate your life, but at least you *have* life, and the cure for a hangover is probably in your kitchen somewhere. There will be birds chirping, a dog somewhere to pet, and a few moments where you can contemplate the pleasant possibility of getting into some sort of adventure that day.

On the other hand, if you live long enough, you'll discover new and exciting ways to wake up that are less than serene, and well before dawn arrives. Weasels in your bedroll: not good. Huns pillaging the city and raping women: very bad. Vampires breaking through your hotel-room door and sinking their fangs into your newly healed neck before you can move: It doesn't get much worse than that.

I was in Room 403 of the Hotel Monte Vista, where Freddy Mercury once stayed. I'd sung a bit of "Bohemian Rhapsody" to myself before slipping underneath the sheets and getting snuggly with the comforter. I fell asleep wondering if Scaramouche would do the fandango.

The vampire attached to my neck was improbably strong. The door to my room was completely destroyed;

he had plowed right through it and attacked me before the sound could rouse me sufficiently to defend myself. Hotel thresholds offer no barriers to vampires.

On the fourth floor and cut off from the earth, I had a limited amount of magic stored in my bear charm. I used some of it to strengthen my right arm and punch him in the temple; it broke three of my knuckles but successfully knocked him off my neck for a moment. I activated my healing charm and began to speak the spell of unbinding as he hissed and came after me again.

I had no leverage, and the thrice-cursed snuggly comforter, so welcoming before, was now effectively keeping me in place for the vampire's dining pleasure. He was on me again before I could get my legs free and employ some basic martial arts. I kept him from my neck, but just barely, using more magically enhanced strength. It was like wrestling Leif—even worse, for this lad was stronger and therefore older—and I knew from experience I would not be able to maintain it for much longer, especially with three broken fingers. My charm was running out of juice rapidly. He slapped me hard to make me stop the unbinding, and it worked. I had to start over.

<Atticus, what was that noise?> Oberon asked from next door. He was spending the night in Granuaile's room.

Vampire trying to kill me.

He began to bark, and I heard Granuaile moving, already up, roused by the noise of the shattering door. I wanted to shout at her, say no, stay in your room, stay safe, but to do that I'd have to stop my unbinding for the second time.

As my magic ebbed away, I saw that I would have to make a choice. Either I could keep the vampire from my neck for a few seconds longer and use all my magic on boosting my strength, or I could let him at my neck and save enough to energize the unbinding, hoping he didn't kill me before I could do it. I chose the latter, seeing no other winning scenario, and once there was nothing between my neck and the vampire but my weak human strength, he plunged down and tore at me again, my blood spilling onto the pillow as much as it spilled into his mouth. I resolutely kept speaking but knew he'd opened me up good, and I could feel my life draining away.

A snarl and an abrupt pressure announced the arrival of Oberon: He jumped on top of the vampire's back, and thus on top of me, and did his best to bite through the vampire's skull. It successfully distracted the vampire, because he tore loose from my neck, hissing, and coldly threw Oberon—all hundred and fifty pounds of him—straight through the open door to slam forcefully against the wall in the papered hallway. I heard his bones break and a pained yelp, closely followed by a startled scream from Granuaile, who was out there, and then the sound of my friend crumpling to the floor.

He had saved my life, because that gave me enough time to finish my unbinding and turn the vampire into a gory accident. He squelched and folded inside his suit until he was naught but a legendary dry-cleaning bill in the middle of the room. I tried to get out of the bed to help Oberon and instead tumbled into the carnage on the floor, too weak to keep my feet. I was still bleeding from the neck, and I had no magic left to heal myself.

"Call a vet!" I managed weakly. They were better last words, I supposed, than many others. I could see Granuaile kneeling next to Oberon, and he wasn't moving. I couldn't hear him in my mind either. Granuaile looked up from Oberon's still form at someone's approach in the hall. Her mouth dropped open.

Leif Helgarson strolled casually into the room, hands in pockets, a smirk on his misshapen face. It widened into a broad smile when he saw the remains in which I wallowed.

"Congratulations, Atticus," he said. "You have just killed a vampire nearly as old as yourself. That was Zdenik, erstwhile lord of Prague and, briefly, the state of Arizona."

No wonder he'd been so strong. "You . . . sent him here?" I said.

Leif removed his hands from his pockets and held them up helplessly. "Were you not the one who told me to orchestrate the deaths of my rivals? I have merely done as you suggested. Thank you for playing your part."

The oxygen leeched out of the room at his words, and all I could breathe in was horror. What he'd done to Oberon and me—and possibly Granuaile—was all for his worthless territory games? The edges of my vision were going black; my blood was still leaking out of my neck, and I could not think of anything to say that would adequately convey the depth of my revulsion and loathing for him now. If I had the strength left, I would have unbound him on the spot; having no recourse, I fell back on Shakespeare. Leif would recognize it and understand the context properly. With my remaining few seconds of consciousness, I quoted Benedick from *Much Ado About Nothing*, who spoke these words to his former friend: "You are a villain: I jest not." And then I collapsed into a pool of my own blood.

Chapter 20

I dislike Dreams—the sort with a capital *D*, full of portent and maybe even fiber, brimming with symbols and glowing sigils and mysterious choruses in the mist. The beings who arrange such nocturnal calls to one's noggin rarely have anything cheerful to say. And I suppose it makes sense. Supernatural beings are too busy to visit humans in their heads and speak unto them, "Congratulations. Upon your waking, you will get some." They have to say something weighty to make it worth the effort, so they drop bombs on you, announcing that you will be afflicted with sundry punishments for past transgressions, or you must journey far, far away to retrieve a Magic McThingie with which to slay the Dark Lord and save the village or world or galaxy. And, to be fair, they often imply that, should you succeed, you will get some. They just leave out the part that you will probably be too emotionally and physically maimed to enjoy it.

I was already feeling pretty maimed in both ways, so the beginning of a Dream immediately upon my collapse was a clue that my life would get worse before it got better. On the positive side, it meant I'd probably get to continue having a life. The figures in Dreams don't often bother with the soon-to-be-deceased.

I was no longer in a mixed cocktail of my own blood

and Bohemian vampire goo but rather hale and whole in a jungle immediately following an afternoon shower. Broad leaves dripped with moisture, and sweet, spicy oxygen filled my lungs. An animal noise of some sort directed my attention upward, and I spied a golden langur monkey pointing down at me from the canopy. The leaves diffused the sun and bathed the jungle floor in soft, dappled light and perhaps lent the monkey an expression of amusement. A rustling to my left tore my gaze away from him, and I took a step back when I saw the head of an elephant emerge from the foliage. I took another step back when I realized the elephant head wasn't attached to an elephant but rather the body of a man—a bare-chested man with four arms and an impressive belly. Underneath this, salwar pants of orange silk covered his legs until they ended at his sandaled feet.

The elephant's trunk twitched and a tranquil voice with a Tamil accent purred at me, its eyes narrowed in curiosity. "Do you know me?"

"You look like Ganesha," I said. I used to sell busts of the Indian god at Third Eye Books and Herbs. Rebecca Dane probably still had some in stock.

"I am he. Lord of Obstacles." One of his tusks was missing. He placed one pair of hands on his hips and clasped the other pair in front of him in a prayerful attitude.

"Fabulous to meet you," I said, trying to sound nonchalant about it. "Would there be any obstacles to me waking up right now so I could help my hound?"

A swish of leaves behind me was my only warning. I turned in time to see a shaggy wreck of a man rap me on the skull with a yew staff. "Pay attention, Siodhachan!" he spat. "You're cocking it up again!"

"Ow! Archdruid?"

He disappeared into the jungle and Ganesha sighed heavily. "That was one of my colleagues. He is trying to be helpful by pulling an authority figure out of your mind and using it to direct your thoughts, but it is less than subtle. Please forgive us."

"Um," I said, rubbing my head gingerly, "I suppose. Who are we talking about, exactly? Or what?"

"We were speaking of obstacles."

"Right. At the risk of reigniting the wrath of my old archdruid, would there be any obstacles to us having a beer while we talk?"

Two cold, frosty flagons appeared in a couple of Ganesha's hands, and he offered one to me. "It is a Dream. I don't see why not." The beer was a hoppy pilsner with a crisp finish, and it tasted of trust and serenity and a love for learning. Ganesha's trunk sank into his flagon, and he drained the entire draught in one go. Elephants aren't supposed to be able to drink using their trunks, but Ganesha didn't care. He was a god, this was a Dream, and so he was going to suck down a beer through his trunk if he wanted. He *ahh*ed in satisfaction, and then the flagon simply disappeared.

"Refreshing," he said. I agreed that it was and then fell silent, waiting for Ganesha to speak. I might be hosting the party in my head, but he was throwing it, so I figured he should set the agenda if I wasn't going to be able to wake up soon.

"We would like to congratulate you on your recent death," Ganesha began.

"My faked one, I hope you mean?"

Ganesha gave a soft trumpet of amusement. "Yes."

"Thank you, I feel pretty good about that death."

"I was particularly amused by Indra's role in the affair."

"He doesn't know it was all a sham, does he?"

"No. He and the rest of the gods with, ah, shall we say, a lesser understanding were completely taken in.

However, I represent a number of others with a keener sight, and you have piqued our curiosity."

"May I ask who these others are?"

Ganesha chuckled. "Let us simply say that we are all employed in Human Services."

Oh, gods. I wouldn't be getting into a pun contest with these guys. I sensed other presences nearby in the jungle; they were out of sight but clearly not out of my mind. Whoever they were, they wished to remain anonymous for the moment. Perhaps they were the other Indian gods, but I suspected they were from other pantheons and Ganesha had somehow been elected spokesperson.

"And why are you curious?"

"We wish to know what you will do next regarding Hel."

"Can you not simply read my mind?"

"We could if you had made a decision yet." The elephant's mouth turned upward around the single tusk. "You have been otherwise occupied."

"You have a gift for understatement," I said. "So I assume you would prefer one course of action over another, and you would like me to commit to that course now?"

"A clever deduction," Ganesha observed.

"And if I would rather think about this later?"

"Then I would be forced to admit that this is a Dream from which you may never awaken."

"I see." Ganesha was the friendly face of a rather unfriendly ultimatum: Do what we say, mortal, or you're toast.

"Any advice you'd like to share with me right now? A helpful hint about what you and your cronies would like me to do?"

"We don't see the point," Ganesha admitted, somewhat sheepishly. He raised his hands, palms up, in a gesture of helplessness. "You have been given advice before—very good advice, I might add—and you ignored it. You were even advised not to get yourself involved in this vampire situation, and now look where you are. Unconscious and completely drained of magic with only the most tenuous grip on your life."

"Is my hound alive?"

"That is irrelevant," Ganesha said.

"It's relevant to me!"

Pain bloomed on the top of my head as the spectre of my archdruid returned to discipline me. "Pay attention, Siodhachan!" he shouted, and then added as he dove back into the jungle, "You're cocking it up again!"

"Gah! Damn it, that hurts! How do you do that?"

"Let us focus, please," Ganesha said, "and see if we cannot remove the obstacles to your continued existence."

Right. I could do that. "Allow me to start by saying that I am incredibly open to persuasion if you don't like my answer," I said.

"Understood." Ganesha tilted his head down in the barest of nods, and the tiny smile returned around his tusk.

"Right now I feel that, while Hel richly deserves a shank between the ribs on her hot side, I have seen more than enough of her and all the Norse for the time being. I have an apprentice to train and a friend in the hall—"

"So you will pursue her later?" Ganesha interrupted.

"Much later. Like, after Granuaile is a full Druid in her own right. The whole point of faking my death was to give myself the chance to train her. It would be silly to toss that away now. And, speaking of which, I hope you guys won't go blabbing to all your buddies that I'm only *mostly* dead."

Ganesha stared at me in silence for a few moments,

and the jungle rustled with nervous energy. The gods, whoever they were, must have been conferring.

"That is satisfactory for now," Ganesha finally said. "We will be in touch. Farewell." He turned his back on me and strode into the jungle without giving me a chance to reply.

"Wait!" I shouted, chasing after him. Leaves sawed at my face and arms as I crashed into the undergrowth. "I have questions! How do I know this is real? What if it's just a dream with a lowercase *d*? What if I change my mind about Hel tomorrow?" I stopped. Ganesha was gone, but I still felt presences in the jungle. I turned right and circled around to where I thought they were lurking. I felt them leave as I ran madly through the vegetation, yelling, "Why doesn't everyone use the metric system? What happened to all of the yeti? How come I've never seen my archdruid in Tír na nÓg? Could he be the Most Interesting Man in the World? Why aren't people from Trinidad and Tobago called Tobaggans? Do you know any Vogon poetry?"

I broke through into the tiny clearing where I'd first appeared. The golden langur monkey screeched and pointed at me. He looked like he was laughing. Then he abruptly vanished, no sound effects or anything. Perhaps he'd been the avatar of a god all along. Or maybe I was just waking up from the Dream.

Chapter 21

Hospitals are buildings of death and give me the fantods. Unlike a field of heather and a benevolent sun shining upon me, they do not give me the sense that the day will bring me joy; they give me the sense that the day will be my last, and I will die cut off from nature. Consequently, when I woke up in the Flagstaff hospital, I couldn't wait to get out.

Granuaile was there and restrained me with a hand on my chest.

"Lie back, sensei. You're okay."

"Oberon?" I asked, my voice tight.

"He's okay too. Well, he's not okay, but he's alive, anyway. Most of his ribs were shattered on the right side and his shoulder too."

The breath I'd been holding whooshed out of me in relief, and tears escaped from my eyes. "Thank the gods," I said, choked up. "I didn't want to lose him."

"I know," Granuaile said, and tears spilled down her face as well. "I didn't want to lose him either."

"What happened?" I asked. "I thought I was finished." I'm sure Granuaile hadn't seen any hint of the Dream on my face while I was unconscious. There had been no gods in the room with their fingers on a red button. Only a traitor.

"When you collapsed, Leif healed up your neck with his little vampire tricks."

"What? How did he do that?" If it was a magical process, my amulet should have prevented him from doing anything to me. I checked to make sure my amulet was still around my neck, and of course it was. Perhaps the healing wasn't magical but rather a radical biological process.

"I didn't see exactly what he did. He squatted down next to you and his body blocked what he was doing—I was still in the hall with Oberon. But when he stood up, you weren't bleeding anymore—in fact, your neck looked perfect."

My fingers drifted up from my amulet and found no bandages, no scabs or puncture wounds.

"You were still out but not losing any more blood," she added, "and that allowed us time to get you over here."

"What about cops? That room was unholy."

"Leif just charmed anyone who came by to forget about it. Then he called up some ghouls to take care of the remains. They were already in town. He summoned them from Phoenix right after he called Zdenik to say he'd found the world's last Druid."

"He told you all this?"

"Yes." Her eyes drifted up, remembering. "He said he was dreadfully sorry that Oberon was hurt, and he hopes you'll be able to forgive him someday."

I shook my head. "That's not going to happen."

Granuaile nodded shortly to indicate she'd heard but then continued with the air of someone who had to recite their lines before they forgot them. "He also said you don't have to worry about him doing this again. He'll take care of the rest of the vampires by himself."

"Good. I want nothing more to do with him. Wait."

She was blinking rapidly and seemed disoriented. "Did he charm you to make you say all that?"

My apprentice glanced down at my face, confusion in her eyes. "Say what?"

"That bastard! I'll unbind him on sight, just like any other vampire."

Granuaile looked as if she was going to say something more, but the scowl on my face must have made her reconsider. Before I could soften and ask her what she was going to say, a doctor wafted into the room like a cotton cloud cut in the shape of a lab coat, trailing two squat nurses in his wake. He had short, light brown hair and a pair of rimless glasses perched on his nose, over which he peered at me with what looked like suspicion.

"Ah, Mr. Collins. Feeling better, are we?"

I blinked at him, not recognizing my new name for a moment. "I'd like to go outside," I finally said.

"Oh-ho!" he exclaimed, a false gaiety coloring his tone. He tried to chuckle companionably, but it didn't endear him to me. "It's far too soon for that." The badge on his coat read *O'Bryan*. An unusual spelling for an Irish name. At another time and place I might have been interested in the history of it.

"We have to figure out what's going on with you first," the doctor said.

For the first time, I realized they had an IV in me, and little expensive boxes were beeping and compiling data on my vitals. I had no magic left whatsoever to speed my own healing, and a glance at the window indicated I was several floors above the earth. I was utterly at the mercy of the American health care system, and the thought made me shudder and the little expensive box beep faster. I clutched at Granuaile's hand as she tried to back off and make room for the doctor.

"Whoa. Calm down. What was that?" O'Bryan said.

"Vitamin D deficiency. Get me outside," I said.

"Miss, I'll need you to excuse us for a moment," one of the nurses said to Granuaile, and she tried to pull away again. I held on.

"She's not going anywhere," I grated, "unless it's outside with me!"

Dr. O'Bryan flicked his eyes at the nurse, telling her to back off and let Granuaile stay where she was for now.

"Perhaps we can arrange a trip outside a bit later," he said, "but I need to ask you some questions about your condition first, and we need to get you stabilized."

"I'm stable and conscious, Doctor, and of sound mind. I'll be checking out immediately. I refuse care. Get this IV out of my arm now."

The doctor's tone became patronizing. "Mr. Collins, we haven't even established your insurance information or a proper check-in yet—"

"There is no insurance information. All bills will be paid by the law firm of Magnusson and Hauk in Tempe, phone number 480-555-8675. I will wait here long enough for you to call them and confirm that they are financially responsible for my bill, but that's it. I'm out of here. Now, are you going to remove this IV or shall I?"

Granuaile proffered her cell phone to the doctor. "Here. You can call them."

That got to him. Helpless patient in bed? He could ignore that. Granuaile in his face? He couldn't hack it. He held up a defensive hand and annoyance tightened his voice as he said, "That's not my priority right now."

"It isn't?" Granuaile replied, still holding the phone up. "You made it sound like insurance was the most important thing, or some kind of payment for your care. That's fair, we understand, and we're giving you what you need so you can take care of it and get us out of here. That way you can see patients who actually need you."

"Just let me ask Mr. Collins here a couple of questions about his condition."

"No questions are necessary, Doctor," I said. "Again, I refuse your care. All that remains is for you to unhook me from this IV and all these monitors and settle the bill."

O'Bryan was visibly irritated now. Doctors aren't used to losing control of conversations in hospitals. If I had any juice left, I would have simply cast camouflage and walked out, but since I was completely drained, I had to play by their rules long enough to get out of there. If I simply yanked out the IV, he'd probably order me restrained, and the nurses looked burly enough to manage it in my weakened condition.

I already knew what he wanted to ask: How did you get to be so drained of blood when I can't find where or how it got out? And if I allowed him to ask me that, there was a fairly decent chance I would scream, "AN EVIL FUCKING VAMPIRE SUCKED ME DRY!" and then the restraints would come out for sure, followed shortly by a trip to a padded cell and little cups of Jell-O spiked with Thorazine. I had to remain calm or I wouldn't be able to help Oberon.

"Mr. Collins. You are in no condition to self-diagnose—"

I interrupted before he could go any further. "Granuaile, call Hal right now please and ask about the possibility of suing this man for continuing treatment after I have refused it."

"Now, hold on, that's just—"

"The American way," I finished for him. "It's no fun having lawyers on retainer unless you can use them on people. So what's it gonna be, Doc? Do you want to call my lawyers and get paid, or should I call my lawyers and sue you?"

Abruptly, I was too much trouble to deal with. He

clenched his fists and exhaled noisily, then turned to the nurses. "The patient has refused our care. Get him ready to check out." He flicked his gaze to Granuaile and said, "Miss, if you will follow me and give me that payment information, we'll settle the paperwork."

"Certainly," she said, and this time when she pulled away I let her go. The nurses loomed over me and began tearing off those monitor things and removing the IV. They didn't speak to me. I didn't rate bedside manners, because I'd gotten pissy with the doctor.

"Where are my clothes?" I said. After I asked the question, it occurred to me that perhaps I didn't have any. I doubted they'd delivered me to the hospital soaked in blood, or else I would have had the police to deal with on top of the doctor. Still, the nurse on my right gestured to a small nightstand in the corner with a heinous plastic lamp on top of it. As soon as I was free of their tentacular monitoring apparatus, I sat up and swung my legs over the bedside. There I paused; I was still light-headed and weak from blood loss. No doubt they had pumped some replacement fluid in, but it wasn't enough. No matter; I'd heal well enough once I could get outside and away from this clinical gray box of death.

I pushed myself forward and rose cautiously to my feet. A draft from the aft signaled that my dressing gown was open, but I didn't care. The nurses could take shots with their camera phones and upload them to their Flickr stream for all I cared, just so long as my face wasn't in it.

A wave of dizziness rolled over me when I took a step, but it was one of those gentle rocking swells and not a thirty-foot-tall fist of Poseidon. I could do this. I shuffled over carefully and leaned against the nightstand for support as I opened the drawer. Then I nearly fell over when Granuaile spoke from behind me.

"Nom nom nom!" she said.

I looked around for the cookies she must be referring to and then realized, belatedly, that the room was bereft of delicious baked goods. The only thing on display was my backside, and apparently she thought it looked tasty. I blushed and retrieved the folded set of clothes, then turned around so that the hospital gown could afford me a shred of modesty. The nurses exited silently and I asked Granuaile if the doctor was satisfied.

"He's pissed and Hal wants you to call him, but, yeah, we're clear to go. You need some help getting dressed?"

She knew I'd say no. Her mouth was quirked up to one side and she was quite clearly teasing me.

"I'll manage, thanks," I said. I held up the jeans. "Did you put these in here?"

"Yep. You're welcome."

"Thanks." I pulled out a mostly white shirt with uncertain ambitions about achieving a pale green. It looked a bit more designer than I was used to. "Where'd you get this?"

"Flagstaff actually has some decent shops," she said. "I noticed you liked henley shirts, so I found you one in 'creamy dill.'"

"What? Are you making that up? Sounds like a salad dressing. A vaguely pornographic one."

"It's the fab new color, Atticus. All the Irish Druids will be wearing it today." She grinned at me impishly.

I tossed my head significantly at the door and said, "I'll be out in a couple of minutes."

She spun on her heel, hands on hips, and sashayed slowly out of the room, allowing me to check her out too. I couldn't figure out what she was up to. Didn't we talk last night in Granny's Closet about the need to stop flirting? Was she defying me? Or was this not flirting at all but an attempt to lighten my rather grim mood? I pushed the matter out of my mind, because I had to get to Oberon.

I leaned against the bed for support as I tugged on the pair of jeans, then pulled on my creamy-dill shirt with a small shudder. There was a pair of sandals for my feet. Once I slipped into these, I made my shaky way to the door, where Granuaile was waiting, beaming her best smile at the frowning nurses. I draped an arm around her shoulders.

"I'm not quite steady yet. Help me get out of here?"

"Sure, sensei."

I was proud of myself. I only drifted to the left and stumbled twice on the way out. And I didn't run my fingers through her hair even once.

Outside, a couple of trees and a decorative expanse of sod surrounded a sign that said FLAGSTAFF MEDICAL CENTER. The grass felt so good underneath my feet, cool and welcoming, and the touch of Gaia's strength was soft and warm as it replenished me.

"Ahh." A smile of relief spread across my face. "Granuaile, you have no idea how awful it is to be so cut off from the earth once you're bound to it."

"That was less than a day, Atticus. Surely you've gone longer than that."

"Oh, yes. Prison sucked more than a little bit."

"What? How did anyone ever manage to imprison you?"

"They caught me in a hospital like this, drained of magic. Aenghus Óg sent a succubus after me in Italy, and she nearly got me, because, you know, *damn,* she was fine. Long story short, I had to hack her up with Fragarach in a crowded plaza, and Italians, gods bless 'em, tend to object when people slice up hot women. I was already running low on the cobblestones, not enough juice left to cast camouflage, and then I had a mob after me and they beat me up pretty good. The *polizia* saved me from getting killed and took me to the hospital to heal up before they beat a confession out of me. They marched me from my hospital bed to their car and straight into a concrete cell."

"Where was Fragarach during this time?"

"I let the *polizia* take it from me."

"No way!"

"It was a calculated risk. They weren't under the control of Aenghus Óg, like Fagles was, and the ironic thing about being locked away from the earth is that the Fae couldn't find me. They had no idea where I was."

"What about your necklace?"

"That was more troublesome. They did their best to take it, but it's bound to me and not dependent on power to stay there. They cut the chain to try to remove it that way, but that didn't work either; the amulet and the charms all remained around my neck. So I was a very suspicious lad. After about a week they took me out to this dusty courtyard to get some exercise, and once I got my shoes off that was all I needed. I filled up my bear charm and camouflaged myself, went ninja and stole back Fragarach from their evidence room, then walked out. Haven't been back to Italy since."

A mischievous grin played at the corners of Granuaile's mouth. "What was your name at that time?"

"I am wanted there under the name of Luigi Fittipaldi. Very dangerous man but assumed to be much older now. This was back in the early seventies."

"Did you wear those wingtip collars and everything?"

"Well, you know, I always try to blend in. . . ."

She laughed. "That's fabulous. All recharged?"

"Yeah," I said, and followed her to where the new SUV was parked. "Thank you, by the way, for watching over Oberon and me. I'm glad you weren't hurt."

"You're welcome, sensei. We going straight to the vet's?"

"No, we have a couple of stops to make first."

We drove to the Winter Sun Trading Company on San

Francisco Street to pick up some necessary herbs, and once I'd blended them and bound them properly, we scooted south of the railroad tracks to Macy's European coffeehouse on Beaver Street to pick up some hot water for tea and one of their famous San Francisco cappuccinos. I made a large cup of modified Immortali-Tea for Oberon—altered to accelerate healing—and, after one more quick stop at a grocery store, we were ready to visit the vet.

Said vet appraised me accusingly, clearly thinking I must be at least partially responsible for Oberon's condition. Her name was Dr. April Flores, and I wished we could have met under better circumstances. She was very sharp and I would have enjoyed talking to her about more pleasant things than wounded doggies.

"Your dog is lucky to be alive," she said. "I haven't seen trauma like this before. What was he doing attacking a bear anyway?"

I glanced at Granuaile and she shrugged apologetically. It was the best cover story she could come up with, but I thought it was at least somewhat plausible. Except that neither of us looked like we'd been attacked by a bear, so Oberon could hardly have been indulging a protective instinct. And encounters with bears in northern Arizona, while not unheard of, were rather infrequent. Dr. Flores was having trouble swallowing the story, and I didn't blame her. But it was more believable than the truth.

"Dogs will be dogs," I said, a meaningless phrase that nevertheless allowed me to avoid lying. I'm not normally averse to lying, but since Dr. Flores was a nice person who clearly loved animals, I was trying to avoid accumulating any more guilt ferrets.

Dr. Flores frowned, fully aware that I hadn't answered her, but led us to a room in her clinic. "He won't be able to move for some time. I have the bones set, but those will take a while to heal, especially his shoulder. He also has a punctured lung and a bruised spleen."

She opened the door and I saw Oberon lying on a table on his left side. His exposed right side was shaved and bandaged; he looked awful. But he saw me and his tail began thumping against the table.

<Atticus! You're all right! Nobody would tell me anything, because they didn't know any better!>

"Hi, buddy. Good to see you." I entered the room and squatted down so I was eye level with him, putting a paper sack and the tea on the floor underneath his head, just beyond the edge of the table. His eyes followed my hands as they disappeared from his view and then came back up to scratch his head gently. Granuaile and the vet began to murmur behind me about recovery time, but I blocked them out and gave all my attention to Oberon.

<Hey. What's in the bag?>

Maybe a little something for you.

<Animal, vegetable, or mineral?>

Former animal, now deceased.

<Is it succulent and juicy?>

You will have to judge for yourself.

<Well, what are we waiting for? All rise for the Right Honorable Judge Oberon—>

I need to have you drink some tea first.

<Aww! That smelly stuff?>

Maybe smellier than usual.

<You are a terrible salesman, you know that?>

I snorted and then remembered I wasn't alone in the room. I looked back at Granuaile and Dr. Flores. "May I have a few minutes with him, please?" I asked.

"Don't move him," the veterinarian said. Her eyes dropped down to the bag and added, "And no food."

<Okay, that was a buzzkill right there.>

"Right," I said, smiling in what I hoped was a reassuring manner. Granuaile smirked as she exited, knowing full well that I planned to ignore those instructions. Once they were gone, I searched for and found a bowl to pour the tea in.

I need you to drink this, Oberon, I said as I filled the bowl. *All of it. It's important. You'll get better quicker. How do you feel?*

<Everything hurts, but I am glad you are here now.> He began to lap up the liquid. <This tastes like depressed teenage flowers that want to rebel against their parents by smelling like feet dipped in stinky cheese.>

I'm sorry, Oberon, but you have to drink it all.

<I know, I'm just saying that most dumps are fresher than this.>

I have andouille sausage in the bag for you when you're finished.

Oberon began to lap up the tea with more gusto.

<I think I'm feeling better already!>

Good. I'm so sorry you got hurt, Oberon. That's not what I wanted.

<There is always a price to pay for badassery, Atticus. But the benefits outweigh the drawbacks. I didn't want you to die.>

That started a tear rolling down my cheek. *And I didn't, because of you. You saved my life. Thank you.*

<You're welcome. Hey! Does saving your life erase all my negative sausages?>

Oh, most definitely. You were at negative sixteen, I believe? Well, now I owe you sixteen sausages.

<Oh, that's gravy! What kind?>

What kind do you want, buddy? You name it, I'll go get it. Keep drinking.

<Okay. You remember that one time you took me to Scotland and you let me try those sweet wild boar sausages from that gourmet place? Can I have some of those?>

The ones you made up a song about?

<Yeah! That's right, I did! I think I forgot it though. How did it go?>

Oh. I think it went like this:

A Scotsman often is a bore
But he sure can cook a boar
This is now my favorite store
I can't wait to eat some more
Boar sausages!

<Oh, man, that was a classic! I have a gift for lyrics. That should have won a Grammy. It's not as good as "Horseradish Tastes Like Death and Sorrow," but I don't think I'll ever top that one.>

Oberon finished the tea and I put the bowl down on the floor. *How do you feel now?* I asked him.

<I feel like seeing what's in the bag,> he replied.

I mean physically, Oberon.

<It still hurts, Atticus, but maybe not as bad.>

That sounds about right. I couldn't give you much in the way of pain relief, because I don't know what the vet is going to be doing. But you're going to be healing now much faster than the vet will expect. Now that your bones are set, you'll be better in a few days rather than a few weeks, and that pain is going to be all gone.

<Is that vampire all gone?>

Yes, he is. Thanks to you, I was able to unbind him and then the ghouls ate what was left. But, look, Leif is no longer our friend. He set that vampire on me and put both you and Granuaile in danger.

<Leif did that?>

Yep. He betrayed us and went to the dark side. So if you smell him or any other vampire coming, you let me know, okay?

<Okay.>

I picked up the bag and pulled out an andouille sausage for him, and he whined softly.

<There was seriously only one in there?>

You have to take it easy right now, I explained as I fed it to him. *The doctor probably has you pumped full of pharmaceuticals and you really shouldn't have anything.*

<So this means you're spoiling me, right?>

Can't help it. You're the best hound ever.

Oberon's tail thumped a few times and his mouth partially opened, seeming to smile at me.

Chapter 22

I didn't want to leave Oberon, but there was nothing more I could do for him for a few days; he simply needed time to heal. In the interim, there was plenty for me to do in Kayenta, and I'd promised I'd be back today. The last thing I needed was to give Coyote an excuse to mess with me because I wasn't holding up my end of the deal.

Before we got out of range of the cell phone towers in Flagstaff, I put in a call to Magnusson and Hauk as we drove north on Highway 89. Hal didn't want to believe that Leif had set Zdenik on me. His growly voice crackled on the phone, but his skepticism came through clearly.

"That doesn't sound consistent with his character," he said.

"He doesn't have the same character anymore, Hal. Not since he came back from Asgard. Or maybe he's been playing us all for fools the whole time. That's possible too."

"So now he thinks he can retake the state for his own again?"

"That's what he told Granuaile. But he charmed her first to make sure she'd tell me."

"Unbelievable."

"Believe it. Has he been in to the offices?"

"No, he's been away on leave since he left for Asgard."

"Well, I tenderly suggest you turn that into permanent leave, and when it comes to my records, he's no longer my attorney, okay? I don't want him to have access to my files at all, and I'm telling you right now that if I see him again he's going to die for real. You can tell him I said so. I'm sorry I ever put him back together in the first place!"

"You know, I have excellent hearing, Atticus."

"I'm sorry, I didn't mean to yell at you, Hal. I'm just angry."

"You're not hunting him now, are you?"

"No, I have other pressing business, but Leif needs to stay out of my way forever."

"All right, send me a signed letter firing him to make it legal in case he makes a fuss, but I'll close your files now. Thanks for letting me know; I'll alert the Pack to watch out for him."

Granuaile drove in silence for a few minutes after I hung up, letting me have a good sulk as I stared out the passenger side window, but eventually she spoke up.

"I've never seen you like this, so you're going to have to coach me a bit," she said. "Do you want me to let you brood in silence, or would it help for you to talk about it?"

"Huh. You know, I haven't had anyone to talk to in so long, it didn't occur to me. Sorry."

"It's kind of scary to think of what you consider to be a long time. How long are we talking about?"

"I've been drifting around for centuries since my wife died."

Granuaile took her eyes off the road briefly to study my face. "I was wondering about that. I thought you must have tied the knot at some point."

"I've tied the knot many times, in one way or another," I explained. "Aenghus Óg chased me away from many of my relationships—I came to believe that it was his punishment for me; he'd let me stay somewhere long enough to love someone and then he'd bring the pain. Maybe my falling in love was a way for him to find me, since that particular emotion was his demesne. Just when I thought I'd lost him for a while, he'd find me again, and then my choice was to stay, fight, and possibly lose everything, or run and abandon the people I'd come to love. I always ran, always lived in the present, because my future was never guaranteed. That made me a terrible husband and a worse father. But one marriage lasted a very long time, and Aenghus Óg wasn't the one to end it. I was married for more than two hundred years to a woman in Africa named Tahirah. We had many beautiful children, and I got to see them grow up and have children of their own. Only grandchildren I've ever seen."

Here I had to stop. Granuaile let the silence stretch for some time before she timidly asked a question.

"The ones you left behind . . . did you ever go back?"

"Secretly, yes. Sometimes they were worse off; sometimes they were better off. I figured out a way to help the ones who were worse off, but there was never any question of continuing the relationship. Even if they were willing, I couldn't."

Silence fell again for a few moments as she considered this, and then she said, "I . . . well—wait. How did you deal with the depression? I mean, how are you even functioning?"

"I ran from it. I'm still running. Most people don't have a choice about picking up and leaving. They're stuck—or believe they're stuck—where they are, and they don't see a way out or the possibility of a better tomorrow. I always have somewhere to go, a new life to live, a new language and culture to learn about."

"So you don't know what happened to your families?"

"I know what happened to all of them, unfortunately. They lived their lives, and now they're gone."

Granuaile puffed some air past her lips and blew a wisp of hair out of her eyes. "You know, most of the time I'm able to ignore how old you are, but sometimes I get a sense of the enormity of it. . . ."

"Yeah. It's not really the sweet carefree deal that it seems. There are dues and blues. And you can't avoid it either. If you remove yourself from human relationships and all the baggage that comes with them, you're removing yourself from humanity entirely. The pain and regret and embarrassment are all repaid in joy, however brief and infrequent that joy may be. I've seen what happens when you try to set yourself apart."

There was silence while Granuaile considered this. Then, delicately, almost too soft to hear, she asked, "Can I ask what happened to Tahirah?"

"Sure." Such an easy word to say. But I had to take a deep breath and divide my mind in order to answer, stripping away the emotions and memories until only the raw words were left. My voice was flat and toneless as I said, "We were ambushed by a Masai war party. Tahirah took a spear through her chest and died before I could even attempt to heal her. And when I saw her dead eyes—eyes into which I used to look and find peace—my reason fled and rage took over: I cast camouflage on myself and cut them all down. They thought they were being slain by a demon. It wasn't my finest hour."

For a time there was nothing but the soft, rolling rumble of the engine and the whistle of gusting winds. Then Granuaile whispered, "I'm sorry, Atticus."

"Yeah. Me too." I paused. "You know that saying about how time heals all wounds? It's not always true."

Granuaile nodded, acknowledging that I probably knew what I was talking about.

"I couldn't bear to stay there after that, where every place and every person was a reminder of her. If you spend two hundred years in an area, every tree and every rock becomes familiar, and every step brings a new memory shaped like cut glass. I took my eldest son aside—his name was Odhiambo—and told him as far as the tribe was concerned I was dead too. Without his mother, there was no life for me there anymore. He was chief now; Tahirah had run the things that needed running, because I had no desire to lead. He tried to argue with me at first; I had been giving him, as well as the rest of my family, Immortali-Tea, and my leaving meant that they would begin to age normally. To me, that was all to the good. The eternal youth of my family had begun to wreak havoc on social structures that normal people take for granted, such as having children before the age of thirty or forty—or, indeed, having them at all. Tahirah and I kept having children, but they rarely married and had children of their own. And of our few grandchildren of childbearing age, none of them was the least inclined to start their own family. There was always time for that later, you see, because I was giving them all the time they wanted to be selfish.

"I had already decided some decades earlier that administering Immortali-Tea to my whole family had been a colossal mistake, but while Tahirah lived I never dared suggest we let nature take its course with her children and grandchildren. With her gone, however, it was abundantly clear that despite my family's advanced age, their development had been severely stunted in crucial ways. They looked down on people who aged normally. They rarely took physical risks, or even wished to exert themselves. A sense of entitlement had bloomed within them. And so I thought the best gift I could give them at that point was a chance at normalcy, painful as that might be.

"Odhiambo disagreed vehemently. He wanted me to teach him how to make Immortali-Tea, even though he knew very well he'd have to become a Druid to do it and he was far too old to begin the training; then he wanted me to make a vast supply and leave it for the village. But he gave up soon enough, seeing that I was determined, and so I wished them all harmony, shifted away from there, and returned to Europe at about the time its monarchs were discovering that the world might be round and full of vast resources to exploit."

"So, ever since then, it's been a month here, a year there, then move on, like a rolling stone and all that?"

"Pretty much. This is the longest I've stayed in any one place."

I waited for her to tell me I was selfish and irresponsible, or that I was the most epic deadbeat dad ever. I searched for signs that she was thinking it. Aside from looking a bit sad, her face was inscrutable; I lost some time as I focused on the freckles high up on her cheeks, and they blurred out and went wonky, the way things do when your eyes wonder what the hell you're doing. She kept her gaze focused on the road, lost in her own thoughts.

"Ten years later I returned," I continued, as if I hadn't paused and stared at her for three minutes. "Though I took care to go in camouflage. By listening and inference, I learned that Odhiambo was dead, as were several others. They'd committed suicide, Granuaile. Couldn't stand the thought of aging. And they were angry with me for leaving—not because they missed me, but because they missed my miracle elixir."

"Well, that's just . . ."

"Yeah. One of my daughters was out alone collecting roots, and I showed myself to her so that we could talk and catch up. At first she was glad to see me, but when I made it clear I wasn't staying or reversing their aging, she turned sullen and never smiled. She made no inquiries into my welfare, and perhaps I deserved that. But then I learned I was commonly cursed by my own family, as was Tahirah, for together we had ruined their paradise on earth, their own land of ceaseless summer."

Granuaile shook her head slowly and frowned, her judgment clear, but said nothing.

"That was when I decided I would never share Immortali-Tea with anyone again. To my children and grandchildren, I was nothing more than a tit engorged with the milk of eternal youth, and while I had Tahirah by my side, I'd been willing to ignore that unpleasant reality. It made me wonder, though, if perhaps that was all I had been to her as well. I don't know now if she ever loved me, you see? Perhaps she only loved being young and keeping her kids young once they reached adulthood. I tell myself no, there was no way she could have fooled me like that for two hundred years, what we had was real—but the doubts won't go away. There will always be a blemish on the memory."

"Don't doubt it, Atticus," Granuaile said. "Never doubt that she loved you."

"Why?"

"Well, because I—" She stopped abruptly, unsure of how to continue. Her hand flailed at the air to brush that attempt away, and then she began again. "Because you're right. She couldn't have faked it for two centuries. Nobody could. You would have seen it in her eyes if she was faking, but you never saw that, did you? You said yourself you found peace in her eyes. I know it turned to shit eventually—if there's anything I learned from studying philosophy, it's that everything turns to shit—but you had two hundred years of bliss before that, and you might be the only guy who ever got that. Ever."

That was a comforting way to look at it, and I nodded to indicate that she'd made a good point.

We exchanged one of those cheerless, halfhearted, tight-lipped smiles where your eyes apologize for the past and your upturned mouth indicates hope for a better future. It's an odd way to reassure someone, but somehow it seems to work across cultures and outlast dynasties. It works well in the cab of an SUV too.

After a few more miles of silent driving, Granuaile opened her mouth to speak, made a tiny noise, and then closed it again. Uncertainty.

"What is it?" I asked.

"I have something to share with you, but I don't want you to be angry with me."

"No one ever wants their sensei to be angry with them. It tends to lead to dire punishments, like being forced to read *Candide*."

She smiled nervously, unsure if I was joking. "Right. Well. In the interest of not hiding anything . . ."

"Yes?"

"My stepfather is an oil executive in Kansas."

"I know, you've mentioned it before."

"I hate him," she spat, fingers tightening on the steering wheel.

"I had surmised as much. Where's the hidden part?"

"While you were in Asgard, I underwent the *Baolach Cruatan*."

That got my attention. The *Baolach Cruatan* was a test of courage and cunning administered to new initiates by elder Druids, and not everyone passed. Those who failed died. I hadn't been sure when or even if it would happen to her, but the fact that she was sitting next to me meant she'd passed it. "Congratulations on your survival," I said. It was a practice of Druidry that had made Saint Patrick's job of converting the young much easier; as far as initiation ceremonies go, a short dunk in some cold water was a much more attractive option than an uncertain trial in which you would undoubtedly be scared shitless and perhaps die. "Who tested you?"

"Flidais and Brighid."

"Both of them? You saw them both?" Breakfast with Coyote hadn't been her first meeting with an immortal after all. Granuaile nodded.

"Wait," I said, a spark of irritation flaring at her for the first time in my memory. "Two members of the Tuatha Dé Danann visited you and you failed to mention this to me? Did you not think it was relevant somehow?"

"I was ashamed because of what happened—"

"Okay, stop right there," I said. "I don't care what happened, because the fact is, you survived. The mistake you made was letting your emotions dictate this choice not to tell me of it. I just got finished working out a scheme with the Morrigan to fool the Tuatha Dé Danann into thinking I'm dead, and now you tell me they've seen you?"

"They saw me weeks ago, when you were in Asgard, before you faked your death."

"I understand that. But when they hear that I've died, they're probably going to wonder where my apprentice is—the one that survived the *Baolach Cruatan*. They may even want to take it upon themselves to finish your training."

"But we just faked my own death," she protested.

"No, I didn't stage that to fool the Fae, because I didn't know you'd come to their attention yet. Bottom line is, you need to tell me whenever you run into any gods, because you might not be seeing the bigger picture. If Brighid has taken a personal interest in you, she will probably send Flidais to the crime scene and then we'll be found. Flidais will hunt us down."

Granuaile clenched and unclenched her fingers on the steering wheel, obviously distressed.

"I'm sorry," she said.

I didn't accept her apology right away; a bit of extra guilt on this issue would be good for her. I pointed at the iron amulet currently dangling on a gold chain outside her shirt. "Look, have you been wearing that amulet all the time, including whatever sack time you got last night in all that madness?"

"Yeah, I've gotten used to it."

"Good. There's a chance Brighid might not be able to divine your presence if you keep wearing it. It's not bound to your aura yet, but its close proximity might help quite a bit. And if that does work, she might really believe you're dead and never send Flidais to look for you."

"Or she'll remember I was wearing it during the *Baolach Cruatan* and send Flidais anyway," she replied.

This made me smile. "That's the way to think."

Granuaile frowned. "Do you seriously think Flidais can track us from my old car to the new car, through the two different restaurants, over to the hotel, then to the hospital and the vet's, all the way up here to the rez?"

"I don't know. But she doesn't have to do it that way."

Her hands left the steering wheel in a gesture of helplessness. "How else would she do it?"

"You have a marble of turquoise in your pocket."

"Oh . . . she'd just ask Sonora."

"And Sonora knows exactly where you are because of that marble."

She pouted. "I have to give it up, then?" I nodded and tried not to be distracted by her lips, extended and puckered. I was supposed to be angry with her. "But I can't just throw it out the window!" she said.

"I know. Pull over."

She obliged and we got out of the SUV. She walked around to my side and I put out my hand, palm up.

"Let's have it."

Granuaile reluctantly dug the marble out of her jeans pocket and grimaced. "Can't I say good-bye first?"

"We're on the Colorado Plateau. Sonora won't hear you."

"We're not going to leave it here, are we?"

"No," I said, removing my sandals. "I'll ask Colorado to return this piece of Sonora through the earth, and then I will explain very carefully that we wish to keep your existence a secret from anyone who asks, especially the Tuatha Dé Danann. Colorado will spread the word to all the elementals worldwide. They've been keeping my whereabouts secret for centuries now, so this won't be difficult."

"Does this mean I can't talk to Sonora now?"

"Yes, but you can always get a new marble next time you're down there. And you wouldn't have been able to talk to him outside of his range, anyway."

"*Her* range."

"Hmm? Oh, right. Her range. What were you going to tell me earlier before we got distracted by trust issues?" Granuaile was watching me place the wee piece of Sonora on the ground, a wistful expression on her face. My question caught her off guard.

"Trust issues?" She looked up with alarm. "You don't trust me now?"

"You kept secrets from me. Not personal secrets— keep those all you want. I mean you kept something from me you knew damn well I should have known. And I must assume you convinced Oberon to keep quiet too. There aren't any laws against suborning hounds, but there ought to be."

"Atticus, I'm so sorry!" she said. "I was trying to explain and you cut me off. Will you let me finish?"

I nodded once. "Go ahead."

"Okay, mental gearshift. I was telling you about my stepfather. His name is Beau Thatcher. He's a giant dick in a suit, and I was thinking about him after I went through the *Baolach Cruatan*. Before as well, to be truthful. And that's what I was leading up to. I never told you the complete truth about why I want to be a Druid."

"All right," I said. I clasped my hands together and waited.

She took a deep breath before continuing. "Basically, I want to be the opposite of him. His nemesis. I want to completely destroy his company and drive him into bankruptcy. He laughs when people get upset at oil spills. He laughed hardest at the Gulf oil spill, because the journalists got shut out, the local biologists were bought out, and the company went on to post obscene profits. Massive die-offs and extinctions in the Gulf and wetlands ruined for decades, and he *laughed*, sensei."

"As you said, he's a dick in a suit."

"But it makes me so angry!" she cried, clenching her fists. Then her voice softened. "Angry enough that it kind of scares me. Don't you ever get to feeling that way about people like him?"

"Sometimes. But preventing ecological disaster isn't a Druid's primary function, Granuaile. Gaia has outlasted dinosaurs and she will outlast the dicks in suits as well, whatever they do to her. This oil spill or that will be overcome, given enough time. Protecting the earth's magic is what we're for. That's why the Tuatha Dé Danann became the first Druids—it was after that episode in the Sahara that I told you about, when a wizard took the elemental's power for his own. Gaia recognized that she needed champions among humans to prevent that from happening again. And so the children of Danu were chosen to become those champions. Marbles like these," I said, pointing to Sonora's turquoise, "appeared beneath their feet. And when the Tuatha Dé Danann picked up those marbles, the elementals began speaking to them and teaching them and eventually guided them in binding the first human to the earth. But you don't see the Tuatha Dé Danann jumping around trying to prevent the clear-cutting of the Amazon or the damming of the Colorado River."

"Well, why not? Don't they revere nature? Don't you?"

"Of course. They—and I—revere all life. Even if significant portions of that life seem too stupid to live, we have to let them live anyway. Unless they try to directly kill us."

Granuaile squatted on the ground beside me and considered the marble. It was an excellent opportunity for me to stare at her without getting caught, so I did. She spoke after a few golden moments of sunlight on a troubled brow. "I think I see what you mean. When Sonora was speaking to me and pointing out the plants and animals that lived along the Verde River, she loved the gnats and the boring little weeds as much as the native trout and the sycamores. She made me love them all too. I wanted to keep them all safe." She looked up and had one of those teary smiles on her face, and it was ridiculously precious. It quivered and crashed into a sob after a few moments. "I couldn't do it though. I had to kill this javelina, and I was so mad at the goddesses for making me do it." She paused, took a deep breath, and wiped the tears from her cheeks. "But I think I understand the wisdom of that whole process now." The smile returned, but weaker. "It's good. You can't just say the words and be accepted. You gotta have the great responsibility before you get the great power."

It was easy to see why she'd passed muster in Brighid's eyes. With that range of emotion at her command, she would be a fierce protector of the earth—and most likely a badass. The *Baolach Cruatan* required quick thinking and didn't allow weapons, so she either killed that javelina with her bare hands or made do with what was around her. Something didn't add up, however.

"Look, I'm glad you had that revelation, but I still don't understand why you'd refrain from telling me about this—about meeting Brighid and Flidais in particular."

"Well, there was so much uncertainty in my mind about what happened. I didn't know if I'd behaved in a way that would make you proud, and—you know what? It doesn't matter. I shouldn't have done it. You're completely right, and I'm sorry. It won't happen again."

"Fair enough," I said. "Apprentices have kept secrets from their masters since the whole system began. It's an annoying but persistent tradition, and everyone does it. I did it when I was an apprentice. The archdruid beat me bloody and called me a poxy shitweasel, because that's how he communicated. I'm hoping I don't have to do that here to communicate how important it is that you never neglect to mention the appearance of a god again. Do I?"

"No," Granuaile said, shaking her head. "I am well aware how badly I've screwed up, and I hope you'll forgive me."

"Considering how brilliant you have been in all other respects, I believe I can do that. And regarding your stepdad, I understand, believe me. If you still want to take down your stepdad's oil company after twelve years, I'm not going to stop you. It won't take you long, though. Think of what else you'd like to accomplish."

"Right now I'd like to find a safe place for me to finish my training."

"Yeah," I said, "I'm working on that." A silent conversation with Colorado sent Sonora's turquoise into the soil, and Granuaile gave a tiny, wistful "Oh." Shortly afterward, a new marble arose, a whorled sphere of rough sandstone in a range of earth tones, kind of like a gas giant in miniature.

"Colorado would like to say hi," I said, and her face brightened as I picked up the marble. "But no more English. You need to use your Latin headspace for him— I mean, her. I'm holding on to this until you're ready."

Disappointment washed over her features for a moment as I pocketed the marble, but then it cleared away, replaced by determination.

"I'll be ready soon, sensei," Granuaile said.

I grinned. "I'm sure you will be."

Chapter 23

We stopped to check on the coal mine well before dark this time; it was running again, though not quite at full capacity. Some equipment was still en route, no doubt, but they were determined to scrape out everything they could as soon as they could. Whatever I did today I would most likely have to do again tomorrow, or soon thereafter, and again and again until their costs finally exceeded their profits.

Corporations might be harder to kill than gods.

I left Granuaile in the SUV with her laptop and promised to be back in a couple of hours. Security around the mine was beefed up. Dudes in starched uniforms patrolled the gates. They had a dog, and that made me smile. There isn't a dog in the world who will bark at me if I don't want him to.

Camouflage on, I slipped through the entrance and headed for the working machinery. As before, I seized up the engines with a binding that made them useless. After the first one, however, the worker radioed what happened and a signal went out to shut down all machinery immediately, before the strange failure could spread. They seemed to think some exotic additive was being squeezed into the fuel tanks by hippies, because they started to siphon gas out of the tanks, pump in a detergent, siphon that out, and then replace it with new gas. This amused me as I made my way from machine to machine, carefully opening the engine compartments and locking up the cylinders while they were busy worrying about the gas. What would they think happened this time? Would they cling to the same theory, reasoning that they hadn't caught the sabotage in time, or would they invent new theories?

I was fairly certain that local environmental activists were going to be questioned about these mysterious machinery breakdowns. The hassle would annoy them, of course, but I wiped away my guilt by imagining that they'd also enjoy the schadenfreude of a coal company losing money. I was certainly enjoying all the cussing they were doing.

This, I hoped, would be proof enough for Colorado that I was serious about keeping things shut down. Perhaps now he'd work on moving that gold for me and getting me out from underneath Coyote's paw.

Chapter 24

The sun was setting behind the sandstone buttes of Tyende Mesa as we drove up to Coyote's claim site. Crows scattered at our approach, and I wondered what had attracted them to the area.

The first hogan was completely finished now in terms of protection, and work had begun on building an administration building for the mine. Coyote was waiting for us and hurried over to say a few words out of earshot of the rest.

"Welcome back, Mr. Druid. You get all your errands finished?"

"Yep. If I'm right, those vampires you mentioned should start to disappear."

"Huh. That a fact?"

"Near as I can tell."

"Good. And when d'ya think I'm gonna see that gold start to appear?"

"Still working on that, don't worry. I don't suppose you took care of those skinwalkers while I was gone?"

"Shit no. Ain't my problem."

"Ain't mine either. The deal was to put gold under this mesa, not make the area safe."

Coyote spat on the ground, squinted at me, and repeated himself. "Huh. That a fact?"

"You know it is."

"All right," Coyote said, seeing that others were approaching. It was Ben Keonie and one of his crew. "My work is done here for today. See you 'round, Mr. Druid. Miss Druid." He looked into the SUV and realized someone was missing. "Hey. Where's your dog?"

"Never you mind," I said. "Your work is done here for the day, whatever that was. Sweet dreams." He ignored me and turned to Granuaile.

"Whatja do, leave that dog back in Flagstaff?"

"Did you leave us anything to eat in there," Granuaile replied, pointing at the hogan, "or did you hog it all?"

Coyote spat again and idly scratched his chest. "So it's like that. All right. Have it your way. Damn Druids." He turned and stalked off to a black work truck. I wondered what happened to the blue one he'd had a few days ago.

The temperature was dropping rapidly as the sun sank below Tyende Mesa. Granuaile and I hurried up to the first hogan. Ben Keonie greeted us with a smile, but he and his crew member looked disappointed when they didn't see Oberon with us. Ben, for his part, had been looking forward to another bout of tug-of-war, and apparently Oberon's friendly ass-sniffing had made him popular with the entire crew. They accompanied us back to the hogan.

Racks of bunk beds filled one side of the hogan now. Sophie Betsuie was lying in one, eyes glued to an e-reading device of some kind, but she looked up long enough to wave at us.

There was a standard fire in the middle of the room; the lava rocks were gone. Frank Chischilly sat on a metal folding chair on one side of a card table, reading the collected works of Edgar Allan Poe by the light of a kerosene lantern.

He saw me looking at the book and said, "Guess I can't get enough spooky shit right now, heh heh." He slipped a bookmark between the pages and closed it, rising to meet us, hand outstretched to shake. "How ya doin', Mr. Collins, Miss Collins."

We settled at the card table with him and Granuaile said, "It's starting to look a bit homey in here."

"It's a bit more comfortable," Frank agreed, nodding. "Going to enjoy it while we can. We start the Blessing Way tomorrow on the second building." He jerked his thumb in the direction of the unfinished structure.

"Had any trouble from the local wildlife?" I asked.

Frank knew what I meant and shook his head. "Not for us. I heard that some climbers disappeared up on the mesa yesterday, and I doubt we'll ever find 'em. The skinwalkers showed up and spent some time issuing threats last night, but they didn't try nothin'. This hogan is totally protected now. They can't get at us in here."

"Those sound like famous last words," I said.

Frank chuckled hoarsely. "They do, don't they? I've always wanted to say somethin' good when I go. Like 'Free Leonard Peltier!' or 'I've got your boarding school right here!' "

We chatted amiably for a few minutes before Frank suggested a card game to pass the time. "You know how to play pinochle?" he asked.

"Sure do," I said. "Learned how when I was in Ohio one time."

"Teach me?" Granuaile asked.

"Me too," Ben chimed in. He grinned at Granuaile, perhaps to reassure her that she wouldn't be the only newb at the game. Or perhaps he was smiling because she had the same effect on him that she did on me, and on most men. He offered to grab us a drink out of a cooler nearby and we thanked him. I surreptitiously waggled my eyebrows at Granuaile and she muttered at me through clenched teeth.

"Shut up, sensei."

Ben heard it and asked, "Why do you call him sensei if he's your brother?"

"Oh," Granuaile said, startled to be reminded of our assumed roles, then covered admirably with the truth. "He's teaching me martial arts, and so I call him that to keep from descending into sibling rivalry. It goes easier when I think of him as the instructor, you know?"

Ben nodded. "Makes sense," he said, handing us each one of those canned iced teas.

We had the first hand dealt, I'd won the bidding, and I was just about to name diamonds trump when the torn-metal scream of a skinwalker startled us. Ben managed to spill tea on himself, and he started cussing but choked that back at the sound of a thunderous impact and cracking, splintering wood coming from the west, where the new admin building sat unfinished. The sounds of destruction continued as I rose to walk to the west wall. I put my face up to a log and held it there, then concentrated on unbinding the cellulose in front of my right eye for a short time. The wood obediently compressed and parted to create a peephole for me—it was sort of like the opening credits of a James Bond movie, except that I didn't get to look at provocative silhouettes. I cast night vision and saw the blurring shape of one skinwalker going Hulk on the construction materials. He couldn't touch us inside the protected hogan, but everything outside had become fair game. He'd have those logs split up into kindling in no time. Where was the other skinwalker though?

The answer came shortly, from behind me. To the east, where the trucks and Granuaile's brand-new SUV were parked, crunching metal and shattered glass announced a skinwalker special on free demolition services. I kept watching the first skinwalker dismantle the construction materials as Ben and the others hurried to the opposite end of the hogan to press their ears against the walls. The skinwalker I could see looked fully healed now, and I assumed the other one was as well from the sound of things. While their strength might be on the low end of vampiric, their speed was still far in excess of what Leif or I could manage. There was no way for me to beat these guys, unless I got in a lucky strike with Moralltach. That was far from a guaranteed win however. I knew from experience how quickly they could take me down and chew me up. They were simply too fast; I had to slow them down somehow.

"That was my SUV, wasn't it?" Granuaile said, reacting to a noise that had a new-car crunch to it. "Damn it, how am I going to explain that to the insurance company?"

"Maybe you lost control and rolled it?" Ben suggested.

"Possible, but it's probably going to have claw marks or handprints or something on there, and then what am I going to say? If I get that little gecko on the line and tell him that a skinwalker smooshed my SUV, is he going to cut me a check? I kind of doubt it."

Frank Chischilly stood next to me and spoke in low tones. "Makes me wonder why they didn't do this before."

"They're not under the Famine curse now," I explained in the same quiet voice. "I think that kept them pretty single-minded. Now they're healed from their injuries, they want us to leave their territory, and they're making it expensuie for us to stay." Sophie Betsuie climbed down from her bunk to join us as I continued talking to Frank. "They're more dangerous like this. Clever. If we don't leave after this, I bet they'll start coming down off the mesa and messing with people down in the flats, adding a human cost on top of the one we've already lost."

"That could be really bad," Frank said. "Lot of ranches along the base of the mesa."

"They're all protected by the Blessing Way, right?"

"Yeah, but those people don't necessarily know to stay inside from sundown to sunup. An' even if they do, the skinwalkers could go after their sheep an' shit like that. Ruin their livelihoods. Some of them are barely scrapin' by as it is."

Sophie caught the end of this conversation and added, worry in her voice, "My grandmother lives below the mesa."

Gods Below. How could Coyote drive off and say his work was done here?

Frank hooked his thumbs in his belt loops and sighed. "You got any ideas on how to stop 'em, Mr. Collins?"

Sophie looked confused. "Why are you asking him?"

"Well . . . he's pretty smart," Frank said.

This intelligence flabbergasted her. Sophie cast a bewildered gaze at me, trying to discern how Frank's assessment could possibly be true—and, even if it was, how I could know more about skinwalkers than did a *hataałii*. Her eyes flicked down to my tattoos, and disapproval floated over her features like storm clouds. Perhaps she thought anyone who spent that long under the needle couldn't be all that bright. "Well, I'm pretty smart too," she finally said.

"What has Mr. Benally said about this skinwalker situation?" I asked, hoping to distract attention from my questionable IQ. Sophie, Ben, and the rest might know all about the skinwalkers, but they didn't know what I was other than a strange man who could make a rock disappear and a good guy to have around when monsters jumped on the roof. Gods knew what they thought Coyote was. As far as I could tell, none of them apart from Frank knew they were working with one of the First People.

"He's kinda hopin' I'll take care of it, like I said a few days ago," Frank said. "But I don't have any ideas. Except you should call your grandma," he told Sophie, "and tell her to lock herself in until this is over."

Sophie pulled out her cell phone and walked away from us for some privacy. As she did so, the demolition noises from the east increased dramatically, and I figured I'd better investigate. The ear-shredding screams were revving up there too. I opened a peephole in time to see both skinwalkers attempting to lift Granuaile's SUV above their heads, quivering and shrieking as they did so. The remains of the other trucks lay strewn about like a parts graveyard.

"The good news is, that wasn't your SUV you heard earlier, Granuaile," I said. "The bad news is, it's going to be dropping on us soon if they're planning what I think they're planning."

"Please say you're just teasing me again."

The skinwalkers got the SUV over their heads, and they looked at each other and nodded, beginning a countdown. While I marveled that those unholy noises could be coming from human throats, I also admired their strategy: They might not be able to touch the hogan now, but the Blessing Way did nothing to protect against damage from mundane objects.

"Not kidding!" I yelled. "Everybody move to the other side against the wall, now!" Granuaile rounded up a very confused Sophie while Frank and Ben got the crew moved over quickly enough. I turned around and looked up at the beams above us. With the earth piled on top, there was a chance the roof would absorb most of the force with a few cracks and splinters and allow the vehicle to slide off the roof. Then again, a half-ton vehicle thrown with force would probably exceed the stresses allowed for in the building code. I wondered what would happen to the Blessing Way ward if the structural integrity of the hogan was breached. Would that provide the skinwalkers a hole in the magic to jump through? Better not to find out. I decided to go for the Gregor Samsa option and let the apple sink into the back—or, in this case, the SUV into the roof. A crescendo of rage from the skinwalkers told me Granuaile's ride was on its way, and I began whispering bindings to strengthen the beams, leaving the targets until last.

The SUV hit almost right on top of me, just past the wall, where the space between beams was widest. I hurriedly looped the target for the binding around the area as the beams and trusses began to crack and splinter apart, then I energized it, which just barely kept the whole mess from dropping down on my head. A few startled screams reached me from the other side of the hogan, but I blocked these out; the structure was still unstable and slowly sinking down upon me. There wasn't enough material to support the vehicle, magically strengthened or not. The roof of the SUV could be seen clearly, and wood splinters littered the floor. I couldn't do any more to strengthen the existing construction . . . unless I made the SUV a part of it. Yes.

Large portions of modern automobiles are made of synthetic materials—fiberglass body panels and plastic everything. But the chassis and most of the undercarriage, thankfully, are still made of materials mined from the earth. The hood and the well of the front tire descended into the hogan, and it was there that I saw the metal I needed. I unbound and promptly rebound to the cellulose in the strained timbers whatever metal I could scavenge, the same way I had bound the silica from the lava rock to the logs of the wall a few nights ago. It turned those broken, splintered logs and beams into steel-reinforced rattan. It was enough to stop the cracking and splintering and support the weight of the vehicle. Barely.

The skinwalkers were disappointed that Granuaile's shiny new vehicle didn't fall through—so disappointed that they took inhuman leaps to land on top of the undercarriage of the SUV and start jumping up and down on it in an attempt to make it happen. The Blessing Way ward didn't flow over the foreign object, as I'd feared. But my bindings didn't allow the SUV to budge either. Frustrated there, the skinwalkers began to tear away at the muffler and all those other thingies underneath a car I never learned about, to get into the passenger area. That wouldn't end well for us if they succeeded. They could bust through the windows and slaughter us all, or just tear through the roof with that inhuman strength of theirs and drop down onto the floor.

I moved off the wall and focused on the steel frames of the bunk beds. I unbound the screws as I ran, not having time to find a screwdriver and disassemble them politely, and yanked one of the support poles free. To Frank and everyone else, it must have looked like I simply tore a hollow tube of steel from the frame of a bed with my bare hands. Drawing on the earth—bless them for sticking to tradition and not pouring a foundation here—I found the crossbar for the passenger cage and thrust upward on it with the pole, using all the strength Colorado allowed me, which was rather a lot. The SUV creaked and lurched upward at my prodding, sending the skinwalkers tumbling gracelessly off the vehicle and onto the edges of the roof, where they promptly got burned by the light of the Blessing Way and let go, falling to the ground to get burned some more. Their tortured howling was far louder than anything they'd screamed before, but now I rather enjoyed it. I allowed Granuaile's SUV to sink back to its former resting place and gestured to Frank to hurry over so I could tell him something. Sophie, I noticed, had missed all of this. She was crouched down near the wall, facing away, still trying to talk her grandmother into retreating indoors, where it would be safe.

Frank shuffled forward and I told him, "Threaten them in your language."

"With what?"

"I don't know. Make something up. We need to intimidate them right now so they won't keep attacking all night. Tell them we have spears made of light. Whatever you think will scare them."

Frank began to shout something incomprehensible, and I asked Ben Keonie if I could borrow his knife again. He handed it over without question, and I began to whittle quick stakes out of a small pile of firewood. Granuaile came over to squat down beside me and looked up at her SUV embedded in the roof.

"Easy come, easy go, eh?" she said.

"Let's hope they got burned bad and Frank can talk a good game," I said to her. "They're a whole lot smarter than they were before, and I don't have anything to throw at them. This magic is beyond me."

"Can't Colorado pump you up to match them?" she asked. "Seems like you're holding your own so far."

Her tone lacked concern, and that concerned me. "No, Granuaile, it's the Navajo magic that's far more effective than mine," I said. "Whatever spirits are driving those men, they are *old*. They are able to juice up those bodies more than Colorado can juice up mine. I might be stronger, but they're much faster. All I'm doing is using the leverage Frank provided us. Druids aren't omnipotent—not even close! Gaia gives you an edge over the average person, but it will always be your wits and your paranoia that help you see the sunrise more than brute strength or speed. If magic was the answer to everything, you wouldn't need a twelve-year training period in languages and lore to become a Druid. It's your mind that matters. Clear?"

Chastened, she nodded. "Clear."

"All right. Listen," I said in a lower voice as I continued to sharpen stakes. "Fear is a weapon. Leaders use it to manipulate the people they lead and to cow other nations. Your enemies will use it to manipulate you. So that means you might be averse to using it yourself, because in your experience it's only bullies and bad guys who use it. But I'm using it right now to manipulate the skinwalkers, because it's not exactly the kind of ethic that stands up when your survival is on the line. Frank is threatening them with light, because they've been burned by the Blessing Way ward and they don't want to get burned again. That *might* prevent them from attacking us further, or it might just delay the next attack; we'll see. But is it only the light from the magical spectrum that scares them?"

"Well, the way you ask that, I'm going to say no, but what do you mean? That we can go out there with flashlights and scare them away?"

I gave her a tiny shake of my head, then jerked my chin toward the fire pit.

"Oh . . ." she said. "If we're sitting in a structure made of wood, why haven't they burned us out and picked us off?"

"Exactly."

"They must be really scared of fire. But you would think the human side of them wouldn't have a problem with it."

"I don't think the human side of them is running the show right now."

As if to confirm that, the skinwalkers roared defiantly at something Frank said.

"They don't sound very scared," Granuaile observed.

"Rage is a tonic for fear. They have plenty of both, I think. I need you to set up a chair or tables under your SUV so we can get to the cab area, all right?"

Looking at her SUV sagging into the structure, she considered the assignment doubtfully. There wasn't enough space for someone to crawl inside, and broken glass lined the edges of the windows, which were slightly compacted from the impact with the roof. But she shrugged and said, "Okay, sensei."

"Thanks."

As Granuaile moved underneath her vehicle and Ben came forward to ask if she needed any help, Sophie Betsuie finally communicated enough information to her grandmother to hang up, turn around, and see what had caused all that unholy racket. And she promptly freaked out.

She knew at a glance that there was no possible way the roof could continue to support that vehicle, yet two people were walking right underneath it. She heroically shouted at them to move out of the way and demanded an explanation. "Why didn't it fall through?" she wondered aloud.

No one had an answer for her. I wasn't about to explain that I magically reinforced the roof with steel. Granuaile doggedly continued to set up a makeshift access to the cab area, ignoring Sophie's assertions that she'd be squashed like a roach.

I called Ben Keonie over and asked him a question. "Are you guys required to have a fire extinguisher in a structure like this, considering that you have a fire pit in here and all?"

"Yeah, we have a small one stashed in that locker over there," he said, gesturing near the door.

"Excellent," I said. "Would you mind grabbing it for me?"

"What are you planning to set on fire?" he asked.

"Skinwalkers. Extinguisher is just in case." He looked at me as though I might have gone mad, but then he shrugged and moved to get the extinguisher. I gathered up the stakes I'd made and dumped them on the floor of the hogan underneath the SUV's roof, ignoring the escalating argument between Sophie and Granuaile and the continued shouting match in Navajo between Frank and the skinwalkers outside. I started for one of the kerosene lanterns to extinguish it but then had a better idea.

"Hey, Ben, do you have extra containers of lamp oil in there too?" I asked.

"Yeah," he said.

"Great. Need some of those."

I dumped a whole container of the lamp oil over the stakes and then started handing them up to Granuaile after she got herself perched on a chair.

"Just sort of arrange them in the center of the roof area," I said. "They need to be touching one another." I would have preferred to bind the stakes to the SUV's roof so that they would point upward, but the manufacturer had lined the roof with a synthetic material I couldn't work with, and it was impossible to get in there and tear it out. The stakes would simply have to serve as kindling.

"I can't get them to always lie on top of one another," Granuaile reported. "We need to throw some in from the other side too. Plus a lot of them are rolling to the front, because it's not exactly level in there."

"Okay," I said, "I'll get over there," and I went to get another chair. Sophie protested.

"Look, we heard your dire warnings, and if we die it's not your fault, okay?" I said. Sophie threw up her hands and turned her back on us, muttering about idiots.

"Hey, Mr. Collins," Frank interjected, "whatever you're gonna do, you might wanna hurry. They ain't buyin' what I'm sellin'."

I hopped up on the chair and asked Granuaile to hop down from hers and hand me some stakes. No sooner was I up there than the SUV shuddered. The skinwalkers had leapt on top of it again, taking advantage of the dead space in the Blessing Way ward. This time they'd be ready for unexpected shifts and were hanging on; taking such care would slow them down, but they were also determined to rip through the chassis to get to us.

I tossed a few more stakes in the window and saw what Granuaile meant. Most of the stakes had rolled down to where the roof met the front windshield. But I could fix that, since no one could see what I was doing. I bound the stakes together end to end and then cross-wise so that they spanned the roof in a rough grid—or a grill would be a better image. A grill primed with kerosene. A tearing noise and starlight above me indicated that the skinwalkers had punctured the cabin. They were wrestling with the seats now.

"Need a lighter, quick!" I said. "Or matches!" This was one of those times I wished Druids could do neato things with fire. Maybe I should try to figure out how to make friends with a phosphorous elemental.

Ben and Frank patted themselves down helplessly and looked around. Granuaile didn't have anything, I knew. "How'd you guys get the lanterns lit without matches?" I asked.

The driver's seat disappeared with a shriek of metal, and a skinwalker in human form dropped down onto the roof. I saw a flash of orange eyes and ducked as he took a swing at me through the window.

"Here!" Someone pressed a lighter into my hand. It was Sophie. I didn't have time to thank her. I bobbed back up and socked my left hand through the window, not caring if I hit him or not. He dodged back easily and began to turn, considering an exit out the passenger side, because the confined space wasn't to his advantage. And then I lit the nearest stake and watched the flames travel along my improvised grill, even as the second skinwalker landed next to the first.

They burned and screamed and climbed on top of each other in an attempt to escape, which only made it worse. They eventually exited through the roof and forgot, in their haste, that the roof of the hogan was still warded. The Blessing Way burned them again and they tumbled off the hogan, howling.

Frank grinned at me as their cries of pain faded; they were clearly retreating.

"Think that got 'em," he said.

"For the night, anyway," I agreed. "They'll be back tomorrow night. We didn't do any permanent damage to them, but now they have this hole in your ward, and they'll probably just sit back and make new ones until they can get to us."

Ben Keonie offered me the fire extinguisher. "Ready for this?"

I looked at the fire and the smoke billowing out of the windows. "Yeah, good idea," I said.

Chapter 25

Dawn brought us a scene of chaos. The site looked like the aftermath of a natural disaster, except that we all knew there was nothing natural about the destruction. Sharp knives of wood lay strewn about like Van Helsing's personal weapons depot, and vehicles had been forcibly disassembled into their component parts. All that was missing was a gloomy heavy metal band to film a music video in the ruin, wind blowing dramatically through their spectacular manes of product-laden hair as they humped their guitars and lovingly fondled their favorite minor chords.

When Sophie, Ben, Frank, and the crew saw what was left of their trucks, they began to chirp "Fuck" in various registers like a small flock of birds—perhaps a new species of finch. The calls were varied and delivered with gusto. Granuaile joined in the morning chorus when she saw the skeleton of her ride nestled in the magically reinforced roof of the hogan.

"Fuckity fuck fuck!" she sang.

Sophie was especially dismayed to see that all the surveying stakes for the plant site down in the flat had been pulled up and destroyed. "We're going to have to start all over," she moaned. "And it'll probably just get torn up again. This project is doomed. Fuck."

Cell phones came out and voices began asking friends

for a ride into town. I wondered if anyone was going to call Coyote—Mr. Benally—and let him know that the skinwalkers had trashed the site. I wondered if Coyote would make an appearance today at all.

Trucks began showing up to collect us after about a half hour. Granuaile and I climbed into the bed of a Ford half ton along with Sophie Betsuie. Frank got to ride shotgun, and he directed the driver—a friend of his—to drop us all off at the Blue Coffee Pot for breakfast. The place was hopping again, because the coal mine was shut down for the second time. It was good to have visual confirmation of my success; Colorado should be in a good mood when I settled down to have another chat.

Once we were seated near a window with cups of strong coffee in front of us, I asked Frank if he could tell me anything more about skinwalkers and how they operated—anything at all that might help me understand them better. I carefully did not imply that this knowledge might help me to defeat them somehow, because Sophie had never been told I was anything but a geologist. But, surprisingly, Frank tilted his head at Sophie and said, "She can actually tell you more'n I can. She's got some privileged information regarding those two."

"You know them?" I said.

"Maybe," Sophie admitted. Her fingers danced nervously around the edges of her coffee mug and she eyed Frank, asking him if it was truly okay to share this information with me. He gave her a nod to go ahead.

"It's speculation, *not* hard fact," she stressed.

"Understood," I said.

"I only know this because of my clan," she began. "And all the workers, including Ben, are from my clan, if that helps you understand why we're on board with Frank here. There was a murder about ten years ago, and it was a big deal. Divorced woman killed in her home. So, uh . . . wait. I need a pen."

She fished a retractable gel pen out of her jacket pocket and then grabbed a napkin out of the dispenser lying on the table. Before she could continue, the waitress arrived to take our order, and we paused to do that. It was a bit depressing for me, because I had nothing to order for Oberon; I asked for an extra side of bacon anyway in his honor.

When the waitress departed, Sophie began to write on her napkin. "All right," she said, "I don't want to say the names of the dead or attract the attention of those who may still be living"—and here Frank nodded sagely at her caution—"so I'm going to just show you these names and explain from there. You don't read them aloud or anything, okay?"

Granuaile and I murmured our agreement. Sophie flipped around the napkin and pointed with her pen to the name at the top, which read *Millie Peshlakai.*

"This person was the murder victim, distantly related to me and the rest of the crew. She was only about forty, and the cause of death was clearly violent. Nicest lady. Nobody could figure out why she'd ever be a target. And these two here," she paused, pointing to the names *Robert* and *Ray Peshlakai,* "were her sons. Twins in their late teens. They disappeared. Haven't been seen since the day their mother was found. Most people figured they were kidnapped by their father, and they thought he'd done the murder too. He's a bad sort, lives up in Utah. But once they tracked him down and interrogated him, it was obvious he had nothing to do with it. Ironclad alibi and everything. So the murder's been unsolved all this time, and we still don't know what happened to the boys."

"So you think . . . ?" I said.

"Anybody can start followin' the Witchery Way

whenever they want. But there's only one way to become one of those things we've been dealin' with," Frank rasped. "Only one way to make your soul so black you attract a spirit from First World and gain powers nobody oughtta have."

Sophie circled the two boys' names and then drew an arrow to their mother's name. "You have to kill a family member," she said. "You become pure evil."

Chapter 26

"Hold on a second," I said. "If they're so evil, how come they haven't been going around killing people?"

" 'Cause they haven't had to go around anywhere to do that," Frank explained. "Plenty of people climb Tyende Mesa for the hell of it. You know how those climbers are. They see a rock that looks cool, an' their life won't be complete until they manage to stand on top of it. They bring their pitons an' rope an' shit an' walk around town smiling at everybody 'cause there's a decent chance they'll fall down an' go *splat*. Well, for the last ten years, some o' them people never came back. They don't go splat, they simply disappear, gear and all."

"The skinwalkers are burying them?"

"The bones, maybe. After all the meat's off 'em."

"They're *cannibals*?" Granuaile said.

"Aw, I don't know for sure," Frank said. "But cannibalism is part of the Witchery Way that they follow. Besides that, I don't know what else they'd be eatin'. Ain't like the shepherds 'round here been missin' sheep. Nobody's missin' their veggies or their breakfast cereals. So what are they eatin' up there? It ain't delivery pizza."

"People have been vanishing on the mesa and nobody notices?"

"O' course somebody notices. Funny thing is, that only attracts more of 'em, because they think the rock's a challenge. And then o' course you get their relatives comin' out to search for 'em, and they disappear too."

"Why doesn't the tribe close off the mesa?" Granuaile asked. "They wouldn't have to give any specific reason. Just say it's too dangerous."

Frank shrugged. "Guess they like the revenue that climbers bring in. Hotel taxes, dining, souvenirs, all that. They go up there at their own risk. And most o' the council don't believe in skinwalkers anyway. After last night I think they'll start believin' though."

Sophie chuckled. "I swear we have leaders like everyone else: Some of them are genuinely bright, but some of them aren't exactly the sharpest tools in the shed."

"The sharpest tools . . . oh!" I said. "That's it, that will work! Frank, I know how to slow them down."

"What? How?"

"Caltrops. They won't be expecting them after having clear ground for days now. They'll run right into them, and they're barefoot. We've already seen that they're suckers for booby traps."

"Psssh. They ain't runnin' at us anymore. Their tactics have changed."

"They will if we lay out some bait."

"Like what? Prime rib?"

"Like me. I'll surround myself with caltrops and ring the dinner bell, and they'll come running."

"That ain't gonna stop 'em. They'll fight through the pain to get to you and then deal with the injuries after you're all tore up. The First World spirit will guarantee that."

"They won't be able to fight through it if the caltrops are poisoned."

Three jaws dropped and three pairs of eyes stared at me, and the waitress appeared with our food. No one said anything until she'd brought back some syrup for Granuaile and refilled our coffee.

"Poisoned?" Frank said. "You gonna dip 'em in bleach or something?"

"Or something, if you get me to a drugstore. I can whip up something pretty good."

"A geologist who can mix poisons?" Sophie said.

"He's a Renaissance man," Granuaile explained as she poured syrup on her pancakes, and I shot her an amused glance. Yes, I was a Renaissance man. And a man of the Enlightenment, a Victorian man, a Postmodern man . . .

Frank squinted at me doubtfully and wagged his head back and forth slowly. "I don't think that's gonna work," he said.

"Why not?"

He sighed and took a stab at his omelet. "I don't care what kind o' poison you got, they ain't gonna step on one and keel over dead. They're gonna keep going based on momentum if nothing else. And skinwalkers have a hell of a lot o' momentum. They're gonna get a shot at you, and one shot's probably all they're gonna need. Poison might get to them eventually, but not before they get to you."

"Maybe. I'm betting that anything traveling that fast is going to fall down and go *boom* as soon as it runs into an obstacle. They'll not only get one in their feet, you see, they'll fall down and get punctured multiple times. Once they're down with that much poison in them, they won't be getting up. But even if they don't fall down, Frank, they're going to be stepping mighty ginger right away; they'll slow down to manageable speeds, enough for us to get a shot at them."

Frank wasn't convinced. "I don't know. I can still see 'em dodging around 'em or something like that. What about trying a net?"

"They'll see it coming and dodge. Or they'll tear through it. Come on, they were chucking trucks around last night. Caltrops are easy to make and tough to avoid. We could finish this up tonight."

Sophie was chewing on a piece of toast and nearly choked. Frank pounded her on the back to help her out. She took a drink to clear her throat and then she said to me, "You just got done reminding us that they were throwing trucks around, and now you think you can finish them tonight with caltrops?"

"The poisoned caltrops only slow them down so we can pop 'em with a gun. Or my sword."

"I've been meaning to ask you about that," she said, "so thanks for bringing it up. Why do you have a sword?"

"In case of the zombie apocalypse. You never run out of ammo with a sword."

Granuaile snorted in amusement, and Sophie flicked her eyes at her in annoyance before returning to me. "Look, I don't know what you are, but you're more than a geologist, if you are one at all. I've met lots of geologists on different projects like this, and they're all tiny sunburned men with fetishes for geodes. They wear floppy hats and carry baggies for soil samples around with them. You don't look or behave like a geologist, and Frank doesn't treat you as one. Neither does Mr. Benally. And geologists don't make rocks disappear like you did the other night. They keep them and build little shrines to them. So stop patronizing me and tell me what you really are."

Since she was already in a state of disbelief, it was difficult to think of something she would accept. She wouldn't buy the truth, and I didn't want to give it to her anyway. I wanted to say, "I'm the Doctor and this is my companion," but I doubted Sophie was a fan of the long-running BBC series. Forget the TARDIS and the sonic screwdriver, the Doctor's best gadget was the psychic paper. I can't tell you how many times I wished I had some. In absence of that, one of my favorite strategies to deflect attention from the fact that I'm a lying bastard is to accuse someone else of being a bigger one.

"Sophie, you may have noticed by now that Mr. Benally is full of shit," I said.

In a voice as dry as the mesa, she said, "Yeah, I noticed that." Frank's shoulders jiggled up and down as he laughed silently.

"Well, he never should have introduced me as a geologist. I'm more of a project troubleshooter."

"No kidding?" That earned me a wry twist to her mouth. "I'd say the project is in some pretty deep trouble at this point."

"Hence the reason Mr. Benally has left everything up to me. Since your part of the project cannot continue until we get the area stabilized, I suggest you enjoy a day or two off. That is, if you can help me get this straightened out tonight, Frank?"

Frank looked up from his omelet, surprised. "Who, me?"

"First, we need to get a buttload of nails."

"A buttload? How much is that?"

"Uh . . ."

Granuaile rescued me with her superior knowledge of indefinite units of measurement. "I believe that's slightly more than a shitload but much less than a fuckton."

"Precisely, thank you."

"What?" Frank put down his fork, lost.

"Then I'll need you to take me to a drugstore to pick up the poison."

"What are you gonna use, rat poison or something?"

"No, nothing like that. I can combine several pharmaceuticals to make what we need. We don't have time to go out and gather the proper plants to do it from scratch."

"I wouldn't think so. But ain't you gonna need a prescription?"

"Nah, I just need a getaway car. Can you lay hold of a ride for us?"

Frank smiled and rediscovered his appetite. "Sure, I got a nephew in town. He's sittin' over there on his ass," he pointed with his fork across the dining room to a table full of middle-aged men, "because the coal mine's shut down."

"Oh. Has he seen you sitting here?"

"Yeah, he's seen me."

"Why hasn't he come over to say hi?"

"He's bein' polite. Sees his uncle talkin' to a stranger, probably thinks we're doin' business."

"And so we are. Don't let him get away, though."

"I won't," Frank assured me. Filled with a new sense of purpose, I downed half my coffee at one draught. It was good, strong stuff, the kind that Louis L'Amour used to say could float a horseshoe. Nobody ever drank weak coffee in his books. It was probably why they were so anxious to shoot people at high noon. Which reminded me . . .

"Think you can get hold of a gun, Frank? Might come in handy."

He studied me and took his time chewing. "Yeah, I have an old six-shooter tucked away somewhere."

"Attaboy."

"I think it'll give you all the chances of a mouse against a sidewinder," he said, "but you're welcome to it. I think some antipersonnel mines would work better."

"Or horny toads with frickin' lasers strapped to their backs," Sophie suggested, and I smiled. No wonder Oberon liked her.

Frank called over his nephew after we finished eating and introduced him to us as Albert. He had his hair cropped short in a crew cut and wore a blue-and-gray flannel shirt tucked into his jeans.

"Say, their car is in the shop," Frank said, pointing a finger at us and admirably skipping the details. "Wouldja mind drivin' us around a bit?"

Albert shrugged a shoulder. "Sure, I don't have nothin' else to do." He flashed a grin past Frank. "Hey, Sophie."

"Hey, Albert."

"You out of work too?"

"Yep. For the day, anyway," she said.

"Aw, that sucks. Man," Albert shook his head and held his hands half clenched in front of him, picturing someone he'd like to strangle, "if they catch the damn hippie who gunked up all the engines, I hope they haul his nuts backward and yank 'em out of his—" He stopped midsentence as he saw Granuaile clutch at my arm and heard her make a tiny noise. "Oh. Sorry, miss." He took in my tattoos and his eyes lingered on the triskele on the back of my hand. Then he spied my necklace and noticed my hair, which admittedly can look a bit unkempt at times. "Are you a damn—I mean, are you guys hippies?" Granuaile's fingernails dug painfully into my arm at his question.

"No," I assured him. "But we are frequently mistaken for hippies. No worries, happens all the time." Granuaile was now pounding at me with her fist. I glanced at her and beheld an expression of barely restrained mirth. Her face was blushing red because she neither dared take a breath nor release one, convinced she would laugh inappropriately and embarrass Albert. I rose from the table to make way for her to get by. "Will you excuse my sister? She really needs to go to the restroom."

Granuaile nodded somewhat manically, her lips pressed tightly together and a tear welling up in her left eye as she stood.

"Oh, sure." Albert scooted over to stand next to

Frank, and Granuaile hurried away toward the restrooms, hand over her mouth and making wee whimpering noises. "Is she going to be okay?" he asked.

"Yeah, she'll be fine," I said, brushing away his concern with a wave. "These episodes just happen sometimes."

The entire restaurant heard her when she closed the door—a long, sustained high note followed by a gasp and another long note.

Albert made a face. "Man, are you sure?"

Chapter 27

I've often been flabbergasted by modern pharmaceutical ads on television. The list of side effects for some maladies often sounds worse than the condition they're supposed to treat. Once I even heard "heart failure" listed as a side effect, and I wondered how that happened. Heart failure sounds like a pretty major event to me, and if you're willing to risk heart failure in order to avoid the mild discomfort of some other condition, then may the gods shield you from harm, since you're obviously seeking it out.

I sought out a drugstore because most every medicine is actually a poison: The dosage is simply much lower. I prefer working directly from plants, of course, but scooping up a few bottles of pills will work when I'm in a hurry, and in this case I was in quite a hurry indeed.

"Sensei," Granuaile whispered to me on the way out of the Blue Coffee Pot to Albert's truck. "I heard you say you don't have a prescription for all these drugs you need, right?"

"Right."

"That means you're going to steal them, aren't you?"

"Yep."

She sighed in exasperation. "Things like that don't matter to you, do they?"

We paused to climb into the back of Albert's truck.

Frank rode shotgun and told him where to go. Once we were on our way, I picked up where we'd left off. "Not when people's lives are at stake, no. I never steal for mere personal gain, if that makes a difference. Well, I take that back. There was that one time in Egypt. And a few years ago I stole some art and precious gems from a businessman in Hong Kong just so he would have a really bad day, and that gained me quite a bit of satisfaction. But I called the cops after a couple of days and told them where to find everything, along with a note telling him not to be such a vag badger. He got most of it back."

"What? Why didn't he get all of it?"

"The cops kept some and told him that was all they found."

"No!"

"Yes. I had to steal the stuff again and give all the crooked cops wedgies. Look, if it makes you feel better, we can make a list of what I pull out of this place, look up the costs elsewhere, and then reimburse them with an anonymous envelope of cash later."

"That would make me feel better."

"Okay, that's what we'll do."

"Thank you." She gave me a couple of patronizing pats on the shoulder. "You're a very considerate sensei."

"I'll say. I haven't done half the things I'm supposed to yet. Usually there's a ritualistic leeching after the second week, and here we are three months or so along."

She squinted at me doubtfully. "You're kidding, right?"

"Lucky for you there aren't many leeches in this part of Arizona."

She cringed a little. "Seriously?"

"But I suppose we can let that slide since I made you eat a steer sack."

"Shut up!" I shook with laughter and she scowled at

me, folding her arms across her chest. "Auggh! You can be so immature sometimes!"

At a quarter to nine we pulled up next to a drugstore to make sure we were out of range of any surveillance cameras, and I got out and walked around to the back. As I left them there, I heard Albert say, "I can't believe I'm doing this."

Once out of sight of Frank and Albert, I cast camouflage on myself and concentrated on the door. Locks aren't that difficult when you can bind the metal inside to the unlocked position. Security systems are another matter; I'm not sophisticated enough with electronics to tackle those, and much of it is dead plastic anyway. I would doubtless trip something as soon as I walked in, so it would have to be a dash to get everything I needed before the cops arrived.

The first thing I did was grab a plastic bag, and then I went hunting among the shelves. I wasn't familiar with brand names, so I had to scan active ingredients to find what I needed. I was trying to find the various chemical components of *Atropa belladonna,* the plant known commonly as deadly nightshade. Chew one leaf as an adult and you're toast; the collected tropane alkaloids mess with your nervous system so that it can't regulate involuntary activities like sweating, breathing, and heart rate. But isolate and regulate the dosage of those alkaloids, and you can turn an extremely deadly plant into a medicinal one. I found atropine, scopolamine, and hyoscyamine all sitting on the shelves under various brand names. According to the dosages, it looked like we'd have to hit another store to make enough poison for a decent spread of caltrops. I picked up a package of surgical gloves on my way out; I didn't want to get any on my skin once I began combining these.

I returned to the truck bed and didn't dissolve my camouflage until I was in it. Granuaile had heard the rustle of the plastic bag and knew I was there, but Albert and Frank jumped a bit when I tapped on the back of the cab window.

"Let's go," I hollered, and Albert peeled out of there with admirable haste. We passed a police car with flashing lights heading toward the store as we drove deeper into town. Frank directed us to a hardware store, and once we got out of the back and could talk, I explained we needed to visit one more drugstore.

"Sure, don't see why not," Frank said. "First one went without a hitch."

Feeling saucy, we walked into the hardware store—which smelled like pressboard and paint—and asked for a buttload of nails.

"We actually have those on sale," the sales associate said without blinking at our denomination.

Granuaile leaned over and whispered in my ear, "Ask if he sells them by the fuckton."

Nails and a good stash of drugs in hand, we were (or I was) perhaps too confident when we hit the second drugstore. It wasn't time for them to open yet, but I surprised a pharmacist who had arrived early to do some paperwork. The alarm to the building was already turned off, but she raised plenty of alarm when the back door seemed to open and close all by itself and my camouflaged form cast a shadow on the floor. She was fast. She made it to the phone and dialed 911 before I could render her unconscious with some deft kung fu. I can't quite do a Vulcan nerve pinch, but my Druid Doomhold is fairly quick and leaves victims with nothing more than a dire need for aspirin. I looked at her name tag, which read *Gina Wachtel.*

"Sorry, Gina," I said. "I do not envy you the headache you will have when you wake up, but until then, rest well, and dream of . . ." I trailed off. What do pharmacists dream of? Caribbean vacations paid for by Glaxo-SmithKline? Sample packs of Percocet?

Her emergency phone call was still a problem. Even though I hung up, dispatch would send somebody out regardless, so close on the heels of the previous visit to the other drugstore. The cops would come running, assuming that the same perpetrator was going Full Stupid with another hit, and they'd be right. I didn't have much time.

I knew what to look for, thanks to my experience at the first store, and I filled up my bag much faster. Though I got out of there in record time, I still heard sirens approaching as I hoofed it for the truck parked next door. Frank and Albert looked distinctly nervous sitting in the cab; they were in front of a convenience store, in full view of security cameras.

Tossing the bag of camouflaged drugs into the back of the truck, I said, "Granuaile, hop out and go into the store to buy a couple of fountain drinks. I'll join you in a moment."

"Got it, sensei." As she clambered out of the bed, I made sure to camouflage the other bag of drugs too. Since they wouldn't move now, they'd be completely invisible to anyone looking into the bed. I dissolved my own camouflage and startled Frank when I rapped on his window.

He rolled it down and said, "About time. Let's go."

"No, these are probably the same cops coming as before. They saw your truck leaving the scene of the last call and might be curious. We're going to let them be. So the story is, my sister and I are hitchhikers from Flagstaff headed to Colorado. You're taking us as far as Teec Nos Pos. Albert's got time, because the coal mine's closed, right?"

"Well, yeah, but, shit, don't you have the drugs in the back?" Albert asked.

"They're hidden. Don't worry. Let them look." The police car showed up as I said this. I tapped the door a couple of times and grinned, performance mode on. "I'm going inside to get a drink, be right back."

"I'll be damned if you are! I'm not going to jail for this!" Albert yelled.

Frank held out a hand and shook his head. "Cool it, nephew. It'll be okay."

"Uncle Frank, what the hell—"

"I know he looks like a dumbass pretty boy, but, trust me, there's more to him than that. Just calm down and play it like he said."

Albert seethed but subsided. Grateful for Frank's vote of confidence, I strode to the convenience store entrance as the police car pulled up right next to the truck and two officers got out. One went running to the back of the drugstore and the other approached Frank's window. Better him than Albert, I figured.

The convenience store smelled of stale tobacco and bleach solution, with a top note of all-beef hot dogs and stale buns. Granuaile was standing next to the fountain drink machine with two cups, looking indecisive. I grabbed one from her and murmured the plan in case we needed it, as I filled my cup with unsweetened tea. Turned out we needed it.

The police officer was waiting for us as we exited the store. He was a wee bit pudgy around the gut, stark physical evidence that police work was more about pushing paper than chasing down bad guys. Frank and Albert were out of the truck and standing near one of those freezers full of bagged ice. Both doors to the truck were open.

"Morning," the officer said to us from behind sunglasses. He gestured to the truck. "Were you two riding in this vehicle?"

"Yes. Is there a problem?"

"May I see your IDs, please?" Ah. He was one of *those* guys. We handed them over without a word. He considered them carefully for a time and then looked up at us. "Where you folks headed?"

"Colorado," I said. "We hitched a ride out of Flagstaff."

"Told ya, Gabe," Frank said.

"An' I heard ya, Frank," the officer said without turning his head, annoyance clear in his tone. I fought to suppress a smile. Frank had followed the plan. Tell the officer a simple story, and then we would come out of the store and independently verify the story. If he was truly suspicious, he'd assume we merely had our story straight, and that was true. Detective Kyle Geffert would never believe anything out of the mouth of Atticus O'Sullivan. But this officer was in a hurry, just covering the bases, and not especially worried about what appeared to be a dumbass pretty boy and his sister; our simple story, therefore, told simply, took on the veneer of truth, especially when it corroborated what Frank said—and Frank was somebody he knew and probably trusted as a *hataałii*. I tried to look as dumb and guileless as possible.

"Need you folks to stand over there," he said, gesturing to the ice cooler, "while I search the vehicle."

"Oh. Okay." Without questioning, I meekly shuffled over to stand next to Albert and Frank, and Granuaile followed silently. There was no need for us to talk to Albert and Frank. If we were hitchhikers, we wouldn't commiserate like friends. Officer Gabe stood there a moment to size us up, and then he ducked into the truck cab. He straightened a moment later, holding up a bag from the hardware store.

"You got a whole lotta nails here. What they for?"

"Tree house," Albert volunteered. "For my kid." Good one, Albert.

Officer Gabe grunted and resumed his search. He opened the glove compartment, looked behind and under the seats. No giant stash of drugs. He didn't see anything in the truck bed either.

"All right," he said, waving at the truck. "Everything seems to be fine. Sorry for the inconvenience. Have a nice day." Without another word, he turned and went to join his partner at the back of the drugstore. More sirens were approaching—an ambulance, no doubt, for the unfortunate pharmacist who'd been rendered unconscious by a mysterious apparition.

Albert waited until Officer Gabe was out of earshot and then turned to me. "Where'd you put 'em all?"

"No worries, Albert," I said. "Let's go have a nice day, build a tree house or something." The drugs were precisely where I'd left them in the bed of the truck, nicely camouflaged.

"But you still got 'em, right?"

"Absolutely."

"Well, how'd you hide 'em?" When I just shrugged and grinned, he turned to his uncle. "Where'd you find this guy? He's too weird for me."

After that, it took some convincing for Albert to drive us to Frank's house, where Frank fetched his old six-shooter for me to use.

We had one more stop to make before we could return to the mine site. At the big box store we picked up two five-gallon paint buckets, a large mixing bowl, a slotted mixing spoon, and two bottles of olive oil. Frank also snagged some food for lunch and some ice and drinks to restock the ice chest at the hogan.

Albert dropped us off at the devastated mine site and waved good-bye uncertainly to Frank. He seemed reluctant to leave his uncle all alone with the crazy white people with uncanny talents for breaking and entering and drug concealment.

I was wondering why we were alone at all. Where was Coyote?

We found a couple of unbroken shovels, and we grabbed these to dig a small hole, into which we dumped all the nails. I summoned Ferris, the iron elemental, and showed him how to bind two nails together in such a way that the pointy parts always stuck up no matter how it landed. It was basically a clever twisting; it could be done non-magically with a pair of pliers and lots of patience, but an iron elemental could do it much more quickly. Once Ferris knew what to do, he made me look like a slowpoke. The scattered nails in the hole leapt and jumped about, twisting themselves into caltrops, and I left Frank and Granuaile to fill up a five-gallon bucket with them while I turned my attention to crafting the poison.

It took an inordinate amount of time to get through the packaging and open the capsules into the mixing bowl. Thanks to Ferris, Granuaile and Frank finished with the caltrops long before I got all the pills out and emptied. Frank busied himself at the hogan while Granuaile joined me sitting on the mesa a short distance away.

"Tell me what you're doing, sensei?"

"Mixing poison. But you mean how, right?"

"Right."

"Okay. Are you comfy? This is going to take a while."

"I'm as comfy as I can be."

"All right, I'll bind your sight again and we'll go into details. How are you on your chemistry?"

"Not so good," she admitted. "Kind of clueless, actually. Do I need to get a clue?"

"If you want to be able to do the sort of thing I'll be showing you here, yes. Normally you'd go get some nightshade and let nature do all the work for you. Not that poisoning caltrops to take out madly fast shape-shifters is normal. But we don't have the time to do this conventionally. I can't shift across to Europe from here and get back before this evening. So what I'm going to do is look at the structure of these alkaloids, synthesize copies, and then distribute them in an oil base, creating a deadly ointment for our skinwalkers."

"You're doing this down at the molecular level?" she asked.

"Yep. Much of what I do in the physical world is at that level. Take the engine sabotage as an example. To fuse the pistons to the cylinder walls, I first unbind the steel on the surfaces of both, letting the elements mix a bit, then I rebind them so that it becomes a solid piece. There's a lot of molecules involved in that, but you can make it go faster by using macrobindings that determine shape and allowed molecular structures."

"A macro? So what you do is craft one binding that executes multiple tasks?"

"Exactly. Macros are your friends. If I had to bind everything individually, we'd be here forever, right? But I'm going to create three macros to make this poison and you'll see."

"Oh, so"—she pointed a finger at my necklace and waggled it around—"your charms are like macros."

"Yes. Except they execute far faster than they would if I had to speak them aloud. I took the trouble to make them because I'm paranoid and I'm always looking for an edge. They're bound to trigger words in my Old Irish headspace; I think the command and it happens. If I need a target for a spell like camouflage or night vision, then I add that, but otherwise it targets me by default. And the shape-shifting ones all include the macro to shrink or expand the necklace, depending on the form I choose."

"That is legit, sensei. I know what these do over here on this side," she said, indicating my right, where all the shape-shifting charms were, "but what's over here on the other side of your amulet?"

She put her hand gently on the left side of my face. "Turn your head so I can see them better." She squinted and leaned in closer, examining the tiny hammered patterns in the silver charms. It brought the top of her head close to my jaw, and I admired the sun-kissed vermilion highlights in her hair and the scent of strawberries and *damn* I wished the Diamondbacks would get a lights-out closer, because they kept losing all those close games by one or two runs due to a shoddy bullpen. She trailed her fingers down the side of my neck, and I reflected that I didn't like the swimming-pool remodel at Chase Field very much; the old tile pattern was much more attractive while the pool area was under the sponsorship of a different company.

"These little patterns are neat, sensei, but I don't know what they mean." Her fingers left my skin and she leaned back, and I nearly sighed with relief. It's tough to think about baseball when it's not in season. Spring training wasn't for another couple of months.

"Okay, starting from the amulet and going outward, you have camouflage, night vision, faerie specs, healing, and I don't have a name for the last one. Soulcatcher, maybe."

"Soulcatcher?"

"I've never used it," I admitted. "I don't even know if it works."

"What is it supposed to do?"

"It's supposed to save my life. But in order to test it, I'd have to die."

"Oh!" she laughed. "Well, I can see how you'd be reluctant to give that one a test-drive." She frowned abruptly as something occurred to her. "Why have it at all, then? I mean, why not put on a different charm, like one for unbinding vampires?"

"I think I'm going to pursue that," I said. "Recent events have pointed out how useful a charm like that would be. But still, if I start now, even with all the experience I've had, it'll be at least fifty years before I can complete it."

"Why so long?"

"Trial and error. I have to construct those macrobindings to execute from a silver charm via mental command in close proximity to a cold iron amulet. There are no instructions in Druidic lore to guide me through how to craft such a thing. Each of these charms is unique. So each time I test it, I'll have to have a vampire in front of me to target. That's going to be a bit dangerous. I didn't realize how dangerous they were, honestly. I'd always avoided them as a matter of course in my efforts to keep myself inconspicuous whenever I tried to settle somewhere. But to answer your earlier question, I mostly keep the soulcatcher around because I worry about accidental deaths. When I began working on it, the Morrigan and I weren't quite as chummy as we are now, and Aenghus Óg was still a dire threat."

"I see. Do you think it'll work?"

"Honestly? Considering how many times I've failed with other charms, no. I had to test them multiple times and change the bindings until I figured out something that worked. This hasn't been tested at all. It's kind of a Hail Mary."

Granuaile smiled. "But you've hailed Mary before."

"Not through my own efforts," I reminded her. "Ready for poison?" I darted a quick finger at the mixing bowl.

"Yep. Let's do this."

I spoke the binding that allowed Granuaile to see with my eyes in the magical spectrum, and then I gradually zoomed in my focus until I could see the various alkaloids on the molecular level—or, rather, a magical proxy for them. I couldn't really zoom in my eyes like a micro-scope.

"Okay, have you ever worked with design software where you can do a series of actions, record them, and then bundle them together for later use?"

"Yeah, I've done that. Photoshop."

"Exactly. So that's what I'm going to do here. See this molecule? That's atropine. This one's scopolamine, and this is hyoscyamine. It's all just carbon, nitrogen, hydro-gen, and oxygen in a specific configuration. We have plenty of those elements around. The inactive ingredi-ents in the pills, which form the majority of the material you see in the bowl, are full of those same elements. So we construct a macro that says to rebind the available material here until it's all one of those three poisons."

"Won't there be leftover stuff?"

"Yes. A few bits of carbon or hydrogen. Neutral non-active ingredients."

I painstakingly constructed the macros and then, be-fore energizing them, zoomed back out and turned off the magical spectrum so that Granuaile could see what happened.

"Watch closely."

"Watching."

I energized the bindings and the powder in the bowl stirred and poofed a wee bit.

"Wait. Is that all?" Granuaile said. "Nothing hap-pened."

"Everything happened. That was a bowl of three per-cent poison and ninety-seven percent random crap that they put in pills to make you feel like the price you're paying is worth it. Now it's almost one hundred percent poison. I never would have been able to do that before I took chemistry."

"You got a degree?"

"No, I sat camouflaged in the classes and bought the

texts. This is now an extremely toxic mixing bowl. Would you mind terribly opening a bottle of olive oil? I don't want to risk tearing these gloves at all." She returned shortly with an opened bottle for me. "Pour slowly while I stir?"

"Sure," she said. "Why the olive oil?"

"It acts as the carrier. This is basically going to be a thin ointment. Once this is all mixed and the alkaloids are distributed evenly, we'll coat the caltrops with it and we'll be good to go."

We worked in silence for a few minutes as we mixed the alkaloids with the base. When I was satisfied, I said, "Lovely. Now we just have to coat the caltrops with it without accidentally poisoning ourselves."

"That sounds perfectly relaxing, sensei," Granuaile said. She put on two pairs of gloves, and we arranged a procedure where we coated small batches of caltrops in the bowl, fished them out with the slotted spoon, let the excess oil drain, and then placed them into the second bucket. It was monotonous labor made edgy by the knowledge that a careless splash could kill us. We finished with only a couple of hours to spare before sundown. We hauled the weaponized caltrops up to the hogan, where Frank was sitting cross-legged on the floor in some kind of meditation. We tried to be quiet as we raided the cooler for cheese and crackers and ice-cold cans of tea.

Frank heard us anyway and grunted as he opened an eye. "You all ready, Mr. Collins?"

"As ready as I can be," I said, nodding.

"Good. So am I." His other eye opened and he began to clamber to his feet.

"You are? For what?"

"For killin' skinwalkers, o' course," he said, brushing dust off his knees.

I held up a hand. "Frank, I didn't ask you to take part

in this. You oughtta get out of here, actually; give your nephew a call."

"Naw, I'm doin' this with you. How many more chances am I gonna have to get me a piece of skin-walker? Think I'll keep my gun. You slow 'em down for me and I'll plug 'em good."

I exchanged a worried glance with Granuaile. "Frank, I can speed myself up enough to have a chance of hitting them. You're not going to have an advantage like that. You only had the one chance to call Monster Slayer."

"I know. But you can't speak my language. What if they wanna talk before killin' us? Whattaya gonna do then, play charades? Look, son, this is what bein' a *hataałii* is all about. I'm s'posed to protect my people from evil. Now, this evil comes from First World; it's a Diné thing, and it's threatening Diné people, and I'm damned if I'll let someone else take care of my problems for me. I'm goin'."

There is no arguing with pride. Jesus and the Morrigan couldn't talk me out of going to Asgard, and I wasn't going to be able to talk Frank out of doing this. I gave him a tight little nod and began to worry about how I would protect him.

"All right, Frank," I said. "I have a bit more business to conduct before we do this. Excuse me?"

He and Granuaile nodded at me and I exited to find a shady spot—not too tough near sundown. Underneath a shaggy-barked juniper, I sat on the ground and took the opportunity to have an overdue conversation with Colorado.

//Druid greets Colorado / Harmony//

//Harmony// came the reply.

//Coal mine stopped / Will monitor / Query: Move gold now?//

//Yes / Coal stopped / Gratitude / Keep coal mine quiet / Will move gold//

//Harmony// I said.

Colorado agreed.

Not for the first time, I reflected that the earth is so much simpler to deal with than people. On the other hand, the earth never gets my jokes.

Chapter 28

Frank and I chose a spot near the south butte, facing the north butte from whence the skinwalkers always appeared. With the approach to our backs defended, I took the five-gallon bucket of poisoned caltrops and carefully scattered them in front of us in a half circle, backing up as I went. I spread them out over fifteen feet or so to make sure the skinwalkers would not leap over them. Frank surveyed the scatter pattern uncertainly.

"Awful lot of places for them to step without hitting any," he observed.

"You can head back into the hogan if you want," I said. "Granuaile would probably appreciate the company." Her SUV in the roof was still a weakness, but the hogan provided more protection than did the open air. We had re-rigged the fire trap on the roof, and she was ready with a lighter if she needed it.

"Hell with that," he said, his bravado returning. Then it faded as he considered the caltrops again. What looked like a lot of defense confined in a bucket was somewhat sparse when spread out on the ground. "Are you sure that's the whole buttload?"

"Yep. Look. Let's say they get through—I don't think they will, but let's pretend. You stand sideways and protect your throat and guts, okay? You also protect your femoral artery that way. Just try to push or roll them into the caltrops."

"And shoot 'em."

"Right. And I'll try to stab 'em." I had Moralltach with me, but I hadn't told Frank about its magical properties. It occurred to me that perhaps I should. "Frank, whatever you do, don't cut yourself with my sword, okay? Even by accident."

"Is it poisoned too?"

"Something like that. It's enchanted with some Druidic hoodoo. You won't walk away."

"So if you hit 'em with that, they're dead?"

"Right. Not instantly, though. Takes a few seconds to work."

"Huh. What happens if the skinwalkers push us onto the caltrops?"

"Then we are most likely not going to live much longer, because they will tear us apart if we're on the ground. However, if you find yourself with the luxury of time, you can try this." I pulled from my pocket one last unopened box from my drugstore raids: a single disposable dose of physostigmine salicylate. It was the only one I'd found. "That contains a syringe with the antidote for tropane alkaloids. Stab yourself with it and press the plunger." Frank grunted, shoved it into his front pocket, and then thought better of it and moved it to his back pocket.

"Shouldn't ever have a needle next to your johnson," he explained.

We watched the shadows lengthen as the sun sank below the sandstone of Tyende Mesa. It was beautiful and quiet and hid an evil against which I had no magical defenses.

Frank looked down at his shoes and scuffed the ground a bit. "I'm gonna say some stuff. Prayers. Get myself in balance, *hózhǫ,* in case this don't work out the way we want. So, you know. Don't mind me."

"Good idea," I said. I could probably do with some prayer myself. But praying to Brighid or any of the Tuatha Dé Danann would probably be unwise at this point, since I was supposed to be dead to them. Praying to the Morrigan would probably do me no good. I noticed that she hadn't shown up to help out when that one skinwalker snacked on my neck. True, I hadn't died, thanks to Coyote, but she had warned me before about much lesser threats than that one. It suggested that I'd failed somehow to be specific enough in the wording of our deal. She had already made clear that she preferred to honor the letter of agreements rather than the spirit of them. If I called to her now, she might think I wanted her to pay a social visit, and that sounded about as blissful as cuddling with a porcupine.

I could certainly use some balance in my life. There had been little enough of that since I'd decided to fight Aenghus Óg—though even the smidgen of balance I'd achieved as a fugitive was a joke: If my inner peace was a calm sea, then my constant paranoia was the wind that chopped the surface. My two centuries with Tahirah were probably the closest thing to peace I've ever had.

Once the sun set, I cast night vision on Frank and myself. He stood as I had suggested, protecting his vitals. He held his gun in his right hand. I centered myself and placed myself en garde with Moralltach.

"Here, kitty kitty," I said softly. "Come on, evil kitties."

They attacked a few minutes later. We heard them snarl, and that was all the warning we got before a couple of blurs rushed at us, so fast that we didn't have time to say anything obvious to each other like "Here they come" or "Weapons hot!" It was more of a single

Doppler-shifted cat screech; we heard them from a distance and they seemed to nearly catch up with the sound and bawl right in front of us with that unholy, shornsteel sound. Suddenly they were visible, scrabbling and braking on the dirt not ten yards away and trying to backpedal as they hit the caltrops and the maddened charge died within them. Frank raised his gun and fired six times, but they saw his arm move and they actually dodged, their bodies blurring and sustaining those feline *rrreoowr* sounds you hear in catfights. They came to a halt outside the range of the caltrops, two panting bobcats with problems in their paws. They rolled onto their backs and began to shake and twitch all over. At first I thought they were trying to dislodge the caltrops in their paws, but then I saw the bobcat pelts slough away and two naked men remained on top of them, steaming in the cool night air, as if they'd been born that way. They had caltrops stuck in their palms and on the soles of their feet, but these they calmly plucked out and tossed away, ignoring the blood and making no further sounds of pain. They stood, picked up their bobcat skins, and regarded us with orange glowing eyes. It was my first really good look at them, and I was surprised at their slight stature. They were extremely lean, with the physique of long-distance runners, so bereft of fat on their frames that their muscles looked a bit too well defined—I thought I could see individual fibers, and there were definitely prominent veins standing out against the skin. They probably weighed a hundred pounds, if that. But I don't think I've ever seen more burning hatred in a pair of eyes, not even those of demons. One of them spat out something in Navajo.

"Frank. What did he say, Frank?"

"He said, 'You and the white man will die tonight.'"

The two skinwalkers turned and jogged back the way they came, carrying their bobcat skins rolled up underneath their arms. They showed no ill effects whatsoever from the caltrops.

"I don't get it," I said. "They should be staggering around and having trouble breathing at this point. They each had four or five caltrops in them, enough poison to kill them twice. They should be dying, not trotting away for a bottle of Gatorade or whatever it is they're doing."

"I told ya it probably wouldn't work, but you wouldn't listen to me."

"Well, now what?"

"Well, now we're fucked, white man."

Chapter 29

From the unnatural quiet, a thin, muffled voice rose in query. "Sensei?" It was Granuaile in the hogan. "You still alive out there?"

"Yes!" I called, my voice echoing back to me off the butte in front of me. "For the moment, anyway," I added in softer tones.

Frank snorted and said, "You got that right." He pulled some bullets from his jacket pocket and began to grimly reload his six-shooter. "Don't know why I'm reloading. It ain't like I'm gonna hit anything."

"Is it safe to come out?" Granuaile called.

"No! Stay in there until sunrise unless I say it's safe. We're not finished. Round two coming up."

The metallic *click* and *whir* of Frank's gun served to order my thoughts. I had clearly underestimated the powers of those First World spirits. Physical healing, like what they did after getting shot and speared, is a very different process from breaking down invasive poisons, and I hadn't thought they would be able to do it. Their magic was so alien to me, and I had to admit I was outclassed by it. Those First World spirits were able to turn very wee men into killing machines . . . which made me wonder.

"Frank?"

"Yeah?"

"Why did they take off? I'm asking because I figure you must have better insights into First World psychology than me. I mean, after they casually plucked my brilliant plan to destroy them out of their hands and feet, why didn't they dance past the remaining caltrops and take us out?"

His gun now fully reloaded, Frank squatted down on his haunches to consider. I could hear everything, from the rustle of his jeans to the slight shift of gravel underneath his boots. Places like this, so far from the ambient noise of cities, were a feast for the ears.

" 'S a good question, Mr. Collins." He peered up at me. "That name of yours don't suit you very well. Ain't your real name, is it?"

"No. I don't tell many people my real name. But you can call me Atticus if you want, when we're alone like this."

"Atticus? What kind o' name is that?"

"Ever read *To Kill a Mockingbird* by Harper Lee?"

"Naw, but I've heard of it."

"Well, there's a man in it named Atticus Finch. Brilliant man—and a brave one. Stood for justice in the face of sheer stupidity, despite what it cost him and his family. I know he's just fictional, but he was the kind of man I'd like to be. It's the kind of name that leaves you room to grow. I need a name like that. Reminds me that I'm not perfect."

Frank sounded mildly incredulous. "You need a reminder of that?"

"Well, yeah," I admitted. "Sometimes I get to feeling pretty smug, because I've managed to dodge the wrath of a few gods. But days like this remind me I'm not all that hot. And the name helps. No matter how old I get, I keep running into people who are smarter, nobler, and kinder. I really ought to start listening to them and telling my pride to shut up. I had gods tell me not to go to

Asgard. I had witches tell me not to go to Flagstaff. You told me this plan wouldn't work. But I barreled ahead anyway for my own reasons. I still have plenty of growing to do."

"How old are you, anyway? Twenty-two?"

"I know I don't look it, but I'm older than you, Frank. Quite a bit older."

Frank grunted and considered my original question. "All right, Atticus who's older 'n me. The only reason I can think of for them leavin' like that is that they're cookin' up some other way to kill us. Some way they think will work better, more surefire. Because there's one thing about those caltrops, something I didn't think about before: Those skinwalkers are gonna have to look where they step if they wanna get through 'em. And if they have to do that, then they can't be lookin' at us at the same time. That ain't somethin' they'd be willin' to risk, not with you standin' there with a badass sword in your hand and me with a gun in mine. So they're gonna come back soon with some way to get around the caltrops."

"Of course!" I said, a grin splitting my face. "Frank, you're a genius!"

"Hell yes I am. What are you talkin' about?"

"They have a bird form," I explained. "Don't know what kind of bird, but I bet they went to get their bird skins. Or feathers. Whatever."

Frank peered up at me. "How do you know that?"

"My hound and I tracked them the other day, after that first night's attack. Found bird tracks. Big ones."

Frank frowned. "Only big birds around these parts are carrion birds. Crows and ravens and shit like that."

"These weren't crows. Didn't have that smell."

"That smell? You can tell birds apart by smell?"

"Well, yeah. I'm a shape-shifter, Frank." A new plan gelled in my head, and I carefully resheathed Moralltach before removing the scabbard altogether as a prelude to removing my clothes. Once that process began, Frank required an explanation.

"Uh, why are you gettin' naked?" he asked.

"Can't change forms with jeans and a shirt on, can I? Clothes get in the way when you want to fly."

"Are you shittin' me right now?" He rose from his squatting position.

"Nope. I'm even starting to feel smug again. Switch places with me, Frank, need you on my left."

"What? Why?"

"Are you left-handed or right-handed?"

"Right."

"That's what I thought, so I need you on my left."

"You ain't makin' no sense at all," he said as he exchanged positions with me.

"Well, trust me, Frank. Hate to throw your own words back at you, but I'm not just a dumbass pretty boy. Sometimes I'm kind of smart and pretty. I have a plan."

"Hope it works better than the last one."

"Me too. All right, tell me what kind of big birds you see out here besides ravens and crows."

"Vultures. They call 'em turkey vultures, to be exact."

"Yes, that works. And they're pretty big?"

"Damn big."

"And they're black, I'm guessing."

"You guess right. Heads are red, but rest of 'em is black."

"So that's their plan, Frank. They're going to put down their bobcat skins and put on their vulture skins, and then they're going to glide right over those caltrops and drop down on top of us like airborne ninjas."

Frank looked up. "Shit, you're right. It's damn sneaky, and it's precisely what an air spirit from First World would want to do."

"And once they're in this circle with us, we don't stand a chance of matching their speed."

"That's for sure," Frank agreed. "If they get in here, we got ourselves a snake's chance in a typing contest."

"So this is what we do." I explained my new plan, which involved him getting back down on his haunches and placing his right arm as flat as possible on the ground.

"You know I ain't no spring chicken, right?" he said.

"Spring just this once for me, Frank."

Frank's eyes were on mine but then shifted over my right shoulder to the northeast, past the looming wall of the northern butte. "They're coming. At least one of 'em is. Don't see the other one." He squatted down as I instructed, and I inched forward so that my toes and the pads of my feet rested on his right forearm. The bulk of my weight was still on my heels, but I could shift forward in an instant.

"Don't cut yourself on the sword," I reminded him, though I was the one holding it at the moment.

"I'll remember," Frank assured me.

Grasping Moralltach firmly in my right hand, I looked up to the sky to spot the skinwalkers. The stars are so bright outside cities; it's like those allergy commercials where they apply a blur filter and then wipe it away to imply that the entire world will be better if you swallow their pills. It is naturally clear like that inside the boundaries of the Navajo Nation—no drugs necessary. And so I spotted the skinwalker after only a few seconds' search.

His companion—or, rather, his brother—was there too, spiraling down onto our position on the south face of the southernmost defile of the Tyende Mesa, and once they had descended far enough, I asked Frank if he was ready.

"Ready," he affirmed.

"Now," I said, as I dropped Moralltach behind me

and triggered the charm that would shift me to a great horned owl. My feet turned into talons and my arms into wings. Frank rose from his squat and lifted his arm over his head, effectively launching me skyward before the nearest skinwalker had time to register what was happening.

Turkey vultures, for all their bulk, are not built for aerial combat. They are scavengers, built to eat dead meat quickly and contract few (if any) diseases from digesting said meat. They are constructed to glide for eons in search of immobile snack foods. So when they encounter a flying predator used to snatching extremely mobile prey like rabbits and mice, they are hopelessly outclassed—even if they have First World spirits juicing up their systems.

I tangled with one of the vultures and it screeched in a combination of rage and astonishment, like a high school boy might when a teacher boldly confiscates his bag of Cheetos. It tore at me with its talons and pecked at me with its beak even as I tore at it—I felt bits of rib meat and my stomach being torn away—but I activated my healing charm and did my best to get hold of its neck with my talons. It thrashed desperately; its wingspan was as great as mine, if not greater, and we began to fall, since neither of us could beat the air sufficiently when we were beating each other. But I managed to roll around to the top and lock on to its neck with one taloned foot and yank upward, and this had a singular, unexpected effect on the creature. The vulture skin made a sucking, popping sound and the human fell from underneath it, screaming, to fall headfirst and splatter wetly on the mesa strewn with poisoned nails.

It did not immediately move afterward and pretend that nothing had happened. It did not, in fact, move at all. *Victory!* I thought, since the vulture skin was still in my talons. I let it drop harmlessly onto Tyende Mesa.

But the other skinwalker saw his brother broken on the ground and cried out, abandoning subterfuge and diving straight for Frank, perceiving him to be the softer target.

They didn't have unnatural speed, I saw, in the air: They could move only as fast as the air would allow the physiognomy of their forms. As bobcats they could take advantage of unnatural musculature. As vultures they could rely on aerodynamics only—their stronger shoulders would allow them to flap more than vultures normally do, perhaps, but it wouldn't allow them to fly at peregrine-falcon speeds.

The *hataałii* saw the skinwalker coming and thrust Moralltach high above his head to make landing difficult. I tacked about and adjusted my course before diving after it. Owls dive faster than vultures; they are designed to do so. I hit him at an angle from above, talons first, and bore him to the ground, barely missing the blade of Moralltach. The creature shrieked and began to bubble and buck bizarrely underneath my grasp. It was more than I could hold on to as an owl, so I shifted directly to a wolfhound and quickly moved to lock my jaws on the back of its neck. As I did so, it shifted as well, from a vulture to a human with the vulture skin and feathers lying on top, but it seemed involuntary. My cold-iron aura, I realized, was causing the transformation to the natural human form; that was why the first one had fallen out of his skin once I'd clutched him in my talons and why the skin of the bobcat had rippled as it chewed on my neck before Coyote shot it.

The neck I was after wasn't so scrawny anymore but was still within the compass of my jaws. The problem now was that there were human limbs and musculature to deal with, and he had a speed and will to wield them viciously. Even as Frank yelled a "Hyaaah!" and brought Moralltach clumsily down across the back of the skinwalker, the creature's left arm buffeted me backward. This gave him time to roll over and kick Frank powerfully in the gut before I could descend upon him again. Frank staggered backward, Moralltach sailing from his hand as he reflexively sought to cushion his fall and protect his head. He fell outside our circle and onto the waiting caltrops—or so I imagined, judging by peripheral vision and what I heard, which was a dismayed "Shit!" I was too busy tearing after the skinwalker's throat. The creature punched my ribs so mightily with his right hand that I heard them crack.

In the movies, you go flying away into the night after a shot like that, landing ruinously against a rock or cement wall, and somehow your mere flesh and bone shatters said rock or cement and you get up afterward and brush dust off your shoulders as the soundtrack swells dramatically. In reality, what happens is that your lungs empty of all air and you fall over—and if you do fly into a rock wall, it will shatter your bones long before you shatter it.

My healing charm was already working on the flesh the other skinwalker had torn as a bird, but it did nothing to reinflate my lungs. As I lay gasping, the cursed thing—Robert or Ray Peshlakai, if Sophie was right—staggered to his feet to finish me off. Instead, he collapsed on top of me, further injuring my ribs as black ruin suffused his entire twitching body, spreading from the wound that Frank had delivered with Moralltach. Unlike my Fourth World poisons, the Fae enchantment on the sword was more than the First World spirit could heal—Fae magic being as alien to First World as the other way around. He died with a hoarse cry of terror, and I think I might have joined him—partly because it was the only sound I could manage and partly because watching a head shrivel and turn black right next to yours is profoundly disturbing.

I couldn't kick him off me, nor could I struggle out from underneath him, injured as I was. I would have to shift back to human to help Frank and call Granuaile for help.

Shifting with bone injuries is never a great idea, but I didn't see what choice I had. The transition nearly turned the cracks in my ribs to breaks, and my half-strangled cry of pain, when added to all the other cries in the night, caused Granuaile to call out from the hogan.

"Atticus? You all right?"

I didn't answer right away. I would be fine eventually, but I was worried about Frank and trying to recover my breath. He rolled back into the circle, several caltrops sticking out of his back and perhaps more elsewhere that I couldn't see. His right hand fumbled into his back pocket for the antidote I'd given him.

"Yes!" I managed to say, trying to encourage him. I shoved the blackened corpse off me with revulsion and winced at the pain the exertion caused. I began to crawl toward Frank. His hand was shaking as he took the box out of his pocket. He dropped it to the ground in front of him and gasped—his breath was wheezy and un-steady already.

"Let me help, Frank," I said, shutting down my pain to allow me to move faster. He had three caltrops lodged in his back and I yanked these out as quickly as I could, being careful about the points, then reached for the an-tidote. The box was mashed up a bit, and that worried me. I remembered how he'd fallen. "No, no, no . . ." I breathed, my fingers scrabbling at the box to get it open. The syringe inside was broken, crushed when Frank's full weight had fallen on it.

Frank's elbow trembled and unlocked on him and he collapsed, then rolled over, clutching his chest. His breath came in short gasps and he was in obvious distress.

"Hold on, Frank, I'm going to try something," I said, discarding the useless antidote. I reached for the side of his neck, intending to heal him directly in spite of the risk to myself—if I caused him any harm while using magic, my own life would be forfeit. He clutched at my arm and the ghost of a smile passed his lips as his eyes flicked to the dead skinwalker.

"Got . . . the fucker," he whispered.

"Yeah, you got him," I agreed. "Just wait a sec, I'm going to fix this."

But his hand left my arm and returned to his chest, his eyes squinting shut in pain. This was wrong. The poison shouldn't be acting this quickly. I should have time to break down the toxins so the ambulance could get here. I should be able to keep him alive until he got to the hospital, where they'd have the antidote for alkaloid poisoning.

"Frank, are you having a heart attack?" My fingers sought the pulse in his neck and found it, but then it disappeared even as all the tension drained from his limbs.

"No!" I flung his hand away from his chest and began CPR. There are no bindings to restart a stopped heart. All healing depends on a functioning circulatory system, and all life needs a will to live. I began shouting at him as I pressed his chest. "Frank, come back! I have something to tell you! Don't go, Frank! There's so much I can teach you, and I need you to teach me! Frank! Breathe!"

A chill wrapped itself around me, and I scrambled away from Frank and turned on my faerie specs, dreading what I would see but needing the confirmation. Frank's *ch'įįdii* was there, looking at me. It was a pale, weak, nebulous thing compared to Darren's, barely more than a whisper of breath in the cold, and it meant

Frank wasn't going to come back. It also meant that most of Frank, gods bless him, was already in harmony with the universe. I knelt there, defeated, and stared at it. It returned my stare with cold equanimity.

"All right, then, Frank," I said softly, holding out my arm and letting the *ch'įįdii* wrap itself around me and disperse. "Those were good last words. Go and be at peace."

Frank's *ch'įįdii* was merely the smallest wisp of a ghost, and if it had any power to affect the living, I can't imagine it was capable of doing much beyond bringing on a bad mood. It wasn't the only *ch'įįdii* hanging around, however. When I turned around to see the *ch'įįdiis* of the skinwalkers, I flinched backward. Their *ch'įįdiis* were gothic horrors, larger than the men themselves, and far, far worse than Darren's. They pulsed and writhed with disharmony, and I realized that they each had two sets of eyes. There were two things attached to those bodies, and they were intertwined as well—a black menace and a blacker one.

"Well, hello there, First World spirits," I said. "Guess you're bound to those men a bit closer than you'd wish right now."

The nearest one—the one Frank had killed—lunged in my direction. I was beyond the length of its metaphorical chain, however, and grateful for it. I wasn't anxious to plunge my arm into that darkness; it wasn't a simple *ch'įįdii* to disperse but a being with its own identity and a sense of purpose.

The rumble of an engine and the yellow cones of headlights tore my gaze away from the spooky eyes in the darkness. I dispelled my faerie specs but kept the night vision.

"Granuaile!" I called. "It's okay to come out. See who's in the truck."

I retrieved my clothes, moving a bit gingerly due to my

injured ribs. I pulled on my jeans but left off the shirt, since my wounds weren't fully closed and still rather bloody. I wiped some of the blood off with the shirt and focused my efforts on closing up the skin.

When the truck engine cut off, I heard two doors slam. Then Granuaile's voice rang out, raw with anger.

"You got a lot of nerve showing up now, you bastard!"

It was Coyote. And he'd brought a friend.

Chapter 30

I searched frantically for Moralltach. I didn't know what Coyote's intentions were, but his arrival at this particular moment spoke of calculation on his part. He was far too conveniently present after the skinwalkers had been dispatched. Stepping carefully around the caltrops, I found the sword and picked it up, then minced my steps again going the other way so that I could give Coyote my two cents' worth.

"Now, calm down there, Miss Druid," he was saying. "I ain't the bad guy here, not by a long shot."

"Well, you're damn sure the coward here," she said.

"Coward, you say? Who let himself get chopped to pieces for the sake of your master? Who let himself be a doggie treat for a giant hound from Hel? Was that a coward that did that?"

"Where have you *been* while we've been dealing with your mess?" she demanded, ignoring his retort.

"I wouldn't mind hearing the answer to that myself," I said as I approached.

Coyote turned and spied me coming. "Ah, Mr. Druid. A good evenin' to you."

Apparently we didn't have to worry about using fake identities in front of this stranger. "Whatever, Coyote. Where have you been?"

"I been down to Many Farms, messin' with the many

farmers. Runnin' some errands on your behalf while I was at it."

"On my behalf?"

"Yeah, but we can talk about that later. How are the skinwalkers?"

"You know very well how they are, or you wouldn't be here."

Coyote grinned shamelessly. "That's right. You kilt 'em for me, just like I knew you would. You got some o' that noble shit in your aura, you know that?"

"I can't see my own aura, Coyote, only the white glow of my magic."

"Well, it looks like a really pompous yellow. Most self-important color I ever did see."

"Frank is dead, Coyote," I said, and Granuaile gasped. "You brought him in on this project, and now he's gone because of you."

"You're lookin' at it the wrong way, Mr. Druid. Two skinwalkers are gone because of him. That *hataałii* over there was one o' the best men I knew. He did what was right for the Diné. And that's what I'm doin' too." He turned back to his truck, and his boots crunched on the gravel of the mesa as he walked to the bed. The man who'd gotten out of the passenger side of the truck had said nothing, but a tiny smirk on his face indicated that he found our irritation amusing. His hair was long and straight underneath a white cowboy hat. He wore blue jeans and boots, a black undershirt, and a blue denim jacket over it. He held what looked like a *jish* in his right hand. Perhaps he was another *hataałii*. Granuaile followed close on Coyote's heels.

"And what about Darren Yazzie?" she asked.

"Look, Miss Druid," he said as he pulled a red plastic gasoline container and a thick manila envelope out of the back. Most of the good humor had bled out of his tone and now he sounded tired. "I didn't know they was gonna get kilt. But I sacrificed myself twice and saved Mr. Druid's life while I was at it. So I'll be waitin' for a thank-you note or maybe a nice batch of cookies from you. I think I've earned a coupla cookies." He stalked away from the truck and headed for the nearest skin-walker corpse. The anonymous second man kept pace with him.

"I don't make anyone cookies!" Granuaile growled at his back.

"Ain't it time you learned?" Coyote said over his shoulder. "You 'n Betty Crocker can bake someone happy."

Granuaile balled her fists and started after him, and I put a hand on her shoulder.

"Hold on, Granuaile, he's just pushing your buttons."

She shrugged off my hand and whirled to face me, pointing at Coyote's back. "I'm going to kick him where it counts and give him a sad sack. I'm tired of his chauvinist bullshit and his cavalier attitude about people dying for him while he runs off and hides somewhere."

"Well, you're welcome to try that a bit later when he's not expecting it," I said in low tones. "Right now I want to see what he's up to and meet this other guy, so hang back a bit and follow my lead, okay?"

She gathered herself with some effort and exhaled, letting the anger go for now. "Okay, sensei."

We followed Coyote and his friend up to the nearest skinwalker body, the one Frank had killed with Morall-tach. We stayed outside the ring of caltrops. Coyote hardly spared the body a glance. He directed his gaze above it, where the *ch'įįdii* was. I flipped my faerie specs on to take another look. If anything, it looked worse than before. The seething blacker portion of the spirit was overwhelming the darkness of the *ch'įįdii*.

"Ah, yes, this is one of the old ones," Coyote said. "He's tryin' to break loose. Give 'im all night and he'll probably manage it. The *ch'įįdii* will start to disperse, and then he'll be free to go find some other black soul to turn into a skinwalker. Can't let that happen."

"Nope," said the mysterious man.

The last time I'd looked at Coyote in the magical spectrum was back at a high school courtyard in Mesa. We'd been fighting a fallen angel together, and at the time I'd found him somewhat mesmerizing to look at; he was a kaleidoscope of shifting colors, an infinite potential of shapes confined to this human form only so long as he willed it. He still looked that way, but what surprised me was that the nameless man beside him looked precisely the same.

"Hey, Coyote, who's your friend?"

"That's Coyote. Coyote, meet Mr. Druid."

"Howdy, Mr. Druid," the man said. His voice was deep, like Michael Clarke Duncan's, a low resonant bass that you felt as much as heard.

"Hi," I said, then frowned at Coyote. "What do you mean?" I asked. "Is he from another tribe?"

"Nope, he's from the Diné," Coyote replied, obviously enjoying my confusion. "You don't know our stories as well as you should. Most tribes have only the one Coyote, but in some versions of the *Diné Bahane'*—the tale of Emergence—there are two."

"I'm Great Coyote," the deep voice said. "Or sometimes Coyote Who Was Formed in the Water."

"And I'm the one the Diné call *Áłtsé Hashké*," Coyote said, then tossed his head at his companion. "He definitely has the better reputation. I get blamed for everything."

"Two Coyotes?" I said. "What should I call you? Black Hat and White Hat? I can't call you both the same thing."

Coyote in the white hat said, "I tell people sometimes

that my name is Joe," he said. "Does that work for you?"

"Very well," I said, and turned to Coyote in the black hat, who'd apparently been playing me for a sucker much longer than I thought. "And what about you?"

"You ain't gonna call me by my real name, so just keep callin' me Coyote and that way you won't get confused."

It was no wonder, I thought, that Frank hadn't been sure which one of the First People Mr. Benally was. His comment that they were "capable of trickin' a fella pretty good" made much more sense now. To my magical sight, Coyote and Joe looked exactly the same. There was no way to tell them apart. Only in the visible spectrum did they appear any different, and I'm sure that was by choice.

"Gotta thank you, Mr. Druid," Coyote said. "Haven't been able to get a shot at these boys in a long time."

Joe nodded. "That's right. This time we should be able to take care of them."

"Take care of them how?" I gestured at the red gasoline containers. "You going to burn the bodies?"

"Well, for a start. If we stopped there, then the First World spirits could take off," Coyote explained.

I was lost for a moment, but then I nodded. "Oh, I see. Because they're bound to the *ch'įįdii* and the *ch'įįdii* are bound to the bodies."

"Right. So if we just burn 'em and disperse the ghosts, then they'll hightail it to Window Rock or someplace, turning regular assholes into superfast shape-shifting cannibal assholes."

"Don't you have a ritual to combat these guys?"

Coyote lifted his hat and scratched his head. "Well, Mr. Druid, it's all defense and no offense. It's protection like the Blessing Way, and there's some exorcism in the Enemy Way—but there's nothin' to kill 'em with. All the killing rituals are on their side—'cause they're practicin' *Áńt'įįh,* the Witchery Way. Sometimes we get lucky and can turn their own spells against 'em. But these guys got smart and stopped doin' ceremonies like that a long time ago, stopped spreadin' their corpse powder around. Ain't a doubt in my mind these spirits were behind that. They used their speed and strength to kill people and left me an' the *hataałiis* nothin' to work with."

"So how do you kill them?"

"You *can't* kill 'em," Joe said, his voice cut with a note of impatience. "They're damn spirits. All you can do is send 'em somewhere else—somewhere safe."

"An' that means sendin' 'em back to First World," Coyote said. "These things have been playin' around up here for far too long. Once we get 'em back there, they'll be stuck."

"Why would they be stuck?" Granuaile asked. "Is there flypaper for spirits down there or something?"

Joe laughed and squatted down on his haunches to untie his *jish*. "That'd be nice, 'cause then they wouldn't bother us when we visit. But Coyote means they won't be able to leave First World again. The doorway to Second World was closed long ago, an' now only he an' I can go back there an' return again." He peered up at Coyote. "We're gonna need to get these caltrops outta the way, though, before we can start."

Granuaile said, "There's a couple of brooms in the hogan. I'll go grab them." As her footsteps crunched behind me, I felt foolish standing there with a naked sword, so I gingerly crept back into the circle, keeping my distance from the skinwalker's body, and recovered the scabbard. I sheathed Moralltach and slung it over my back. Coyote tossed his manila envelope onto the ground behind him; whatever was in there wasn't important to him right now.

Inside Joe's *jish* were some feathers, rattles, pouches of

herbs, and two sacred buckskins. He divided the contents with Coyote.

When Granuaile returned with two brooms, we carefully brushed all the caltrops to the south side against the wall. She saw Frank there and quietly said, "He was such a sweet man. How did he die?"

"Heart attack. They didn't get him, though. Other way around."

She didn't reply, only nodded, and then leaned her broom up against the wall of the butte. The two Coyotes were murmuring to each other in their own language. When they finished, Joe set off toward the other skinwalker, who had fallen to his death some thirty yards away to the west. Coyote stepped closer to the blackened one that Frank had killed and motioned us over.

"Wanna tell ya somethin' in case somethin'—well, just in case, all right? See, in the beginnin', me an' Joe weren't much differ'nt than that thing you see there." He pointed at the boiling blackness of the First World spirit. "Except we were a whole lot sexier, o' course. First Man and First Woman, they were spirits of the air too. We were people of mist, if you wanna think about it that way. An' as we rose up through the worlds, we changed, an' these bodies were given to us by the Holy People." He tossed his head toward the spirits before continuing, "These fuckers, however, came up with us from First World, but they never got their bodies. They're unevolved, see? Unless you wanna count the fact that they've turned from plain ornery to pigshit evil. Thing is, like Joe said, we can't do anything to 'em when they're spirits. So we're gonna give 'em bodies. Their own bodies, not somebody else's body they can possess and turn to the Witchery Way. Then we step on 'em."

"Beg your pardon?" Granuaile said.

"They're insects," Coyote said. "Not sure what kind.

Could be ants, could be those hard-shelled bigass beetles, could be dragonflies or locusts, but insects no matter what. When we get through with this ceremony, they'll be bugs, and we can kill 'em easy and send 'em back to First World. They won't be coming back, though. So you two can help by kinda standin' over there." He pointed to a space between the two skinwalker corpses. "Once they're bugs, they're gonna try to get away—they'll skitter around or fly or somethin'—and we could use your help to chase 'em down."

"What if they do get away?" Granuaile asked.

Coyote shrugged. "Ain't that big a deal. What's the average life span of a bug? They'll die eventually. A bird will eat 'em if we're lucky. They'll be on the slow train to First World instead of the express, that's all. The important thing is they'll be mortal and won't be able to harm anyone after this. We're gonna get started now before the *ch'įįdii* start to disperse, all right?"

He bent down and grabbed a pouch of corn pollen and an eagle feather.

"Um—" I said, but Coyote started to sing before I could form a coherent question, and I knew he wouldn't stop for my benefit now that he'd begun. Joe's voice joined in from over by the other skinwalker, and that left Granuaile and me with nothing to do but worry.

My apprentice asked the philosophical question first. "Is he trying to create something out of nothing, sensei? Can he do that?"

"I'm not sure," I said. "Maybe."

"But how?"

"I don't know. Let's go stand over there where he asked us to."

Granuaile kept talking as we moved. "Don't you know how the stories went? How did First Man and First Woman get their bodies? You can't tell me you don't remember."

"Well, I'm fairly certain the process didn't involve gasoline," I said, watching the two Coyotes sprinkle gas on the skinwalkers' bodies as they sang and danced around them clockwise.

She snorted. "That's a safe bet."

"I understand why they're doing it: They have to un-bind the spirit from the *ch'įįdii* before they can shove it into a body. It just seems to be a very modern way to do it. You'd think they'd use some pine or juniper or some-thing."

Granuaile frowned. "Yeah, that *is* weird. He seemed like he was in a hurry, though."

"True. And it's not an important part of giving the spirit a body. The buckskin has a lot to do with that." Both Coyotes had set the bodies on fire now and the spirits were billowing, straining to get away. They defi-nitely did not like the light. Nor did they want to be bound to those *ch'įįdiis* anymore.

"What do they do with the buckskin?"

"In the *Diné Bahane'*, there are a few different stories where the Holy People gave spirits a corporeal form. Usually they covered up corn or special stones with sa-cred buckskins and then invited the Wind to blow un-derneath the skin. *Nílch'i* was the name of the Wind, and it always had to blow four times—four was an im-portant number. But the idea was that you had a Breath of Life thing going on there, like you see in many crea-tion stories."

"Oh, cool." Granuaile flashed a quick smile at me. "I like how certain ideas seem to be almost universal."

"I dig that too. It's cool how almost every culture has some sort of trickster figure like Coyote, who's always cocking something up—oh, shit." I paled.

"What?"

"This could be very bad." The Coyotes had unfurled their sacred buckskins over the burning bodies and briefly let them rest on top, smothering the flames before lifting the buckskins and letting the Wind blow underneath them for the first time. The resulting plume of smoke and ash was made worse by the enraged *ch'įįdiis* and spirits.

"Coyote is one of the First People, not one of the Holy People," I pointed out. He didn't have the same powers of creation. Granuaile understood right away.

"Oh, shit," she breathed, as the Coyotes dropped the buckskins a second time and lifted them again, inviting the Wind to blow. In my magical sight, I saw the *ch'įįdiis* weakening and the spirits straining mightily to break free.

"Yeah. And there's a whole series of tales where Coyote tries to imitate Badger and Wolf and so on, and every time he does, he fails spectacularly."

"Fails as in nothing happens, or fails as in something explodes?"

The Coyotes dropped their buckskins a third time, and when they rose again to invite the Wind to blow, the *ch'įįdiis* were almost gone. The spirits would be free the next time they raised those skins. Or they'd be trapped inside the form of a bug.

"Depends on the story. A bit of both." Without realizing it, I had drawn Moralltach and set myself in a defensive stance.

"Gah! Can't we do something?"

"Hope nothing happens," I said, watching the buckskins fall for the fourth time. But when the Coyotes lifted them from the fire, something happened: Instead of smoke and *ch'įįdiis* and spirits, giant locusts the size of half-ton pickups erupted from underneath them, and the source of that torn-metal skinwalker scream became woefully clear. It was also clear we would not be stepping on these bugs.

"Run for the hogan!" I shouted over the noise, giving

her a tiny shove in that direction. She would have to run around, because Coyote's locust was between us. I began a charge at it but then halted as it fluttered enormous wings—the sound and wind was like a helicopter taking off—and leapt out of the fire. It pivoted and seized Coyote with its front legs and bit off his head, hat and all. A fevered glance backward showed that Joe was also abruptly on the menu. Occupied as they were with their Coyote Crunch 'n' Munch, the horrors didn't forget about us. They shifted their giant back legs a bit and fixed their nasty compound eyes on our progress. Granuaile and I were next.

Chapter 31

I admit that I froze, and it wasn't just because I was scared. I was woefully unprepared.

Locusts of Unusual Size weren't supposed to exist. I had seen a large insect fairly recently, but it was a type of assassin beetle called a wheel bug, and it wasn't really a bug at all but rather a demon using that shape to scare the bejesus out of people. Demons don't belong on this plane, and Gaia has no trouble giving me an assist in dealing with them. I could use Cold Fire on them or summon the local elemental to throw down for me—which is what Sonora had done in that case. But these weren't demons; as far as Gaia was concerned, they were natural creatures—just big'uns—so that meant magic was off limits, and Colorado wouldn't lift a pebble to help me fight them directly. I turned off my faerie specs since they wouldn't help me anymore, but left night vision on.

Normally bugs don't grow more than six inches in length, due to the limitations of their tracheal systems, and all that heavy chitin they have to lug around has got to be a drag. Coyote had screwed that all up. He gave these bugs plenty of Wind—way too much, in point of fact—and those old First World spirits took full advantage of the chance to be on top of the food chain. The spirits of these locusts hadn't been raised on a diet of grains but rather on human flesh whenever they could get it. If they lived to reproduce, cities would have to invest in antiaircraft batteries to protect their citizens from swarms. Locusts would descend on small towns and eat people like corn on the cob. Did FEMA have a contingency plan in place for something like that?

I found myself missing Mr. Semerdjian and his garage full of rocket-propelled grenade launchers. And again I missed Fragarach—I doubted Moralltach would make a dent in the locusts' armor. It was green and sleek and looked like it was made of that impenetrable counter-top material. But . . . maybe I could pull a Rancor? You don't find hard, chitinous exoskeleton on the inside of a bug. I almost immediately discarded that thought, because those multiple mandibles—blades and feelers and way more moving parts than a mouth should have—were alarmingly efficient at chewing up Coyote. But after checking to make sure Granuaile was still running for the hogan, I charged anyway, yelling as I went to snare its attention.

When one doesn't have Fragarach handy, the answer to strong armor is stronger blunt force; a baseball bat will do more damage than a sword blade. Confined to a large, bulky body, the spirit didn't have unnatural speed anymore—it had the speed of a grasshopper, to be sure, but that wasn't impossible for me to match. Boosting my speed and strength and transferring Moralltach to my left hand, I bent down and scooped up a stone the size of a softball, like a shortstop on a 6–3 play. First base in this case was the locust's left eye. I whipped it at him, but he saw it coming and flinched away. Rather than hitting his eye, the stone caught him on the side of the mouth, knocking the lower half of Coyote's body loose with a slurping noise, which was quickly followed by a keening screech. One of those little twitching max-illa thingies was hanging loose and slack now, and the creature leapt away, fluttering its wings with a low rumble of thunder.

"Aw, he got a widdle toof ache."

The spirits probably had to deal with pain in a whole new way now that they had their own physical housings—dealing with it, period, would be a new sensation for them. I figured they'd let their human hosts feel most of the pain before—even with the fire, they'd fled the light more than the heat—but now they didn't have a choice. Casting a quick glance at the hogan, I saw Granuaile disappearing around to the east side, where the door was. That seemed like a good idea, with one hopper distracted and the other one still munching away on Joe, so I swerved in that direction myself.

I swerved too soon.

The locust decided that the best way to deal with pain was to go after the thing that caused it. It wasn't the correct lesson I'd wanted it to learn from the experience—but, then, if they weren't used to feeling pain, then they weren't used to fearing it either. The sound of its wings gave me a warning, but it was in the air so quickly that it was almost on me before I could spot it—directly above my head.

"There are only three things you can do when something falls from the sky," my archdruid used to say. "Get out of the way, get underneath some shelter, or give it some reason to change its mind about falling on you." Then he threw a pissed-off rooster at me.

I had no shelter from the locust except for the hogan, which might as well have been in New Zealand for all the good it would do me now. Trying to scramble out of the way when the hopper literally had the drop on me would only give it more convenient access to my flesh. So I would let it fall on top of my sword.

I dropped to my back, using my left arm to cushion the impact while thrusting Moralltach directly above my face and locking my elbow. If Coyote's demise offered any clue, it wanted my head. It tried to brush aside the sword with a leg as it fell, but instead of properly doing so by slapping the flat of the blade, its leg caught the edge and neatly severed itself. That meant it took the point directly in its nasty ten-part grasshopper gob, falling directly down the blade until Moralltach erupted through the back of its head and kept going—*gahh*—

I hit my own head on the rock of the mesa and lost a fraction of a second there, during which the damn thing continued to slide down my sword. I admit that I lost my shit at that point, because the hilt didn't stop anything and my hand and forearm disappeared into its mouth while its heavy, ichor-filled body thumped against mine like the world's heaviest water balloon. It was dead and already turning black from Moralltach's enchantment, but I couldn't move. Something was dreadfully wrong with my hand and arm—I couldn't move either of them, and it hurt like hell. My blood was leaking down my arm, and though I logically knew I had won, my instincts were screaming that I was being eaten by the grossest thing in the entire world—which pretty much meant that I was screaming, period.

Hoppers have more than just mandibles; they have a labrum and labium and maxillae with segmented palps like spider's legs, plus antennae waving around and those gods-awful alien eyes that stare without emotion while they eat your corn or wheat grass or whatever. I can reliably report that seeing any part of your body in the grasp of such mouth parts will freak your shit right out. Give me a shark with straight up-and-down teeth every time if I'm going to be eaten; don't give me these chitinous plates and stubby appendages that come in from the sides and tickle as they feed you into a crop before you go to a proper stomach.

I bucked and tried to yank free, but something inside

had pierced me and held me fast, and I had such poor leverage that I couldn't get out from under the creature anyway. My ribs reminded me that they weren't in good condition either. I shut down the pain in hopes that it would allow me to think. A throbbing buzz startled me—perhaps the locust wasn't dead after all? But then I remembered that there was another one . . .

I turned my head and saw the second locust's head approaching, six long legs splayed out from the sides; its perfectly working mouth parts were covered in Joe's blood and twitching in anticipation of sampling mine. Its dead eyes were fixed on me and I'm sure it had no trouble locating me by sound, because I was hollering incoherently in an attempt to die angry at maximum volume. Anger was kind of taking a backseat to fear, unfortunately, but I don't think even my eternally irate father could keep his edge if he was unable to move or defend himself from becoming the main course on the all-night bug breakfast menu.

A bright light overhead distracted me—

"All right, I heard you," Granuaile said. She was holding aloft one of the kerosene-soaked stakes we'd prepared to defend the SUV in the hogan; she'd lit it up as a makeshift torch. Standing directly to the left of my head—or to the right of the dead locust's head—she kept her eyes on the other locust and breathed, "You'd better tell me they're still afraid of fire though, or we're toast."

The locust had stopped advancing. It remembered what fire was very well.

"Do you have any other weapons?" I asked.

"No, just this and a spare in my pocket. Get out of there."

"I can't. I'm stuck."

"What do you mean, you're stuck? Unstick yourself."

"I seriously can't. I'm hooked on something inside its head."

"So do some magic."

"Like what? I can't think of anything." Frank Herbert said that Fear is the mind-killer. He was a wise man.

"Well, look—I sort of can't help you right now. Trying to outstare the spooky bug."

It was inching closer. Much too close for my comfort. It made little clicking and fluttering noises as it moved. I think most of the noise came from its mouth.

"Be careful, it's much faster than you think."

Granuaile lunged at the locust with her torch and was rewarded with a small cringe and an unholy screech. But it didn't fly away and leave us alone. We were too much like Lunchables, and this stalemate couldn't go on forever.

"You have another stake, you said?"

"Yeah."

"Light it up and go for the wings."

"Oh! Right." She pulled another stake out of her pocket and lit it by touching the soaked end to the flame of her other one.

"Excellent. Throw the one you just lit over its head far back enough to hit the wings. Lob it like you're playing Skee-Ball."

She switched the torches in her hand so that she could throw right-handed; the newly lit torch was flaring brighter and had a better chance of catching.

"Weapons hot," she said drily. Oh, what a fabulous Druid she was going to be, when she could make puns under pressure!

"Fire at will," I responded in the same tone.

She tossed the torch in a low arc over the locust's head, and it backed up a couple of steps, then stopped, forgetting perhaps that it wasn't a spirit anymore and it had a big, physical body behind its eyes. It cocked its head, almost as if to say, "Ha-ha, you missed," and then found out Granuaile hadn't missed after all.

I couldn't see precisely how the torch landed, nor could Granuaile, but the locust certainly reacted. It hopped back—it wasn't going forward when Granuaile still had the other torch—and fluttered its wings a tiny bit, landing only twenty yards or so away. It repeated this a couple of more times, hopping to either side, but that didn't help. Then it leapt up high in desperation and tried to fly with a full extension of its wings, but that resulted in a crazy spiraling crash back to the mesa, its wings on fire, fanned to a cheerful blaze by its own efforts. We saw that the stake had lodged itself point first into the joint where the wings attached to the thorax. The noise it made wasn't threatening or terrifying now but rather comforting. It hadn't ever heard of stop, drop, and roll, so all its flailing did nothing but feed the flames more oxygen. The fire continued to spread along the locust's body and I was able to return my attention to my predicament.

"That was excellent, Granuaile. Feel like tearing apart this head for me now?"

"Um," she replied. I looked up at her and she wasn't paying attention to me at all. Her gaze was directed back at the hogan, and I followed the line of her sight until I spied a large crow resting on the roof of the hogan. Its eyes were red, but they faded to black even as I watched.

"Good evening, Siodhachan," the Morrigan said.

"Have you been there all this while?" I asked, outraged.

"I only just arrived."

"A bit late, wouldn't you say?"

"I would say in good time. Introduce me to your brave young apprentice."

"Oh, I do beg your pardon. My manners must have

been consumed by this locust, along with my arm. Granuaile MacTiernan, meet the Morrigan of the Tuatha Dé Danann, Chooser of the Slain, also known as Badb, Macha, or Nemain when occasion calls."

The crow flew off the roof toward Granuaile and sort of melted in midair until there was a naked woman with milk-white skin striding toward her, hand extended.

"Pleased to make your acquaintance," the Morrigan said.

"Likewise," Granuaile managed, shaking the Morrigan's hand. "I think we prayed to you on Samhain."

The Morrigan smiled. "Yes, you did. Please continue praying to me, as I'm the only one of the Tuatha Dé Danann who knows both of you are alive."

The locust's screeching ceased and clued us in that it had finally died, though its body continued to burn. The Morrigan tilted her head down to look at me.

"You will find, once you are free, that your tattoos are badly damaged. You will need to have them touched up, and I am the only one who can do it now. Call me when you are ready."

She took a step or two back and raised her arms in preparation to shift back to a crow. "Wait!" I said. "Aren't you going to help me out of this?"

"You're perfectly capable of figuring it out on your own, Siodhachan, now that you have time to think," she said, and then nodded once to Granuaile. "Farewell."

She shifted to a crow and left us there. Oh, were we going to have a talk later.

"Wow," Granuaile said.

"Yeah."

"I just shook hands with a naked goddess. What was that she called you? She-ya-han? Does that mean dumbass in Old Irish or something?"

"No, that's my real name. Maybe it does mean dumbass, though. Keep calling me Atticus. Watch out—step back about ten yards, will you?"

The Morrigan had been right. Now that the creature was dead and I wasn't so panicked, I could think and use Druidry to get myself out of this. Still, I needed to see what I was doing. There was an awful lot of blood and now ichor oozing down my arm, and I was starting to feel a bit light-headed. My healing had stopped. I tried to retrigger my healing charm but nothing happened. That meant the healing knots on my hand had been badly marred. I could still ask Colorado to heal me, and he would, but not having the agency to do it myself was a problem.

//Colorado / Druid needs healing / Please//

//Healing// the elemental said, and there was harmony.

Granuaile was out of the way now, so I crafted a binding between Moralltach's blade and the northern butte. Rather than the butte moving to the sword, Moralltach would cut through the locust's head to get to the butte. All I had to do was let go of the hilt. I energized it and Moralltach ripped through the head, splitting it open down to just above my hand. I dissolved the binding while it was still flying and the sword fell to the ground.

"Great. Now, Granuaile, can you tear off this half?" I gestured with my left hand to the right's side of the locust's head.

"Seriously?"

"Yeah. My hand is stuck in there and I have to figure out what's causing it."

"This is so gross. I'm going to have nightmares."

"Me too, believe me. Blame Coyote."

"Oh, I do." Her nose scrunched up in disgust, she grabbed hold of the chitinous edge of the head and pulled, ripping the gooey flesh down the middle and spilling a sludge of ichor onto my face. I spluttered and coughed.

"Gah! Sorry!" she said.

"Had to be done. It's all right," I croaked, trying not to vomit. I felt air on the inside of my forearm. "Can you see my hand?" I asked.

Granuaile peered closer. "Yeah, it's there. Something's sticking through your palm a little bit."

"Ah, that would be why I'm having problems healing, then. It's pierced me through the back of my hand."

"That circle and triskele governs your ability to heal?"

"Yep."

"And you must have blocked the nerves there or you'd be in severe pain."

"Right. But it also means I can't do much with it right now. Would you mind pulling it off there?"

"Okay." Grasping me by the wrist, she pulled my hand off the obstruction with a squishy sucking sound. When my hand fell away, we could see what had been keeping it there: the locust's left mandible. It had broken off—aided in part by my thrown rock, no doubt—and been shoved up into the mouth along with the sword hilt and my arm, and then when I tried to yank my hand loose it had been waiting there like a spearhead.

To get out from under the bulk of the beast, I bound the top of its thorax to the ground on my right. This effectively rolled the carcass over and allowed me to stand and shudder.

"I really need to get cleaned up," I said.

"There's all that ice in the chest," Granuaile said.

"Good thinking. All the way around, really," I said. "And thank you."

"You're welcome, sensei."

"Will you do two things while I'm washing up? Go get that manila envelope over there and let's see what's inside. Then bring out another stake and set this one on fire too."

She nodded and I went to wash off my arm and my

face. I had no idea how long it would take the Coyotes to respawn and come back, but I suspected it would be before dawn, and I wasn't planning to be around when they did. Let them figure it out on their own and clean up their own mess. Colorado had moved the gold under the mesa, so as far as I was concerned we were square. Time for me to get out and live the life of a dead man, like I'd always wanted.

The ice water was refreshing. It wouldn't wash away my guilt over Frank's or Darren's death, but physically I felt better not to have bug juice all over me.

Granuaile came in, left me the envelope unopened, and took out a few stakes to burn the carcass of the second locust.

Having only one functioning hand, I cheated and un-bound the envelope with a bit of magic, then shook out the contents. It was a set of official tribal documents and a lease on a trailer in Many Farms, giving permission for a white male and white female to live among the Diné. So that's what he'd been doing—arranging a place for me to train Granuaile. I noticed it said we had black hair, which was probably a good idea. Too many people had seen a couple of redheads in the area, and if I wanted the peace to train her right, it was time to pretend I wasn't Irish for a while. We'd have to get a whole new set of documents from Hal, though, and Coyote hadn't been able to resist having fun with our new names.

I hadn't planned on staying in the area, but the idea had some appeal now that I thought about it. Reservations don't get much satellite surveillance, and there wasn't a gauntlet of security cameras recording your every move. Besides that, I needed to stay nearby to keep a close eye on the coal mine. And I could make trips down to the valley every couple of weeks to work on the wasted land around Tony Cabin and then reward myself with fish and chips at Rúla Búla.

"So what was in the envelope?" Granuaile asked, returning inside.

"New identities and a place to live, courtesy of Coyote. See for yourself." I handed her the sheaf of papers.

A giggle escaped Granuaile's lips and she covered them up with her hand. "You're going to spend the next twelve years as Sterling Silver?" she asked.

"Yours isn't much better," I said.

Her laughter cut off abruptly as her eyes found the blank with her new name in it. "Oh, that bastard. He put me down as Betty Baker."

"Let's get him back by stealing his truck."

Her eyes flicked to the big black truck Coyote had driven onto the site, and she nodded. "Yeah!"

After retrieving Moralltach, I turned on the truck's ignition with a binding—there was no way I was going to search for keys in Coyote's remains—and Granuaile got us on the road back to Flagstaff. There was a hound down there who needed some hugs.

Epilogue

April Flores didn't want to let Oberon go.

"I've never seen a dog heal so fast from a broken shoulder," she said, "not to mention the ribs. He shouldn't be able to walk for a few more weeks, but now it's like nothing ever happened to him. I keep thinking it's some kind of miracle. I'd like to keep him for some more tests—no cost to you, of course. Just some X rays and things like that—"

"Sorry, but we really must be going."

<I heard *that*!> Oberon said. <Outside that door there are oodles of poodles to ogle!> He barked once to punctuate the sentence for the veterinarian's benefit.

"What happened to you?" Dr. Flores asked, pointing to the bandages on my right hand. I couldn't tell her I'd fought a giant locust any more than I could tell her Oberon had fought a vampire, so I stuck to the original lie.

"I hunted down that bear."

"Congratulations," she said, clearly not believing me. She petted Oberon regretfully and wished him farewell and no more encounters with "scary bears."

<See how she's keeping her voice low, Atticus? If Granuaile had admitted me under the name of Snugglepumpkin, she'd be in dog-whistle territory right now.>

Your sample size is still too small. You haven't made it past mere coincidence yet.

<You know what would be cool? We should experiment on the Borg Queen. Once she hears my name is Snugglepumpkin, resistance is futile! Though I'm not sure if she's a dog person. Or a person at all. Whatever. We're going to Scotland, right, for sixteen succulent boar sausages?>

Right. Gotta dye my hair and take some pictures first, but then we can take off for the Scottish Highlands.

<I smell sheep already!>

I watched Oberon's gait carefully as we exited the vet's office. *You look like you're doing okay, no limping. How does that shoulder feel?*

<I get a little twinge of pain, but it's not that bad. Not sure I want to run on it yet. That nasty tea of yours sure helped.>

Good, I'll make you some more. Need you to feel perfect again so we can go hunting.

<That's right! You feel that subtle shudder in the wind? Around the world, squirrels are cringing in fear right now and they don't know why.>

We ran errands in Flagstaff—getting more herbs for Oberon's tea and some for myself, plus a particularly inky hair dye that would completely ruin me for a while. Dyeing my own hair didn't scare me as much as saying good-bye to Granuaile's: The sun wouldn't shine on it the same way anymore, and she'd probably remind me uncomfortably of the Morrigan. But then I thought it might be a good thing for us to be unattractive to each other for a while, and this alteration of our appearance would be a blessing. Coyote had probably done me more favors than he actually intended. I knew he'd gotten us a place to live so I could keep the coal mine closed and his gold mine open, not out of any sense of guilt for tricking me or any other sense of obligation.

Granuaile didn't like the dye job at all. We got a hotel suite so we could do it properly. She looked terminally depressed when she emerged from the bathroom with raven hair and, as a result, rather Goth by accident. She didn't want to get her picture taken.

"Aughh!" she said miserably, looking in the vanity mirror in the truck of the cab and fingering a wavy curl near her temple. "This sucks more than anything has ever sucked before. You know what we look like? A couple of emo douche bags."

"Well, look at the bright side, Granuaile. Emo Douche Bags would be a great band name."

<That's brilliant! It's already the unofficial name of more bands than I can count.>

We spent some time at one of those office/print stores where you can use the Internet and fax and so on, sending our new likenesses to Hal at Magnusson and Hauk and asking him to work us up some new IDs.

"You hardly had time to get used to the ones I just gave you!" he grumbled on the phone. "I can't get these overnight, you know. It's going to take a few days."

"Understood. We're going to get out of the country for a while and then come back to get ourselves settled in these new names. They should last us a good decade or so while I'm training Granuaile."

"I'm looking at these forms right now. You're going to let people call you Sterling Silver?"

"I didn't pick the names, I swear. It was Coyote."

"Before you go," Hal said, "thought you might like to know that Leif has severed all ties with our firm."

"He's left the state?"

"No, just our law firm. He's still very much in the state. He's back in charge too, from what I can tell. There may be a few stragglers here and there in the corners, but no one is going to give him any trouble after the coup he pulled. Antoine and the boys are well fed right now," he said, referring to the local ghouls. "And I delivered your message. He knows he's supposed to stay out of your way. He asked me to express his deepest regrets. Believe that if you want."

I thanked Hal, assuring him I'd be back in touch in a week or so, and rang off. In a way it was soothing to have Leif back in charge; like a despised dictator, he was easy to hate, but at least he provided stability. Much as I wished to hunt him down for what he did to Oberon and me, letting him live (or continue in undeath, whatever) would keep Arizona a slightly safer place to train Granuaile. And I had already seen what happened to people when they pursued vengeance above all else. Besides, no matter how I tried to rationalize Leif's actions as self-serving, there was the undeniable fact that he had saved me from bleeding out and gotten me to a hospital. Had he wanted me dead, all he had to do was nothing at all. Saving me had to count for something, even if he was the one to imperil me in the first place. Still, I planned on creating a new charm for my necklace as soon as I could set up a new shop in which to work metals. My experience with Zdenik proved that a mental command for unbinding a vampire would be extremely useful.

Silversmithing, I decided, would be my next cover job—it would fit my assumed name if nothing else. I'd do some farming too and maybe get some sheep or goats for Oberon to tend. Now that I was free of all obligations and everyone who wanted me dead thought I already was, I could consider such things.

We drove Coyote's truck up to Hart Prairie, a beautiful place on the west side of the San Francisco Peaks largely watched over by the Nature Conservancy. There was a tether to Tír na nÓg there, and it was there that Granuaile experienced her first shift to another plane.

We spent very little time in Tír na nÓg—I shifted us

to Scotland right away, before any faeries could spot us and report that the Iron Druid bloke wasn't dead after all.

Those few days were probably the best time I've ever had in Scotland. Oberon was able to run confidently after another three days of healing—he called it "Intensive Sausage Therapy." And I got back the use of my hand after three days of healing as well; the Highlands elemental was only too happy to help me out with that. The tattoo was indeed ruined on the back of my hand, however, and I wasn't looking forward to having the Morrigan touch it up.

Once we were fully functional, Oberon and I shifted to the southern hemisphere, where it was summer, while Granuaile stayed behind to tour castles and politely deflect the come-ons of randy Scottish lads. Or maybe she didn't deflect them; I don't know, it's her business anyway, and she deserves whatever happiness she can find.

There was plenty of time for me to think as I stalked Australia with Oberon on a sunny day in Queensland. Though I usually try to live in the present and avoid dwelling on the past, I found time there to gnaw on some regrets. I wished I hadn't been tricked into killing Zdenik and the two skinwalkers; I mourned the deaths of Darren Yazzie and Frank Chischilly, and it was a shame that Hel had escaped—especially since she took the widow's body with her. I was worried about what Hel was up to more than anything else at this point, but as there was very little I could do about it until Granuaile was trained, I decided I would not let the daughter of Loki steal away the few moments of sunshine afforded to me now. Ganesha's mysterious League of Jungle Gods seemed to want me to lay low anyway. The omniscient deities all knew I was still around, of course, but Jesus and that lot weren't the types to share information with the pantheons who'd like to cast my ashes into the sea.

That meant nobody was looking for me, and for the first time in millennia I could ease back on my paranoia and relax.

Oberon and I found a field of red clover and we flopped down onto our backs for an epic wriggling session. Wriggling around in clover is one of the finest perks of walking the world as a hound. It's not the same when you do it as a human.

Oberon sneezed and then we rested, legs in the air, enjoying the sun on our bellies.

<This field is awesome, Atticus,> he said.

<I agree.>

<Will there be clover like this at Many Farms?>

<No, it'll be a much drier place than this. But I'm sure it will have its own charms, as any place does. It will have plenty of room for you to run, unlike at the house in Tempe.>

<Excellent! Think there will be any French poodles in Many Farms?>

<I doubt it. Mostly working dogs. They tend sheep up there, you know. Not enough grassland to support cattle. We can maybe get you a small herd to look after if you like and make lamb sausage.>

<Oh, I like the sound of that! "Snugglepumpkin's Sausage Farm.">

<Why not Oberon's?> I asked.

<We can continue the Great Snugglepumpkin Experiment that way. When all the ladies come to the sausage stand, you will introduce me to them and we can compile mounds of irrefutable data.>

<Yeesh. I really need to give you another bath.>

<Maybe so. You were going to tell me a story about a samurai.>

<I'll probably have to reconsider that. I'm worried about what that story would do to your psyche.>

<Aww! Hey, you know what, Atticus?> Oberon said,

rolling right side up, ears perked, bath and story forgotten. <I think the clover on the other side of the field looks even more luxurious than this clover right here. I think we should race each other to the other side and wriggle around in that clover to see if it's true.>

<Now, that's a hypothesis worth testing! You're on, buddy!>

<Let's go!>

I cannot tell you how wonderful it feels to run when you no longer have to do it.

Acknowledgments

Since the first three books came out blam-blam-blam, I never really got a chance to say thanks to the readers. So I want to thank *you*, first, for your support of the series, and for buying books, period. Authors don't get to keep writing unless readers buy 'em, and this book wouldn't have been possible without you buying *Hounded* way back when and telling your friends to go buy it too. Many of you have said howdy to me on Facebook, Goodreads, Twitter, and on my blog, and I appreciate you taking the trouble! You're all very kind.

My family is incredibly supportive and pretends not to notice when I walk around talking to my imaginary friends; thank you for the love.

Tricia Pasternak is my editor at Del Rey, and I think she's five kinds of brilliant. We agree on things like the greatest Metallica song ever recorded and the potential for mayhem inherent in a bag of marshmallows. She is my shepherd through the Valley of the Shadow of Doubt, and I am so grateful for her encouragement, guidance, and the unseen work she does to make each book the best it can be.

Thanks also to the scads o' fabulous people at Del Rey who contribute to the series' success: Mike Braff, Nancy Delia, David Moench, Joe Scalora, Scott Shannon, April Flores, and Gina Wachtel, among many others.

Evan Goldfried, my agent at JGLM, deserves bounteous thanks for all his advice and help.

Thanks to Detective Dana Packer in Rhode Island for tips on how to fake a death scene. Anything that sounds stupid or implausible is entirely my fault, and if you try to fake a death in her jurisdiction she *will* find you.

Sincere gratitude to Tammy Gwara for uncomfortable conversations about poison chemistry. She will probably never come over for dinner at my house now.

Mihir Wanchoo is a font of Indian stories, so thanks to him for the heads-up on the very interesting history of Indra.

To the Confederacy of Nerds—Tooth, Martin, Andrew, Alan, and John—thanks for the laughs and the Insanity Points.

As in my other books, I do try to set these fictional events in the real world as much as possible. However, this particular story inserts two more drugstores into Kayenta than it currently has; the town's pharmaceutical needs are handled by the Tribal Health Office. While the Double Dog Dare Gourmet Café in Flagstaff is entirely fictional, you can visit the Winter Sun Trading Company, Macy's European coffeehouse, and Granny's Closet "for reals." They're all spiffy places, and writing about them took me back to my happy college days at NAU.

The Navajo creation story, the *Diné Bahane'*, is a constantly changing and evolving work meant to be performed orally by a singer and tailored to the audience and purpose for the ceremony. The written versions, therefore, often differ significantly in the details—and my fiction, while based on a couple of well-documented accounts, should definitely not be viewed as an authoritative source on the subject, nor should the ceremonial procedures depicted herein be construed as genuine. In some versions of the story there are five worlds instead of four, but since four are taught at Diné College in the Navajo Nation, I went with that. My source for the two

Coyotes, the spirits of First World, and more was the version Hastin Tlo'tsi Hee (Old Man Buffalo Grass) told to Aileen O'Bryan in 1928, originally published as Bulletin 163 of the Bureau of American Ethnology of the Smithsonian Institution in 1956, but now available under the title *Navaho Indian Myths;* I also consulted the work of Paul G. Zolbrod, *Diné Bahane',* published in 1987 by the University of New Mexico Press.

I'm indebted to Karen, Mervyn, and Leah Harvey for helping me out with the pronunciation of words in *Diné bazaad,* the Navajo language, which you see at the front of the book. Any errors are of course mine and not theirs.

extras

about the author

Kevin Hearne is a native of Arizona and really appreciates whoever invented air-conditioning. He graduated from Northern Arizona University in Flagstaff and now teaches high school English. When he's not grading essays or writing novels, he tends to his basil plants and paints landscapes with his daughter. He has been known to obsess over fonts, frolic unreservedly with dogs and stop whatever he's doing in the rare event of rain to commune with the precipitation. He enjoys hiking, the guilty pleasure of comic books and living with his wife and daughter in a wee, snug cottage.

Find out more about Kevin Hearne and other Orbit authors by registering for the free monthly newsletter at www.orbitbooks.net

if you enjoyed

TRICKED

look out for

THE MINORITY COUNCIL

by

Kate Griffin

I had been in Deptford, hunting vandals.

Not your nice vandals, not the kind who trashed a park bench or burnt out a car.

These were the vandals who painted, on the walls of the houses, signs that sent all who looked on them, quite, quite mad.

They said they did it to show us the truth, and the truth was we were all being tricked. We were all insane, all of us who thought that the world was safe, and ordered, and had a purpose. They knew, they had seen, they were trying to make us understand.

I said, pull the other one, it's got bells on, you're just going around screwing up people because you're screwed up in turn and besides, if the world really is as dark as you think it is, then I'll take the illusion any day, thank you.

They answered, and who the hell do you think you are, jimbo (or words to that effect), you come swaggering on in here in the middle of the night and you're all like, Stop being vandals or else – well we know people, you know, we can do you.

I made a few pithy comments, along the following lines:

My name is Matthew Swift. I'm a sorcerer, the only one in the city who survived Robert Bakker's purge. I was killed by my teacher's shadow and my body dissolved into telephone static and all they had left to bury was a bit of blood. Then we came back, and I am we and we are me, and we are the blue electric angels, creatures of the phones and the wires, the gods made from the surplus life you miserable excuse for mortals pour into all things electric. I am the Midnight Mayor, the protector of the city, the guardian of the night, the keeper of the gates, the watcher on the walls. We turned back the death of cities, we were there when Lady Neon died, we drove the creature called Blackout into the shadows at the end of the alleys, we are light, we are life, we are fire and, would you believe it, the word that best describes our condition right now is cranky.

Would you like to see what happens when you make us mad?

They seemed to understand.

When they were gone, I walked along the river, heading east with the turning of the tide. Sorcerers in the big city go mad too easily; their hearts race at rush hour, their heads ache when the music plays in the clubs below the city streets, they breathe a mixture of carbon monoxide and lead nitrate fumes, and fresh air, clean, country air, brings on wheezing. I have always been careful to avoid the madness, but the river, on a clean, cold night inclining to winter, was a draw and a power that couldn't be resisted.

So I walked. Over muddy quays drained down to the bed, past timber warehouses and cement factories, beneath the white bulbous lights of brand new apartment blocks and over crooked paths between cracked tarmac roads. Past shops with brown-eyed mannequins staring emptily out from reflective window-panes, through the smell of Chinese take-away guarded by a forever-saluting golden Nazi cat, across car parks to shopping estates where the average price of the average good was £14.99 and this month's material of choice was polyester or plywood, past little chapels wedged in between the building society and the sixth-form college where, If You Believed It, You Could Achieve It. (Classes rated 'Satisfactory' by the Schools Inspector.) I kept the river to my left, paused to watch a flight of twin-bladed military helicopters following the curve of the water into the centre of town, leant out over a balustrade to see the silver towers of Canary Wharf catching cloud in their reflective surfaces, watched the train rattle away beneath Greenwich Hill, felt the shock as we crossed the Prime Meridian. Ley lines exist but, like all of magic, they are formed where life is thickest, and where meaning is imposed by man. Life is magic; magic grows where there is most life.

Quite how I ended up at the pier, I don't know. But my feet were starting to tingle with a dry heat that might at some point become an ache, and even the curry houses and not-quite-Irish pubs were closing for the night. At the Millennium Dome, an exercise in civil engineering somewhere between a white pleasure palace and a blister in a wasteland, the gigs were ending, doors were opening, and people dressed to honour their chosen band were tumbling out towards Tube, bus and boat. Signs were going up at stations announcing the times of the first and last trains, as a warning to all who might linger too long. The footpath under the river to the Isle of Dogs was closed, a sign politely suggesting that travellers try alternative routes: access only between 8 a.m. and 10 p.m. Monday–Saturdays, please do not ride your bikes in the tunnel.

I hadn't realised I'd been waiting for the boat back to the centre of town, but when it came, I boarded it, a catamaran that offered a full 30 per cent off the price of its fare, already 130 per cent higher than I had expected to pay. I paid anyway, and boarded a vessel built for a hundred and fifty tourists, now holding a crew of three and a cargo of twelve. A group of friends at the front wore T-shirts announcing that Life Is Punk, sported haircuts that in previous times would have been used to indicate rank in warrior tribes and were now worn to cause distress to difficult mothers, and talked loudly and with sweeping gestures about the brilliance of this and the horror of that. They seemed to be of that age when things were either one or the other, with no middle ground.

Near the back of the boat, a man was embracing a woman to keep off the cold wind from the river as we churned towards the west, and said nothing, and didn't need to. In the middle section, two women, carrying guides to Londra, leant out of the window and gleefully claimed to identify the Tower of Westminster, Buckingham Palace, the London Eye and Hampstead Heath.

I stood alone on the deck and tasted salt and smelt the river and felt the engine beneath my feet and knew that tonight there wasn't much I couldn't do, though I didn't feel like doing much anyway.

Then she said, "Sometimes people come here to get clean."

At first I hadn't realised that the voice had been addressed to me, but when I felt an expectation next to me, I looked round, and there she stood, hands on the railing, hair flicking back and forward around her face, tangling in the wind, her eyes sliding over me like oil across silk. We stammered, "What?"

"Not physically clean," she added, with a shrug. "More ... clean inside. The river, washing away our sins." I had nothing to say, but this didn't seem to bother her. She held out one hand and added brightly, "Meera."

We shook her hand, fingers sticking out of the fingerless gloves that hide the scars on the palm of our own hand. "Matthew," I said. There was a tingle on our skin as they touched hers, an aching at the back of our teeth. Her eyes locked onto ours, and they were the colour of fresh chestnuts, flecked with yellow, and, for a moment, it could have gone any way.

Her fingers tightened, before releasing their grip, and she looked away, back at the river and the city rolling by. "I could tell," she explained, casually, as if announcing breakfast. "The street lights dim a little when you pass them."

"Is that why we're talking?"

She grinned, and shook her head. "No."

"Then why?"

"We're the only people at the back of this boat who are alone. I thought maybe we could be lonely together."

She said that she was a risk analyst, working in the Isle of Dogs. Most nights, the people in her office went out drinking together – champagne, clubs, music. Sometimes they had teamwork evenings – paintballing, rowing, learning to play the ukulele . . .

"The ukulele?"

"It's a very easy instrument. Put us all together and get us playing: teamwork and music. Paintballing didn't work so well. A lot of very aggressive men in my office."

Tonight her colleagues had decided to go to a stripper joint and, for the first time, they'd invited her.

"And?"

"It was loud and dull. It didn't interest me."

So did she just leave?

Yes. She'd made sure to be seen first, sat around with the boys, made the right sounds – even paid £50 to a Ukrainian for a dance – and once everyone was too drunk to notice or care, she'd snuck away, down to the river.

"It's where I'm me," she'd explained.

I said nothing; confessions of an innermost nature were never our strong point. We passed Rotherhithe, new brick apartments and converted wharves whose names – silver, guns, pepper – told their histories, along with the black cranes still bolted into their walls. She said, "I've got an aunt who's a witch. Or a wise woman. Both, I think. She's from Chennai, practises there. I got into it through her."

"Do you do a lot?"

"She taught me petty glamours and enchantments. Beauties, cheap charms, precious dreams – nothing special. That used to be the extent of it. What about you? Why are your eyes so blue?"

I hesitated. "Complicated."

"I'm interested."

"Very complicated."

"Your shyness only makes the story grow in my imagination. How much stranger can the truth be from what I'm imagining?"

"Truth is stranger than fiction," I suggested.

"I'm seeing dragons," she retorted. "Dragons and volcanoes and adventures and demi-gods. Am I close?"

"Everything except the tectonic activity."

"And you're not shy," she added, the brightness never leaving her voice. "Sad, maybe? Or is it fear? But not shy."

We fell silent. Tower Bridge, all blue metal and pale yellow stone, was swinging into view round the bend of the river. To the north the lights in the windows of Wapping were out, apart from the occasional fluorescent kitchen and the blue-grey of a late-night movie.

Finally I said, "Used to?"

"Used to?" she echoed playfully.

"You said 'That used to be the extent of it.' As in, that's no longer just what you do, with your magics. What's changed?"

She made no answer. At length she said, "Give me your hand."

I hesitated, but there was a seriousness in her face that hadn't been there before, even though the smile remained in place. I put my hand in hers. Through her gloves I could feel her skin cold from the river wind. There was a colour in the whites of her eyes, a yellowish stain that didn't belong, but which I couldn't place. She took a deep breath, and when her lungs were full, breathed just a little deeper and I felt the change.

It started with a sound. First a fading, as the chugging of the boat receded, leaving only the lapping of the water against the boat's hull; then a growing, as new sounds slipped in to take their place, as if they'd always been there, but had been drowned out by the noise of the here and now. A creaking of masts, a rattling of cloth, a flapping of sail. I listened, and heard the sound of voices calling out from the waterside, calling in East End accents for the dockmaster to come quick to the wharf, for that bloody old fool to mind his feet, for the sailors and dolly girls to clear the way, for the ship docked from India to wait her turn because there's ten tons of meat what will spoil over here unless it's run quickly down to market. And looking towards the banks, in the converted warehouses that lined the docks lights were springing up behind the windows, flickering candlelight and lamplight, and the water around us teemed with a hundred craft, fishermen guided by a single burning point of light slung over the end of their boat, pilots and watermen with their little vessels stained sewage-sludge green, the silent cranes on the sides of the river now in full motion, wooden wharves running out into the water from a place where stone embankment should be. I opened my mouth to speak, but Meera's fingers closed tighter around mine in a command for silence and as we passed beneath Tower Bridge, a bare shadow overhead, I could see the craft swarming around the Tower of London and the sky above it was full of a thousand cawing ravens, spiralling like a tornado overhead, unseen by any but her and me, and I looked upriver and London Bridge was sagging under the weight of houses clinging to its sides, half-timbered houses and crooked clinging shacks.

I said, "Meera . . ." but my voice fell away into nothing, a fog was rising off the river, smothering the boat but somehow through it the sounds kept coming, wooden wheels on cobblestones, dogs barking in the night, the ringing of church bells announcing the hour, a watchman's rattle, a donkey's bray of distress, the roar from an inn on the south bank. "Meera!" I begged. "You've got to stop!"

She didn't hear me. Her face was lit up with delight, her eyes bright, flecked with yellow, her fingers so tight in mine they hurt. A glow to the north caught my eye and, as I watched, flames sprang up in the darkness behind a skyline of crooked cramped houses leaning against each other for support, and they spread, and overhead London Bridge was crammed with faceless dark shapes of people pressing against each other and children crying and women screaming and the sky was full of ashes and the stars were blacked out by smoke and I said, "Meera! You have to stop, you've gone too far, we'll . . ."

Then the boat jumped to one side, bumping against something below and there was a barge with a canopy and a pair of men pulling at the oars, and they wore doublets and stockings and shoes with buckles on and flat caps and looking up onto the bridge there were heads, four heads all in a row, stuck on spikes, tongues hanging loose, eyes rolled upwards, ragged zigzags around the still-dripping necks where the axe had struck a dozen times in an attempt to break the spine, traitors' heads stuck on spikes and the shallow banks were stained with fresh raw sewage and not so far off at all, the place where the city stopped, and there was a boy on the bridge, and I heard a shout.

And for a moment, just a moment, I looked up, and met a stranger's eyes. He couldn't have been more than nineteen years old, in a rough cap, his face smeared with dirt and sawdust, and, God help us, he wore a dagger in his belt and a pouch on his hip and iron buttons and as he leant out across London Bridge and looked down towards the river, he saw me, and I saw him.

I felt the deck beneath my feet grow cold, arctic cold. My breath was slow, too slow, condensing in the air, sensation was going out of my feet and fingertips, there was a weight on my back, a pressure pushing me down and the river below was wide and dark and black, ready to pull us in. We gritted our teeth and with all our strength, with every ounce of power in us, grabbed hold of Meera's wrist and pulled our fingers free. Her breath was steam on the air, her face was lit up in wonder and delight. I shook her by the shoulders and tried to shout, but my words were lost in the fog. I pushed her against the rail of the boat and, in that moment of confusion, forced her hands together with a sharp clap.

There was a noise too low to be heard, but I felt it. If whales wept, that would be the sound they made; if oceans talked, it would have been their language. It passed straight through our belly and out the other side, a ripple on the air that tore the fog around us to shreds, and for a moment it all ran backwards. The boy on the bridge darted away, the houses stretched out across the night, candles flickering in the windows, rats scurried away beneath horses' hooves, fires rose and blazed and fell, leaving a cloud of ash, chimneys grew, smoke stained the sky, stone embankments advanced along the muddy banks, searchlights briefly swept the air and, far off, bombs blasted onto the docks of the East End before even that illusion was shattered and, with an unclenching, a letting out of breath, time returned to its normal place. I staggered as the spell broke, bumping into Meera who in turn caught hold of the railing for support. She was breathless, her face shimmering with sweat, but she was grinning, and her shoulders shook with a barely suppressed laugh. Our catamaran was passing beneath Southwark Bridge, towards the silver spike of the footbridge between St Paul's and the Tate, engines slowing now as it moved in to dock, unperturbed by everything I'd witnessed.

And she was saying, "Did you see? Did you see did you did you see?"

"Meera!" I rasped. "You can't do that, you can't, you mustn't, how did you do that?"

She clapped her hands together like a child, almost bouncing on the spot. "It's here! It's all here it's all here if you just look the city built on layers and layers can you hear it? Can you hear it all the time it's always there can you see?"

The cold night felt warm in comparison to where we'd just been. My legs were shaking. "Not possible," I stammered. "No one should be able to do that, no one! How did you do that?"

"Don't be a misery," she retorted. "Wasn't it incredible?" She opened her arms wide and for a moment I thought she was going to do it again. I caught her fingers in mine and pulled them back close.

Somehow the action had put us not a breath apart, her hands in mine. We hesitated, a strange tugging in our belly. She paused too, looking straight into our eyes, unafraid. Very few look into our eyes and are not afraid. What I'd meant to say somehow didn't happen. Instead I heard myself say, "It was ... yes. You're right. It was. Incredible. Promise me – promise me you'll never, ever do it again."

"Why?"

"That kind of power – that sort of magic – isn't meant. You can't do it. You'll burn. You'll go too far and stay too long and you'll burn. Promise me you won't."

She took an instant too long before she answered playfully, "Aw. It's sweet that you care."

Perhaps we could have said something else.

But the moment passed.

"I can see it now," she said. "You're the kinda guy who stands up when a woman enters the room, and doesn't like to see ladies walk unescorted back to the bus stop. A regular knight in shiny armour."

Our fingers were still tangled together, and didn't show any sign of letting go. Her eyes crinkled as she smiled. "Did I scare you?" she asked softly, as the boat chugged round the bend towards the Oxo Tower. "Back then, were you scared?"

"Do I get points for lying?" I asked.

"You care *and* you want points? I'm beginning to think you have an ulterior motive."

"I didn't mean . . ."

"Wouldn't be talking to you if you did."

"Is this how you talk to every stranger you meet on the back of a boat?" I asked.

"Yes."

"See – that scares me."

"But you're the first one I ever did magic for," she added. "Were you impressed?"

"Honestly, yes. Never do it again."

"Were you scared?"

"Honestly, yes. And may I add, as we're standing here, never, *ever*, do it again."

Her eyes widened; she stepped half a pace back as if trying to get a better look at me. "Oh, my God!" she exclaimed. "You weren't scared for yourself, were you?"

"I'd be pretty thick if I wasn't."

"Yes, and unfortunately, being pretty thick, you're not quite smart enough to lie well."

"I study the art when I can."

She laughed, and her fingers tightened in mine. "We're nearly at the end of the line," she said. "You're sweet. Some guys try to be sweet because they think it'll make women go gooey inside. They think 'Well shit, I ain't got brains, I ain't got brawn, I ain't got nothing worth saying so I'll try being sweet.'"

"Most people don't think I'm 'sweet'," I said, struggling with the word.

"What do they think?"

"Most people don't get much past the job description."

"What's the job description?"

"Protector of the city," I answered with a shrug.

"See what I mean? That's so sweet you could spin it onto a stick and call it candy floss. Don't try too hard, though. You'll spoil the effect."

Our boat was slipping in sideways by the next dock. Above us, directly overhead, the London Eye, built as a temporary Ferris wheel to last forever, was lit up pale violet, its dark capsules turning at a glacier's crawl through the night. Across the river, the Houses of Parliament were brilliant sodium orange, with flecks of blue and green cast onto its towers. The river was rolling east, washing away the smells of the city, great ridges and swells beneath its surface, like invisible smooth backs of whales.

Meera asked where I was going.

I said I didn't know.

She said she didn't live far.

I said I had work to do.

She said, "Yeah, of course you do, work, at this hour."

I wanted to say, look, it's not like that, but there are a lot of really good reasons why I should head into town now and find a nice homeless hostel to spend the night in like I usually do, or a doorway out of the wind or something and it's been lovely meeting you, but seriously, careful with the magic because that's the kind of shit that you don't want to screw around with and while it was great, it was deadly, please don't do that again. So yeah. Bye. See you around, maybe. Perhaps. Sometime.

What I found myself saying was, "Yeah, well."

After such inspiring prose, she would have been well within her rights to walk away.

She didn't.

And neither did we